PETE
YOU CAN'T

REGINALD Evelyn Peter Southouse Cheyney (1896-1951) was
born in Whitechapel in the East End of London. After serving
as a lieutenant during the First World War, he worked as
a police reporter and freelance investigator until he found
success with his first Lemmy Caution novel. In his lifetime
Cheyney was a prolific and wildly successful author, selling, in
1946 alone, over 1.5 million copies of his books. His work was
also enormously popular in France, and inspired Jean-Luc
Godard's character of the same name in his dystopian sci-fi
film *Alphaville*. The master of British noir, in Lemmy Caution
Peter Cheyney created the blueprint for the tough-talking,
hard-drinking pulp fiction detective.

# PETER CHEYNEY

# YOU CAN'T KEEP THE CHANGE

DEAN STREET PRESS

Published by Dean Street Press 2022

All Rights Reserved

First published in 1940

Cover by DSP

ISBN 978 1 915014 09 2

www.deanstreetpress.co.uk

# CHAPTER ONE
## EASY MONEY

THE Chinese clock on the mantelpiece struck seven.

A beam of May sunshine, following a sharp shower, pushed its way through the crack between the heavy velvet curtains, slanted obliquely across the big settee, stayed for a moment in the long, expensively furnished bedroom then, apparently disheartened, disappeared, giving place to a fresh shower.

The door between the sitting-room and the bedroom opened slowly. Effie Thompson's red head appeared, followed by the rest of her. She stood in the doorway, one hand on hip, her green eyes narrowed, scanning the disordered room, noting the trail of trousers, coat, waistcoat, shirt and what-will-you that lay between the doorway and the settee.

She sighed. She walked quietly about the room, picking up the clothes, folding them, laying them on a chair.

On the settee, Callaghan lay stretched out at full length. He was wearing a sea-green silk undervest and shorts. One foot sported a blue silk sock and a well-polished shoe; the other merely a suspender which hung precariously from the big toe.

His hands were folded across his belly. He slept deeply and peacefully. His broad shoulders, which almost covered the width of the settee, descended to a thin waist and narrow hips. His face was thin and the high cheekbones made it appear longer. His black hair was tousled and unruly.

On the floor beside the settee was a big, half-empty bottle of *eau-de-Cologne* with the stopper beside it.

Effie Thompson replaced the stopper and stood looking down at Callaghan's face. She looked at his mouth. She wondered why the devil she should be so intrigued with that mouth.

Callaghan grunted.

She went out of the room closing the door behind her gently. She walked across the sitting-room out into the corridor. She went into the electric lift and down to the offices two floors below.

As she walked along the passage that led to the main door of the offices she found herself wondering why Callaghan had been on a jag. She expected it was a woman. Whenever something started—or ended—with Callaghan there was a jag. She wondered whether this was the start of something or the ending of something . . . or somebody . . .

She said a very wicked word under her breath.

Nikolls was sitting in Callaghan's room, with his chair tipped back on its hind legs. He was smoking a Lucky Strike and blowing smoke rings. Nikolls was broad in the shoulder and inclined to run to a little fat in the region of the waist-belt. His face was round and good-humored; his eyes intelligent, penetrating.

As Effie Thompson passed him on the way to Callaghan's desk he began to sing "You Got Snake's Hips." Simultaneously, and with amazing speed, he switched his chair round and aimed a playful smack at the most obvious portion of her anatomy. She side-stepped expertly—just in time. She said:

"Listen, you damned Canadian. I've told you to keep your hands to yourself. One of these days I'm going to kick you on the shins."

Nikolls sighed.

"Look, honey," he said plaintively. "Be human. Why can't a man take a smack at you now an' again. It's natural—ain't it?"

She sat down behind the desk. She began to tidy the litter of papers.

"Why is it natural?" she asked.

Her green eyes were angry.

Nikolls fished about in his coat pocket and produced a fresh cigarette. He lit it from the stub of the old one. Then, with the cigarette hanging out of the corner of his mouth, he heaved a sigh which, intended to be tragic, sounded like a whale coming up for air.

"Every guy has got a weakness, honey," he said. "Ain't you ever learned that? Every normal guy, I mean. O.K. Well, my weakness is hips. I go for hips. I always have gone for 'em an' I always will. In a big way I mean."

He shifted the cigarette to the other corner of his mouth.

"Some fellas think ankles are the thing," Nikolls continued, almost dreamily, "other fellas go for face, an' fancy hairstyles, or poise, or a nice line in talks but with me it's hips, an' I'm gonna stand up an' tell the whole cock-eyed world that when it comes to hips you got every dame I ever met lookin' like somethin' you find under a rock when the tide goes out. An' I'm gonna tell you somethin'. Just before I die I'm gonna take one big smack at you an' then I'll pass out happy."

She pushed a tendril of red hair back into place.

She said: "Nikolls . . . I've never heard any one talk such rot as you do. You . . ."

He grinned at her.

"Oh, yeah?" he said. "Looky . . . maybe you wouldn't mind if somebody did take a smack at you, so long as it was the right guy . . . Now, if it was Slim . . . ?"

She reddened, flashed an angry look at him.

He blew a smoke ring.

"Say, how is the big boy?" he asked. "Is he conscious yet?"

"He's snoring his head off," said Effie. "Clothes all over the bedroom. He must have had a head last night. He's used half a bottle of *eau-de-Cologne.*"

Nikolls nodded.

"That one certainly did drink some liquor last night," he said. "Plenty. An' he was as happy as a sandlark . . ."

She shut a drawer with a bang.

"The advent of a new lady friend or the end of an old one," she said.

She looked at Nikolls. He grinned back at her mischievously.

"You're sorta curious, ain't you, honey?" he said. "Well, I don't know a thing . . . Slim never talks about dolls to me. He's a very close guy. Mind you, I've seen him around with one or two very sweet numbers. But still that wouldn't interest *you,* would it, honey?"

She flushed.

"It certainly would *not,*" she said.

One of the telephones on Callaghan's desk jangled. She took off the receiver.

"Yes . . . This is Callaghan Investigations. I'm sorry, Mr. Layne, I've been trying to get Mr. Callaghan to call you all day. No . . . he's in conference at this very moment. I can't disturb him. I'm very sorry, but he's just concluding a most important case. Will you speak to his first assistant, Mr. Nikolls . . . Thank you, Mr. Layne . . . hold on, please . . ."

She passed the receiver on its long cord to Nikolls. He shifted his cigarette to the other side of his mouth and tilted his chair back to a perilous angle.

"Is this Mr. Layne . . . ? This is Windemere Nikolls. What can we do for you, Mr. Layne? . . . I see . . . yeah . . . I'm ahead of you . . . well what's the stuff worth? . . . One hundred thousand . . . You don't say . . . Say, Mr. Layne, if you'll let me have your number I'll get Mr. Callaghan to call you right back directly he comes out of that conference he's at right now. I'll do that . . . 'Bye . . ."

He threw the receiver back to Effie Thompson who caught it neatly and replaced it. He got up.

"It looks like some big business is startin' around here, sister," he said. "You tinkle through to Slim an' wake him up. I gotta talk to him."

The telephone jangled again. She picked up the receiver. Nikolls heard Callaghan's voice, brusque and rather acid, coming through from the flat above.

Effie said: "I'm glad you're awake. I came up and looked at you, but I thought it was more than my life would be worth to disturb you."

Nikolls got up and took the receiver from her hand.

"Hallo, Slim," he said. "Say . . . what she really meant was that she just had to come up an' look at them green silk underpants of yours. Yeah . . . it makes her feel good . . . but don't tell her I said so. Look . . . do you want to listen to business? . . . OK. I'm coming up . . . All right."

He hung up.

"He says you're to telephone down to the service to send him up a big pot of tea . . . very hot an' very strong . . . an' then you can go home, sister . . . maybe one night when I ain't busy you an' me could go to a movie . . ."

"Like hell," said Effie. "D'you think I'd trust myself in the dark with you?"

Nikolls grinned.

"Why not, honey?" he said. "I'm swell in the dark an' I'm just as dangerous in the daylight anyhow. I remember once some dame in Minnesota . . ."

The telephone jangled again. She said as she reached for it:

"I'd get upstairs if I were you. That's him and he's in a very bad temper if I know anything about Mr. Callaghan."

"Maybe you're right," said Nikolls.

He went to the door.

Effie said into the telephone in a very smooth, cool voice:

"Yes, Mr. Callaghan . . . Yes . . . he's just left the office . . . he's on his way up . . . and I'm ringing through to service for the tea. And is there anything else? . . . Very well . . . Good-night . . ."

Callaghan came out of the bathroom and stood in front of the mirror carefully tying a black watered-silk bow. When this was done he put on a double-breasted dinner jacket and went over to the corner cupboard. He produced a bottle of whisky, a water carafe and two glasses.

He poured out the whisky. He drank four fingers neat and swallowed a little water afterwards. Nikolls came across and helped himself.

Callaghan said: "What's the story, Windy?"

He lit a cigarette, inhaled deeply and began to cough.

Nikolls said: "It's some lawyer guy named Layne. They've been tryin' to get you all afternoon. The firm's Layne, Norcot, Fellins, Treap and Layne. They're good lawyers—act for a lot of swells. This Layne is the head man. The case is a steal . . . somebody's pinched about a hundred thousand pounds worth of first-class ice from some guy in Devonshire. They've had the police on it but they don't seem satisfied. I don't know any more details. They want you to go in on it. Layne wants to see you. I said you'd ring back. He's waiting at his office. It's in Green Street just off the Park."

Callaghan looked at his watch. It was eight o'clock.

"Ring through and say I'm coming round now," he said. "I'll be with him in ten minutes. And you stay around downstairs in case I want you."

Nikolls nodded. As he got up the house telephone rang. He answered it. Callaghan was looking out of the window.

Nikolls put his hand over the transmitter.

"It's a dame," he said. "Her name's Vendayne—Miss Vendayne. She says that she believes the Layne firm have been trying to get into touch with you. She says she wants to see you urgently. What do I say?"

Callaghan grinned.

"Funny business," he said. "Make an appointment for tonight somewhere. Anywhere she likes—if it's in London."

Nikolls talked into the telephone. After he had hung up he said:

"It's O.K. She says for you to meet her at Ventura's Club, near Shepherd's Market, at ten o'clock."

Callaghan lit a fresh cigarette.

"What did she sound like?" he asked.

Nikolls grinned. He waved his big hands dreamily.

"She had one of those voices, Slim," he said. "You know . . . music an' promises of rewards an' all that Omar Khayyám stuff . . ."

"You don't say," said Callaghan. "Windy, you're getting poetic."

"Yeah . . ." said Nikolls. "I'm like that sometimes . . . but I sorta spoil myself. I'm always poetic at the wrong times. Just when I oughta be spoutin' poetry I find myself tryin' to take a smack at some dame an' I get all washed up."

He got up.

"I'll wait downstairs in the office," he said. "Maybe you'll come through later?"

Callaghan nodded. He put on a black soft hat and went out. As the bedroom door closed behind him, Nikolls reached for the whisky bottle.

Callaghan reopened the door.

"Help yourself to a drink, Windy," he said.

He grinned.

Nikolls cursed softly to himself.

"Why in hell didn't I wait?" he muttered.


Mr. Layne, of Layne, Norcot, Fellins, Treap and Layne was very thin, very dignified. He looked extremely ascetic and rather uncomfortable.

Callaghan, seated in the big chair on the other side of the lawyer's desk, lit a cigarette with an engine-turned gold lighter.

Layne said: "I am afraid it's rather an extraordinary case, Mr. Callaghan."

Callaghan grinned.

"I gathered that," he said. "When somebody steals £100,000 worth of jewellery it is a job for the police, not a private detective." He looked at the lawyer. "That's obvious, isn't it?" he asked.

Layne nodded. He put the tips of his fingers together and looked over them at Callaghan. He said:

"Mr. Callaghan, I think I'd better give you the whole story from the beginning. I should like to point out to you that it was not my idea to employ a private detective in this case. During my legal experience I have always found the services of the police adequate."

Callaghan said: "You don't say . . ."

He flipped the ash from his cigarette.

"In a nutshell," said Mr. Layne precisely, "the position is this: My client is Major Eustace Vendayne. You may have heard of the Vendaynes—a very old Devon family—very ancient indeed. Major Vendayne lives at Margraud Manor, a delightful estate near Gara in South Devon.

"He is—or was," the lawyer went on, "the life owner of some extremely valuable antique jewellery, which came into possession of the family in rather unique circumstances. One of the Vendaynes sank a great deal of Spanish shipping at the time of Queen Elizabeth, and he was allowed to retain a percentage of the captured booty. He left directions as to its disposal after his death in his will.

"He directed that the head of the Vendayne family should be owner and trustee of the jewellery in his lifetime. He was to keep it intact in safe custody and allow it to be worn on the proper occasions by women members of the family. If he attempted to sell it, it was to pass immediately to the next male in line to whom it would go, in any event, after his death.

"Should any member of the family have no male heir by the time he was twenty-five years of age, and if there were no other male member of the family existing, then the holder was entitled to dispose of the jewellery as he saw fit. You understand?"

Callaghan nodded.

"The present owner and trustee of the jewellery is my client," said Layne. "After his death it goes to his nephew Lancelot Vendayne, who, being over twenty-five years of age, being unmarried and having no heir, is entitled to dispose of it when it comes to him after my client's death—should he wish to do so.

"Some eleven weeks ago," the lawyer went on, "thieves broke into the Manor House, opened the safe and removed the jewellery. They were either very lucky or they had some means of knowing that on that particular night the jewellery would be in the house, because only the day before it had been brought over from the bank vault at Newton Abbott—where it was usually kept—for the purpose of a private exhibition which was to be held at the Manor.

"When the theft was discovered Major Vendayne informed the local police at once. The matter was taken up by the County Police and after a week's delay the services of Scotland Yard were requested. It seems that up to the moment the authorities have discovered nothing.

"The jewellery," Layne continued, "was insured for £100,000, which, believe me, does not represent its true value. Major Vendayne, of course, made a claim on the Insurance Company, but for some reason or other—and I must say I fail to understand this—the Company do not seem inclined to meet the claim promptly. They have during the past three or four weeks made all sorts of vague excuses, and, quite candidly, at the moment I have no information as to when they propose to settle the claim.

"This," the lawyer went on, "is where Mr. Lancelot Vendayne comes into the story. As the next owner of the jewellery, and the one to whom it would actually belong in its entirety with power for him to do as he liked with it, he is, naturally, most perturbed about the situation. After all he was entitled to regard it almost as being his own property. My client is fifty-five years of age and has a weakness of the heart. He is not expected to live a great deal longer.

"To cut a long story short," said the lawyer, "Mr. Lancelot Vendayne has become more and more perturbed about the attitude of the Insurance Company. It had been arranged between him and Major Vendayne—and I think the young man's attitude was most generous— that when the claim was settled he should receive £75,000 and my client would be entitled to keep the remaining balance of £25,000.

"Two weeks ago Lancelot Vendayne went down to the Manor House and saw my client. He suggested to him that as the police seem to be doing very little in this matter it was time that outside help was brought in. Apparently," said Mr. Layne, looking at Callaghan over the top of his pince-nez, "Lancelot has heard about you. Your reputation," he continued with an icy smile, "has evidently preceded you. He insisted that my client should retain your services and that you should endeavour to find out if possible, first of all, what happened to the jewellery, and secondly why the Insurance Company are taking up the attitude which they have adopted."

Callaghan said: "I can answer the second part of that question now. I've done a lot of work for Insurance Companies. I know their methods. They just don't like the claim. They're stalling for time."

The solicitor said: "So I gathered. But Lancelot Vendayne —and for that matter my client—would like to know *why.*"

The lawyer got up. He crossed over to the fireplace and stood, his hands behind his back, looking at Callaghan.

"Would you like to take up this case, Mr. Callaghan?" he said.

"Why not?" Callaghan answered. "It sounds an interesting case. I like the idea. I shall want a retainer of £250. If I get that jewellery back I'll put in a bill. It'll be a big bill. If I don't get it back, I'll put in a bill not quite so big."

The lawyer nodded.

"That is agreeable," he said. "I'll have the cheque sent to you to-morrow. I expect you'll want to go down to Margraud. I believe there is an excellent train service. Will you go to-morrow?"

"Maybe," said Callaghan, "and I never use trains anyway."

He lit another cigarette.

"Mr. Layne," he said, "supposing you tell me something about the Vendayne family, or isn't there a family?"

The lawyer nodded. A little smile appeared at the corner of his mouth. Callaghan thought it was a cynical smile.

"Oh, yes, Mr. Callaghan," he said, "there is a family. I will describe it to you. There is my client—Major Vendayne—who as I have told you is fifty-five years of age, with a not very good heart. Then there is his eldest daughter, a most charming young lady—Miss Audrey Vendayne. She is I think thirty years of age. There are two other daughters—Clarissa aged twenty-eight and Esme aged twenty-five. They are all extremely attractive. Clarissa and Esme," the lawyer went on, "are thoroughly modern young women. In fact, I suppose that people of my generation might possibly consider them a trifle wild. They have what I believe is called, in these days, temperament as well as looks."

Callaghan said: "I see. They're all good-lookin' and attractive. But Clarissa and Esme are a trifle wild and they've got temperaments. Audrey is good-looking, but she hasn't got a temperament and she's not wild. What has *she* got?"

Layne said very coldly: "Miss Vendayne is a most charming, agreeable and delightful young woman. She is unlike her sisters merely in the fact that she is not at all wild and has no temperament to speak of."

"I see," said Callaghan. "I'm sorry I interrupted."

He grinned amiably at the lawyer.

"These three ladies and my client live at the Manor House," continued the lawyer. "The only other member of the family living, as I have already said, is Mr. Lancelot Vendayne. He does not live in Devonshire. He lives in town."

Callaghan nodded.

"Do you know his address?" he asked.

"He lives at the Grant Hotel, in Clarges Street," replied the lawyer. "He is an interesting young man and has made, I believe, considerable money on the Stock Exchange. He is a lucky gambler they tell me. He plays golf and has a fondness for night clubs. He is quite a nice sort of person. In the evening he is usually found at the Ventura Club, where he drinks a great deal and plans fresh raids on the stock market. As I told you, he is responsible for your being called in on this unfortunate business."

Callaghan got up. He stubbed out his cigarette.

He said: "Thanks for the information. I'll probably go down to Devonshire some time. Maybe to-morrow. You might let Major Vendayne know I'm coming. I'll telephone the Manor when I'm on my way. I'd like to stay there. I shall take an assistant with me."

"Very well, Mr. Callaghan," said the lawyer. "I'll inform my client. He'll expect you. I wish you good luck."

Callaghan said: "Thanks."

He picked up his hat and went out.


It was nine-thirty when Callaghan finished his dinner. He came out of the Premier Lounge and turned down Albemarle Street. He walked into Bond Street, through Bruton Street, through Berkeley Square into the region of Shepherd's Market. He turned into the long mews that bisects one corner of the Market and turned into the passage on the left. At the end of the passage the entrance of The Ventura Club formed a *cul de sac*. Over the door was a green "blackout" shaded light. On each side of it a miniature tree in a tub.

Callaghan paused before the entrance and produced his cigarette-case. He was lighting the cigarette when the woman came out of the shadow beside one of the tree tubs.

She said: "Mr. Callaghan?"

He looked at her. She was tall and slim and supple. Callaghan had a vague impression that she was very well dressed and that she emanated a subtle and discreet perfume. There was a peculiar quality in her voice that was, he thought, extraordinarily attractive.

He said: "Miss Vendayne, I imagine? Somehow I thought I'd find you inside . . ."

She shrugged her shoulders.

"I didn't know where to make an appointment to meet you," she said. "I discovered that your office was off Berkeley Square. I thought this would be as good a place as anywhere."

Callaghan said: "Why not?"

There was a pause. He stood, inhaling his cigarette smoke, looking at her. After a moment she said:

"Can we go somewhere? I want to talk to you."

Callaghan grinned in the darkness.

"I rather imagined you did," he said.

He turned and began to walk down the passage into the mews. He could hear her high heels tapping just behind him.

In Charles Street, they found a wandering taxi-cab.

Callaghan said: "There's a not-too-bad club I know near here. Would you like to go there?"

He stopped the cab. In the darkness he could almost feel her shrugging her shoulders.

They drove to the club in Conduit Street. On the way he amused himself trying to identify the perfume she was wearing. After a while he gave it up.

When the cab stopped, Callaghan helped her out. She drew her arm away quickly as her foot reached the pavement. He paid off the driver. As he turned away from the moving cab the moon came out and he saw her. He had a sudden picture of a white face, half-hidden by a short veil, framed with dark hair, of two large dark eyes, a straight and attractive nose with sensitive nostrils and a superbly chiselled mouth. Callaghan, who liked looking at women's mouths, thought that hers was quite delightful. He remembered Nikoll's wisecrack about her voice . . . "music an' promises of rewards an' all that Omar Khayyám stuff. . . ." He wondered if Nikolls was right.

His eyes wandered quickly over her. She wore a coat and skirt that fitted as a suit *should* fit. She had style, Callaghan thought. He wondered about Clarissa and Esme . . .

The cab disappeared. They stood for a moment looking at each other. Then Callaghan said:

"I wouldn't do anything you didn't want to do. You don't seem awfully sure of yourself. You look to me as if you'd rather be somewhere else."

She smiled. It was a small smile. Then she said arrogantly:

"I would. I'm not used to having heart-to-heart talks with private detectives whom I don't know. But as I'm here I'd better go through with it."

He grinned at her.

"Too bad," he said. "It must be awful for you. Come inside. Maybe you'll feel better after a drink."

They went up the stairs to the first floor. The club was a one-room affair—a big room with a bar at one end. It was empty except for the bar-tender. Callaghan led the way to a table and, when she was seated, went to the bar and ordered *fine maison* and black coffee. When he got back to the table she said:

"I suppose the best thing I can do is to say what I've got to say and be done with it."

Callaghan smiled at her. She noticed his white even teeth.

"That's always a good idea," he said. "Only the devil of it is that when we've said what we've got to say, very often we're *not* done with it."

She smiled. It was a very cold smile.

"You're fearfully, clever, aren't you, Mr. Callaghan?" she said. "I've heard that about you. I suppose I ought to be rather frightened or something . . ."

Callaghan said: "I wouldn't know."

He sat down.

The bar-tender brought the brandy and coffee. He offered her a cigarette and, when she refused, lit one for himself. He drew the smoke down into his lungs, exhaled it slowly through one nostril. He said:

"Well . . . ?"

He was grinning amiably.

She looked towards the window. Then she said: "I *would* like a cigarette, please."

He gave her one and lit it. As he held up the lighter he thought that Miss Audrey Vendayne had something—as Nikolls would say—even if she was finding it a little difficult to bring matters to a head.

She smoked silently for a moment. Then she said very quickly:

"Mr. Callaghan, I don't want you to handle this case for my father. I don't think it's necessary."

"I see," said Callaghan. "I suppose you've got a good reason for wanting me *not* to handle it?"

"The very best of reasons," she answered. Her eyes were cold. "The matter has been put into the hands of the police," she went on. "I think the police are very efficient. I do not see why the services of a private detective are necessary."

Callaghan said nothing. There was a pause. He began to sip his coffee.

"Of course," she went on, "if you go out of the case now . . . if you give it up—although you haven't even started it—I think you ought to have some sort of compensation."

Callaghan shook the ash off his cigarette. Then he looked at the glowing end for quite a while. One corner of his mouth was curled up in an odd sort of smile. He could sense her feeling of impatience.

He said: "I think that's very nice of you. Very sporting. The devil of it is I've already seen Mr. Layne—your father's lawyer. I've practically accepted the case."

He looked at her. She was looking towards the window. Callaghan thought that even if, as Layne had said, Audrey Vendayne was not wild and had not a lot of temperament she still had plenty of *something*. Anyway, Callaghan had little opinion of the abilities of lawyers to sum up character.

Her glance returned to him. She said casually:

"Possibly. But I don't see any reason why you can't be bought off the case. Can you?"

Callaghan looked at her for a moment. Then he began to grin wickedly.

"Of course, Miss Vendayne, I'm always open to be 'bought off' a case. What compensation would you suggest? And I think compensation is a hell of a word. I like it. Having regard to the fact that there's nothing to compensate me for, I think it's good."

She flushed. She said quietly:

"You're making fun of me?"

"I never make fun of a woman who is as serious as you are," Callaghan answered. "I was merely curious about the compensation."

She nodded. She looked down at the table and made as if to pick up the little glass of brandy. She did not. Then she looked at him and said:

"I don't think my father should be worried any more about this business of the jewellery being stolen. He's been terribly harassed about it. And he's not well. He should be left alone. It doesn't matter sufficiently."

"No?" queried Callaghan. "I should have thought that a hundred thousand pounds worth of jewels would have mattered to any one."

"That is a matter of opinion," she said. "*I* don't think it matters."

Callaghan nodded.

"Excellent," he said. His voice held a definite tinge of insolence. "So *you* don't think it matters. And where do we go from there?"

Her eyes blazed.

"I wonder has any one told you that you can be fearfully impertinent, Mr. Callaghan?" she said.

He grinned.

"Lots of people have, Miss Vendayne," he answered. "And I suppose I should be considered even more impertinent if I said—*so what!*" He blew a smoke ring and watched it rise in the air. "If you've got a proposition I'm listening," he went on. "I suppose we didn't come here to discuss my ability to be impertinent."

She shrugged her shoulders.

"You're perfectly right," she said. "Very well then, briefly, my proposition is this. I am willing to pay you two hundred pounds immediately if you decide *not* to take the case."

Callaghan said softly: "Mr. Layne offered me two hundred and fifty to handle it. Your offer would have to be over his."

She said: "I'll give you three hundred."

"Done," said Callaghan.

She looked at him for a moment. Then she began to open her handbag. She stopped suddenly and said:

"How do I know I can trust you?"

"You don't," said Callaghan.

He lit another cigarette.

She said something under her breath. It sounded like "pig" . . . Then she opened the bag and took out a packet of banknotes. She extracted six fifty pound notes from the pile and pushed them towards Callaghan. He put them in his waistcoat pocket.

She got up.

"Good-night, Mr. Callaghan," she said.

Callaghan stood up.

"Thanks for the money," he said. "But aren't you going to drink your brandy, Miss Vendayne? Or don't you drink with strange men?"

He stood looking at her.

"*Good*-night, Mr. Callaghan," she repeated.

She walked to the door and went out. He could hear her high heels tapping down the stairs.

Callaghan sighed. He sat for a moment, looking at her undrunk glass of *fine maison* and the now cold cup of black coffee. He walked over to the bar and ordered a brandy and soda. He drank it, put on his hat and went out.

It was eleven o'clock when Callaghan came into the office. Nikolls was seated at the desk in the outer room playing patience.

Callaghan said: "Windy, you can get around and do a little fast work. Go round to the garage and hire a car. Go home, get a few hours' sleep, pack your bags and get down to Devonshire. Stay at an hotel near—but not too near—Margraud Manor, near Gara Rock. You should be there early to-morrow morning."

Nikolls said: "That suits me. I could do with some sea air."

Callaghan went on: "Collect all the local rumours about the Vendayne family. There are three daughters—Audrey, Clarissa and Esme. Clarissa and Esme are supposed to be a little wild. Check on them. Find out if they've got any boy friends locally, how they spent their time and all the rest of it. Understand?"

Nikolls said: "I've got it. Did you see the Vendayne dame?"

"I saw her," Callaghan replied. "The eldest one. She paid me three hundred pounds to throw the case."

"Marvellous," said Nikolls. "Here's once we get paid for *not* doing something."

Callaghan went into his office. He sat down at the desk. Nikolls ambled in and stood looking at him.

"You'll meet me the day after to-morrow," said Callaghan. "You'd better wait for me around six o'clock at the Clock Tower in Newton Abbott. Have your bags with you. I'll pick you up. Have that information about the Vendayne family by then and don't let any of the local wise-guys get on to you. Understand?"

"I got it," said Nikolls. "I'm practically there."

He went to the door. When arrived he turned and said:

"Am I dreamin' or does this case stink?"

"I don't know," said Callaghan, "but I don't think you're dreaming."

Nikolls fished about in his coat pocket for a Lucky Strike. He said pleasantly:

"*I* think it's a nice case. The eldest Vendayne doll hands you three hundred to walk out on it an' you're not walkin' out. She can't say anything because quite obviously she don't want anybody to know she's paid you to throw it. Nice work. You make both ways."

Callaghan said very softly: "I don't remember asking your opinion, Windy."

Nikolls flushed.

"Sorry," he said. "Me . . . I always talk too much."

"Don't worry about that," said Callaghan. "I can always stop that if I want to by knocking a few of your teeth down your throat. By the way, you'd better pack a tuxedo. And when we get to Margraud go easy on those Canadian tales. Sometimes people like the Vendaynes don't appreciate 'em."

Nikolls said: "I'll be so Fifth Avenue it's gonna hurt. So long, Slim . . ."

He went out.

Callaghan leaned back in his swivel chair and put his feet on the desk. He lit a cigarette and smoked it slowly. Then he took his feet off the desk, reached for the desk pad and wrote a note to Effie Thompson. It said:

*"Effie,*

*"Directly you get here telephone Gringall at the Yard. Tell him I'd like to see him. Afternoon if possible. Tell him that I've been retained in the Vendayne jewellery steal.*

"S. C."

He put the note in the right-hand drawer of her desk in the outer office.

Then he put on his hat and went out.

He walked across Berkeley Square towards the Ventura Club.

## CHAPTER TWO
## ENTER GABBY

Meet Mr. Ventura.

If you have ever seen a picture—taken in his prime—of Mr. Al Capone and you care to imagine the face a little fuller, a little more smiling, then you will have an adequate idea of Mr. Ventura; who, as he would be the first to admit, was invariably one jump ahead of the market and by the use of much foresight managed to stay in that enviable position.

At an early age Mr. Gabriel Ventura—Gabby to his friends—had discovered the efficacy of being all things to all men—and a few women. It was perhaps for this reason that all sorts and conditions of ladies and gentlemen found their way into the expensively furnished, well-appointed Ventura Club.

You could get anything you liked there if you knew how to ask for it.

On the other hand if you were up from the country and merely dropped in for a drink and to look at pretty women, no one would even try to take you for your pocket book.

If there had been odd rumours about the Ventura Club, and if, on occasion, Scotland Yard had taken more than a passing interest in what went on within its elegant portals, that was no affair of Gabby's. He believed in living and letting live, although, it has been said, he was not so keen on the letting live part.

If Gabby had made good at a time when most West End Night Club proprietors were trying to get enough money to get their shoes soled, it was because he had "vision." Gabby liked to think of himself as a Napoleon of night life, but a Napoleon with more "vision" than the original boyo. Gabby did not intend to end up on a St. Helena masquerading under the name of Dartmoor or Portland.

He had a series of mottos, which had assisted him during a career not entirely devoid of incident. One was: "Play 'em along and don't lose your temper." Another: "The sucker always comes back for more"; and another: "A wise man *might* trust a man but only a mug trusts a woman."

So there you are.

It was nearly twelve o'clock when Callaghan arrived. He left his hat with a pretty girl in the cloak-room. He walked along the passage, went through the heavy velvet curtains and stood looking round the main floor of the club. Whenever Callaghan had been in the Ventura Club he had always looked at the large tastefully furnished room with a certain admiration for Gabby.

Other club proprietors sunk their dance floor a few feet and had a raised balcony on which the dining tables were set around the edges of the room, with a higher band platform at the end, and the furniture was always gold or chromium. Gabby did not do anything like that. He was original. His dance floor—an excellent one, not too big or too small—was raised two feet off the main floor, and the dining tables set on the lower level that surrounded it. The furniture was antique oak and comfortable. An air of luxury, even of good taste, pervaded the atmosphere.

The band—a series of hand-picked *maestros* from the East End— played in a balcony about eight feet off the dance floor. At the moment it was resting, looking about it with that peculiarly vacant expression of face adopted by swing players on the slightest excuse.

On the right-hand side of the room, in charge of a tall slim brunette and a shorter plump blonde—two ladies who lost nothing by contrast—was the bar. Gabby, in a faultless tuxedo, white marcella evening shirt and collar, was leaning against the far end smoking a Green Upmann. He smiled and waved his hand when he saw Callaghan.

Callaghan went over. Gabby said:

"Hallo, Slim. You're looking fine. One of these days when you want to do me a good turn just let me know who your tailor is. He certainly knows how to cut clothes."

Callaghan cocked an eyebrow.

He said: "You don't do so badly yourself, Gabby."

Ventura shrugged his heavy shoulders.

"It's a tough game, Slim," he said. "It's all very well for you fellows, but this war's doing me no good at all. Nobody's got any money." He sighed. "I get very worried sometimes."

The sigh blended into an angelic grin which curved Gabby's lips and showed a set of teeth on which a dentist had expended much platinum bridgework.

"I suppose you're still drinking whisky?" he concluded.

Callaghan nodded. Gabby ordered a large whisky for Callaghan and a gin and soda for himself.

He said: "So you're on the war path again, hey, Slim? It's funny, but I always know when you're looking for somebody. What's the matter? Has one of my clients been getting in bad?"

Callaghan shook his head. He drank a little whisky. He said:

"I want to see Lancelot Vendayne. I've got a job through him—rather a nice one. I feel I'd like to buy him a drink. Do you know anything about him, Gabby?"

"Plenty," replied Ventura. "I don't know what I'd do without him. He spends money around here. That boy's clever. I wish I had his brains. And," he continued, "he's not only clever, but he's a gentleman. It sounds almost impossible, I know"—he grinned at Callaghan—"but it's a fact. He comes of an old family and actually makes money on the Stock Exchange. Can you beat that?"

Callaghan did not say anything. He finished his whisky.

"He'll be in," said Ventura. "He's usually in soon after twelve. But whether he'll have a lot of time to talk to-night, I don't know."

Callaghan said: "Why won't he have time to talk?"

Gabby grinned.

"We've got a little poker game on—just three of us upstairs, at half-past twelve," he said. "Why don't you join in, Slim? If your luck's in you might win something."

Callaghan said: "It's an idea."

He looked round as Ventura's eyes went towards the entrance curtains. Through them came a young man.

"Talk of angels . . ." said Gabby softly.

Callaghan was looking at Lancelot. Vendayne was nearly six feet tall. He had broad shoulders, thin hips. His face was open, his brow frank. He had that kind of wavy auburn hair that women like to run their fingers through. He came over to the bar. Gabby said:

"Good evening, Mr. Vendayne. In case you don't know, this is Mr. Callaghan—Mr. Slim Callaghan of Callaghan Investigations. He wants to have a little talk with you."

Vendayne shook hands. He said:

"I'm glad to meet you, Callaghan. You've probably been hearing about me. Let's go and talk."

He led the way across the dance floor to a table on the other side of the room. He signalled a waiter, ordered drinks. He said:

"So you've seen old Layne. He's a nice old boy, isn't he?"

Callaghan said: "I saw him this evening. He gave me an outline of the situation, but there are one or two points I want to talk about. According to Layne my client is your uncle, but I take it you're the person that's really responsible for me coming in on this job?"

Lancelot nodded.

"Yes," he said. "I forced the situation because the situation has got to be forced. I don't like it."

He offered his cigarette-case to Callaghan and lit their cigarettes. He went on:

"When I heard that the jewellery had been stolen I was naturally perturbed, because, as I expect Layne told you, under the original deed, when my uncle dies and the jewellery comes to me I can do what I like with it. The deed said that the last male member of the family who was over twenty-five years of age, and who had no existing heir, becomes actual owner of the jewellery."

Callaghan nodded.

"I should have sold the stuff when it came to me," said Vendayne, "because, quite candidly, I don't see the use of having a pile of antique jewellery simply being used at occasional dinner parties or at private exhibitions. I've been told that if the stones were re-cut and re-set by experts to-day they would probably double their value. I imagine myself being worth a couple of hundred thousand," he went on, "because as you probably know the doctors don't think that my uncle is going to live more than another four or five years."

He leaned back in his chair and smiled happily.

"That suited my book excellently," he said. "I'm not in need of any money now. I've been rather lucky during the last year or two, and I'm a half partner in one of the few stock-broking businesses that are making any money. But I look forward to retiring in eight or nine years' time, and having a good time."

Callaghan said: "You could have a pretty good time on £200,000."

Vendayne nodded.

"I shouldn't have had all that," he said, "because I should have done the right thing by the girls."

Callaghan said: "Oh, you'd have done that . . . ?"

"Obviously," said Vendayne. "I'm perfectly certain that the old boy's not going to be able to leave anything very much to them when he departs from this earth, and I must say they'd probably think it a bit thick if I had all that money and they had to take jobs as governesses or something. Because without money they'd never be able to keep Margraud going. No, I'd made up my mind that if I could have got £200,000 out of the sale of the jewellery I was going to give 'em a life interest in the income from £30,000 each. Even then I should be doing pretty well. I'd still have £100,000."

Callaghan said: "Quite."

"You can imagine," said Vendayne, holding up his glass of whisky and looking through it, "that I didn't feel quite so good when I heard about the robbery. I went down right away and saw my uncle. He'd already had the County Police in, and within ten days they'd got the Yard people in. The Chief Constable, who is rather a friend of my uncle's, had come to the conclusion that it was an astute job, and that the people who did it knew their way about. He thought they were probably first-class international crooks who knew the value of that stuff."

Callaghan said, "You thought the police would get the stuff back?"

Vendayne nodded.

"That was our first idea," he said. "After all, we thought it would be impossible for them to dispose of jewels like the Vendayne collection—that is, of course, unless they were going to have the stones dismounted or re-cut, but that would cost 'em some money. We didn't think they'd go to that trouble. When Scotland Yard came in, they thought the crooks' idea might have been to do a deal with the Insurance Company, who would certainly have paid about £20,000 to cut their loss and get the stuff back. But Scotland Yard drew a blank. It's nearly three months, and they're just where they started.

"The next thing," Vendayne went on, "was the attitude of the Insurance Company. They haven't suggested that they're not going to meet the claim, and I imagine their assessors have been pretty busy in the meantime trying to get a line of where the stuff is." He looked at Callaghan with a smile. "I'm probably teaching my grandmother to suck eggs," he said, "but you know that Insurance Companies' assessors are pretty good, and if they can't find out who's done the job and where the stuff is, I don't think anybody can.

"About three weeks ago," he continued, "I thought it was time we did something. I wondered what would be the best thing to do. Then one night some friends of mine were talking about you. I thought it would be a pretty good idea to have you in on this—for obvious reasons."

Callaghan finished his whisky.

"The obvious reasons being that you think I might force the hand of the Insurance Company?" he said.

Lancelot grinned.

"That's right," he agreed. "I don't know how you're going to do it, but quite obviously the Insurance Company have got to do something fairly quickly. They've either got to say they're not going to pay or they've got to pay. I want you to speed up that process. I rather imagine," he said, "that with your technique we shouldn't have too much difficulty with the Insurance Company."

Callaghan said: "That's very nice of you."

He lit another cigarette.

Vendayne said: "Have you got any ideas about this thing?"

Callaghan nodded.

"I'm going down to Devonshire," he said. "I'm a great believer in atmosphere. I like to see the places where things happen. Sometimes I get an idea."

Vendayne said: "Well, I hope you'll let me know how things go."

"Of course," said Callaghan. "Why not? By the way," he went on, "Gabby was just talking about a little game of poker that you had planned for to-night. He suggested I join in. Do you mind?"

Vendayne said: "The more the merrier. Three's too few for good poker anyway. Four's much better. What about it? We usually play upstairs."

"All right," said Callaghan.

He signalled the waiter. Ordered more drinks.

The ornate cuckoo clock in the corner made a whirring noise and struck three. Gabby yawned.

"I don't know about you gentlemen," he said with a smile that took in every one. "But I suggest we call it a day—or a night. An' I think I'm losing."

Callaghan said: "That suits me. I'm losing a little too, I think."

Gabby raked in the counters. He said:

"I lose fifteen pounds, and, Slim, you lose twelve. Mr. Rains wins nine pounds and Mr. Vendayne eighteen."

Vendayne said: "You had bad luck, Callaghan. I hope it will go better next time."

Callaghan smiled. He put his hand into the breast pocket of his coat and produced a leather wallet. He placed it on the green baize table and flipped it open. Inside the wallet were sixty new fifty pound notes—Audrey Vendayne's contribution.

Lancelot Vendayne looked at the wallet. He said, with a smile:

"You came prepared to lose a lot."

Callaghan picked up one of the notes. He handed it to Vendayne.

"Will you change that and take twelve pounds?" he asked. "Then if Gabby gives you six and pays Rains we're all square."

Vendayne picked up the fifty pound note. He looked at it and said:

"There's something very attractive about a fifty pound note."

He threw it over to Ventura.

"There you are, Gabby," he said. "You can do the paying out and give Mr. Callaghan his change."

Callaghan finished his drink. He got up and went to the corner of the room. He got his hat, walked back to the table and picked up the little pile of five and one pound notes that Ventura had put down for him.

"Good-night," he said. "And thank you for the game."

Ventura said: "Use the back stairs, Slim. You'll find the door open at the bottom."

Callaghan nodded. He put on his hat and went out. He walked slowly through the black-out in the direction of Berkeley Square: He looked very happy.

Up in his apartment he gave himself four fingers of whisky neat, and began to walk up and down the sitting-room.

He was thinking about Audrey Vendayne. A hell of a woman, he thought. He imagined that there might be a spot of trouble with the lady at some time or other. She was that type. And she didn't like him.

Callaghan began to grin. He was not averse to being disliked by very pretty ladies at any time.

Well . . . what was she playing at? Whatever it was it was important. Sufficiently important for her to take chances about. And she'd taken a chance. And it hadn't come off. Definitely, he thought, it had not come off . . .

He went into his bedroom and undressed. Then he walked into the bathroom, sat down on the stool and began to rub *eau-de-Cologne* into his hair.

He was still grinning.

Chief Detective-Inspector Gringall looked out of the window of his office in Scotland Yard. The sunshine on the Embankment made him feel contented. He took a short pipe from his pocket and began to fill it from a dilapidated tobacco pouch.

The telephone on Gringall's desk rang. Fields got up from his desk, walked across and answered it. After a minute he put his hand over the mouthpiece and said:

"It's Effie Thompson, Callaghan's secretary. She says he would like to see you somewhere around three o'clock. She says he's been retained in the Vendayne jewellery steal."

Gringall nodded.

"Tell her I'll be glad to see him," he said.

Fields did so and hung up. Gringall went back to his desk, sat down and began to draw fruit on the blotter. He drew a tomato and a banana and regarded his handiwork with his head on one side.

"Ring down and find out who's handling that Vendayne job," he said. "And ask whoever it is if they'll let me have the folder and any notes there are."

Fields nodded.

"Walperton's handling the case," he said. "And as far as I know nothing's happened."

Gringall said: "Well, it will now . . ."

Fields grinned at his superior.

"You mean Callaghan?" he asked.

Gringall smiled.

"Yes, Fields," he said. "I mean Callaghan."

He began to draw a pineapple.

Callaghan awoke at twelve o'clock, put his hands behind his head and looked up at the ceiling. He spent five minutes doing this, then, with a sudden movement, threw off the bedclothes and swung out of bed. He wore the top part of a pair of violet shantung silk pyjamas.

He walked over to the window and looked out. He stood there for a moment yawning. Then he went into the sitting-room and telephoned down to the office.

He said: "Good morning, Effie. Did you get Gringall?"

She said, yes; the appointment was made for three o'clock.

Callaghan said: "Ring Parvell & Co., the Insurance Assessors in Eastcheap. Ask 'em if they'll let you know which Company covered the Vendayne jewellery. Whether the risk was fire and theft or just theft."

She said: "Very well. Oh . . . by the way, Mr. Ventura of the Ventura Club's been on the telephone. He asked if he could have a word with you. He said he'd drop in here, at the office, if that would be convenient for you."

"That's all right," said Callaghan. "Tell him to come round at two-thirty. I'll be down by that time."

Effie Thompson went on: "Just a moment, please, Mr. Callaghan. There's some mail here. There's a letter from a firm of lawyers asking you if you'll go in on a blackmail case. Their client's too frightened to go to the police apparently; and there's an inquiry from a cement firm. They want to know if you'll investigate some office leakages."

"No," said Callaghan, "I won't. And tell the other people—the lawyers—to get their client to go to the police. They know damned well that blackmail cases always finish up at Scotland Yard—one way or another. Tell 'em a private detective only prolongs the agony. Anything else?"

"Yes," said Effie. "There's a cheque for two hundred and fifty pounds from the Vendayne solicitors. They say it's a retainer and for expenses. They limit any further bill to three hundred and fifty pounds."

"Do they, hell . . ." muttered Callaghan. "All right. Acknowledge the cheque and pay it into the bank."

She said: "I've already done both things."

Callaghan said: "You're too, too wonderful."

He hung up.

Callaghan went into his office at a quarter-past two. He was wearing a dark blue pinhead suit, a blue silk shirt with a soft collar and a black tie. As he went through the outer office Effie Thompson noticed that the suit was new. She began to wonder about Miss Vendayne.

He sat down at his desk and lit a cigarette. He drew the smoke slowly down into his lungs, sending it out through one nostril. Effie Thompson came in from the outer office with her notebook in her hand.

"I got through to Parvell's," she said. "The Vendayne jewellery was insured by the Sphere & International Assurance Company. Their firm has covered it for the last two hundred and seventy years. They consider it a good risk and if anything under-insured. The jewellery was covered for theft *and* fire."

Callaghan said: "Thank you, Effie."

A bell sounded as the outer office door opened. She went out. After a moment she returned and said:

"Mr. Ventura."

Gabby reflected the first promise of spring. He was wearing a light grey suit, the exquisite cut of which took at least three inches off his stomach; a cream silk shirt and collar, a crepe-de-chine tie in a nice shade of oyster with a cornelian and diamond pin stuck in the middle of it. A grey soft hat matching the suit swung in his fleshy right hand.

Callaghan said: "Well, Gabby, what's eating you? Sit down." He looked at Ventura's stomach. "You've got too much weight on your feet anyway."

Ventura dropped into the big leather armchair. He took out a silk handkerchief and inserted it with difficulty between the tight silk collar and his neck.

He said: "I think I'll have to go on a diet or something."

Callaghan nodded.

"Did you come round to tell me that, Gabby?" he asked.

Ventura wriggled a little in his chair. He said:

"Look, Slim, I know you and you know me. I suppose we might even go so far as to say that we're friends."

Callaghan lit another cigarette.

"We might," he said. He grinned. "The question is whether anybody would believe us."

Ventura said: "Now, don't be tough, Slim. I suppose you've still got that Randall business sticking in your mind?"

Callaghan was still smiling amiably.

"That and a few other things," he said. "There's a lot of things about some of the clubs that you've run in your time that I don't like, Gabby."

Ventura said softly: "Look, Slim, I got to make my living and my clubs are pretty good these days. Look at the way I run the Ventura."

"I know," said Callaghan. "And what about that other dump of yours, the little place—The Gilded Lily? The last time I was in there it stunk so much of marihuana that I almost needed a gas mask, but still. . ."

He looked at Ventura inquiringly.

Gabby said: "You're a hard case, Slim, and you're not making things any easier for me. I came round here because I wanted you to do me a favour."

Callaghan said: "That's what I thought. What's the favour?"

"Nothing much," said Gabby. "Look, Slim, here's how it is: I just want you to tell me something without asking me any questions. This is sort of a personal thing, see? Well, it's like this . . ." He wriggled his chair a little nearer to Callaghan's desk. "You know me, Slim," he said. "You think I'm tough, but maybe I have my soft moments."

Callaghan said: "You're not trying to make me cry, Gabby, are you?"

Ventura wrinkled his nose.

"I wish you wouldn't always take a poke at me," he said.

He flushed.

"All right," said Callaghan, "I won't take a poke at you. You're a soft-hearted feller an' well, where do we go from there?"

Ventura said: "Last night I lent somebody some money—£300 to be exact—no names no packdrill. I lent this certain person six new fifty pound notes. All right. Well, I parted with that dough because I fell for a hard luck story, see? And then do I get a surprise!"

Callaghan said: "Go on, tell me. I can hardly wait."

"Well," said Ventura slowly, "you came in last night to see young Vendayne. You came into that poker game with us, and, so help me

God, when we were settling up you pushed one of my notes back at me. When I saw the number on it I nearly had a fit."

Callaghan said: "It would be very tough if you did have a fit, Gabby."

"Well," said Ventura, "I wanted to know if you'd tell me where you got that note from, Slim. Last night when you opened your case I saw there were six new fifty pound notes. You gave me the top one. I had the idea that the other five might have been mine, too."

"What you really mean is," said Callaghan, "that the other five might have been the money that you did this good turn with."

"That's right," said Ventura.

Callaghan looked at the ceiling. After a minute he looked at Gabby. He was smiling. He said:

"I'm afraid I can't help you a lot, Gabby. I got that money from Gortells, the wine merchants that supply the Safety Valve Bottle Party. I needed £500, and when I want money after the bank's closed I always go to Gortells for it. I sent 'em a cheque round and they cashed it. I paid a bill with the other two hundred."

Ventura got up.

"I see," he said.

"You don't sound very satisfied, Gabby," said Callaghan.

Ventura shrugged his shoulders.

"What the hell!" he said. "I was a mug to come round, anyway."

Callaghan said: "You always were a mug, Gabby."

Ventura was at the door. He turned quickly. His eyes were very hard, very cold. He said:

"Maybe I'm not always going to be a sucker. So long, Slim."

" 'Bye, Gabby," said Callaghan.

He walked over to the door and watched Ventura leave through the outer office. He caught the look in Effie's eyes as the night club proprietor passed her.

He said: "You don't like Mr. Ventura, do you, Effie?"

She said: "I do not. I think he looks like a white-slaver, don't you, Mr. Callaghan?"

Callaghan said: "I wouldn't know. I've never been white-slaved. Have you?"

He took his hat off the hat-stand.

"I'm going down to see Gringall, Effie," he said. "Maybe I'll be back, maybe not. I'm going down to Devonshire to-morrow. I don't know how long I'll be there. I'll keep in touch with you."

She said: "Very well, Mr. Callaghan." When he got to the door she added very calmly: "I hope the weather keeps fine for you, sir."

It was five-and-twenty to three when Callaghan went into Gringall's office. Gringall was looking out of the window, smoking his pipe. He said:

"Hallo, Slim, you're looking well. What—another suit! How you private detectives make money!"

Callaghan said: "I've got a patient tailor, Gringall. And congratulations on getting that promotion. Chief Detective-Inspector Gringall sounds nice, doesn't it?"

Gringall went to his desk and sat down. He nodded towards the chair on the other side.

"I gather you're going to ask a favour," he said. "That's why you brought my promotion up. I suppose you're thinking that I got my step up over the Riverton case, and I suppose that you're also thinking that you pulled that out of the bag for me when I couldn't do it."

Callaghan said: "Nothing was farther from my mind, Gringall."

Gringall said: "I'm sure of that."

He looked at the ceiling. Callaghan sat down and lit a cigarette. He said:

"Look, Gringall, I wanted to ask your advice . . ."

Gringall looked over at Fields, who was grinning at him.

Callaghan said: "What's the joke?"

He looked from one to the other.

"Fields and I were both thinking the same thing. Whenever you come down here and ask my advice there is always a lot of trouble for us all almost immediately afterwards."

Callaghan said: "Well, there's going to be no trouble this time."

He blew a smoke ring, watched it sail across the office.

He said: "I always put my cards on the table and there's one thing I don't like doing . . . I don't like bucking up against the official police forces."

Gringall said: "Oh, no? If you had to serve one year for every time you've bucked the official police forces as you call it, you'd probably never see daylight again. I nearly brought a charge of 'obstruction of a police officer, etc. . . .' over that last little job of yours."

Callaghan said amiably: "Let's let bygones be bygones."

"We will," said Gringall. "So you've come here to ask some advice because you don't want to go bucking against the official force, and I gather you've been retained in the Vendayne case."

Callaghan nodded.

"That's the trouble," he said. "Here's a case where the police have been working for something like three months, and nothing's happened. Then old man Vendayne decides to put me in. Well, what chance have I got? If you boys down here couldn't get away with anything, what am I going to do?"

Gringall said: "I had the folder sent up this morning when your secretary rang through. Walperton has been handling the case, and as you know he's one of our best officers. Well, the whole thing's so simple that it hurts."

He got up, walked over to the window. He stood with his back to it looking at Callaghan.

"Whoever it was had this jewellery were a pretty fly crowd," he said. "The job was done very nicely. Walperton doesn't know how they got into the Manor House, but he thinks they got in through a french window at the back. The catch had been forced but the funny thing was that there weren't any prints on the window or on the sill or anywhere else, and if they'd made any footmarks on the flower-bed outside they'd covered 'em over before they left. The safe was just opened. It wasn't cracked. Whoever opened the safe knew the combination. There were no prints on the safe. There's the story."

Callaghan shook his head.

"That's not an easy one, is it? I feel a little sorry for Walperton," he went on. "Tell me something, Gringall. What's the matter with the Sphere & International Assurance Company? They're being a little sticky about paying the claim, aren't they?"

Gringall shrugged his shoulders.

"What would you do?" he said.

Callaghan nodded.

"You mean their idea is it's an inside job?"

"That's right," said Gringall. "I should think that was their idea. Yet," he went on, "the servants at Margraud Manor have all been there for donkey's years. There's no reason to suspect any one of them."

Callaghan said: "I suppose it was an old safe?"

"A Climax," said Gringall. "Old, but still very good. Why?"

Callaghan grinned.

"You know as well as I do," he said, "that a smart bunch of crooks could very easily get at somebody who used to work in the Climax factory. Maybe those boys had that safe combination before they ever went down to Devonshire."

Gringall said: "Perhaps you're right." He relit his pipe. "You know, Slim," he said, "I think you've come to the wrong place. You really came here to find out why the Insurance Company are holding up that claim. Well, I don't know, and Walperton doesn't know, but they do know. Why don't you go and ask them?"

Callaghan said: "Tell me something, Gringall. Have they had anybody in on this job?"

Gringall nodded.

"Two of the smartest assessors in this country," he said. "Both hand-picked men who know the history of every jewel thief in this country, and that doesn't seem to have done much good." Gringall looked at the ceiling. "Now if you are as wise as I think you are . . ."

Callaghan grinned.

"What would you do, Gringall?" he asked.

The police officer said: "Well, it's only an idea, but I should think the Insurance Company might like to put you in themselves on this."

Callaghan said: "You mean, I could investigate this job for them, too."

He was smiling.

"Something like that," said Gringall.

Callaghan got up.

"I'll be getting along," he said. "Thank you for being so nice."

He had reached the door when Gringall said:

"Just a minute, Slim. Maybe I've given you a good tip. If by any chance, in the course of your investigations either for the Vendayne family or the Insurance Company—*if* they decided it was worth their while to employ you—you become in possession of knowledge of a criminal act or acts having taken place in connection with this steal, I take it you'd let us know about it?"

Callaghan said: "Of course. 'Bye Gringall."

He closed the door quietly behind him.

Fields said: "Like hell he'd let us know, sir."

Gringall looked at his subordinate.

"How do you know?" he said. "He might if it was worth his while."

He took off the telephone receiver and rang Room No. 12. He said:

"Is that you, Walperton? Listen to this. Callaghan's been retained by the family in that Vendayne job. And I've got an idea he's on his way to the Sphere & International Assurance to try and get them to put him in as well. So you can look out for fireworks."

Walperton said: "I will, sir. And if Mister Callaghan gets in the way I'm going to make things hot for him."

"Do," said Gringall. "Only while you're on the job, Walperton, make certain he doesn't make things hot for you instead. Good-bye . . ."

He hung up. He looked at Fields.

Fields said: "I feel sorry for Walperton."

Gringall nodded.

"Me, too," he said

He began to draw a lemon.

## CHAPTER THREE
## MEET THE GIRLS

CALLAGHAN pulled the Jaguar into the side of the road by the Clock Tower at Newton Abbott. Fifty yards away, standing in the entrance of the Golden Hind, was Nikolls.

He strolled towards the car. He said:

"Hallo, Slim. The women around here have got nice hips. I've never seen so many nice shapes . . . It must be the cream. . . ."

They went into the bar. Callaghan ordered two double whiskies. They sat at a little table in the corner. When he had finished his drink, Callaghan said:

"We've got to play this easily, Windy. We're working for the Insurance Company as well."

He grinned sardonically.

Nikolls said: "My God . . . what a set-up. How did you pull *that* one?"

He picked up the empty glasses and went over to the bar. He returned with the glasses filled.

Callaghan said: "I saw Gringall. A *D.I.* named Walperton is handling this case. He's just where he started. Gringall suggested that I had a word with the Sphere & International—the Company who covered the insurance. I took the tip. I told them that I was in the case for the Vendayne family. After a lot of flirting with the situation they asked me if I'd come in and represent them too. They said that the Vendayne family's interests were *their* interests. Clever . . . that . . ."

Nikolls said: "You're tellin' *me*. So the Insurance people don't like it."

Callaghan shrugged his shoulders.

"They're in a jam," he said. "Layne, the Vendayne lawyer, must have written 'em just after he'd seen me. He said that unless they paid up within a month he was going to bring an action. They're hoping that before the month's out I shall have got something that'll help 'em. If I haven't, they've got to pay."

Nikolls nodded.

"Still, it ain't really ethical, Slim, is it?" he asked. "Why, dam' it, you're actin' for everybody."

"Why not?" said Callaghan. He was smiling pleasantly. "If this robbery is all square and above board what have the Vendaynes got to be afraid of? If it's not . . ."

Nikolls lit a cigarette.

"*I* think it stinks," he said.

Callaghan's grin broadened.

"You've got a theory, Windy?" he said accusingly.

Nikolls grinned.

"It's stickin' out a foot. Little Audrey is the girl. She's pinched the stuff so that the claim could be put in. She's pinched it an' hidden it in the back garden or somewhere. That's why she paid you that money to keep out of the case. Besides . . . I know *why* she pulled the job."

"I'm still listening," said Callaghan.

"I got around plenty yesterday," Nikolls began. "I got out to Kingsbridge an' Gara, an' around Totnes. I been in all the pubs around Prawle and Hallsands. I learned an awful lot."

Callaghan raised his eyebrows.

"Such as . . . ?" he queried.

Nikolls took a large gulp of whisky. He continued:

"This Vendayne bunch are a sort of institution in this county. Especially around Gara. They been living here since Noah's Ark or somethin'. Everybody knows 'em. The old boy—the Major—is a honey. Nice an' affable an' quiet an' aristocratic—a real guy. He's nutty about the family, an' he's nutty about Margraud Manor, which is a helluva place an' must cost a lot to keep goin'.

"O.K. Well, he ain't got a lot of money. He's got about four thousand a year, an' what's that worth these days to keep up a place like Margraud ... sweet Fanny Adams ... Well, a year ago the Manor House is practically fallin' to pieces, an' he's mad keen to have it done up. It's goin' to be an expensive job but he wants it done. So does Audrey, an' it looks like Audrey got a scheme to get the Manor repaired. She sold the old man the idea to mortgage the place and get it repaired with the dough he got for the mortgage. Well, he got £20,000, and he did the whole lot on the repair bill.

"Well, that mortgage was the shortest one I've ever heard of. It was a 6½% mortgage for one year. Now how was the Major goin' to pay that mortgage off in a year? Where was the dough comin' from to pay £20,000 plus 6½%?

"But do you know what the joke is, Slim? He's paid it off. I went into Exeter and looked it up. The satisfaction of the mortgage is recorded on the original deed. Well, what's the answer to that one?"

Nikolls drank some more whisky. He went on:

"There's another funny thing. Layne is the family lawyer, ain't he? Well, you'da thought a job like that woulda been handled by the family lawyer. Well, it wasn't. Some lawyer in Exeter put that mortgage through. The name of the firm was endorsed on the deed."

Callaghan said: "I'm still waiting for the theory, Windy ..."

"Little Audrey is my theory," Nikolls grinned. "The old boy is sorta simple, see ... simple an' nice. I reckon Audrey tells him to go inta this mortgage business knowin' that she can pull a fast one. She thinks that she's gonna wait a few months an' then pinch the jewellery. She thinks that the Vendayne reputation is so goddam swell that the Insurance people will pay up on the nail. Then when they pay up she reckons the old man can pay off the mortgage out of the insurance money."

Nikolls picked up the glasses, went to the bar, ordered the same again and wandered back. He said:

"Audrey is just too sweet. Everybody likes Audrey. She plays golf an' sails a boat and is nice an' county an' all that. Half the boyos around here have tried to get themselves engaged to that baby but she ain't havin' any. She's sorta remote if you get me ... goes for long walks an' all that sorta stuff. Maybe Audrey is just the sort of quiet momma who would try an' pull a fast one. She could get away with it, too."

Callaghan nodded.

"She might . . ." he said. "Because it doesn't matter a damn what the Sphere & International people *think*. If they've got nothing tangible by the end of this month they've *got* to pay even if they are practically certain that it's an inside job done by somebody who was planning a fake claim."

Nikolls nodded.

"Sure," he said. "An' by what I can hear of the old Major he'd never suspect anythin' was wrong in a million years. He's one of those guys who believe in everybody, an' if somebody tried to tell him that Audrey had pulled a fast one he'd probably challenge 'em to a duel or somethin'."

Callaghan finished his third whisky.

"It's a nice story, Windy," he said. "But there's one thing we don't know. Even if Audrey did think that the Insurance Company would pay on the stolen jewellery, they haven't done so, have they? All right, where did the Major get the money to pay this mortgage off with?"

Nikolls shrugged.

"That's easy," he said. "Maybe the old boy or Audrey have borrowed the dough on the strength of the Insurance Company paying. Maybe it was a personal loan from somebody they know."

Callaghan nodded.

"Perhaps," he said. "But I don't think so."

He blew a smoke ring.

"Tell me about the other girls, Windy," he said.

Nikolls began to grin. He stretched himself back in his chair and switched his cigarette to the other side of his mouth.

"There's a pair for you," he said. "A pair of honeys. Look . . . let's take Clarissa first of all. She's the next eldest to Audrey. Well, Clarissa is something to look at, they tell me. She's tall an' she's got a figure that was just made for knitwear. She's got dark, auburn sorta hair an' eyes that look as if they couldn't say scram to a kitten, an' she ain't too fond of Esme either . . ."

Callaghan asked: "What about Esme?"

"That baby's a handful," said Nikolls. "The stories they tell about Esme is just nobody's business. Boy, I could write a book about that dame. She's got a big trouble. Her trouble is that she keeps fallin' in love all the time, but she don't fall in love with the right guys. She just goes for anything that is big an' bronzed and blue-eyed. She likes 'em with lots of muscle an' no brains. There's a sorta perpetual war goin' on between Clarissa an' Esme. Every time Esme gets herself a new boy friend, Clarissa tries to muscle in an' pinch the sap off her. Them girls must see a whole lotta life one way an' another."

Callaghan grinned.

"High spirits," he said, "and a spot of temperament."

"Temperament *plus,*" agreed Nikolls. "Last year—a couple months before the War broke—Esme falls for a good-lookin' young fisher-man from Beesands. She falls like a ton of bricks. There was plenty of trouble about it. She swore she was goin' to marry this fishin' guy or die in the attempt. Things got so tough that the old boy had to send her off for a trip. So she went off on a cruise to South Africa for six months. I reckon the old boy thought that a spot of travel would be good for his little daughter. Well . . . he was wrong. She's been a bit worse since she's been back. That baby is just a natural flirt. Anytime she sees somethin' in pants she does a couple backfalls an' thinks he must be the one an' only . . ."

Callaghan smoked silently for a moment. Then:

"What do Clarissa and Esme do with themselves when they aren't at home? How do they spend their evenings, for instance?"

"I was comin' to that," said Nikolls. "Yesterday evenin' I got talkin' to some guy who keeps a little pub on the Totnes-Plymouth road. He said that he'd got sorta intrigued with seein' Clarissa and Esme drivin' past at night as if the devil was after 'em—they both got little cars those two—an' he took the trouble to find out. It seems as if there's a dump a few miles past him—a roadhouse called The Yard Arm. This Yard Arm hang-out usta be a farmhouse, an' some smart guy took it an' turned it into a roadhouse with a restaurant an' bar an' everything. Well, it looks as if Clarissa an' Esme put in a whole lot of time around that dump."

Callaghan asked: "Where are your bags, Windy?"

"I got 'em parked over at a news-shop around the corner," said Nikolls. "I better go put 'em on the car. I've garaged the hired car at Kingsbridge. I thought it would be sorta central if we wanted it."

Callaghan nodded.

"You get the bags on the car," he said. "I'll be with you in five minutes."

He finished his drink and went out into the street. He walked until he came to the post office. Inside he bought a registered envelope.

He went over to the desk and took a telegraph form. He wrote on it:

*"With the Compliments of Callaghan Investigations to Miss Vendayne."*

He took out his wallet, extracted six fifty pound notes, folded them in the telegraph form and put the package in the registered envelope. He addressed the envelope to:

> *"Miss Audrey Vendayne,*
> *Margrand Manor,*
> *Near Gara,*
> *Devon."*

He waited while the clerk wrote out the receipt; then he went back to the car. Nikolls was reading an evening paper.

Callaghan got in and let in the gear. He said as the car started:

"I think this might be very interesting."

Nikolls grinned.

"That's what I thought, but I didn't like to say so. I get shy sometimes."

It was seven-thirty when Callaghan braked the car to a standstill outside the pillared portico of Margraud. As he went up the stone steps, followed by Nikolls, the door opened. Framed in the doorway stood one of the oldest, most venerable butlers that Callaghan had ever seen. His hair was white and his face radiated that good-nature and good manners peculiar to Devonshire people.

He said: "If you will let me have your keys, sir, I'll get your things unpacked. The Major thought you'd like to go up to your rooms and change. He said he'd like to see you in the library at a quarter to eight if that was convenient to you. Dinner is at eight."

Callaghan nodded. He asked the butler what his name was. The old man said:

"My name is Stevens, sir." He paused for a minute. Then he went on: "I'm very glad you've come, sir. We're all a little worried about this thing—the servants, I mean."

Callaghan said: "Quite." Then he added with a smile. "I shouldn't worry if I were you, Stevens. After all what have *you* got to worry about?"

He followed the old man up the broad stairs.

Callaghan sat in a big chair on one side of the library fireplace in which a cheerful fire was burning. On the other side Major Vendayne stood, one elbow resting on the mantelpiece, looking at the detective.

Callaghan thought that if the Vendayne jewellery steal was an inside job, he would bet his last half-crown that Major Vendayne knew nothing about it.

He looked much more than his fifty-five years. His figure, although straight, was thin; his face frail and ascetic looking, with that high flush on the cheekbones often associated with heart cases.

Callaghan said: "I understand that your lawyers have written to the Sphere & International and given 'em a month to pay. Otherwise they're going to issue a writ. I think that was a wise thing to do."

Vendayne sighed. He said:

"I wonder." He paused for a moment; then went on: "They're a very good company. As you know, the insurance of the jewellery has been in the hands of the Sphere & International for nearly three hundred years. That's what is so worrying. I feel they must have some reason for not having paid the claim before."

Callaghan shrugged his shoulders.

"When a hundred thousand pounds worth of jewellery is stolen, Major," he said, "any Insurance Company has got to go through certain processes before they pay a claim. First of all they've got to try and find the jewellery. You probably know as well as I do that even if the police are working on a case the Insurance Company put assessors on the job. Well, it seems as if in this case nothing's happened. I expect you'll find they'll pay the claim before the month's out, Major, unless . . ."

Vendayne looked at Callaghan.

"Unless what?" he said.

"Unless during that time the company get an idea that this robbery was an inside job and that somebody interested financially in that jewellery had a hand in stealing it. There have been fake insurance claims, you know, Major, before now."

"I suppose there have," said the Major. "But it's rather a terrible thought to have in one's mind. The only people living in this house are myself and my three daughters. Naturally none of us could possibly have had anything to do with it. Beyond that there are the servants, every one of whom has practically grown up with the family. We know everything about them. It's quite impossible to associate this robbery with any of them."

Callaghan said: "You haven't had an odd man or woman working about the place—a jobbing gardener, a housemaid—someone who stayed for a few weeks—who might possibly have got the combination of the safe and given it to associates outside?"

"No," said the Major, "we have not."

Callaghan said: "You know, Major, there are one or two things about this robbery which aren't too easy. It was a coincidence that whoever stole that stuff knew it was going to be in the house that night. It was another coincidence that they knew just how to get into the house without disturbing anybody, and the third coincidence is that they knew the combination of the safe. I don't like it."

Vendayne said: "What do you propose to do? Have you got any ideas as to how you're going to start on this thing?"

Callaghan shrugged his shoulders again.

"How can I?" he said. "You have got to remember that this robbery took place three months ago. Directly you had reported the matter to the local police they would have inquired about any strangers in the vicinity. They would have checked up on everybody, and whoever it is has got that stuff isn't in any particular hurry to sell it."

Callaghan took out his cigarette-case and lit a cigarette.

"I gather I've come in on this mainly through your nephew, Lancelot Vendayne," he said. "And I don't think the idea's a bad one. After all, the fact that you've put a private investigator in on this job while it's still being handled by the police shows the Insurance Company that at least you're doing your best. It would be funny if we found that jewellery . . ."

Vendayne said: "It would be wonderful. The jewels have been in this family for hundreds of years. I should hate to feel that they were lost to us, more especially to Lancelot who, as you know, would have been the actual owner under the terms of the original will."

He sighed.

"Well, we must hope for the best, Mr. Callaghan," he said. "In the meantime, come into the drawing-room. I want you to meet my daughters."

Callaghan stubbed out his cigarette.

He said: "I've been looking forward to meeting them."

He followed his host.

Clarissa Vendayne was standing in front of the fireplace in the large oak panelled drawing-room, drinking a glass of sherry. She was tall, slim. Her face was very white and her large brown eyes rested humorously on Esme, who was sprawled in a chair by the side of the fire. Audrey Vendayne, who was writing a letter at a table by the french windows, got up as the Major and Callaghan entered the room.

Vendayne said: "These are my three daughters, Audrey, Clarissa and Esme. My dears, this is Mr. Callaghan, who I hope is going to find the jewellery for us."

Callaghan smiled. His eyes took in Esme, who was arranging her skirts demurely, then wandered to Clarissa, who was looking at him under deep lashes over the rim of her sherry glass. Audrey was not smiling. It was with a certain amount of difficulty that she kept the hostility out of her eyes. Callaghan gave her an extra smile.

Esme said to Clarissa: "We'll finish our conversation afterwards. I'm never rude in front of guests."

Clarissa made a face.

"No?" she said. "And may I ask how long have you been so courteous?" She said to Callaghan:

"We're an extraordinary family, Mr. Callaghan. You'll probably realise that in a day or two. We have only one serious trouble—Esme."

Esme said: "Mr. Callaghan, my sister can't help it. Being a bit of a basket—I mean."

Vendayne said: "Children, *please!*"

Audrey said: "Esme, your language is foul."

Esme picked up her glass of sherry from the small table beside her.

"Are you trying to tell me, Audrey, that Mr. Callaghan has never heard the word basket before?"

Audrey said: "Mr. Callaghan has probably heard a lot of things. But he doesn't have to hear them at Margraud."

Esme said: "Well, I always think it's best for a detective to know the worst, and Clarissa is a basket."

Clarissa said: "Don't repeat yourself, darling. For myself, I think it's just too, too thrilling to have a detective in the house."

She shot a slow smile at Callaghan.

"For once," said Esme, "I agree with you. I imagine he'll take you out on to the balcony this evening and drag the whole of your past life from you."

Clarissa said: "That would be interesting, but I think not possible. He couldn't possibly stay here as long as that would take."

Vendayne said: "Mr. Callaghan, you mustn't take my little girls too seriously. They don't mean anything."

Callaghan said: "I'm sure they don't. By the way," he went on, addressing the three women, "are you going to be in to-night?"

Clarissa said: "I knew it. He's going to cross-examine us. It's going to be like the district attorney in the gangster films."

"Not necessarily," said Callaghan. "But I want to talk to you all about what happened on the night of the robbery. I want to know where you were, if you heard or noticed anything. It's just a matter of routine, of course."

Esme said: "I'm fearfully sorry, Mr. Callaghan. I'd love it, but I've got an appointment to-night."

She looked at Clarissa.

Clarissa said: *"That* reminds me that I think I have too. Would to-morrow do, Mr. Callaghan?"

"To-morrow would be excellent," said Callaghan.

Esme said: "Perhaps it would be a good idea if you deal with Audrey to-night. I've often thought she *was* a bit mysterious."

Clarissa said: "Definitely."

Audrey said: "You two are ridiculous."

Stevens came in with sherry glasses. A minute afterwards Nikolls arrived. The Major introduced him.

Nikolls said: "I don't know what you think, ladies, but I reckon this is goin' to be one of the most interestin' cases in my life."

Clarissa favoured him with a long look.

"Mr. Nikolls," she said, "you look to me like a man who's had a great deal of experience. One day we must get together in the flower garden and you must tell me about it."

Nikolls said: "Why not? Let's do that."

Stevens reappeared and announced that dinner was served. They went into the dining-room.

On the way Nikolls whispered to Callaghan: "Slim, I always thought this was goin' to be good. Now, havin' seen these babies I *know* it's goin' to be a *riot!*"


The first shadows were beginning to fall. Callaghan stood at the far edge of the rolling lawn behind Margraud Manor. In front of him on the other side of the neatly clipped hedge, the fields rolled down to the edge of the cliffs a mile and a half away.

Callaghan turned and began to walk towards the house. Between the lawn and the covered veranda that ran round the back of the house, a series of terraces rose one above the other. Callaghan, who had an eye for atmosphere, stood there with the cool evening wind on his face, thinking that if he had a choice between owning the Vendayne jewellery or Margraud, he'd have the Manor House.

Nikolls came round the side of the house. Callaghan went to meet him.

Nikolls said: "I like this. This is the sort of life I go for. Nice air, nice women an' nice food." He grinned at Callaghan. "Clarissa and Esme don't like each other much, do they?" he said.

"Not so you'd notice it," said Callaghan. "I wonder what the war is between those two."

Nikolls said: "I've got an idea that Clarissa is one of those babies who just *have* to queer other dames' pitches."

Callaghan nodded.

"I thought that too," he said. "After all, the easiest thing for two women to quarrel over is a man."

"I've just been walkin' around the garage," Nikolls went on. "The gardener is pumpin' up a tire of Esme's car, and when he's done that he's goin' to fill the tank of Clarissa's roadster. Those two are goin' places."

Callaghan said: "Listen Windy. Go back to the garage and hang around. When Esme comes out ask her if she can drop you at Kingsbridge. Wherever she's going to it's ten to one she'll have to go through the town. Ask her to drop you there. If she does, get the hired car out of the garage, get over to this Yard Arm place. Have a look round and see if you can pick up anything."

"O.K.," said Nikolls.

He went off.

Callaghan walked up the terrace steps towards the house. He sat down in a low chair on the balcony. He lit a cigarette and began to blow smoke rings. A soft voice said:

"Mr. Callaghan."

Callaghan got up. It was Audrey Vendayne. Looking at her in the half light Callaghan thought that except for the temperament she had a great deal more, in his opinion, than either Clarissa or Esme. He liked the lines of her slim black dinner frock.

He said amiably: "It's a lovely evening, isn't it?"

She said coldly: "Possibly, Mr. Callaghan, you can imagine that I didn't want to talk to you about the evening."

"No?" said Callaghan. "What did you want to talk about?"

"Three hundred pounds," she said. She smiled cynically. "I've always been led to believe that private detectives are rather strange people," she went on, "but I couldn't imagine even a private detective having the effrontery to do what you did."

Callaghan knocked the ash off his cigarette. He said slowly:

"You mean taking that three hundred pounds from you to keep out of this case and then going on with the job?"

"That is what I mean," she said.

Callaghan said: "Miss Vendayne, I think you're stupid. Whatever personal opinion you may have of private detectives they're usually considered to be intelligent. You must admit it was particularly stupid of you to try and bribe me to keep out of this investigation."

He drew a mouthful of smoke down into his lungs and exhaled it slowly through one nostril. He continued:

"Quite obviously if a private detective wasn't straight, he'd do what I did—keep the money and still go on with the job." He grinned. "After all, I was paid £250 yesterday by your father's lawyers. If on the other hand the detective was an honest man; supposing—if such a thing were possible—and he wanted to do a straight job of work, then his best plan would be to play you along to find out just why you wanted him to lay off the case. You couldn't squeal anyway."

Her eyes flashed. She said:

"I told you my reasons for not wanting you here."

"Maybe," said Callaghan. He was smiling. "A lot of people tell me things, but I don't *have* to believe them."

She looked at him. Her eyes were wide with amazement.

"Mr. Callaghan," she said, "are you trying to tell me that I'm a liar?"

"No," said Callaghan. "I'm not trying to tell *you* anything, but I'm going to state some facts to you, and you can think 'em out. When you rang my office the night before last and made that appointment to meet me at the Ventura Club, I wondered why."

He paused.

She said: "How *very* interesting."

Callaghan grinned.

"I'm going to be still more interesting," he said. "I'll tell you why you did it. You had a reason for making that appointment to meet me at the Ventura Club, the reason being that before you saw me you wanted to see Gabby Ventura. You thought it would be a good thing to have a little ammunition to bribe me with if necessary."

Callaghan stopped talking. He flicked the ash off his cigarette and looked at her. One corner of his mouth was wreathed in a cynical smile.

"Well?" he queried.

She said nothing. He continued:

"You got to the Ventura Club early and you borrowed £300 from Gabby Ventura. Then you waited outside till I came along.

"Strangely enough," said Callaghan, "I went back to the club later. I wanted to see Lancelot. I got into a little poker game with Lancelot and Gabby and another man. I lost some money, and I paid my losses with one of the fifty pound notes that you gave me."

Callaghan's grin broadened.

"Yesterday morning," he went on, "Gabby Ventura came round to my office trying to find out where I got the note from. He said he'd lent somebody some money the night before. Naturally he was very interested to know just how and why that fifty pound note had got into my hands."

Callaghan's grin altered. It became almost angelic.

"And you don't like being called a liar, do you, Miss Vendayne?" he concluded.

She stood looking out over the terraces. She said nothing. Callaghan stubbed out his cigarette and lit another.

"The joke is," he said, "I don't really disbelieve you. Immediately I saw your father I could understand any daughter wanting to save him any trouble. He's a sick man. All I say is that your technique wasn't too clever. If I were you I'd remember in the future that even if you think private detectives are dishonest as a tribe they're seldom unintelligent. At least this one isn't."

She said: "Mr. Callaghan, why should you believe that I am interested in anything you think?"

"That's just another bluff," said Callaghan. "You're fearfully interested in what I think, and I know it. The trouble is that you're one of those people who've still got to learn that honesty is the best policy."

His smile showed his white teeth. He said:

"I'll make a little bet with you. Before we're through on this job, you'll tell me what's on your mind."

"Really," she said sarcastically. "And, of course, you know *why* I shall do that."

"I can make a good guess," said Callaghan. "Believe it or not I can be quite useful when people are in tight corners, and I've got an idea you're in one."

She turned on her heel and disappeared through the french windows.

Callaghan walked down the terrace smoking, appreciating the evening air.

## CHAPTER FOUR
## THREE'S A PARTY

SOMEWHERE in the Manor House a clock struck eleven. Callaghan thought that the chimes, brassy and resonant, possessed an almost antique note that might well be associated with a headless ghost that wandered playfully about the dark, oaken corridors.

He lay stretched out on the four-poster bed in his room, looking at the ceiling, wondering why he disliked oak panelling even when it was relieved by tastefully selected chintzes.

After a moment he concluded that he was not really thinking about panelling or chintz; that his mind was concerned with Audrey Vendayne.

After all, you've got to know a man like Gabby fairly well to borrow three hundred pounds . . . if you are a woman.

He got up, switched on the light, straightened his tie. He went over to the corner cupboard and took out a bottle of rye whisky and a glass. He drank five fingers of neat whisky, lit a cigarette and went downstairs.

When he reached the big hallway he began to cough. He coughed for some time. Then he replaced the cigarette in his mouth and walked towards the doorway.

Behind him, in the main passage, a door opened. Audrey Vendayne's voice said: "Oh, Mr. Callaghan."

Callaghan turned. He was smiling cheerfully. He said:

"Hallo . . . Miss Vendayne. It seems to be a nice night. I thought I'd go and look at it. Will you come too?"

She said shortly: "No thank you."

She walked towards him and stopped when she was a foot or two away from him.

Callaghan was thinking to himself. "She doesn't like me a bit. And she isn't quite certain why. She's wondering just how crooked I am and just how much she can play me along. She's fed up to the back teeth about that three hundred . . ."

He grinned amiably at her.

She said: "I've been talking to my father. We've come to a conclusion. It should interest you."

Callaghan said nothing.

"*I* think, and my father agrees with me, that in the circumstances we ought to postpone the claim against the Sphere & International Company. It's quite obvious from their attitude that they think there's something wrong with the claim. Or alternatively the police have not had time to find the culprits. We propose to give them more time. If they fail we can always claim when the position is more definite."

Callaghan said: "It would be a good idea if it worked."

"*What* would be a good idea, Mr. Callaghan?" she asked.

His smile was beatific.

"It would be a good idea if I fell for that line of talk and allowed the Major to fall for it," he said. "If I fell for it I'd pack my bags and get out because there wouldn't be anything or me to do here. Well . . . I'm not going to do that. I'm going to stay here until such time as I get my hands on something tangible . . . that is if I haven't got something tangible now . . ."

She turned away with an angry gesture and moved towards the staircase. She stopped with her foot on the first stair and half turned. Callaghan liked the pose. He thought that she had quite delightful ankles, that her frock hung gracefully, that the poise of her head was as it should be. He noticed that, under the hall light, her hair had auburn tints.

She said: "You're really an impossible person, aren't you?"

"Maybe," said Callaghan. "But the best thing you can do is to stand for my being impossible, otherwise I'm going to tell the Major that you went dashing up to town for the express purpose of touching one of the lousiest night club proprietors in London for three hundred pounds to buy me off with, only a few hours after your own lawyers had put me in on this business. I don't think you'd like that."

She smiled. There was a great deal of dislike in her smile.

"Perhaps I shouldn't," she said. "Any more than you would like my father to know that having accepted the case you took the money from me and kept it."

He grinned at her.

"And you're going to tell him, I suppose?" he asked. "Sticking to that three hundred was about the safest thing I ever did in my life. You just can't do anything about it. It's one of those things you have to stand for and like."

She took her foot off the stair and faced him. Her face was flushed. She said, controlling her voice:

"I suppose it's part of the technique of a private detective to be as gratuitously insolent as possible."

There was a world of contempt in her voice.

"That *is* fairly right," said Callaghan very cheerfully. He drew some smoke down into his lungs and began to cough. "It's these damned cigarettes," he explained. "I smoke 'em all the time and I've a permanent smoker's cough."

She said: "Am I supposed to be interested?"

He grinned at her.

"I forgot—you wouldn't be, of course," he said. "And about being insolent, I've found it's not a bad thing. It gets a reaction sometimes. People are more inclined to tell the truth when they're in a bad temper. Besides which I like looking at you when you're in a temper. It suits you."

She said sarcastically: "You're fearfully clever, aren't you? Quite a psychologist. I suppose you know everything there is to be known . . ."

"I wouldn't say that," said Callaghan. "I just know a little. But I know *one* thing."

He exhaled cigarette smoke slowly.

"To-morrow," he went on, "your father and you and I are going to have a show-down. I'm going to tell you one or two things that might be good for you to hear. Or perhaps you'd rather I had the conversation with *you?*"

Her expression altered. She said quickly:

"I've told you that my father is a sick man. Naturally, I'd do anything to save him trouble . . ."

"Rubbish," said Callaghan amiably. "What you really mean is you're afraid of a show-down. I suppose you've made a fool out of the old boy and you think I might have guessed how you've done it."

She caught her breath. It was almost a gasp of rage. She said in a low voice:

"There are moments when I think I could quite easily *kill* you. I think you are easily the most loathable person I've ever met . . ."

Callaghan said: "Well, that's something. I never mind what a woman feels so long as she's not *quite* disinterested."

She turned quickly and began to walk up the stairs. Callaghan watched her. Every movement spoke of the rage that possessed her.

Somewhere down the passage a telephone bell jangled. After a moment Stevens appeared. He said:

"Mr. Nikolls is on the telephone, sir. He wants to speak to you."

Callaghan walked down the passage to the alcove where the telephone stood. He took up the receiver. Stevens disappeared.

Nikolls said: "Slim, have a good laugh. Esme dropped me at Kingsbridge. I thought *you* could push a car along but that baby's drivin' is an eye-opener. I'm surprised I'm still in one piece."

Callaghan said: "Well . . . ?"

"She dropped me and went off on the Totnes Road," Nikolls continued. "I got the car out of the garage and went after her. I had an idea that maybe she was goin' to that Yard Arm dump I told you about. Well, the hunch was right. She's there now. So's Clarissa. Their cars are both parked behind the place."

Callaghan asked: "Is it still open?"

Nikolls said: "No. But here's the funny thing. I stuck around outside behind a hedge. When the place closed down Esme and Clarissa went out the back with a guy. They walked across a little orchard an' went into some other place—a fairly large sorta cottage at the back. I stuck around for a bit to see if they'd come out, but they didn't. So I tried something. I went up to the back door and knocked. Some guy opened the door, not the guy who the girls had gone in with. I asked him for some water for the car. When he went to get it he switched the light on an' I nearly had a fit. Who d'you think the baby was?"

Callaghan said: "What am I supposed to do—have three guesses?"

"Sorry," said Nikolls. "Well, you remember that boyo who was doorman on that dive of Ventura's, the Backstairs Club, in Soho—Ropey Felliner? Well, it was him. Was I surprised?"

"I bet you were," said Callaghan. "Did he recognise you?"

"He did not," answered Nikolls. "I kept away back in the dark."

"Where are you speaking from?" Callaghan asked.

"I'm in an A.A. box away down the road," Nikolls replied. "About half a mile from the Yard Arm."

Callaghan said: "I'm coming along. I think it's time something happened. If it doesn't, we'll make it. I'll be with you as soon as I can."

"O.K.," said Nikolls. "I'll just stick around an' look at the moon. I'm feelin' poetic to-night, anyway."

Callaghan hung up. He went up to his room and got an overcoat. He rang the bell, came downstairs and met Stevens in the hall.

He said: "Stevens, I may be a little late to-night. Have you a spare key?"

"Yes, sir," said the butler. "I'll go and get it."

Callaghan walked up and down the hall waiting for Stevens to come back. He looked contented. He was intrigued by Nikoll's news that Ropey Felliner was at the cottage behind the Yard Arm. He wondered why.

Stevens came back with the key. As he gave it to Callaghan he said:

"I hope things are going all right, sir, and I hope I'm not too curious, but have you got any idea yet, sir? We are naturally very interested."

Callaghan grinned.

"I've practically got the criminal, Stevens," he said. "I think I know who stole the Vendayne jewellery."

The butler's eyes widened.

"My God, Mr. Callaghan," he said. "Who was it, sir?"

"Santa Claus," said Callaghan, as he went out.


The moon was full. The road in front of the Jaguar was like a grey ribbon. Nikolls came out of the darkness of the hedge and stood in the middle of the road. He got on the running board of the car. He said:

"I got the bus parked in a field three or four hundred yards down the road on the right. The gate's open. How about you parkin' in there, too?"

Callaghan let in the clutch. He drove down the road, through the open gate. He parked the car beside Nikolls's. He said:

"Where's this cottage, Windy?"

"About sixty or seventy yards down the road," Nikolls answered. "On the left is the Yard Arm. There's a sign outside. Just past it is a pathway leading through an orchard. The cottage is on the other side."

Callaghan said: "All right. You'd better look at the moon some more."

He began to walk down the road.

He passed the Yard Arm, found the little pathway running behind it, began to walk across the orchard. He was thinking it was a lovely night and wondering about Felliner. Just in front of him, almost hidden by the trees, was the cottage. It was a large two-storied affair formed, evidently, of two or three cottages knocked into one. The little lawn and the white palings that surrounded it were well kept, and the windows carefully blacked-out. Callaghan pushed open the gate, walked up the short path and knocked on the door. He stood there, looking at the glowing end of his cigarette. After a minute the door opened.

Callaghan, looking past the man who stood in the doorway, could see that the hall of the cottage was luxuriously carpeted, well-furnished. Then he looked at the man. He was about thirty-five years of age; had very sleek black wavy hair, a face that was almost too good-looking, a decided jaw. He was tanned. Callaghan's eyes, straying from the man's face to the side of the cottage doorway, noticed the plate that bore the name of the place. On it was the word: "MALMESBURY."

He said: "My name's Callaghan. I'm staying at Margraud Manor. I understand that Clarissa and Esme Vendayne are here."

The man said: "Yes?"

He raised his eyebrows. The tone of his voice was half inquiring, half insolent. Callaghan went on:

"I don't think the Major's very well," he said, lying easily. "Miss Vendayne's a little bit perturbed about him. She thinks the girls ought to go home."

The other said: "How did you know they were here?"

Callaghan said: "That's my business."

The man in the doorway shrugged his shoulders.

"Well, if you want to be rude . . ." he said.

"I don't want to be rude," said Callaghan, "but why shouldn't anybody know where they were. Or is it a secret?"

The man stood back. Callaghan noticed he was fairly tall and muscular, that he moved easily.

He said: "There isn't any secrecy. Perhaps I sounded a little short. Come in. My name's Blaize."

"I'm glad to meet you," said Callaghan.

He stepped into the hallway. Blaize closed the door behind him. Esme came out of the door on the other side of the hall. She turned her head and spoke into the room behind her.

"My God," she said. "It's Mr. Callaghan. I'm *thrilled*. He's a fast worker, isn't he?" She said to Callaghan: "Don't tell me you couldn't wait till to-morrow to question me."

Clarissa came out from the room. She stood behind Esme. Esme murmured:

"Well, three's a party—sometimes. But I rather think that four's a crowd."

Callaghan said: "I think so too." He went on: "Miss Vendayne asked me to come over and say that she was worried about the Major. She thinks maybe he's going to have one of his attacks. She thought you might like to go back."

Esme's face became serious.

"Oh, dear," she said, "Come on, Clarissa, we'd better go. Good-night, Willie."

She walked straight past Blaize, out of the cottage. Close behind her came Clarissa. She stopped as she reached Callaghan. She said:

"I think you two should know each other. William dear, this is Mr. Callaghan, a veritable prince of private detectives. Mr. Callaghan, this is Mr. Blaize—Mr. William Blaize. I think he's rather a sweet, don't I, William?"

Blaize grinned.

"In case you should want to know why I think he's a sweet," Clarissa went on, "it's mainly because Esme's stuck on him, and as my only amusement in these parts is trying to pinch Esme's young men, there, Mr. Callaghan, you have a logical and deductive reason as to why I think William's sweet. He's awfully relieved that we've got to go. I know he's got an appointment somewhere."

Blaize said with a grin: "I've been wanting to go to Exeter for the last hour, but I'm always a little gentleman." He grinned ruefully. "It'll be about three before I get there."

"Poor William," said Clarissa. "It's just too bad! Good-night, Sweet William. 'Bye, Mr. Callaghan."

She went out.

Callaghan stood looking at Blaize. After a minute he said: "It's nice work if you can get it."

Blaize said: "Exactly what do you mean by that?"

Callaghan said: "I don't know. You probably do. Good-night."

He went out of the doorway and began to walk across the orchard. From somewhere in the vicinity he could hear the sound of Clarissa's and Esme's cars starting. He walked back on to the main road. He waited until he saw the tail lights of the girls' cars disappear. Then he walked down the road through the gateway into the field.

Nikolls was sitting in the driving seat of the hired car, smoking, looking at the moon, his hands behind his head.

"Didn't take long to break that party up, Slim," he said. "How did you do it?"

Callaghan said: "I told 'em the old man was going to have one of his attacks. They decided they'd go home. You'd better go back. Put your car in the garage at Margraud—I left the door open."

Nikolls said: "O.K. You're not comin'?"

Callaghan said: "No, I'm going to have a little talk with Felliner." Nikolls raised his eyebrows.

"What about the other guy?" he asked.

Callaghan said: "There's a rumour he's going to Exeter. I'll wait for a bit and see."

Nikolls said. "I get it. You're gonna use the old system?"

Callaghan grinned.

"Why not, Windy?" he said.


Callaghan got into the Jaguar and sat there smoking. He was listening for the sound of a car. He was wondering about Blaize. He waited ten minutes—then he got out of the car, threw his cigarette end into the damp grass, walked out into the road, keeping in the shadow of the hedge. He began to walk towards the Yard Arm. When he had gone thirty yards down the road, a long low car shot out from the drive on the right of the Yard Arm building and turned left.

Callaghan walked through the orchard. He walked round the side of the cottage. At the back, beside a white painted water-butt, was a door. Callaghan rapped. After a minute he heard some sounds from inside, then the noise of a bolt being pulled. The door opened.

Callaghan said: "Good-evening, Ropey."

Someone from inside the doorway said: "What the hell . . . Callaghan . . . !"

"That's right," said Callaghan. "Come outside, Ropey. I want to talk to you."

Felliner came into the doorway. He was very big. His shoulders were wide. He looked like a boxer. His great hands hung down by his sides relaxed, like a gorilla's. He said:

"Supposin' I don't want to talk to *you*. What the hell do you want? What's going on round here? You're the second guy that's knocked me up to-night."

Callaghan said: "I know. The first one was Nikolls. You didn't recognize him. Your eyes aren't so good as they used to be, are they?"

Felliner said: "Cut it out. What is it you want?"

Callaghan lit a cigarette. He said:

"I want to know what you're doing down here."

Felliner said with a faint grin: "And supposin' I tell you to mind your own damn business?"

Callaghan took the cigarette from his mouth with his left hand casually. Almost simultaneously he moved forward on to the ball of his left foot. His right fist caught Felliner fairly in the mouth. The big man went over backwards. Callaghan stepped into the doorway. As Felliner got to his knees, Callaghan put out his left hand and put his fingers inside Felliner's collar. He helped him to his feet. When he was almost there, Callaghan hit him again.

Felliner went down with a crash. A beam of moonlight came through the doorway. On the other side of the room Callaghan could see an electric light switch. He went across, switched on the light. Felliner had got to his feet. His shoulders were hunched like a bull's. His mouth was bleeding. He stood looking at Callaghan.

He said: "I've always wanted to paste you, Callaghan, and now, by God, I'm goin' to do it!"

Callaghan grinned. He said:

"Well, there's no law against trying, Ropey. I hope you're in better condition than you were when you were working for Gabby, throwing half-cut sissies out of the Backstairs Club . . ."

Felliner said something under his breath. He moved quickly forward.

Callaghan put his hand on the back of a kitchen chair that stood underneath the switch. He spun the chair suddenly towards Felliner. It hit him fairly across the shins.

Felliner swore viciously. He jumped in at Callaghan with an agility that was surprising and swung a left hook. Callaghan caught the punch with his right hand, put out his left hand and caught Ropey's right wrist. His fingers seemed to be resting easily on the pulse.

Felliner began to howl. Callaghan brought over his right hand and took hold of the other's fingers. He exerted a little pressure. Felliner screamed. His forehead was covered with sweat.

Callaghan said: "I'll always back, *judo* against old-fashioned slugging tactics, Ropey. This is one of the sweetest Japanese hand-holds I know. If you try and move anyway at all you break at least two of your fingers. Would you like to try?"

He released his hold and put his hands in his pockets. Ropey went over to the other side of the room and sat down. He was nursing his wrist, massaging the fingers.

"The trouble with you, Ropey, is that slugging has always been your best bet and you think it always does the job. If you're as wise as I think you are, you'll cut out any ideas of rough stuff and begin to think. You're in a bad jam, Ropey."

Felliner said: "I don't know what the 'ell you're talkin' about. You're barking up the wrong tree, I'm tellin' you."

Callaghan picked up the fallen chair. He sat down on it. He was thinking quickly . . . considering the best line of bluff to use. He said:

"Ropey, you know damn well I always know what I'm doing."

Felliner growled: "I don't know what you're talkin' about. It's lucky for you that Blaize isn't 'ere. If he was there'd be some trouble. He'd 'ave you pinched maybe."

Callaghan grinned.

He said: "I wouldn't be too sure of that, Ropey. And since you seem to have become so unintelligent, perhaps you'd like to listen to *why* I think you're in a bad jam. Three months ago some jewellery was stolen from the Vendayne Manor House, see? Well, I don't think it looks too good for you—with your record—being around."

Callaghan took out his cigarette-case, selected a cigarette. He went on: "The police must have overlooked you when they were checking up."

Felliner grinned. There was a look of relief in his eyes. He said:

"I get it. So you're trying to tie me up with that steal, are you? Well, you can't do it. I wasn't anywhere near 'ere when that stuff was pinched. I've only been 'ere three days, an' how do you like that, Mr. bleeding know-all?"

"I don't mind it," said Callaghan. "It doesn't prove anything one way or the other. All right, Ropey, if you're so certain of yourself I'll have a word on the telephone with Walperton, the Scotland Yard man who's handling this job. I think he might like to have a little talk to you . . . that is, of course, if you don't like talking to me."

Felliner said: "I'm not looking for trouble, and I've got nothing to be afraid of either, but I don't want to have any truck with coppers. I don't like 'em, you know that."

"All right, Ropey," said Callaghan. "Well, let you and me be friends, shall we? Maybe that way nobody'll get hurt, at least not any more than they *have.*"

Callaghan got up. He walked round the kitchen table and sat on the edge of it, looking down at Felliner.

He said: "You know, Ropey, you're not the sort of man who gets himself a job in the heart of Devonshire as a caretaker or a servant or whatever you are just because he likes fresh air. That's sense, isn't it? What are you doing down here?"

Felliner said nothing. Callaghan went on:

"For the last six or seven years you've been working for Gabby. You've worked in every club he's had. If there's been any dirty work afoot you've been in it—*well* in it. There's a lot of funny business going on round here and the fact that you're here shows me that Gabby's interested. The best thing you can do is to talk."

Felliner said: "Well, all right. What's it matter anyway? I came down 'ere and I took this job because Gabby told me to."

"I see," said Callaghan. "So Gabby knew the job was going?"

" 'E didn't," said Felliner. "There was an advertisement in a paper. The boss saw it. He told me to answer it."

Callaghan nodded.

"And what were you supposed to do?"

"Stick around an' keep my eye on Blaize," said Felliner. "Gabby thought he was goin' off somewhere sort of sudden. He wanted to know where 'e was goin'. 'E wanted to know anythin' I could find out."

Callaghan got up. He said:

"You take a tip from me, Ropey, keep your nose clean. I've got an idea there's going to be a little trouble flying about in these parts. If I were you I'd keep out of it."

"You're telling me?" said Felliner. "I reckon I've had all the trouble I'm going to have. I'm getting out."

"No, you're not," said Callaghan pleasantly. "You're going to stay put just where you are, and another thing you needn't bother to let

Gabby know I've seen you. Let's keep this little conversation a secret as between friends, shall we?"

He walked over to the door. He stood for a moment looking out at the moonlit orchard. Then he turned and said:

"Ropey, you remember that fellow who was rolled a year ago at the Backstairs Club—the one they found out in the alleyway? Well, I don't believe that case is marked 'closed' yet. The police still want to know who it was threw him out of the window. Maybe you'd like me to tell 'em?"

Felliner said hoarsely: "You're a bastard, that's what you are. If you can't get a thing one way you get it another."

Callaghan grinned.

"That's right, Ropey. We get there somehow and who the hell cares how. Keep your nose clean, and behave, and you're all right. But if you get up against me I'll stick you inside over that Backstairs job, and you know I *mean* it.

"Good-night, Ropey."

Callaghan sat behind the wheel of the Jaguar. He sat there for a long time looking across the fields. Eventually he drew on his gloves, lit a cigarette, let in the clutch.

He drove slowly back to Margraud enjoying the night air. Nikolls was waiting outside the garage.

"I reckon you're a thought reader or something, Slim," he said. "I thought I'd be the first to give you the good news."

Callaghan raised his eyebrows.

"What's happened?" he said.

"Well, it's damned funny," said Nikolls. "You go out to that Yard Arm place an' tell those girls a phoney story about the old man havin' a seizure, an' when they get back here they find it's right. He has."

"Well . . . ?" said Callaghan.

"They took him away," Nikolls replied. "The ambulance got here about half an hour ago. They took him to Exeter. I reckon he's pretty bad, too."

Callaghan said: "I wonder."

Nikolls said: "How do you mean? Do you think it's screwy, too?"

"Why not?" said Callaghan. "Maybe little Audrey wanted the Major out of the way for a bit. Maybe she thinks it'll be easier if he's not around."

Nikolls said: "So you think she's going to do something?"

Callaghan began to walk towards the house.

"She's *got* to do something," he said.

## CHAPTER FIVE
## THE LINE FOR CLARISSA

NIKOLLS reclined in a wicker chair set back behind a little table in Grantley's Café in Kingsbridge High Street. He finished his coffee and pondered heavily. He ordered more coffee with a large portion of Devonshire cream, looked at his wristwatch, observed the morning sun illuminating the new bread and cakes in the Window, considered critically the hip-lines of the two young women behind the counter.

It was ten minutes past eleven. Nikolls fished about in his pocket for a Lucky Strike, found one, put it in his mouth, reread the note from Callaghan:

*"Try and get a minute with Clarissa after breakfast. Make a date with her to meet you at the café in Kingsbridge at half-past eleven. Get there first and wait for her. When she turns up work the old stuff on her. If she seems interested, mention Slapton Sands casually when I arrive. Play it up like hell—I think shell fall for the line.*

*S.C."*

Nikolls produced his lighter and lit the corner of the note. He held it up in his plump fingers and watched it burn. He lit his cigarette from the last corner and put the ashes carefully into the ash tray.

He wondered if Callaghan was right about Clarissa. He realised that Callaghan *was* right about women more often than not. On the other hand, Clarissa was a smart package, ruminated Nikolls. She had brains in her head. All the Vendayne women had brains. The fact just stuck out and hit you when you looked at them. Nikolls, who reduced most problems to terms of betting, thought that it was about six to four on Callaghan. Clarissa came in.

Nikolls eyed her critically as she walked towards his table. He thought: "A hell of a dame, she knows how to walk an' her hips are just right, an' what she don't know about clothes could be stuck up your nose and it wouldn't even make you sneeze."

Clarissa was wearing a sage green tweed coat and skirt over a matching jersey that was tied at the neck with a yellow cord. Pulled well on to one side of her carefully dressed auburn-dark head was a sage green Robin Hood hat with a yellow ribbon to match the neck cord. Her shoes were polished calf-skin. Her stockings beige silk. Her small hands were encased in sleek pigskin driving gauntlets.

She said sweetly as Nikolls got to his feet:

"Hallo, Windy . . . I'm going to call you Windy because I heard Mr. Callaghan do it. And why are you called Windy . . . Windy?"

Nikolls grinned amiably. He said:

"My name's Windemere . . . It's a helluva name but I couldn't do a thing to stop it. My old man usta live around there before he went to the States."

She said: "You're *not* an American, Windy?"

"American . . . *hell,*" replied Nikolls. "I'm a Canadian. I was born there an' so was my ma. I've spent a lot of time in the States though. I usta work for a Detective Agency there until some guy shot Monty Kells who usta be Slim's assistant. Then he cabled for me an' I came over here."

Clarissa said: "Why is he called 'Slim'?"

Nikolls grinned at her.

"Because that's just what he is . . . as slim as they make 'em. He'd slide through or round or under anythin'. There's only one thing that ever gets him beat—" Nikolls produced an air of ponderous gravity— "an' that's what I'm afraid of now . . ."

She said: "I want some coffee, please." She began to take off her gloves. "*Do* tell me, Windy," she murmured angelically, "just what it is you're afraid of."

Nikolls looked out of the window. His face expressed concern and a suggestion of doubt. Nikolls was a very good actor—a fact that few people raised until it was too late.

He looked at her. It was a long searching look. Then he said very seriously:

"Clarissa, I'm very fond of Slim. I'd do anythin' for that guy. To me he's just the biggest guy in the world . . . an' I just don't wanta see him get hurt."

Clarissa's big eyes widened. She leaned across the table, folded her hands together. She said:

"But this is *exciting*. I'm *thrilled*. Tell me . . . *please* . . . Who's going to hurt Mr. Callaghan?"

Nikolls drew in a deep breath of tobacco smoke. He drew it right down into his lungs and allowed it to trickle out of one corner of his mouth. He said quietly:

"You might . . ."

"My God," said Clarissa. "How marvelous! Why might I?"

Nikolls stubbed out his cigarette. He stubbed it out with an air of finality. The air of a man who has made up his mind. He said very quietly, his eyes on hers:

"Clarissa . . . I wanna tell you somethin'. An' if you ever let on I'm gonna cut your pretty throat from ear to ear. Slim's nutty about you, see? Ever since he set eyes on you last night he's gone crackers over you. And get *this;* women fall for that guy like ninepins an' he usually just don't take any notice. He's just like an ice-box where women are concerned. So any time he does give a dame a tumble she's entitled to fly flags an' give herself a twenty-one gun salute."

He shrugged his shoulders sadly.

"Maybe I ought not to have said anything'," he went on. "But I'm sorta worried. You see, when he told me he was chuckin' the case this mornin' . . ."

Clarissa interrupted: "Why is he giving up the case?" she asked.

Nikolls said: "He says it's because he can't get a line on anythin'. But I don't believe it. I believe it's *you.* I watched him lookin' at you last night, after he got back from the Yard Arm—when you were pourin' tea for us all an' I knew."

He stopped suddenly and regarded the cakes in the window. He was watching Clarissa out of the corner of his eye. He noted with satisfaction that her eyes were soft.

"He mustn't give up the case, Windy," she said. "He *just* mustn't. And you needn't worry about *me.* I couldn't do anything to hurt him. I just couldn't. I'm not like that. Besides . . . I think he's terribly sweet. Directly I saw him I thought he was *fearfully* sweet. He's got that look in his eyes, that faraway look . . . you know, Windy?"

Nikolls said softly: "I know . . ."

He was thinking: "By heck . . . Slim was right again. She's fallen for it."

He put his hand over hers as it lay on the table. He said gravely:

"Clarissa, I trust you . . . remember . . . If you take Slim for a ride I'm gonna personally cut your throat . . . that is if he don't do it first . . ."

Clarissa's right hand went to her throat. She smiled happily. Nikolls, looking at her, thought: "Hell . . . she looks as if she'd *like* to have her throat cut . . ."

She said: "This is all too marvellous. Windy, I'll do anything to help. Just *anything* . . ."

Nikolls looked out of the window. Outside, Callaghan was getting out of the Jaguar. Nikolls said:

"Here he is. We better pretend we met by accident." When Callaghan came in, he went on:

"This is funny, Slim. Miss Vendayne just arrived for some coffee. Maybe you'd like to talk to her. I want to take a look at Slapton Sands. They tell me there's some marvellous pike fishin' there." He looked quickly at Callaghan. One eyelid quivered almost imperceptibly. He went on: "They tell me that the fish there just go for everything . . . hook, line an' sinker."

He got up.

"I'll be seein' you," he said.

He gave Clarissa a long look and went out.

Callaghan ordered some coffee. He was wearing a grey flannel suit, a fawn silk shirt and a brown tie. Clarissa found herself looking at his mouth, thinking that it was a very mobile mouth.

She said: "Slim . . . I'm going to call you Slim, and you're going to call me Clarissa . . . I want you to know that I'd love to do anything I can do to help you. Directly I saw you I felt I wanted to do anything I could . . . You understand?"

Callaghan looked at her. His expression was soulful. His features arranged themselves in an expression of almost hopeless passion. He said softly:

"Clarissa . . . you're wonderful. Directly I saw you I knew that you were *different*—yes, that's the word—*different*. Somehow I felt you'd help me. Of course, it's going to be difficult, but . . ."

She said: "Nothing's difficult unless one makes it so."

He smiled at her. It had taken him several years hard work to perfect that smile. He put his hand over hers. He murmured: "Let's talk, Clarissa."

Callaghan sat on a green-painted garden seat on the edge of the lawn that bounded the bottom of the lower terrace. Fifty yards away on the other side of the flower-garden Nikolls, in a multi-coloured sweater—practised putts on the miniature golf green. Over his shoulder Callaghan could see Esme, sitting on the covered balcony that ran past the French windows of the dining-room, reading a book. He thought she was having a little difficulty in concentrating.

He lit a cigarette, got up and strolled down the tiled pathway between the lawns. He stood at the bottom looking out over the green fields toward the sea.

Audrey Vendayne came out of the side door of the house. She walked swiftly down the steps that led between the terraces, along the pathway. Callaghan turned and walked to meet her.

She was wearing a fawn-coloured woolen suit. She was bareheaded. He noticed that the afternoon sun brought out the auburn tints in her hair.

She said abruptly: "As much as I dislike doing it I have to apologise to you. I received the three hundred pounds you registered to me from Newton Abbott, by the after-lunch post. I suppose you've been waiting to see, if I *would* apologise."

Callaghan grinned. "More or less," he said. "But I wasn't worrying about it."

She went on: "I suppose it was part of your technique *not* to tell me that you'd returned the money, when we were talking last night. I imagine it gave you a feeling of superiority."

"It did, rather," said Callaghan.

He stamped out his cigarette, kicked the butt to the edge of the path.

"How's the Major?" he asked. "Have you had any news?"

She nodded.

"He's better," she said. "He is to have complete rest and quiet. I'm glad he's not here."

His grin was cynical.

"That seems to indicate that you don't think it's going to be either quiet or restful here."

She said: "Candidly, I'm certain of nothing while you are here, Mr. Callaghan. In a way I'm glad my father had that attack. At least he will not be worried."

He looked at her. He noticed that her eyes were very blue and very steady.

"I imagine you'll return the three hundred to our friend Gabby," he queried. "I bet he'll be glad to see it come back again. He'll probably wonder what's been happening to it. That three hundred has been playing ring of roses like a playful boomerang."

"Gabby—as you call him—isn't my friend," she said coldly. "If I decide to return the money I shall return it to the person who lent it to me. In any event I don't see what it has to do with you."

"You will," said Callaghan.

She was about to say something but she checked herself. She turned on her heel and walked back towards the house.

Callaghan lit a cigarette and walked across the lawn to Nikolls who was concentrating on a six-foot putt.

He stood watching. Nikolls tapped the ball neatly. It trickled slowly across the velvet green into the hole. Nikoll's sighed. He said:

"I'm marvellous at this game any time I ain't really playing it. As I said before, it's a nice life!"

Callaghan said: "Listen, Windy. I'm going up to town. I may be a day or two: I don't know yet. But you don't have to let anybody here know where I'm going. You might even suggest that I've gone over to talk to the police at Plymouth."

"O.K.," said Nikolls. "How was Clarissa?"

He grinned at Callaghan, who grinned back.

"Clarissa was pretty good," said Callaghan.

"Yeah," said Nikolls. "It's marvellous how the idea that a guy is in love with a dame will make the doll talk."

Callaghan stood looking towards the sea. He said:

"I think Clarissa's scared. I think she's afraid that the business that happened between Esme and the fisherman at Beesands is going to be repeated with Blaize. Esme seems stuck on Blaize, but not in the usual light-hearted way that she adopts towards most of her boy friends. Clarissa thinks this time it might be really serious."

"I get you," said Nikolls. "So Clarissa plays around an' makes out that she's tryin' to queer Esme's pitch and pinch her boy friend, when all the time she's trying to keep her eye on those two just to stop things comin' to a head."

"It looks like that to me," said Callaghan. He went on: "While I'm away you might try and pull one on Esme. Use exactly the opposite tactics to those you used on Clarissa. Give Esme the idea that you don't like me very much. Try and get her confidence. Maybe she'll do a little talking."

"Who knows?" said Nikolls. "I'll try it anyway. When are you goin', Slim?"

"In about ten minutes," said Callaghan. "I'll just take the car out of the garage and disappear. I shan't take any clothes. If Audrey wants to know when I'll be back, say you don't know, but I'll be back."

Nikolls stooped down and picked the ball out of the hole. He threw it six or seven feet from him.

He said: "Audrey'll be pleased to know you're comin' back."

He walked to the ball and putted. This time it stopped three inches off the hole. He kicked it in.

He said: "I thought she looked a bit high-hat when she was talking to you just now. She ain't very pleased with you, Slim. It must be that three hundred."

Callaghan said: "Not exactly. I registered the money back to her at Newton Abbott. She got it this afternoon."

Nikolls raised his eyebrows.

"What was the idea in that, Slim?" he asked.

Callaghan said: "That money came originally from Gabby Ventura. I told her he'd be pleased if she sent it back to him. She said she'd return it to the person she borrowed it from. That sounds a bit odd, doesn't it, Windy?."

"Yeah," said Windy. "But I don't see it."

Callaghan said: "I didn't but I'm beginning to."

He walked away. He walked back to the path that led up to the house between the terraces. At the top he turned to the left past the balcony where Esme was sitting. Her eyes were concentrated on the page in front of her.

Callaghan said: "It's a lovely day, isn't it?"

She closed the book, marking her place with her finger. She looked pale and unhappy. There were circles under her eyes. Callaghan thought Esme was worrying about something.

She said: "The weather is so good down here, Mr. Callaghan, that we seldom take very much notice of it. We're used to fine days."

She smiled at him, one corner of her mouth twisted cynically.

Callaghan said: "Yes, it would be like that. Of course, in London you never know what the weather's going to be like."

He stood, his arm resting on the rail of the balcony, looking at her.

She said: "We're having an interesting conversation about the weather, aren't we? Or is this a prelude to something else?"

"I don't think so," said Callaghan. "I thought I'd like to talk to you, that's all I wanted to ask you something."

Esme took her finger out of the book and put it on the seat beside her. She said:

"Ask on! Aren't you sorry you haven't got a lie detector or whatever they call it fixed on my arm?"

Callaghan said: "I don't believe in lie detectors. They like 'em in America, but I don't. I think you can always tell."

"I expect *you* would be able to in any event, Mr. Callaghan," said Esme. "But I'm curious. Won't you ask your question?"

Callaghan said: "I wanted to know how you liked Malmesbury. It's a nice place isn't it?"

Esme opened her mouth to say something. Then she closed it.

She said: "I don't know . . . I wasn't fearfully interested in it. I wasn't in the Cape very long."

Callaghan was grinning. She went on:

"And may I ask what amuses you so much about it?"

Callaghan said: "I think you're clever. It was on the tip of your tongue to tell me you'd never heard of Malmesbury. I'm glad you didn't do that. I shouldn't have believed you."

He smiled at her and walked on towards the side of the Manor. Esme picked up her book, but she did not open it.

She sat looking over the terraces wondering about Callaghan.


Callaghan went into the garage and tested the air pressure in the tires on the Jaguar. He went back to the main door of the Manor House. Inside the hall he rang the bell. When Stevens appeared he said:

"Where's Miss Clarissa, Stevens?"

The butler said: "I think she's in her room, Mr. Callaghan. I believe she's lying down."

Callaghan said: "I'm going round to the garage in a few minutes. I'd be obliged if you'd tell her I'd like to have a few words with her there."

He went up stairs for his hat and gloves. He was sitting in the car waiting when Clarissa appeared.

She said: "Well, Slim, where are you going to?"

"I'm not quite certain," Callaghan answered. "I think I want to go to Plymouth to talk to the police there. Maybe I'll go on somewhere else afterwards."

Clarissa said hopefully: "Do you want me to come too?"

"No," said Callaghan. "I'd like you to come." He smiled at her. "But I don't think it's indicated. And I want you to do something for me here. Do you ever do anything that's dishonest, Clarissa?"

"Good God, yes," she answered. "I suppose everybody does, don't they?"

He nodded.

"I suppose they do," he said. "But I mean really dishonest, such as grabbing letters out of other people's mail, opening letters—steaming 'em open—listening to telephone calls . . . things like that."

Clarissa said: "Well, I haven't gone in for that sort of stuff much, but I dare say I could if I tried. By the way, whose post is it that has to be watched?"

Her eyes rested steadily on Callaghan's.

He said: "Listen, Clarissa. What I'm talking to you about now has nothing to do with this case. It's just a little thing on the side!"

Her eyes widened.

"You don't mean there's something else happening here?" she asked.

Callaghan began to lie. He said:

"I don't like that fellow Blaize, Clarissa. I can't quite place him, but I've got an idea that I remember his name in connection with something that wasn't quite so good. Ever since I had that talk with you this morning about Esme being stuck on him, I've been doing some serious thinking. I know you don't like him, and I don't."

Clarissa said: "What are you afraid of, Slim? Do you think . . ."

Callaghan said: "I don't think anything, but I don't like Blaize and I think Esme is much too nice a girl, even if she is a bit wild, to get mixed up with a fellow like that. My idea was," said Callaghan, "that you might keep your eye on the post if you can, and if a note or letter comes from Blaize you might have a look at it."

Clarissa said: "That wouldn't be difficult. The post is always left on the tray on the hall table. Everybody collects their own, and Esme's always last down. Besides," she added, "I could get up a little bit earlier—for you."

Callaghan said: "You're a sweet."

"What do I do? Steam open the letters and take a copy? And how shall I know if it's one from Blaize? Sometimes Esme has quite a large post," Clarissa went on. "Imagine me surrounded with letters, steaming them open upstairs in my room."

"I shouldn't worry about that," said Callaghan. "All you have to do is to look at the postmark. The only letters you want to bother about are ones that are posted in the county. Another thing, you needn't steam 'em open."

He put his hand into his breast pocket and produced a leather case. He opened it. Inside were three slim steel instruments rather like darning needles. He took one out, handed it over the side of the car to Clarissa.

"These are nice little things," said Callaghan. "Scotland Yard and the Postal Censors use 'em. Most people don't stick down the top edges of the envelope flap. All you have to do is to push this through the opening at the top, straight along the top of the envelope, turn it round until the top of the letter inside works itself through the slit."

He took a pound note from his note case and demonstrated.

"When you've got the top of the letter in the slit you start turning," said Callaghan. "Then the letter twists round the rod and you pull it out through the side of the flap. You do that very carefully. When you've read it you can put it back the same way—you merely reverse the process."

Clarissa sighed.

"You think of everything, don't you, Slim?" she said.

"I try to," he said. "Tell me something, Clarissa," he went on. "What sort of allowances do you girls have—much or little?"

"Not too bad," said Clarissa airily. "We have enough to get along on. One can always do with more, of course."

Callaghan nodded.

"And I suppose you're all pretty well broke most of the time?" he queried. "Every woman overspends her allowance."

"I wouldn't say that," said Clarissa. "I don't, and Audrey doesn't. Esme's the one who's always broke. How that girl does it I don't know. She's always up to her neck in debt. But why did you ask?"

Callaghan said: "I was just wondering."

He took her hand and squeezed it.

"So long, Clarissa," he said. "Don't forget you're working for Callaghan Investigations."

She smiled.

"I won't," she said. "Perhaps when you come back you'll give me a medal . . . or something?"

He smiled at her and let in the clutch. He backed the car slowly out of the garage, turned it, drove down the drive.

She stood watching it until it was out of sight.

## CHAPTER SIX
## THE END OF THE WEDGE

IT WAS nine o'clock, Callaghan unlocked the door of his apartment in Berkeley Square, entered the flat, threw his hat and overcoat over a chair and helped himself to four fingers of rye whiskey from the sideboard.

He went into the bedroom, undressed, ran the bath, got in when it was half full. Then he turned on the cold tap and let it run. He lay at full length in the bath, his feet resting on the brush board, looking at the ceiling. He was thinking about Audrey Vendayne.

When the bath was almost filled with tepid water, Callaghan turned off the cold tap. He reached out for his cigarette-case which lay on the stool beside the bath, took a cigarette, lit it and relaxed.

He thought that the Vendayne case was beginning to resolve itself into a series of questions. He liked questions, not so much because finding the answers was amusing, but because in the process of trying to find the answers a case was often solved.

Callaghan, whose practice it was to regard investigations purely from the point of view of the people concerned in them, thought that the Vendayne burglary presented a most interesting picture. He was no armchair detective, possessed of a unique brain, a needle point mentality able to discover and assemble infinitesimal points called "clues" obvious to no one—including the reader—but the armchair detective himself.

A case, to Callaghan, was merely a collection of people, some of whom—or all of whom—were giving incorrect information, or telling lies, because circumstances either forced them or led them into the process.

But the fact that they *had* to tell lies; *had* to give false impressions, necessitated a reorientation of their own viewpoints and their own lives. Sooner or later they became exhausted or careless. Then, and not until then, was an investigator able to put his finger on the one fact that would lead him to a possible, logical solution.

Callaghan thought that Audrey Vendayne was an excellent example of this process. In spite of the opinion that Nikolls had formed of the lady, Callaghan himself was not so certain. Audrey radiated a certain atmosphere—an aura of apparent honesty and essential frankness. Also she was inclined to be proud. It was a bad egg to all the tea in China that the things that she had done which, according to his working-out, were not normal actions on her part, were the result of circumstances which made it imperative for her to behave in that way.

As for instance the borrowing of the three hundred pounds and her attitude to him at Margraud. Neither of these things were characteristic of her and they were, therefore, all the more interesting.

He was concerned to find the reasons.

He considered it was his business to continue to create other situations—a verbal or practical—in which people in the case would enmesh themselves. And any situation was better than none at all. Such was the Callaghan system.

It was this system which had been responsible for the motto which Chief Detective-Inspector Gringall had originated for Callaghan Investigations—"We get there somehow and who the hell cares how!"

The system could possibly be criticised as unmoral, to which criticism Callaghan, if asked, would have probably replied that, as most interesting things in life—especially crime—were unmoral, it was an obvious truism that the remedy must, of necessity, be more violent than the disease.

He began to think in terms of blackmail. Life, he ruminated, consisted of fifty per cent of the world trying to blackmail—in some way or other—the other fifty per cent. The hair-line between "moral persuasion" and honest to goodness blackmail was very often a *hair* line.

He switched his mind to the three girls in the Margraud Manor. He thought that Audrey could be a worthwhile opponent in any battle of wits. Clarissa was not quite so clever. If anything she was the most innocuous of the three. Callaghan found himself concentrating on Esme. One of the things that intrigued him was the question of Esme's allowance. Esme was always broke; yet as far as he could see she did nothing that the other two did not do. Here was an interesting question. He wondered if he had already found the answer.

The second question was that of the three hundred pounds. Callaghan remembered what Audrey had said when he had suggested that she might like to return it to Gabby Ventura. He wondered if she were speaking the truth. Supposing she were. This presented another, quite interesting, angle of thought. He thought possibly he might have an idea about that, too.

He got out of the bath, began to dry himself. During the process and when he was finished and sitting on the bathroom stool rubbing *eau-de Cologne* into his hair, he was still thinking about the other questions. Why was Gabby interested in Blaize? Who and what was Blaize? Why were his movements of such importance to Gabby that Ropey Felliner—one time custodian of the alleyway entrance to the Backstairs Club—was sent post-haste down to Devonshire in order to keep an eye on Blaize's movements?

Callaghan thought that this technique was not of the type usually employed by Gabby. Gabby was a tough egg. He either had something on you or he had not. If he had dealt with the situation personally. The fact that he was having Blaize watched by Felliner indicated to Callaghan that Gabby knew little about Blaize. He wondered if he even *knew* Blaize.

He went back to the bedroom, began to dress. During the process he considered another angle of the case—the angle of the mortgage on Margraud. He wondered if Nikolls's theory was correct. Callaghan thought there was something funny about that mortgage. First of all, it was entirely unlike an individual of the characteristics of Major Vendayne to utilise the services of a strange firm of lawyers over an important matter like a mortgage on Margraud. Yet he had done so. But the more interesting part of this question was how had the mortgage been paid off. Where did the money come from? If, as Nikolls had suggested, the scheme was Audrey's, and Audrey had hoped to satisfy the mortgage by the money paid by the Insurance Company under the claim, she had been disappointed. There had been no money. Yet the mortgage *had* been paid.

Callaghan's mind came back to Esme. When he had last seen her sitting on the balcony at Margraud, he had tried a shot in the dark about Malmesbury. The shot had come off. There at least it seemed he had something tangible.

He tied his tie carefully, went into the sitting-room. He lit a cigarette, moved over to the window and stood looking out into the dusk. He stood there for some minutes, his hands in his pockets. Then he turned and went to the telephone. He dialled a Clerkenwell number. After a minute he said:

"Is that you, Blooey? Listen carefully: There's a good-looking young fellow by the name of Lancelot Vendayne. He lives at Grant's Hotel in Clarges Street. He's supposed to have lots of money. Anyhow," he went on, "he's much too good-looking not to have a girl friend. You might get around and find out who she is. And I'd like to know if possible by tomorrow evening. If you come up against anything else in the process, let me know. You got that?"

Blooey said he had got it. Callaghan hung up. He lit another cigarette, drank a little more whisky.

Callaghan went out. He walked slowly across Berkeley Square. He found himself thinking about the characters that made up the "picture" of the Vendayne case. Major Vendayne, Audrey and Clarissa and Esme. These people, with the possible exception of Audrey, were fairly obvious, he thought. Audrey was not obvious. She was not obvious, because one knew nothing of the motives that actuated her own particular line of thought or conduct. Only one thing about her was obvious and that was that she was damned attractive.

Callaghan thought that of the Vendayne women she was easily the winner so far as the sex-appeal stakes were concerned. The fact that her attitude towards life was quieter than that of her sisters meant nothing. Quiet Women were invariably dangerous. Callaghan, who liked his women quiet and dangerous—but not too dangerous—considered that the progress of the investigation might produce some fireworks from Audrey. It would have to produce fireworks of one sort or another.

Then there was Gabby Ventura, Lancelot Vendayne, and William Blaize. Just how these three people came into the pictures was a question which Callaghan could not, at that moment, attempt to answer. Whether there was an actual connection, an actual contact, as regards the case between Gabby and Audrey, Gabby and Lancelot, Gabby and Blaize, was an unknown quantity. Audrey's remark—if it had been truth—about returning the three hundred pounds had unsettled his original conviction about a definite connection between her and Gabby.

Callaghan allowed his mind to dwell on Gabby's career as he knew it. He had no respect for Ventura, merely a grudging admiration. Gabby had a quick brain and a flair for "keeping his nose clean." During the last ten years he had been associated with some of the toughest night haunts in London. Not those near-nice places around the West End which are considered dangerous in war time, but the really tough places—the ones you seldom hear about. Gabby had made money out of these haunts and he had never taken the knock. They had been raided, closed down; there had been prosecutions galore, but it was always someone else that the "blue inks" pulled in—never Gabby. Callaghan thought that if Ventura had cared to use his brains in some legitimate line of finance he might have been one of those people whose pictures one sees periodically in the evening papers and who are called kings of industry. But even if Gabby was not a king of industry he was certainly a small time emperor of underworld finance. Callaghan was intrigued with any connection, no matter how vague, between Gabby and the other people in the Vendayne picture. Gabby presented himself—for a reason which Callaghan could not quite make out—as the centre point of the situation—a rather vague situation.

But he proposed to make the situation clear and to do that quickly. It was time, he thought, that something happened, and if it would not happen of itself then it must be made to happen.

At the corner of Hay Hill he stopped to light a cigarette. Then he went into the phone box and looked up the number of Grant's Hotel in Clarges Street. He dialled the number, asked for Mr. Lancelot Vendayne. After a moment Vendayne came on the line. Callaghan said:

"Good-evening. This is Callaghan. I've just got back from Devonshire. Your uncle's had one of his periodical heart attacks. They've taken him to the Nursing Home in Exeter. I want to see you. Is that possible?"

"Of course," said Lancelot cheerfully. "Has anything happened? I'm dying with curiosity."

"Nothing's happened," said Callaghan. "What about meeting me at the Ventura Club at half-past ten?"

"I'd like to," said Vendayne. "Anyway, even if you've nothing to tell me, we can have a drink."

Callaghan said: "I haven't anything to tell you, but there're one or two things I want to ask you. I'll see you at ten-thirty."

He hung up. As he came out of the phone box he was smiling.

Lancelot Vendayne was leaning up against the bar in the Ventura Club talking to the plump blonde. There were few people in the club and only half a dozen couples were dancing, and few more people finishing late dinners or early suppers. Ventura was nowhere in sight. Callaghan walked over to the bar. He said:

"Let's take our drinks and sit down at a table. I want to talk to you."

Vendayne, who was drinking whisky and soda, ordered another one. He picked up the glasses and followed Callaghan, who was on his way to a lone table in the corner. When they were seated Callaghan said:

"There's one rule that we always stick to in Callaghan Investigations. We never delude our clients—well not much, and only then if we think it's good for them. As you are in effect my client, I think you ought to know that I don't like this Vendayne burglary business at all."

Lancelot said: "Why not?" He was frowning.

"There's nothing about it that looks like a burglary ought to look," said Callaghan. "Just because the police don't pull in somebody over every job that's done that fact doesn't mean that they don't know who it is. It usually means that they just haven't got any evidence. But in this case nobody knows anything about anything—including me."

Lancelot raised his eyebrows. He said:

"I thought the idea was that *you* were the person who was going to find things out."

"Oh, no, you didn't," said Callaghan. "You know why you put me in on this job and it wasn't for that reason at all. You put me in as an additional lever to force the Insurance Company to pay up. You probably knew that old Layne had threatened them with an action if they didn't pay up by the end of the month. I was to be a sort of gesture of good faith."

Lancelot said: "Well, do you think they will pay by the end of the month?"

Callaghan said: "I don't know, but if an opinion's any use to you I think it's very doubtful. The second thing is, I don't think I'd worry the Insurance Company. I'd leave 'em alone for a bit."

Vendayne shrugged his shoulders.

"Either they're going to pay or they're not," he said. "If they're not, I want to know why."

Callaghan grinned.

"That's all right," he said. "Your wanting to know why, I mean. But you realise you haven't any *right* to know why. You have no interest in the Vendayne jewellery until your uncle is dead, and he's not dead yet."

"That's perfectly true," said Vendayne. "I haven't any legal right to do anything at the moment. But what is all this leading up to? I suppose I've a legal right to employ you to watch my interests."

"That's the point I was coming to," said Callaghan. "I want to alter my status in this job. I don't want to feel I'm acting as a lever on the

Insurance Company. I just want to play around and find out one or two things that interest me."

Vendayne shrugged his shoulders.

"That's all right," he said. "I suppose it will come to the same thing in the end."

Callaghan smiled.

"I should think it might," he said. "And there's something I want to discuss with you. It's this—"

He stopped speaking suddenly as if an idea had just come to him. After a pause he said:

"You might tell me something. It's rather a personal question. Were you ever stuck on any of the Vendayne girls, or shall we narrow that down a bit? Were you ever stuck on Audrey?"

Vendayne smiled. He said:

"Well, that's not a bad guess, Callaghan. How did you know?"

Callaghan said: "I didn't know, I just guessed. I could imagine anybody being stuck on Audrey."

Lancelot said: "I was. For quite a little time there was an idea that she and I might become engaged. Then for some reason or other she didn't like the idea, so we weren't. That's all."

Callaghan nodded. He said:

"Did you know that your uncle had mortgaged the Manor House on a mortgage payable in one year at 6½% for £20,000, in order to get the place repaired?"

Vendayne said: "How did you know that? Did the old boy or Audrey tell you?"

"No," said Callaghan. He smiled amiably. "You know we don't sit down on our bottoms all the time and just do nothing, Vendayne," he said. "We get around sometimes. An assistant of mine found the deed and the satisfaction recorded on it in the Registry in Exeter."

Lancelot said: "Well, I knew all about it. As a matter of fact, I thought it was a good idea at the time."

Callaghan nodded.

"And you weren't curious," he went on, "about where the Major was going to get the money to pay off that mortgage with?"

"Oh, yes," said Lancelot. He paused for a moment. "My uncle was in a deal—a share deal," he went on, "and he was perfectly certain that this thing was going to come off and make him three or four hundred per cent profit. The idea was that he would pay the mortgage off on the proceeds of that. He had quite a bit of his capital in this deal."

"I see," said Callaghan. "And the deal didn't come off?"

"I believe not," Lancelot answered.

Callaghan drew his cigarette smoke down into his lungs and exhaled through one nostril. He said, looking at Lancelot.

"And you haven't got any ideas as to how that mortgage was paid off?"

"Not one in the world," said the other. "Until you told me I didn't know it was paid off. I thought naturally that my uncle or Audrey had got it extended. After all a year for a mortgage is a very short term. My uncle's well known in the county and the property is fairly valuable. The mortgagees would have been glad to extend the time."

"Maybe," said Callaghan. "But the fact remains that they weren't asked to extend. The mortgage was paid off in full. You wouldn't know where the money came from?"

Lancelot said: "I would not." He smiled at Callaghan. "And purely from a point of view of curiosity I would very much like to know."

Callaghan grinned.

"So would I," he said.

He got up.

"I suppose I can always find you at Grant's Hotel?" he asked.

"Most of the time," said Lancelot. "Anyway, they can always let you know where I can be got at. Won't you stay and have another drink?"

"No thanks," said Callaghan. "I've got one or two things to do. By the way," he went on, "what do you think of Gabby? Are you and he friendly?"

Lancelot made a wry face.

"Just about as much as a man like me could ever be friendly with the proprietor of a place like this," he said with a whimsical smile. "I come here quite a bit because it's cheerful and amusing. I used to think that Gabby wasn't a bad sort, but now, between you and me and the gate-post, I don't like him very much. I think he's a bit crooked."

Callaghan grinned.

"You don't say?" he said airily. "It's taken you a hell of a time to find that out, hasn't it?"

Lancelot's smile faded. He looked at the table. He said:

"I don't see why you should say that. I don't see why I should be particularly interested in whether Ventura is crooked or not. His character doesn't concern me. I merely use this place as a bar and to amuse myself. Incidentally," he went on, "I didn't like the way you said that."

"No?" said Callaghan cheerfully. "Well . . . what am I supposed to do—burst into tears?"

Lancelot said nothing.

Callaghan went out.

It was eleven o'clock when Callaghan, having negotiated the black-out between Shepherd Market and Soho, walked into the Backstairs Club.

If the Backstairs Club was a little different to the others it was merely in the fact that practically every one who used the Backstairs smoked *marihuana*. The purchase and sale of the noxious weed— together with the "by-products" thereof—and when one considers the effect of a couple of *marihuana* cigarettes on some women one realises that there are "by-products"—constituted its main business.

The club premises consisted of a long room with a very low ceiling and an appalling odour. The room was approached through a passage which was guarded at the far end by a cubby hole in which the watch-dog of the moment sat and scrutinised would-be users.

The odour which was most prevalent at the far end—where the stink of cheap scent and stale *marihuana* smoke was joined by that of oil from the infinitesimal kitchen which stood just off one corner of the room—was entirely lost on the white-faced young gentleman who, seated at an ancient piano, from the keyboard of which at least a dozen ivories were missing, played a hot number called: *"I don't know what it is you've got but I want it,"* and pondered, possibly, on the days when he used to wash at least once a day and shave, at any rate, sometimes.

There were a dozen people seated at the little tables set round the room. They were the sort of people you expected to find in the Back-stairs Club. They had no memories, no hope and no morals. They were not interested in peace or war or any state between those two conditions, because most of them had never known peace, and most of them were continuously at war with something or somebody—the police, their friends, or themselves.

When Callaghan passed through the room they looked over their shoulders with the sudden furtive glance characteristic of people who are never quite certain as to what is going to happen from one minute to another.

Callaghan looked round the room. Sitting by himself at a table at the top was Kittel. Kittel was a tall, thin individual who purported to be an artist. He had a long white face, a bad temper and an addiction to barbituric drugs.

Callaghan walked over to the table. He sat down.

Kittel said suspiciously: "What do you want, Callaghan?"

"Just to talk to you for a minute or two, Jimmy," said Callaghan cheerfully. "And I think I'd like to buy you a drink. You don't look so well. I suppose the war's cut off most of your supplies."

Kittel said: "You mind your own damned business."

Callaghan signalled the bleary-eyed waiter in the dirty apron who was leaning against the kitchen door.

He said: "What you need, Kittel, is a double brandy."

Kittel looked relieved. When the drinks were brought Callaghan said:

"I wonder you come down here. If you had a pound for every time you'd been chucked out of here you'd be a rich man."

The dope grinned cynically.

"I shall never be that," he said. "Although I thought at one time there was a chance of it. I hate this damned place," he went on. "But life's like that. You hate a place, but you go there. You don't want to do a thing, but you do it."

"Quite," said Callaghan. He grinned. "True happiness would appear to consist in not doing all the things we want to do," he said.

He put his hand into the breast pocket of his coat and brought out a note case. He took out five one pound notes. They were new notes. They rustled. Callaghan could see Kittel eyeing them greedily. He said:

"Have you got any use for a fiver, Jimmy?"

Kittel said: "There are times when I think I'd murder someone for five pounds."

Callaghan said: "It's not as bad as that." He looked at his watch. It was half-past eleven. He said:

"I want you to start something around here at half-past twelve. Just hit the waiter or start throwing glasses at the doorman, enough to create a little sensation without the police being called in. Understand, Jimmy?"

Kittel asked wearily: "Is that *all* I've got to do for five pounds?"

"That's all," said Callaghan.

Kittel said: "Give me the fiver."

Callaghan handed over a pound note.

"Where are you living now, Jimmy?" he asked.

Kittel looked at the pound note.

"I'm living at the same place," he answered.

"All right," said Callaghan. "I'll send you round the other four pounds to-morrow when the job's done."

Kittel looked at him. Callaghan noticed that the pupils of his eyes were mere pin-points. Kittel said:

"You're a disbelieving swine, aren't you?"

"You bet," said Callaghan. "Don't forget . . . at half-past twelve."

"All right," said Kittel. "You needn't worry. I need the other four pounds."

Callaghan finished his drink and went out.

It was nearly twelve when Callaghan took his feet off his office desk, stubbed out his cigarette in the ash tray and rang the Ventura Club. He asked for Gabby Ventura.

"He's not down here, Mr. Callaghan," said the voice at the other end of the telephone. "He's upstairs in his own rooms. Perhaps you'd like to get through to him direct. I'll give you the number."

Callaghan said: "Thanks."

He wrote down the number and hung up. After a moment he dialled the number he had been given. Ventura's voice answered.

"Hallo, Gabby," said Callaghan cheerfully. "I want to talk to you. It *might* be important."

"All right, Slim," said Gabby. "Would you like to come round and have a drink?"

Callaghan said: "I'll be with you at twelve o'clock. I'd like to talk to you upstairs. Just you and me."

There was a pause. Then Ventura said:

"You'd better come to the back door. Ring the bell and I'll come down and let you in. Then we shan't be disturbed."

"That'll be fine," said Callaghan. "I'll be with you in a quarter of an hour."

He lit a cigarette and blew smoke rings for a minute or two. Then he dialled Effie Thompson's number. When she answered he said:

"Hallo, Effie. Are you in bed?"

"Yes, Mr. Callaghan, I am," she said. "Can I do something?"

"You can," Callaghan answered, "and you needn't even get up to do it. Just stay awake for a bit. At half-past twelve exactly ring through to Mayfair 995469—that's Gabby Ventura's private number in his flat over the club. He'll answer the telephone. Put on a false voice—a rather common voice—tell him you're Lilly Dells, that you're speaking from the call box near the Backstairs Club. Tell him that Jimmy Kittel's been hitting the dope again and that he's creating murder at the Backstairs. Lay it on thick. Say Kittel's slugged the waiter and knocked out the doorman. And you needn't be particular about your language. Let yourself go a bit. Directly you've said your piece, hang up. Have you got that, Effie?"

"I've got it," said Effie caustically. "You're sure that's all you want done? You don't want me to give an imitation of Greta Garbo as well?"

"No thanks," said Callaghan. "Not to-night."

He hung up.

He waited a moment, then rang the Berkeley Square cab rank. He said:

"Is Fairley on the rank? He is. Tell him to come round to the office and pick me up."

He hung up the telephone, went over to a filing cabinet in the corner of the office, opened it and took out a small bunch of "spider" keys. He put them in his pocket. Then he went downstairs and waited for the cab. When it arrived he handed the driver a pound note.

"Listen, Fairley," he said. "Take me round to the back door of the Ventura Club in Shepherd Market. Then go back to the rank. Wait there until twelve twenty-five and then drive back to the Ventura back entrance. I want you to be waiting for me outside the door at twelve thirty-five. See?"

Fairley said he saw.

Callaghan got into the cab. He lay back in the corner and relaxed. He began to smile.

He was still thinking about Audrey Vendayne.

## CHAPTER SEVEN
## ONE FOR THE BAG

GABBY, at the sideboard, mixed two large whiskies and sodas. He was wearing a blue-grey Glen check suit with a white silk tie. A large diamond pin twinkled in the centre of it. He looked contented, almost cheerful.

Callaghan, sitting in the big armchair on the other side of the table, watched Gabby's precise movements as he handled bottle and syphon. He moved quickly and easily in spite of his bulk and he had a good jaw even if it was concealed by a jowl. Callaghan thought that Gabby could be tough if necessity arose—very tough. He would stick at nothing to attain a desired end. It would be interesting to know, thought the detective, just what "end" Gabby wanted.

Ventura came back to the table with the glasses. He sat down and produced a cigar. He said smilingly:

"I'm getting curious about what you wanted to see me over, Slim. Something important, hey?"

Callaghan said: "Not very, Gabby. Just important to me. Besides which, I've been thinking . . ."

He took out his cigarette-case and lit a cigarette. Ventura regarded the glowing end of his expensive cigar. He said nothing. He waited.

Callaghan went on: "I was thinking I was a bit short with you the other day when you came round to my office and asked me about that £300."

He grinned.

"I thought you were a bit short, too, Slim," said Gabby. "Naturally I didn't believe that stuff you told me."

Callaghan drew the cigarette smoke down into his lungs.

"You know that I'm investigating the Vendayne burglary," he said. "I'm doing the job because Lancelot Vendayne wanted it investigated. The night before you came to see me, his cousin, Audrey Vendayne, made a date to meet me at this club. She waited for me outside. She gave me £300 to keep out of the case. I concluded she'd borrowed it from you. That's why I was glad to take a hand in that poker game and let you see the banknotes she'd given me. Now I've come to the conclusion that I was wrong."

Ventura knocked the ash from the end of his cigar. He said softly: "You don't say, Slim."

Callaghan grinned at him.

"I've got another theory now," he said. "Supposing I made a guess. Supposing I suggested that Lancelot Vendayne lent Audrey that £300 after *he* had borrowed it from you. Would I be very far wrong?"

Gabby said: "You wouldn't be wrong at all. You'd be dead right. I lent Vendayne that £300. I didn't know what for. He told me a hard luck story—that he was in a jam—so I let him have it."

"That was nice of you, Gabby," said Callaghan. "I didn't know you were so kind-hearted. What did you do it for?"

Ventura shrugged his massive shoulders. He smiled wryly at Callaghan. He said:

"I'm not quite certain. I get like that sometimes."

Callaghan said: "When was he going to pay you back?"

"I wasn't worrying about that," Gabby answered. "I expect him to pay it back pretty soon. He said he would."

Callaghan said: "Gabby, you told me Lancelot Vendayne was rather a clever fellow. You told me he was making money. If he was making money, what did he have to borrow £300 from you for?"

Gabby said: "That don't signify, Slim. Anybody can be making money and be short of a few hundred ready, especially when they want it in a hurry."

Callaghan nodded.

"Would you call Lancelot a pal of yours, Gabby?" he asked.

Gabby grinned.

"I wouldn't exactly call him that," he said. "He's all right and he's a good customer. Sometimes I think he's a bit of a bastard."

Callaghan said: "I see."

He glanced at his wrist-watch. It was just after twelve-thirty. The telephone on the desk in the corner jangled. Gabby went over. He took off the receiver. Callaghan could hear a high-pitched almost hysterical voice coming through the telephone—a metallic, common voice. He grinned. He thought that Effie was doing pretty well. Ventura began to talk into the transmitter. He said:

"All right . . . all right." He hung up suddenly. He said to Callaghan: "Sorry, Slim, but I got to get away from here. I've just had a call—some rush business. Why don't you go downstairs and have a drink? I'll be back in half an hour."

"No thanks, Gabby," said Callaghan. "I've said all I wanted to say and I've got a date myself. If you're in a hurry you'd better take my cab. I've got one waiting outside. I can get another."

Ventura said: "That's nice of you, Slim."

He led the way down the dark staircase, opened the back door. Outside, Callaghan's cab driver, Fairley, was standing beside his cab. Callaghan said:

"Take this gentleman wherever he wants to go to. I think I'll walk. Good-night, Gabby."

Gabby said good-night. He got into the cab.

Callaghan walked a few yards down the dark side street, then he turned back. He put his hand in his pocket and brought out the bunch of "spider" keys. In two minutes he had the back door of the Ventura Club open. He closed it behind him, went swiftly and silently up the stairs. He switched on the light in Gabby's room. On the other side of the room was another door leading down to the club. There was a bolt on the inside. Callaghan shot it home. Then he began a systematic search of the room.

He went round opening drawers, taking out the contents, going through them, replacing them in the same order. He worked rapidly, thoroughly. The roll-top desk in the corner on which the telephone stood was open. Callaghan turned his attention to that. One drawer in the bottom right-hand pedestal was locked. He opened it easily with a "spider." There were a bundle of papers in the drawer. On the top of them was an envelope addressed to Gabby Ventura in a sprawling handwriting. Callaghan picked it up. The stamp bore the Kingsbridge postmark. He opened the envelope, drew out the sheet of notepaper inside. He read:

*"Dear Guvner,*

*There's some proper bleedin trubble poppin down here. The boys been on the telephon to-day. He was shoutin his head orf, talkin a lot of stuff about some deal being phoney. And he's gettin ready to get out. He's been packin all day. Sent one trunk to Exeter orlreddy. I think he's goin' abroad. I couldn't get all he said on the telephon but I herd him say there was goin to be a showdown pretty soon and that he was goin to keep the party he was talkin to tied up properly. He said the whole bag of tricks was as phoney as hell. Whatever the showdown is goin to be its goin to be pretty soon because I don't think he'll be here for more than a couple of days. Let me know what you want done. You better let me know quick.*

*Well, so long,*

*Ropey.*

*P.S.—That bastard Callaghan is kickin around here."*

Callaghan sat in the armchair that stood before the desk. He copied the letter on the back of a tailor's bill. Then he put it back in the envelope, replaced the envelope in the drawer, shut it and relocked it. He drew the bolt on the door leading to the club, looked round the room to see that everything was as he had found it, went down the stairs. Outside he began to walk in the direction of Berkeley Square. He was whistling softly to himself.

Callaghan woke up at eleven o'clock. He reached out for the bedside telephone that connected his flat with the office below. He said:

"Good-morning, Effie. You did very well last night. I didn't know you were such a good actress. Congratulations."

Effie Thompson said primly: "Thank you, Mr. Callaghan. I like to be a help."

Callaghan went on: "Get through to Layne—the Vendayne solicitor, Effie. Tell him I'm coming round to see him. I'll be there at twelve. When you've done that, get through to Detective-Inspector Walperton at Scotland Yard. Ask him if it would be convenient to see me at a quarter to one."

He hung up, bathed and began to dress. Five minutes afterwards Effie Thompson rang through to say the two appointments were in order.

Callaghan finished dressing, took the lift down to the offices, read his mail, drank a cup of tea that Effie brought to him. Then he went around to Layne's office.

When the detective was shown in, Layne looked at him suspiciously over the top of his *pince-nez*. Callaghan said:

"I don't want to waste a lot of your time, Mr. Layne, but I want to have a straight talk with you. I suppose that anything that's said in this office can be considered to be 'off the record'?"

The lawyer said: "Rather a strange request, is it not, Mr. Callaghan? May I ask why?"

Callaghan said: "There ought not to be anything 'off the record' between you and me; at the same time there are one or two angles on this business that you don't know. For instance, am I right in supposing that you *didn't* know that your client, Major Vendayne, mortgaged the Margraud Manor for £20,000 at 6½% for one year, and that the mortgage has been paid off?"

Layne's eyebrows went up. "You amaze me," he said. "I certainly did not know."

"I thought as much," said Callaghan. "I thought so because the mortgage was put through by a firm of Exeter lawyers." He went on: "I believe you've written to the Sphere & International and told them that unless this claim is settled by the end of the month, you're going to issue a writ."

The lawyer nodded.

"That is correct," he said.

Callaghan lit a cigarette.

"I want you to do something," he said. "Something that is maybe a little bit odd. You won't like it. It's going behind your client's back."

Layne said: "I don't think I could do that."

"Oh, yes, you could," said Callaghan. "If it were in your client's interests you could do it."

The lawyer pursed his lips.

"Possibly," he said, "But I should have to *know* that it was in my client's interests."

"All right," said Callaghan. "Well, look at the facts. When this jewellery was stolen, I believe I'm right in saying that your client wasn't in a fearful hurry for the claim to be put in to the Insurance Company. The person who was responsible for getting after the Sphere & International—tryin' to get 'em to pay—wasn't the Major, it was Lancelot Vendayne. You can understand that too; he was worrying about whether he was going to get what was coming to him when the Major dies. But the point is that *he* was the person who's been trying to bring pressure to bear on the Sphere & International."

Layne said: "That is correct, but I still don't see—"

"You will," said Callaghan. "Listen. When I went down to Margraud, Audrey Vendayne told me she'd had a word with her father and they had an idea of writing to the Insurance Company and postponing the claim."

Layne looked surprised.

"Really," he said.

"Well, I stopped that," said Callaghan. "Obviously, it would have been a ridiculous thing to do. First of all, it is sticking out a foot that the Insurance Company are already suspicious and any request to them merely to postpone the claim would make them more suspicious."

"Quite," said Layne. "Unless there were some good reason for the postponement."

"Exactly," said Callaghan. "We've got to find a reason. The point is," he went on, "the Insurance Company have delayed paying this claim because they smell a rat, and we don't have to do a lot of thinking to know what that rat is. The only time when an Insurance Company don't pay is when they believe that a claim is phoney. They believe this claim is phoney, and they're not the only ones—I think so, too."

The lawyer said nothing. He looked very grave.

Callaghan went on: "It would be a bit difficult for the Vendayne family—or one or more members of it—if the Insurance Company were to pay this claim and then discover afterwards that there'd been funny business. Somebody might find themselves stuck in gaol."

"I see," said Layne. He put the tips of his fingers together and looked out of the window. "And your idea is?" he queried.

Callaghan blew a smoke ring. He watched it sail across the office.

"My idea is this," he said. "You write to the Insurance Company to-day. You tell 'em that Callaghan Investigations, who were put in on this job to find out what has happened, think they have got a line on where that jewellery is; that, in the circumstances, pending a further report from Mr. Callaghan, Major Vendayne wishes to *withdraw* the claim, as that is the obvious thing to do."

The lawyer nodded.

"I see . . ." he said.

"It's not particularly clever, it's common sense," said Callaghan. "If we really thought we had an idea where that jewellery is, the obvious thing would be for us to withdraw the claim. Doing it that way doesn't look suspicious."

Layne said: "I think I ought to have a word with my client about this."

"You can't," said Callaghan. "He's had a heart attack. He's in a nursing home at Exeter. They won't let him talk to anybody. Anyway," he went on, "you'll be well advised to do what I suggest."

"Shall I?" said the lawyer. "Why?"

"Because if you don't," said Callaghan, "I'm going down to the Insurance Company to tell 'em the same story myself. I feel it is necessary that that claim is stalled for a bit anyway."

Layne said: "Mr. Callaghan, I suppose you realise what you are suggesting? Your attitude suggests that the original claim made against the Insurance Company was a fake claim and that either my client or some member or members of his family knew that fact. That is a very serious suggestion."

"You're telling me," said Callaghan. "And I'm not *suggesting* anything. I'm telling you. The only way out of the job is my way. You've got to do it whether you like it or not. If you don't, I'll do it for you."

"I don't like your attitude but I think you're right," said the solicitor. "In the circumstances, and as I can't get into touch with the Major immediately, I'll do as you suggest, but I'm very worried about this."

Callaghan exhaled smoke slowly.

"What's worrying you?" he asked.

"You're practically suggesting that some member of the Vendayne family is concerned in that burglary, Mr. Callaghan," said Layne. "And the fact that you've told me that it was Miss Vendayne who told you that she had talked to the Major about withdrawing the claim seems to indicate that she was the person. I find it very difficult to believe."

"I expect you do," said Callaghan. "And as for suggesting that some member of the Vendayne family had something to do with this steal, you're entitled to think what you like."

He got up, picked up his hat.

"I'll take it you'll get that letter off to-day," he said. "If I were you I'd write it now and send it round by hand."

Layne said: "I think I will do that, Mr. Callaghan."

Callaghan smiled.

"Nice work, Mr. Layne," he said.

He went out.

Callaghan sat in the waiting-room at Scotland Yard thinking about Detective-Inspector Walperton. It was obvious, he thought, that Walperton was going to be a little difficult, and the business of putting him in the waiting-room for a quarter of an hour or so, to cool his heels, was merely part of the process.

He lit a cigarette and began to consider the letter he had found in Gabby's roll-top desk. A very interesting document, thought Callaghan. And not only interesting but practical—about the only practical thing, the only *fact* that had showed up in the Vendayne case up to the moment.

And Callaghan liked a fact. A fact was a good thing to start working from, and the Ropey Felliner letter was, as he saw it, an extremely illuminating document.

He took the copy of the letter out of his pocket and studied it. He put it back as the door opened and a detective-constable put his head in to say that Mr. Walperton was ready now and would Mr. Callaghan come along.

Callaghan followed the policeman. His face was composed into a picture of beatific innocence. The detective-constable held the door open and Callaghan went in.

Walperton was sitting behind his desk, with the window behind him. The desk was a large one. At the left hand end of it, with his note-book already open and his pencil almost poised, was Detective-Sergeant Gridley, whose reputation for writing shorthand almost more quickly than the English language could be spoken had preceded him so far as Callaghan was concerned.

Walperton was thirty-eight years of age, keen-eyed, round-faced, a thruster. He had heard quite a lot about Callaghan and Callaghan Investigations. He had wondered why it was that Gringall and one or two other of the senior men at the Yard talked about Callaghan with a certain respect. Walperton had no respect for Callaghan. He did not like private detectives. He thought that there was no place in the English legal system for private investigation and he was prepared heartily to dislike any private detective from the word go.

He said: "Good-morning, Callaghan. I understand you've got something to say to me. Before you say it I'd like to make my own position quite clear. In doing so I shall make yours clear too."

Callaghan said nothing. He went over to the wall, picked up a chair that stood there, brought it back, placed it squarely in front of the Detective-Inspector's desk. He sat down, crossed his legs and drew cigarette smoke down into his lungs with obvious pleasure.

He said: "That's what I like to hear. I think there's nothing like having a position made clear. So you get ahead and make it clear, Walperton, and don't waste any time in doing it because I'm very busy." Walperton raised his eyebrows just a little. Gridley, his eyes on his note-book, began to grin.

"All right," said Walperton. "Well, the position is briefly this so far as *I'm* concerned: I understood from Chief Detective-Inspector Gringall that the Vendayne solicitors had retained you in this case. Well, that's all right. It means you're working for the family . . ."

Callaghan interrupted.

"I'm retained by the Insurance Company too," he said. "So I'm working for them as well. It also looks as if I'm working for you."

"I see," said Walperton. "So you're working for the Sphere & International as well. That surprises me a little. Hasn't it struck you that the interests of the two parties might clash?"

"I don't know," said Callaghan. "But I'd like to. Just how could they clash? The Vendayne family want to know where their jewellery is. The Insurance Company want to know too—otherwise they've got to fork out one hundred thousand pounds. So do you. *You* want to know as well—because that's what you get paid for."

Walperton flushed a little. He said:

"I presume you didn't come here to tell me what I get paid for. I imagine you came here to give me some information."

"You're quite wrong," said Callaghan. His smile was angelic. "I don't intend to do your job for you, Walperton, because I don't get paid for doing your job and I didn't come here to help you do it, which is what you hoped I was going to do."

He blew a large smoke ring.

Gridley said: "Do I make a note of this?"

He looked at Walperton.

Callaghan said: "You ought to know better than that, Gridley. Of course, you don't make a note of it. You can't make a note of *part* of what I say, unless you make a note of the whole lot. That's sense, isn't it? It's not only sense, it's police regulations—even Mr. Walperton knows that."

Walperton got up. He went over to the window and turned facing Callaghan. He said angrily:

"I know all about you, Callaghan. You've got medals for teaching police officers their business. Well, I'd like to tell you something, and I've already mentioned it to Mr. Gringall. I'd better tell you here and now. It's this: If I have any reason to believe that you are deliberately obstructing me or any other officer in the execution of his duty, I'll . . ."

". . . Apply for a warrant," said Callaghan. "Also under the old Act, you can apply for one if you have reason to believe that I am 'mischievously giving wrongful or false information to an officer.' But you can't use either of those things unless I'm making a statement. So let's fix just what I *am* doing, shall we?"

He sent a thin stream of tobacco smoke out of one nostril. He went on:

"I'm either just talkin' to you, Walperton—just a little heart-to-heart talk—without any notes being taken of what I say—or else I'm definitely making a statement, in which case we'll get busy on it and we'll take note of *everything* I say and when they're made I want 'em transcribed right away so that I can see they are what I said, and I'll sign the statement. Well . . . what are we going to do?"

Walperton turned and looked out of the window. He was cursing himself for a fool. He realised that, up to the moment, he had played into Callaghan's hands by losing his temper. After a moment he turned away from the window, went back to his desk. He said:

"All right, Callaghan, have it your way. This is a heart-to-heart talk."

He produced an icy smile.

Callaghan grinned amiably. That expression of supreme frankness and candour which came over his face when he intended to lie brazenly, appeared in all its glory. He looked almost winsome.

"That's fine, Walperton," he said. "Now . . . you can believe it or not, but I came here to give you a hand. I know you've had very tough luck with this case. I know you've had nothing at all to work on. Well, I think I've got something for you. It's not much, but it's something . . ."

Walperton, in spite of himself, began to look interested. He said:

"Well, I'll be glad of *any* information, Callaghan." He paused for a moment, then: "You're going to tell me that this was an inside job?" he queried.

"No," said Callaghan, "I'm not. In spite of the fact that the Insurance Company probably thinks that there's been some funny business *I* don't think that it was an inside job."

He stubbed out his cigarette. He was thinking that he would have to have a really *good* story for Walperton. He began to think it out while he was lighting a fresh cigarette.

When that process was finished he said:

"I thought at first that the case was a bit fishy. I thought—just as you and any other sensible person would think—that everything pointed to someone inside Margraud Manor being concerned in that steal. I thought so until I ran into Ropey Felliner."

Walperton said: "Who the hell's Ropey Felliner?"

"He used to work for Gabby Ventura. You ought to send down for his record. It's a sweet one. He was doorman at the Backstairs Club for a long time," said Callaghan. "Well, Felliner took a job at a cottage not twenty miles from Margraud. He's working for a fellow called Blaize. I've got my own ideas about Blaize. I think that this Blaize is a very smart piece of work and I think that he could have told you quite a bit about the Vendayne steal."

*"Could have?"* queried the police officer. "Why 'could have'?"

"Because I don't think you'll pick him up now," said Callaghan. "If you get after that bird—which I think you ought to do—you'll find he's flown."

Walperton made a note on his blotter. "Where do I find this Blaize, Callaghan?" he asked.

He sounded much more friendly.

"You find him at a place called the Yard Arm—a road house between Totnes and Plymouth," Callaghan answered. "He lives in a cottage at the back of the Yard Arm—rather a nice place—with Ropey Felliner as a servant. I should think that if you got a man down there the day after to-morrow—I think he'll be there then—you might get Ropey. I don't think you'll get Blaize. I've had the place watched and it looked as if he was packing up."

Walperton said with a grudging note of admiration in his voice: "You don't waste much time, do you, Callaghan? Is there anything else?"

Callaghan got up.

"Nothing else," he said. "I thought that information would be better than nothing."

"I'm very glad of *any* information on this damned job," said Walperton.

"And I'm very glad to have been of use," said Callaghan.

He grinned at Walperton, nodded to Gridley, picked up his hat and went out.

Walperton lit a cigarette. He said to Gridley:

"What the hell's Callaghan playing at. D'you think he came in here just to give me that information?"

Gridley shrugged his shoulders.

"I don't know," he answered. "But I know one thing an' that is that Callaghan's too clever to give you information that wasn't O.K.

Besides," he went on, "there wouldn't be any harm in somebody going down to this Yard Arm dump and taking a look."

"Perhaps not," said Walperton. "You'd better go down. You'd better go down to-morrow night. Maybe by the day after to-morrow this Ropey bird will be back. See what you can get out of him. You'd better be careful. If he's got a record he might try to be clever, and we've got no charge to make against him."

Gridley said: "I remember Ropey Felliner. He's been in twice on drug charges and once for receiving. He used to be a dope runner for somebody or other."

"Get his record," said Walperton. "Anyhow you won't do any harm by talking to him."

Gridley grinned.

"I don't think I'll do much *good*," he said. "There's only one way to talk to Ropey and that's with a length of lead piping. Still . . . there's no harm in trying."

Callaghan went into the Premier Lounge in Albemarle Street, ordered a salad and a double whisky and soda.

While he was eating he was thinking about Walperton and what Walperton would do. Probably, Callaghan thought, the Detective-Inspector would send someone down to Devonshire. But he would not do that for a day or two. Callaghan had already made up his mind that when Walperton's emissary arrived he should find the birds—both the birds—flown.

After which the detective-officer would make inquiries in the neighbourhood. He would discover that there *had been* a William Blaize and a Ropey Felliner at the Yard Arm cottage. And once this fact was established Walperton would begin to believe the theory that Callaghan intended he should believe—that the Vendayne job was *not* an inside job but a cleverly conceived *outside* job pulled by somebody who had been astute enough to get the safe combination by some extraneous method and experienced enough to negotiate an entrance into Margraud without leaving trade marks all over the place.

He ordered another double whisky, drank it, paid his bill, lit a cigarette and went out into the street. He walked down Albemarle Street, went into the telephone box on the corner of Hay Hill and rang through to the Ventura Club. He asked for Mr. Ventura:

After a minute or two Gabby came on the line. Callaghan said:

"Gabby? This is Callaghan. I'm going to do you a good turn. I looked in at Scotland Yard this morning. A *D.I.* called Walperton had telephoned my office and asked me to. He knew I'd been down to Margraud. Well, this Walperton is a bit of a mug. He talked quite a lot."

Ventura said: "Did he? Well, what did he have to say that would interest me?"

Callaghan grinned.

"Just this," he said. "It seems that they've got a line on Ropey Felliner—you know the slugger who used to work for you. Apparently he's been working at some place near Margraud. Walperton has checked on Ropey's record and doesn't like it. I think they might pull him in. I thought perhaps you wouldn't like that?"

There was a pause. Then Ventura said:

"I don't know that I'd mind it."

Callaghan said: "Don't bluff. I'm doing you a good turn. You get through on the telephone to Ropey and tell him to clear out quick before they get down there and start putting him through it. Well . . . good-bye, Gabby."

He hung up. He stood for a moment outside the call box thinking about the next step. Then he lit a cigarette and began to walk towards the Empire Cable Office in Piccadilly. He spent a few minutes evolving the cable:

*"Harvey Soames*
*Telegraphic Address: Investigate Cape Town.*
*Urgent rush me information William Blaize probably using that name last year check local records check Malmesbury district stop. Five feet eleven inches blue eyes black curly hair well developed slight scar under left ear might be con man check family history. Reply Margraud Manor Gara Devonshire make it snappy good wishes*
*Callaghan."*

He marked the cable "Priority," handed it in, and went back to the office.

IT WAS just before six o'clock when Callaghan went back to Berkeley Square.

He found on his desk an envelope. Written on it, in Effie Thompson's handwriting, were the words: *"Stevens left this."*

Callaghan opened the letter and read the report written in the almost unintelligible scrawl that Blooey affected. It said:

*"Up to the beginning of this year, Lancelot Vendayne was getting around with a young woman called Paula Rochette. Paula is a blonde who lives at Flat 7, 263a Courtfield Gardens. She is a night club artiste and used to work at the Ventura Club. I believe she was introduced to Vendayne by Gabby Ventura the proprietor. Vendayne and Rochette used to get around a lot together until a few months ago. Then it finished. I don't know why. Since then she's tried to get back working at the Ventura but Gabby s not having any. That's all.*

*Blooey."*

Callaghan made a note of Paula Rochette's address on his blotter, tore up the report and threw it into the waste-paper basket. Then he took from his pocket the copy of the letter from Ropey Felliner to Ventura. He read it through carefully, then he got up and went into the outer office. Effie Thompson was putting her machine away. Callaghan took his note case out of his pocket. He extracted five five-pound notes, handed them to Effie. He said:

"Get around to Bond Street as quickly as you can. If you hurry you'll be there before the shops close. I want a piece of jewellery. You can spend all that on it. I want something that looks as if it costs more than twenty-five pounds—something flashy. See?"

She said: "I see. You want something to give to a woman who is not of the class of women you usually give things to."

Callaghan said with a grin: "That sounds all right to me. By the way, what sort of women do I usually give things to?"

She looked at him. Her green eyes were jealous.

She said: "They vary, Mr. Callaghan . . . don't they? There was Mrs. Thorla Riverton and that other woman in the Riverton case and there was . . ."

Callaghan said: "Never mind. Just go and get that bauble before the shops close."

After she had gone, Callaghan looked through the telephone directory and found the number of Miss Paula Rochette, who described herself as an actress. He sat down at Effie Thompson's desk and dialled the number. He asked if Miss Rochette was in. When the voice at the other end asked who it was, Callaghan said it didn't matter, that he wanted to speak to Miss Rochette. Two minutes later a rather high-pitched voice came on the telephone. Callaghan said:

"Is that Miss Rochette? Well, my name's Callaghan. You don't know me, but I know you. I've seen you do your show at the Ventura Club in the old days a dozen times. I used to go every night to watch you. I thought you were *marvellous.*"

Miss Rochette said that was very good news, that she was glad when people rang her up and told her that they liked her show. Her voice was curious.

Callaghan went on: "I often wanted to talk to you. In fact I asked Gabby Ventura if he'd introduce us, but for some reason or other he stalled. He didn't want to do it, which was a little bit tough when you come to think of it."

Miss Rochette said that Ventura was an old devil who would queer anybody's pitch. She asked why it was tough—particularly.

Callaghan said: "Well, to tell you the truth, last time I went round there, I think it was the last night you gave a show there—I bought a little present for you, but owing to Gabby's attitude I never had the chance to give it to you. He said he didn't like patrons meeting artistes at the club."

Miss Rochette said that Gabby was a lousy liar, that he did not mind anything of the sort, that he was just trying to queer her pitch.

"Well, it doesn't matter much," said Callaghan. "The point is I'm at a loose end, and I'd still like an opportunity to give you that mark of my appreciation of you as an artiste. I wonder if you'd like to have dinner somewhere to-night."

Miss Rochette gurgled. She said she would like it immensely. She agreed to meet Callaghan at the Jewel Club off Conduit Street at eight o'clock. Callaghan hung up. He was looking quite pleased with life.

Miss Rochette sat opposite Callaghan at a corner table at the Jewel Club. She was dressed in a very tight-fitting black frock and wore a great deal of imitation jewellery. She was of the peroxide blonde type, and Callaghan noticed that her hair was reverting to its original colour at the roots. He hoped she would have it dyed again soon for her own sake.

At the moment she was giving an imitation of a high-class cabaret artiste, carefully sticking out her little finger when she drank and doing all the things which she considered to be the hall-mark of "class."

She said: "I've enjoyed my dinner immensely, Mr. Callaghan. I must say it's a great treat going out with a real gentleman. In my business too many people try to get funny with you."

Callaghan nodded.

"I know," he said. "It must be tough. But then you see I've always admired you as an *artiste.*"

She said: "It's nice to hear that. Tell me, which of my numbers did you like best?"

Callaghan said: "Don't ask me a thing like that, because I wasn't so much interested in the numbers as the way you put them over."

He put his hand in his pocket and brought out the jewelled clip that Effie had brought. He slid the case towards her. He said:

"You'd have had this a long time ago except for Gabby Ventura. I could never make out why he wouldn't let me meet you. He'd always got some sort of excuse."

"I don't understand it either," she said. "He used to bring a lot of thugs round to see me. Maybe he had some reason. Anyway, Ventura's an old devil. He'd do anything to crab my pitch. I always think . . ."

She stopped talking as she opened the case and saw the clip. She squealed with delight.

"It's just too divine," she said. "I've always wanted one of them, you know." She looked at him archly. "Of course, I ought not to take presents from gentlemen . . ."

Callaghan said solemnly: "That is a gift to an artiste—not a woman."

"I see," said Paula.

She did not sound *too* pleased.

"It's funny," she went on. "I mighta met you a long time ago if it hadn't been for Gabby. But as I was saying he'd always do anything to queer my pitch."

"Would he?" said Callaghan. He signalled the waiter. "I want you to try a cocktail they serve here. It's a very good one. You'll like it."

He told the waiter to bring two double Bacardi cocktails. Miss Rochette said:

"I ought not to drink a cocktail after whisky." She looked at him archly. "I shall be telling you all about my past life in a minute."

Callaghan thought that that was exactly what he wanted her to do. When she had drunk her cocktail he gave her a cigarette. He said:

"It's a small thing, but I wonder why Ventura got rid of you, Paula. I should have thought you took a lot of custom to the club."

"I did," she said. "My show was always a riot there. Lots of people came to see me. All my boy friends too. I used to have a lot of boy friends in those days," she added with a look that was supposed to be demure.

She took her cigarette out of her mouth and looked at it for a moment. She said:

"I've got an idea why Ventura sacked me. I've always hoped I'd have a chance to get back on him."

Callaghan said: "You never know. You might get a chance. Tell me—I'm curious. Why did he sack you?"

She put her fingers to her hair and pushed a blonde tendril back into place. She said:

"It was over some fellow—a fellow called Lancelot Vendayne. He used the club a lot. Gabby introduced him to me. Gabby told me that he was the sort of fellow who'd give me a good time."

"I see," said Callaghan. "So you and Lancelot were friends, eh?"

"More or less," she answered. "For about eight or nine weeks. According to Gabby I thought this Vendayne bird was going to give me a hell of a time. But don't you believe it. He was the meanest thing I've ever struck."

Callaghan said: "Meanness is a bad thing in a man."

"That's right," said Paula. "He was as mean as a monkey. As for havin' money, I don't think he'd *ever* had any money."

"I see," said Callaghan. "Tell me something, Paula," he went on. "Did Gabby and this Vendayne bird quarrel over you?" He looked at her. "I don't see why they shouldn't have," he said seriously. "You're the sort of woman that men would quarrel over."

She simpered.

"Well, I s'pose I am in a way," she said. "But it wasn't over *me*. I don't know very much about it, but there was some share deal on. Vendayne was mixed up in it. I believe he thought he was going to make a fortune in about four weeks. My opinion is," Paula continued, "that Vendayne had got Gabby to put some money into this share business and when it didn't come off he lost his dough, and I think there was a bit of a schmozzle. And *I* got the sack. Gabby said he couldn't afford to run a floor show at the club any more, and that anyway with this war going nobody wanted to see floor shows. I think he was wrong."

Callaghan said: "I'm sure he was."

He lit a cigarette. Paula took out her compact and began to powder her nose and to touch up her too-scarlet mouth. Callaghan watched her. He was rather pleased with Paula. She had given him another piece of the jig-saw puzzle to fit into its place.

And she was an odd sort of person. Paula was definitely *not* the sort of women that a man like Lancelot Vendayne would go for. She was not his type. Lancelot, who liked—at least—the outward appearance of success, would certainly not get around with a woman who was obviously not off the top shelf, who didn't know how to dress, who didn't know how to behave and who wore the cheapest sort of perfume.

He began to think about Audrey Vendayne, who had, for a period, played with the idea of becoming engaged to Lancelot and then had not liked it after all.

Lancelot, thought Callaghan, would probably have started with Paula after Audrey had given him the air. But why?

He thought he probably knew the answer to that one. There was an old-fashioned idea about Gabby Ventura—one not unassociated with night club proprietors—which was that whoever was starring as an artiste in his club, was also *pro tem,* his mistress. Callaghan thought that it would be quite on the cards that Lancelot had gone out to make Paula, merely because, having been associated with Gabby, she might be able to give him some information he required.

And it was just as much on the cards that Gabby was quite prepared to allow such a situation to exist while it suited his book.

Then, when Lancelot's "deal" failed to materialise; when, owing to something or somebody, he was short of money, the first thing he did was to get rid of Paula, and Gabby, true to type, having finished with her as a means of inside information about Lancelot, promptly dismissed her from her job at the club.

And Lancelot thought that Gabby was a crook and Gabby thought that Lancelot was "clever" and a "bastard." And yet, in spite of their obvious dislike for each other, Lancelot was not disinclined to borrow three hundred pounds from Gabby to lend to Audrey, and Gabby was not disinclined to lend it.

A very pretty set-up.

Callaghan said: "Paula . . . there's something about you that gets me. I think you're swell. What would you like to do?"

She smiled. The Bacardi cocktail after whisky was beginning to affect her outlook. Life, in spite of the war, and this and that, appeared almost rosy.

"I think you're pretty good, too," she said. "Well . . . I'd like to go along to the Minnelola Club an' have a drink. An' then I'd like to go along to the Blue Pennant an' have another little drink an' then . . ."

"And then," interrupted Callaghan, "we'll go along to Gabby Ventura's place and show him that Paula Rochette isn't such a back number as he thinks she is."

She laughed.

"That's a hell of an idea," she said. "I like it. Let's do that."

Callaghan signalled the waiter for the bill. He thought the evening was going to be interesting. He said:

"I've got to make a telephone call. I'll be back in a minute."

He went into the call box in the corner. He rang Grant's Hotel. He asked if Mr. Vendayne was in. The clerk said he was.

"All right," said Callaghan. "Well . . . I don't want to talk to him. Just give him a message, will you? Say that Mr. Callaghan will be at the Ventura Club at twelve-thirty, and he'd like to have a word with Mr. Vendayne before he goes back to Devonshire."

Paula leaned back in the corner of the cab and squeezed Callaghan's arm. She said:

"I think this is a marvelous idea—you an' me goin' to Gabby's place an' lettin' him see that little Paula is still gettin' around with the right sort of people."

She smothered a hiccough with difficulty.

Callaghan said: "I think that too."

But he was not thinking that. He was thinking that it would be amusing to watch the reactions of Gabby Ventura and Lancelot Vendayne when they saw Paula with him.

If the association between Vendayne and Paula had been merely what it appeared to be then there was no reason why either Gabby or Lancelot should be unduly interested in the fact that Callaghan was amusing himself by taking around a rather passé night-club turn.

But if, on the other hand, Gabby had put Paula in to keep an eye on Lancelot, and Lancelot had given the lady the air immediately he had realised what Gabby's scheme was—if this were so, then both of them would be *very* interested in the Callaghan-Paula association.

The cab stopped outside the Ventura Club. Callaghan helped Paula out. She was happy. A small bottle of champagne at the Minnelola Club, followed by another small bottle at the Blue Pennant, had put the seal on an ideal evening. And then there was the brooch that Callaghan had given her. Life, thought Paula, was not so bad after all, and even if she was experiencing a little difficulty in enunciating the rather long and "classy" words that she had been using during the latter part of the evening, she was well aware of the fact that she was a perfect lady with everything that being a perfect lady implied.

They went into the club. When they were seated at the table in the corner and another bottle of champagne was ordered, Callaghan saw Gabby standing by the bar. Gabby was looking towards them. His attitude was, as usual, relaxed, but there was a certain stiffness about the stock smile round his plump lips. He came over to them.

"Hallo, Slim," he said cheerfully. "An' hallo, Paula. It's nice to see you around again. How's tricks?"

Paula tossed her head.

"Tricks," she said brightly, "is all right, although why you should condescend to worry about the state of my relatively unimportant existence is more than I can say, Mr. Ventura."

She bestowed a glance on Gabby that was intended to be cynical, proud and indifferent.

Callaghan said: "Why don't you sit down and have a drink, Gabby?"

Ventura sat down. He produced a gold cigarette-case and lit a cigarette. He said:

"It was nice of you to trouble to call through to me about Ropey, Slim, but you needn't have bothered. Anyway, I didn't know what you was takin' about."

"That's fine," said Callaghan. "If you didn't know what I was talking about, then I was wasting my time. But I don't think I was. I bet you got through to Ropey on the telephone or wired him."

He grinned at Ventura.

Paula, who had drunk half a glass of champagne, said acidly:

"Mr. Ventura, you're no gentleman. I've been wanting to tell you that for a long time."

Ventura looked at her. Then he said to Callaghan:

"I don't know what the idea is, Slim—you chasin' around with this floosie, I mean. But I flung her out of this club once an' if she don't keep her ugly mouth shut up I'm personally going to throw her out on her ear. She makes me sick."

Paula stood up.

"Oh, my God!" she said. "So I've got to be insulted, have I? Mr. Callaghan, if you're the man I take you for, if you've got one instink of a gentleman, you're goin' to smack that fat slob's lousy ears right off. The dirty . . ."

"Sit down, Paula," said Callaghan. "You're first-class provided you don't try to talk, and you'll find that sitting down is much easier than standing up."

Paula began to cry. He patted her hand.

Ventura said softly: "Look, Slim. You know me. I'm all right. I never start anythin'. You an' me have always got along. You've used this club for a long time, an' I've always treated you right, haven't I? But don't start anythin', Slim. I'd hate to get sort of annoyed with you."

"You don't say," said Callaghan. "All right, Gabby. Any time you want to get annoyed just start right in. I'll chance what happens."

He was smiling amiably.

Ventura got up. He said:

"O.K. Slim. I reckon that you an' me know just where we are."

"You may know where you are, Gabby," said Callaghan. "But *I* don't." His smile was more amiable than ever. "But I'm going to find out before I'm through."

He stubbed out his cigarette. Ventura got up.

"I'll be seein' you," he said. "And don't let that cheap skirt start anythin' around this club, otherwise I'm going to have her pinched."

Callaghan said: "She wouldn't worry. Maybe she likes being pinched. So long, Gabby."

He watched Ventura as he walked back to the bar, and thence to the pass door at the end of the club that led to the stairway to the flat above.

As Gabby disappeared Lancelot Vendayne came through the entrance curtains. He stood, looking around the dance floor. Eventually he saw Callaghan and Paula. Callaghan thought that Lancelot was looking rather unhappy, rather strained.

He said: "Paula, I've had a very nice evening and so have you. And even if you have a headache to-morrow, you'll still have that brooch."

"Oh, yes?" said Paula. "What're you tryin' to tell me? I s'pose you think the time has come when I ought to do a disappearing act." She snivelled a little. "I don't *understand* you," she concluded.

Callaghan got up.

"Come on, honey," he said. "I'm going to get you a cab and send you home. One of these fine days you and I will meet again and have another little drink together."

He put his hand under her arm.

She said: "It's bloody awful, that's what it is. Any time I meet a man who I think is a real gentleman he walks out on me. I don't understand it. I give up."

She arranged her features into what was intended to be a picture of distressed *hauteur*—a picture which, having regard to the fact that her eyeblack was running down her well peach-bloomed cheeks, was not entirely successful. But she went quietly.

When Callaghan came back Lancelot was standing at the bar. He said:

"I didn't know *you* knew Paula. Paula can be amusing sometimes when she's *quite* sober."

Callaghan grinned.

"You'd be surprised at the things and people that I know, Vendayne," he said. "Let's have a drink."

He ordered double whiskies and sodas.

Vendayne said: "Shall we sit down? I want to talk to you."

They went over to a table. Callaghan drank his whisky and soda. He said:

"I thought you and I might have a little talk before I go back to Devonshire. I'm going early to-morrow morning."

Vendayne said: "And what the hell d'you propose to do when you get there? Tell me that."

Callaghan said: "I don't know. That's half the fun of being a detective. You never quite know *what* you're going to do."

Lancelot drank some whisky.

"That's damned nice for the people who are paying the detective," he said caustically. "I expect the fact that he never quite knows what he's going to do amuses them immensely."

"Possibly," said Callaghan. His voice was insolent. "But why should you worry? *You're* not paying me."

Vendayne sneered.

"Which is lucky for me," he said. "If I *was* paying you I should want some results for my money. As it is"—the sneer became more apparent—"it's quite obvious that you *are* working for the people who are paying you."

Callaghan sighed.

"That shows how honest I am—don't you think?" he asked.

Vendayne put down his glass. He fumbled with his cigarette-case. Callaghan could see that his hands were trembling. He said:

"I've heard about you, Callaghan. You're supposed to be damned clever. Let me give you a word of advice. Don't be too damned clever where I'm concerned. There might be a come-back."

Callaghan blew a smoke ring. He blew it with great artistry right into Lancelot's face.

"There is, of course, always the possibility of a come-back," he said. "But I doubt its efficacy if a rather weak-kneed sonofabitch like you was behind it." He smiled at Lancelot.

Vendayne said: "I see. So that's how it is." He controlled his rising temper with difficulty. "I wonder why you think you can talk to me like that?" he asked.

"I don't know," said Callaghan. "I get that way sometimes. It must be the weather or the war or something. Don't you like it?"

His blue eyes, very cynical, very hard, watched the other.

"I don't like it," said Vendayne. "And what's more I'm not going to stand for it. I . . ."

Callaghan said: "You tell me something." He leaned across the table. "Just how are you going to stop it?" he asked.

Vendayne said: "It might be easier than you think. You *might* be working *very hard* for the people who are paying you. You might even be assisting in something that could put even the clever Mr. Callaghan in a tough spot."

"Dear . . . dear . . ." said Callaghan. "Now I believe you're getting tough. But you've a lot to learn, Lancelot. You ought to take some lessons in bluffing. You're not good at it."

Vendayne's face was white with rage.

"Possibly you'll find out that I'm not *bluffing,*" he said. "Perhaps sooner than you expect. People like you are too prone to think that people like me must be fools."

"I don't think you're a fool," said Callaghan. "I *know* you're a fool. If you weren't you wouldn't be sitting there trying to bluff me. Trying to teach your grandmother how to suck eggs."

Vendayne leaned across the table.

"Really," he sneered. "Well, let me tell *you* something. I began to suspect that you were up to something when you advised me that the claim against the Insurance Company ought to be withdrawn. *Why did you do that?* You know damned well that I created the situation in which you were brought into this case, and I created it because I wanted the screw put on the Insurance Company. I wanted to know why they wouldn't pay. Your job was to find that out. Instead of which *you* are the person who wants the claim withdrawn. Any one might easily think . . ."

Callaghan said quietly: "What might any one easily think?"

Vendayne sat back in his chair. The expression on his face was not amiable. He said:

"They might easily think that the people who ought to have been most keen on the Insurance Company paying aren't too keen. And the reason for their being not too keen was that they might know something about that burglary. And because they were scared when I had you put in they've got you on their side. You're working for them because you're as crooked as they are . . ."

Callaghan said smoothly: "I don't wonder Audrey wasn't keen on you. I don't wonder she gave you the air . . . you cheap sissy . . ."

Vendayne flushed. His face was the colour of beet-root. He muttered:

"All right, Mr. Callaghan. If you wait long enough you'll see who wins. And I don't think you'll have to wait long."

Callaghan lit a fresh cigarette.

"I've told you that you're bluffing," he said. "And you haven't said or done anything to show me that I'm wrong. So I still think you're bluffing. See . . . ?"

Vendayne fumbled in the inside pocket of his jacket. He brought out an envelope. He flung it on the table.

"So I'm bluffing, am I?" he said. "Well, read that, Mr. Know-all!"

Callaghan looked at the envelope. It was addressed, typewritten, to Lancelot Vendayne at Grant's Hotel. The postmark was Exeter.

He opened the envelope. Inside was a sheet of quarto notepaper. He read the typewritten note:

*"To Lancelot Vendayne Esq.*

*Dear Mug,*

*I thought that I was the only sucker in this job. I'm glad you've joined me.*

*Even if the Vendayne jewels hadn't been pinched they'd have done you a bundle of good if and when you got 'em after the old boy passed out. I should think the whole goddam lot was worth about forty pounds. Why don't you get wise to yourself? Love to Mister Callaghan.*

*With best wishes*

*From one Mug to Another."*

Callaghan read the note through twice. He put it in the envelope and handed it back to Lancelot. He said:

"Very interesting. D'you know what I'd do if I were you?"

Vendayne did not answer.

Callaghan continued: "If I were you I'd take that down to Detective-Inspector Walperton at Scotland Yard. That's what *I'd* do. But *you* won't."

Vendayne looked at him.

"No?" he said. "And why not?"

"Because you haven't got the nerve," said Callaghan. "Because you might start something that you can't finish. And lastly because if you did I'm going to make life so tough for you that you'll wish you'd never seen me. Understand?"

"I understand," said Vendayne. "And I'm telling you to go to hell. I'll teach you to call me a sissy before I'm through with you Callaghan."

Callaghan said: "I oughtn't to have called you a sissy. You're not good-looking enough. You're just a plain cheap sonofabitch and you make me sick."

Vendayne jumped to his feet. Callaghan put out his hand and pushed. Vendayne fell backwards over his chair.

Callaghan said: "You run off and get somebody to give you a bromide. You ought not to be out at this time of night without your nurse."

After he had finished brushing his clothes Lancelot Vendayne went back to the bar and ordered a large whisky and soda. He felt he needed it. When he had drunk it he asked the plump blonde behind the bar where Mr. Ventura was. She said he was up in his flat, that she would ring through.

She rang through. She did not get an immediate answer because Gabby was busy sending a wire over the telephone. It was addressed to Ropey Felliner and it consisted of three words:

*"Get out quick."*

## CHAPTER NINE
## LOVE SCENE

CALLAGHAN drove the Jaguar slowly into the garage at Margraud. He got out of the car, lit a cigarette, walked out of the garage, round the east side of the house and stood, at the end of the top terrace, looking out towards the sea.

It was just after six o'clock. The late afternoon sun, still brilliant, gilded the Margraud terraces, turned into sheets of golden velvet the lawns below the terrace steps. Callaghan thought it was a lovely afternoon and an exquisite setting for something—he was not quite sure what. He ruminated that dramatic situations were sometimes the better for a suitable *decor,* decided that the scenery was all right and that only the drama was, at the moment, lacking.

He walked slowly back to the entrance. Stevens was standing in the cool, shadowy hall. He said:

"I'm glad to see you back, Mr. Callaghan. I hope you aren't too tired. Would you like something?"

"You can send a bottle of whisky up to my room, Stevens," said Callaghan. "And where's Mr. Nikolls?"

The butler said he thought that Mr. Nikolls was at Slapton Sands fishing. Callaghan, on his way up the stairs, wondered what Windy was fishing for.

When, half an hour later, Nikolls knocked and put his head round the door, Callaghan was lying on the bed, naked except for a pair of lemon silk shorts, drinking neat whisky, looking at the ceiling.

He said: "How was the fishing, Windy?"

Nikolls grinned. "Not so hot," he said. "I didn't even catch a cold."

Callaghan picked up the bottle of whisky from his bedside table and inserted the cork. He threw the bottle to Nikolls, who caught it expertly, then got a chair and Callaghan's tooth glass, sat down and poured himself a drink.

Callaghan asked: "What's new, Windy?"

"Nothin's new," said Nikolls. "Clarissa has been goddam mysterious, snoopin' about the place like she was chief agent to the Gestapo or somethin'. Audrey has just been around lookin' as if life had declared a blitzkrieg on her just for nothin' at all, an' as for Esme . . ."

Callaghan interrupted: "What's the matter with Esme?"

"Search me," said Nikolls. "That dame is either as dumb as they come or else she's up to somethin'. She's worried sick. I tried that stuff on her like you said, tryin' to get her to fall for the idea that I didn't like you a bit an' that she could rely on little Windy till the cows came home, but she just wasn't buyin' it. She looked at me as if I was somethin' the cat brought in an' scrammed. It's my considered opinion that she don't like *me,* an' she don't like *you* and she don't like anybody. I don't believe that baby even likes herself."

Callaghan said: "That's all right. I don't see why she should like herself either."

He caught the bottle and drank some more whisky.

Nikolls said: "I'm glad to have you back with us, Slim. It's been sorta lonely down here just hangin' around."

"Well, it won't be lonely any more," said Callaghan. "I think something's going to happen any minute."

"That'll be nice," said Nikolls. "I'd like something to happen. I've never been on such a screwy case in my life. I suppose you wouldn't have an idea . . ."

"I've got plenty of ideas," said Callaghan, "but the main thing is, I think I've started a little trouble."

"Swell," said Nikolls. "Anythin' is better than nothin' an' there's nothin' like a spot of trouble to make people start talkin'. I remember a dame I knew in Wisconsin . . ."

"So do I," said Callaghan. "I've been remembering her ever since the first time you told me about her. She was the one with the legs, wasn't she?"

"Correct," said Nikolls. "They was her one redeemin' feature. She got through life on them an' a cast iron nerve . . ."

He sighed at the recollection.

Callaghan blew a smoke ring. He began:

"I went down and saw Walperton at the Yard yesterday. He doesn't like private detectives. I sold him a pup."

"You don't say," said Nikolls. "Maybe he won't like that."

"He won't like it if he finds out," said Callaghan, "but I don't see why he should find out. I told him Ropey Felliner was living over at that cottage at the Yard Arm. I told him about Blaize and suggested that Blaize had a record. I believe Blaize has either cleared out or is just about to clear out, and Ropey Felliner will be clearing out too. I told Gabby Ventura to give him the tip. Gabby pretended that he knew nothing about Ropey, but I bet he got through and told him to get out of here quick."

"I get it," said Nikolls. "Walperton either comes bustin' around here himself or sends somebody down. He finds Ropey an' Blaize are gone. He checks on Ropey's record and finds it as long as a bride's night-dress, after which he comes to the conclusion that Blaize has gotta record too—even if the cops don't know it. He then begins to believe that the Margraud burglary was an outside job pulled by Blaize and or Ropey and or pals of theirs."

He put his glass down suddenly and leaned forward in his chair.

"Hey, Slim," he said, "what's the big idea? What are you selling that boy that phoney stuff for?"

Callaghan grinned.

"What do you mean?" he said.

Nikolls shrugged his shoulders.

"If ever there was an inside job, this is it," he said. "And how could Ropey have had anything to do with it? He's only been down here a few days."

"Quite," said Callaghan. "But Walperton's not to know that."

He blew another smoke ring at the ceiling.

"Windy," he said, "when I came in on this job I thought I was working for Lancelot Vendayne and the Vendayne family. Well, I think I'm working for the Vendayne family now and not Lancelot."

"You don't say," said Nikolls. "What you mean is, you're working for that dame Audrey." He laughed. "I don't blame you either," he said, "I could go for that baby myself. But it wouldn't be so good if Clarissa found out. She thinks you're for *her*."

Callaghan said: "Don't concern yourself with Audrey, Windy. Just get that great brain of yours concentrated on this case. I think I'm beginning to see daylight."

"Yeah?" said Windy. "Well, you've got something on me. This case looks to me as clear as a bottle of ink."

Callaghan said: "We know that Gabby sent Ropey down here to keep an eye on Blaize. Well, you know as much about Gabby as I do. He's a tough egg. If Gabby had known Blaize—known he was a crook—if he'd ever met him before, he wouldn't have sent Ropey down. He'd have come down himself and had a show-down. But he didn't know anything about Blaize, so he sent Ropey down to keep an eye on him, taking advantage of an advertisement that Blaize had put in the newspaper."

"I got that," said Nikolls.

"All right," said Callaghan. "Now, when does Gabby send Ropey down here? He sends him down here *after* the burglary has been committed—not before. So it is only after the burglary had been committed that Gabby is interested in Blaize. Now can you see some daylight?"

"Not particularly," said Nikolls. "Listen, are you trying to tell me it was Blaize pinched this stuff?"

"Why shouldn't he?" asked Callaghan. "It's a free country, isn't it? Anyway, that's my story."

"Blaize won't be here to deny it," said Nikolls. "Well, you think what you like, Slim, but my guess is still Audrey."

Callaghan said: "Windy, there are moments when you're positively thick. Take a look at Audrey Vendayne, and ask yourself whether you really believe that that woman could be mixed up in a burglary."

Nikolls raised his eyebrows.

"Sarsaparilla!" he said. "Listen, Slim, experience has taught me that *any* goddam woman can be mixed up in *any* goddam business no matter how bad it is. Ain't that what women were made for? Look," he said, "you never knew any trouble in this world that some dame wasn't at the bottom of, and the sweller the dame the worse the trouble is. So why not Audrey?"

Callaghan said: "She just isn't the type, Windy."

"I see," said Nikolls. "So she's just not the type! But she's done one or two things that're pretty suspicious looking to my mind."

"I agree with you," said Callaghan. "But that isn't the point. Audrey's attitude may be suspicious; she may have done some things that are suspicious, but that doesn't mean to say she knew anything about the burglary."

"All right," said Nikolls. "What does she want to give you £300 to stay out of this case for? I suppose that was honest."

Callaghan said: "Windy, you answer your own question. Why should she give me £300 to stay out of this case? What's the logical answer to that question?"

Nikolls said: "The logical answer to that question is that she didn't want the case investigated because she'd had something to do with it. She was scared."

"That's all right," said Callaghan, "but that doesn't mean that she had anything to do with it."

Nikolls pursed his lips and whistled.

"I see," he said. "I'm beginning to get it. You think she's scared for somebody else?"

"That's right," said Callaghan. "If you use such brains as you've got, Windy, it wouldn't take you very long to work out who that somebody is."

Nikolls refilled the tooth glass with whisky. He took a long drink.

"I think this is a *nice* case," he said. "Something happens every minute, but nobody gets pinched except maybe Ropey, and that wouldn't hurt anybody."

Callaghan said: "Go over to the wardrobe and feel in the breast pocket of my coat. You'll find a copy letter. It's a copy of a letter that Ropey Felliner wrote to Gabby. I found the original in Gabby's desk . . . Well, read it."

Nikolls read it. "Nice work," he said.

"All right," said Callaghan. "Well, take the operative points in that letter. Ropey says Blaize is telling somebody that the *deal* was phoney. Mark the word 'deal.' So there's been a deal with somebody, and that has to be between Blaize and somebody else, because Blaize is the person who's complaining, and the other person—whoever it is—has given Blaize a raw deal—has twisted him. That could be the only explanation of Blaize saying that the deal had been phoney.

"Now look at the other operative words in that note. Blaize says he's going to keep the other party tied up properly, that there was going to be a show-down pretty soon. What does Blaize mean when he says he's going to keep the other party tied up? Well, it must mean that he's got some sort of hold or lever on the other party and he's going to use it. Probably that's what the show-down is going to be. Ropey says that that show-down is going to take place pretty quickly because Blaize is only going to be down here for a couple of days—that was two days ago."

"I see," said Nikolls. "So you're expecting some fireworks?"

Callaghan lit a fresh cigarette.

"Correct," he said.

He got off the bed, walked over to the wardrobe and began to dress. He asked:

"Where's Esme?"

Nikolls said: "She's around somewhere. She was in early this afternoon. She's been sticking around pretty close the last day or two."

"You don't know where Clarissa is at the moment?" queried Callaghan.

"I believe she's in her room," said Nikolls. "I told you I thought that baby was practising to join the Ogpu, didn't I?"

Callaghan grinned.

"I know," he said. "But in this case we're the Ogpu. She is working for us."

Nikolls got up.

"I'm glad somebody's working for us. Maybe before we're through with this bezusus we'll need it. I'll be around if you want me."

Callaghan walked down the stone steps that led from the lower terrace on to the lawn. At the bottom he took the left-hand pathway, walked parallel with the terrace, turned right at the end. At the end of the path where the wall that surrounded that side of Margraud separated the lawn from the fields outside was a summer-house. Callaghan walked down and stood leaning up against the wall of the summer-house looking out towards the sea, smoking. He stood there for three or four minutes; then he heard the sound of light footsteps on the path behind him. He did not move. Somebody said in a cold voice:

"Mr. Callaghan."

Callaghan turned. He was smiling. He took the cigarette out of his mouth. He said:

"Good-evening, Miss Vendayne."

She was as white as death and her hands were trembling. Callaghan realised that she was fighting a first-class rage. He said:

"It looks as if you're angry with me about something. I seem to be thoroughly unpopular with you. I wonder why?"

"You have the impertinence to wonder why, Mr. Callaghan?" she said. "Anyhow, I don't want to discuss that with you, but I'd be glad if you would do something for me, and it's the last favour I'll ever ask. I'd be glad if you'd pack your bags and get out. There's nothing you can do down here. There's no need for you to stay."

"That's where you're wrong," said Callaghan. "There is an awful lot for me to do down here, and I've got an idea I'm going to stay down here and do it. But why the sudden anger?"

She said: "I've just been talking to my cousin Lancelot on the telephone. It seems he's been making one or two inquiries about you in London, Mr. Callaghan. It seems that whilst you are purporting to be working for Mr. Vendayne and us, in reality you are working for the Insurance Company."

Callaghan put the cigarette back in his mouth and inhaled. He said coolly.

"Let's go into the summer-house. I want to talk to you. You're beginning to make me feel bored."

She looked at him in surprise for a second, then she moved into the summer-house. Callaghan went in after her. He pointed to the rustic bench on one side. He said. "Just sit down there and listen to me, because, as I told you just now, you're beginning to make me feel *very* bored."

She opened her mouth to speak. He put up his hand. She shrugged her shoulders. Callaghan went on:

"During my experience as a private detective, I have met a lot of fool women, but you take the prize. One moment I look at you and think you're clever and the next moment you say something that gives me the idea that you are solid lead above the ears. Now listen . . . you have just accused me of working for Lancelot Vendayne, this family and the Insurance Company itself. Well, why shouldn't I? If this business is straight, then all those people want the same thing—the recovery of the Vendayne jewellery. Why shouldn't I work for the Insurance Company, if the Vendayne family and Lancelot Vendayne are straight?"

She said: "How could Lancelot be anything else but straight? He stands to lose a great deal—"

Callaghan said: "I don't think Lancelot Vendayne *is* straight. Maybe that surprises you." He grinned. "Possibly *you* didn't think he was straight either."

She said: "What do you mean by that?"

"Why did you throw him over?" said Callaghan. "You two were going to be engaged one time. Then you gave him the air. You're a wise girl. I think Lancelot's too clever for you."

He saw that she was fighting to control her temper. He wondered just how much that temper was due to anger and just how much to fear. Either way he proposed to take advantage of the situation.

She said: "I don't think it matters whether I'm a wise girl, whether Lancelot has been too clever for me, or anything else. All that has nothing to do with you."

"It's got a lot to do with me," said Callaghan with an amiable grin, "as you'll see before long. The trouble with you is that you get scared. You start something and you can't finish it. You go rushing around the place being impulsive, doing things before you think. You're stupid. If you hadn't been stupid you'd have taken the trouble to find out something about me before you tried to bribe me to keep out of this case. If you had you might have discovered that I can't be bought anytime . . ." He paused. "Not for money, anyhow . . ."

"I see," she said. Her voice held all the sarcasm she could put into it. "I see. So the great, the clever Mr. Callaghan has a price after all— even if it isn't money. Well, what is it?"

Callaghan grinned at her. His grin was pleasant and cool and quite kindly. He looked at her for a long time.

"You can have two guesses," he said.

She flushed. She began to speak, then stopped herself. After a moment she said:

"I prefer not to understand you."

"That's all right," said Callaghan. "You and I understand each other very well. You think I'm a double-crossing detective who's been grafted by the Insurance Company to snoop out the truth down here, and I think you're a fool woman who could be intelligent if she wanted to, but who is stuck so full of high-falutin' nonsense that, at this moment, you don't know which way you're pointing. Now if you had any sense . . ."

She interrupted. She said coolly:

"This *might* be interesting. I should like to know exactly *what* I should do if I had any sense."

"I'll tell you," said Callaghan.

He leaned up against the wall of the summer-house beside the door, looking down on her. He looked pleasantly impersonal.

"If you had any sense," he went on, "you'd realise a lot of things. First of all you'd realise that if I was working for the Insurance Company to the exclusion of the Vendayne interests I'd have already told 'em that you tried to bribe me to keep out of this case. That fact alone would have sewn the Vendayne family up as far as ever getting any money out of the Insurance people was concerned. Secondly, you'd see that after I got down here and you thought I'd double-crossed you over that three hundred you went into a huddle with your father and the pair of you decided to tell me you were going to *postpone* the claim. I put a stop to that idea. But if you use such brains as you've got you'll realise I did that for the Vendaynes. You'll see why in a minute. The next thing is that the Major has a heart attack. I don't blame him. The probability is that he had the heart attack after you told him what was worrying *you*, and then I imagine he told you what was worrying *him*. I wonder you didn't have a heart attack too!"

He produced his cigarette-case and lit a cigarette. He was watching her. Her eyes were on his and they were interested.

"I'm not doing so badly, am I?" said Callaghan.

He inhaled cigarette smoke and allowed it to trickle out of one nostril.

"The point is," he went on, "when I'm working on a case I like to *work* on it and I like to work for *somebody*. I don't just kick around trying to scrape off odd bits of money. I've discovered that you make much more the other way. In this particular case I don't think that there's a lot of money to be made but I've got other interests . . ."

She said: "Really. May I know what they are?"

"Certainly," answered Callaghan. "I'll tell you. You're my main interest. I like your type of woman. I like the way you dress and walk and behave generally. Even if you do go off the rails sometimes and do silly things I still think I like you . . . quite a lot."

She said: "I think you are the most impertinent person I've ever met. Your insolence is amazing. I suppose you consider I ought to be flattered when you say you 'like' me. Well . . . I don't like *you!*"

"The joke is you *do*," said Callaghan. He was still smiling. "You like me quite a lot and because you do you take an awful lot of trouble to make yourself believe that you don't. That's why you lose your temper so easily."

She said: "I don't see why we should discuss the psychological angles of my character."

"All right," said Callaghan. "We won't. We won't discuss the psychological angles of your character. We won't even discuss the psychological angles of Esme's character or any of the other interesting things about this family. What we will discuss is what's going to happen and what you're going to do. And when I say what you're going to do I mean it. You're going to do what I say and *like* it. Understand?"

She got up. For a moment Callaghan thought she was going to strike him. She said in a low voice: "Don't you dare talk to me like that. I . . ."

He said: "You'd be surprised if I told you what I'd dare to do. But I meant what I said just now. There's going to be a show-down here at Margraud pretty soon and I want it to be played my way. That's the only way that's going to do *you* any good. Otherwise there's a damned good chance of Detective-Inspector Walperton—a most keen, efficient and busy young police officer—coming down here and finding out one or two things that are better left where they are. You're between the devil and the deep sea and even if you think I'm the devil you'll find I'm more accommodating than the deep sea."

She put her hand out against the wall of the summer-house to steady herself. Her face was very white. She said:

"Go on . . ."

Callaghan threw his cigarette end away.

"I've been up to London," he said. "I've done one or two things I wanted to do, found out one or two things. The main thing is:

"I've seen Layne, your father's solicitor. I've persuaded him to write to the Insurance Company and *withdraw* the claim. The Insurance Company are not going to be at all suspicious about that, first of all because I'm supposed to be working for them, and secondly because we've led 'em to believe that we're withdrawing the claim because I've an idea that I know where that jewellery is. That fixes the Company. All they want is *not* to have to pay that claim, and if they don't have to pay the claim their interest in who's done what and why promptly ceases. Understand?"

She said: "I understand."

She took her hand away from the wall and went back to the seat. She sat down. All the while she kept her eyes on Callaghan's face.

"The next thing is Lancelot," he went on. "Lancelot is going to make all the trouble he can. He's started in already by trying to get you up against me. Remember that Lancelot was the one who wanted this business investigated and the screw put on the Insurance people.

I'll bet he's been down to see them and they've said their piece and he doesn't like it—especially as he has decided not to like *me*."

She said: "Is there any way of stopping Lancelot making trouble—as you call it?"

Callaghan said: "I'll find a way to do that."

She looked at the floor.

"I see," she said very quietly.

Callaghan said: "I've got to find ways to stop a lot of things happening. But with luck I might even manage that too . . ."

She got up.

"We shall be late for dinner," she said.

She moved over to the doorway, stood there, looking along the path. She turned suddenly.

"It would be funny," she said in a peculiar, strained voice, "if you really were a friend, if you weren't such a . . ." her voice trailed off.

Callaghan smiled.

"Stranger things have happened," he said. "Anyhow, stop worrying. Worry killed the cat and in any event it's illogical. It never stops things happening and it never helps. Don't worry and don't *do* anything. I think it's time you began to take things easy for a bit. At the moment there's only one thing—or possibly two things—for you to do."

She turned towards him, away from the doorway.

"What things?" she asked.

"First of all, relax," said Callaghan. "You're almost at breaking point now. Secondly, when you've got time to get to it just ask yourself if it isn't possible—having regard to what I've told you—that instead of being your most bitter enemy I might even be almost a friend—shall we say a sheep in wolf's clothing."

He smiled at her. She noticed, once again, the whiteness of his teeth and the firm angle of his jaw. Suddenly, and for no reason that she knew, she began to sob. She stepped back into the summer-house, her head in her hands.

Callaghan said: "Come here, Audrey. Stop crying. Take your hands away from your face and don't be a little fool."

She did as she was told. She said:

"Well . . . what do you want . . . ?"

Callaghan put his hand under her chin and lifted it. He kissed her on the mouth.

He said: "You'd better sit down and arrange your face and your mind. They both need it. I've got one or two things to do. I'll be seeing you."

She said: "Very well . . ."

She produced an infinitesimal handkerchief from her tweed jacket pocket and dabbed at her eyes.

She said vaguely: "I wonder why I did that . . . or rather why I let you do that."

He grinned.

"You didn't do it," he said. "*I* did. But next time I hope you'll be the originator of the idea."

He walked over to the doorway and lit a cigarette. He said, smiling:

"I told you I had my price. You realise now that I'm a most expensive person."

He walked along the pathway towards the house.

When he was out of sight she sat down on the bench and concentrated on being normal.

The process took five minutes. When she had achieved it successfully she decided to cry some more.

## Chapter Ten
## Portrait of Esme

CALLAGHAN came out of the side entrance, walked down the terrace and turned right towards the putting green. He thought Nikolls would be there. He was right. That one, struggling with the intricacies of an eight-foot putt, kept his eye on the ball, hit it smartly and with determination and watched it as it travelled towards the hole. He said, as he put the putter under his arm:

"Maybe you think I'm goin' nutty, but this game's got me bad. One of these fine days when I come into some money or somethin' I'm goin' to give up bein' a detective. I'm goin' to be a golf pro."

Callaghan said: "I don't see any difference so far as *you* are concerned."

"Think of it," said Nikolls. "Out in the open all day knockin' a little white ball about, teachin' beautiful dames how to swing."

Callaghan grinned. He said:

"You're not having such a bad time on this case."

"Correct," said Nikolls. "At the same time all good things come to an end."

He bent down and picked the golf ball out of the hole. He said:

"By the way, Clarissa was talkin' to me just after dinner—I just remembered. She asked me for a good name to call a really bad guy. Well, I didn't like to tell her anything sorta strong. I told her 'sonofa-bitch' was best, that is unless she wanted to call the guy a 'heel.' I got an idea she liked 'heel' best."

Callaghan said: "Where is she?"

"I think she's gone to her room," said Nikolls. "Either that or else she's the one who's playin' the piano in the drawin'-room. You can hear it—but maybe that's Audrey."

He put the putter under his other arm and felt in his jacket pocket for a cigarette. After he'd lit it, he said:

"Where do we go from here, Slim? Do we know?"

Callaghan said: "I don't think we'll have to wait very long now. I think a very nice little situation is blowing up. Stay around, Windy. Don't go on any more of those fishing trips until I say so."

"That's O.K. by me," said Nikolls. "I'm dyin' to get to work. I've almost forgotten *how* to be a detective."

Callaghan said: "I don't think you ever remembered."

He walked away towards the house. As he neared the side entrance, Stevens came out. He said:

"Here's a cable, sir. It's just arrived. I think it has been at Kings-bridge a couple of hours. They had difficulty in finding a boy to bring it over."

Callaghan nodded. He took the cable, opened it, read it. It was from Harvey Soames in Cape Town. Callaghan began to grin. He was half joyful, half satanic. He went into the house, put his head round the door of the drawing-room, looked in. Audrey was seated at the piano running her fingers idly over the keys. She did not see him. Callaghan closed the door softly and went upstairs.

He was half-way down the first floor corridor on the way to his room when a door opened. Clarissa came out.

She said. "Slim, you're a heel. Alternatively, you're a sonofabitch. Personally, I think you're both."

He grinned at her.

"I'm surprised you should have to get your vocabulary from Windy, Clarissa. What's the matter?"

She leaned up against the door-post.

"The only trouble with me is my eyesight—that, and a little synchronisation."

"What's the matter with your eyesight?" said Callaghan. "And who have you been synchronising with or haven't you?"

Clarissa said: "The trouble is my eyes are too good, and as for the synchronisation, I happened to be in the end room of this corridor looking out towards the summer-house some time before dinner. I saw you and Audrey. I didn't know she liked being kissed like that. Was it good?"

"Very," said Callaghan. "Well, how do you think she'd like to be kissed?"

Clarissa said: "Maybe I'll give you a demonstration one day. In the meantime, as I've told you before, I think you're a heel. You make love to me and kiss my sister. Do you think that's fair? But perhaps you were only practising. You *are* a heel, Slim."

He said: "Clarissa, all's fair in love and war. Didn't you know?"

"That's all right," said Clarissa. "But were you and I in love or having a war? You needn't worry, Slim. I've had the idea that you were leading me up the garden path, using me as a sort of 'stooge.' That's what they call it, isn't it?"

Callaghan said: "Clarissa, I think you're fine. I wanted to get you working on my side, and I just didn't know the best way to do it. I thought that was a good approach."

"I see," said Clarissa. "I suppose Audrey's working for you too . . . only in her case the approach has got to be a little more passionate. What do I have to do to get kissed like that? I think it's lucky I haven't got any more sisters."

Callaghan said: "You didn't waylay me to tell me all this?"

She shook her head.

"No," she said, "I didn't. I wanted to ask you something and I'd be rather obliged if you'd tell me the truth. That was all nonsense, wasn't it, that stuff you told me about merely having an idea about Blaize and about your thinking that he hadn't anything to do with the burglary? You're worried about Blaize, aren't you, Slim?"

He nodded.

"Just about as much as you are, Clarissa," he said. "I knew you were putting on an act that night I went over to his cottage behind the Yard

Arm and found you and Esme there. I guessed why you were stringing along with Esme. I realised that you weren't a *natural* gooseberry . . ."

"You were right," she said, "I was frightened for her. She's so silly. Esme's always been the *bloodiest* fool, Slim."

"That's what I think," said Callaghan. "And you've got some news for me?"

She said: "Yes, I've got some news for you. Ever since you've been away I've been snooping about, keeping an eye on Esme and on her post as we arranged. She's had no letters of importance—at least nothing that was posted in this county—but this evening while you and Audrey were indulging in the summer-house somebody came through from Exeter. They wanted Esme. I happened to be in the hall, so I went quickly into Daddy's room where there's an extension from the hall phone. I listened in."

Callaghan lit a cigarette.

"This sounds as if it might be interesting."

"It is *very* interesting," said Clarissa, "and rather worrying. It was a man. He didn't shout or anything like that, but he sounded terribly angry. He told Esme he wanted to talk to her, that the time had come for a show-down. He said she was to meet him as usual at half-past eleven tonight, that if she didn't turn up there was going to be a lot of trouble. I didn't like the sound of him a bit," Clarissa concluded.

Callaghan said: "I shouldn't worry about the sound of people's voices. Words don't hurt very much. Do you know where the 'usual place' is?"

Clarissa shook her head.

"I don't," she said. "I didn't even know there'd been a usual place. I didn't know that Esme had been meeting anybody. Why should she want to meet anybody surreptitiously?"

Callaghan grinned.

"Why does any woman meet any man surreptitiously?" he said.

Clarissa said: "Do you know who the man is?"

"I can make a good guess," said Callaghan.

She put her hand on his arm. She said:

"You know, Slim, you've deluded me, but I'm inclined to trust you. There's something about you I really like. Promise me something— you won't let anything happen to Esme, will you? I'd *hate* anything to happen to her."

Callaghan said: "Don't you worry. I'll try and take care of Esme. I'm learning to be the Santa Claus of this family."

She said: "Like hell you are!—and I learned that from Windy, too. Anyway," she said, "it's probably the first and the last time, but I want payment for my information, and when I say payment, I mean just that. You owe me a lot, Slim. You got that Windy person to tell me a lot of rubbish about you being *fearfully* attracted by me and I fell for it like a schoolgirl. You've probably ruined my life anyway. I might even go into a nunnery or something at any moment."

She came up close to him. She said:

"Mr. Callaghan, I think I've got something in my eye. Will you look, please?"

Callaghan said: "Clarissa, there's something damned nice about you. If it wasn't for Audrey . . ."

"To blazes with Audrey," said Clarissa. "Audrey can look after herself. Just let yourself go for a minute, will you, and don't bring up other women when you're supposed to be kissing me."

After a minute she said: "Is there anything else you want me to do?"

"I don't think so," said Callaghan. "You've done a good job, Clarissa."

"All right," she said. "Only remember . . . I'm relying on you . . . I expect Audrey is too . . . look after Esme . . ."

She went back to her door.

"I think you're rather nice, Slim," she said. "I know you're fearfully stuck on Audrey. I can understand it too . . . If I were a man I'd be stuck on her. She's got something, hasn't she . . . you know . . ."

She made a face at him and closed the door.

At nine o'clock Callaghan went into the smoking-room on the first floor. He rang the bell and sent for Nikolls. When Nikolls arrived Callaghan said:

"Listen to this, Windy: I've got an idea that to-night, possibly about eleven, Esme's going out to keep an appointment with somebody. I'd rather like to be there or anyway in the neighbourhood. The devil of it is I don't know where the appointment is."

Nikolls said: "What the hell! It can't be far away. Where do you keep appointments around here anyway?"

Callaghan said: "Quite. So this appointment's either got to be in a place like Kingsbridge or some place you get to by car, or it's going to be local. The best thing for you to do is to keep your eye on the garage.

It'll be fairly dark by that time, and if you hang about in that thicket on the far side of the lawn you can see the garage doors. If Esme takes the car out, you've got to go after her. When she gets to wherever she's going to you can telephone me."

"O.K.," said Nikolls. "An' supposin' this date is a local date?"

Callaghan said. "The same thing applies. But if it's a local date the obvious place to have such a date is somewhere in the grounds here— at the back of the house. There are plenty of places to meet. There's that stretch of cliffs along by the sea—an ideal place. I'll keep my eye on the gardens and terraces," said Callaghan. "I can do that from the balcony. But don't lose her if she goes out your way. I want to find where that girl's going to."

"All right," said Nikolls. "I'll watch her plenty."

Callaghan said: "There's just a chance that Lancelot Vendayne may be hanging around here to-morrow or the day after. Lancelot doesn't like me very much. He got an anonymous note from somebody. He showed it to me. The note said that Lancelot was a mug. It also said that even if he had inherited the Vendayne jewellery he would have found that it was worth about forty pounds."

Nikolls said: "For cryin' out loud! You don't mean to tell me that we've been chasin' around after some stuff that's worth about two hundred dollars?" His eyebrows went up. "Say, what about that insurance claim!"

Callaghan was grinning.

"It's a nice situation," he said. "But Lancelot isn't going to like it. I've got an idea in my head that the only thing Lancelot cares about is money, and when he thinks he's not going to get what he thought was coming to him, he's going to turn damn' nasty."

"Yeah," said Nikolls. "And Audrey wouldn't like that, would she?" He grinned sardonically at Callaghan.

Callaghan said: "Windy, you're a fool. You're still harping on that old theory of yours about Audrey. You just don't know how wrong you are."

"Maybe," said Nikolls.

Callaghan said: "All right. Keep your eyes skinned and don't miss anything. I'll be seeing you."

He went out.

The moon came up from behind a cloud. Callaghan, seated on the balcony outside the dining-room French windows, could see the lawns and terraces plainly in the silver light. He looked at his watch. It was eleven-thirty. He swore softly under his breath, lit a cigarette, went through the dining-room into the corridor and out by the side door near the garage. He stood there in the shadows smoking.

Five minutes passed. Callaghan could hear the sound of an approaching car coming up the drive. He walked into the moonlight. Nikolls braked the car to a standstill at his side.

"Not so hot, Slim," he said. "That little so-an'-so ditched me. Around ten past eleven she came out to the garage an' got her car out. I gave her a start an' went after her. Believe me she was goin' some. About two miles away I found her bus parked by the side of the roadway. But no Esme!"

Callaghan said: "That's all right. Maybe she has an idea someone was going after her. Which direction did she take? Where did you find the car?"

"She took one of the secondary roads, leadin' off to the left, in the direction of Gara," said Nikolls. "I reckon if she was goin' on foot she was goin' across country. She had to be. I drove down the road for a coupla miles more an' there wasn't a sign of her."

"All right," said Callaghan. "Put the car away and stay put."

He went back into the house. He found Audrey in the drawing-room. She was sitting at the writing table playing patience. He said:

"You ought to be in bed. You look tired. Why don't you call it a day?"

"I am tired," she said. "But I don't want to go to bed. I feel I shouldn't sleep. Do you want something?"

"Yes," said Callaghan. "I want to know what Esme usually does with her spare time. Does she ever go for walks? If she does, has she got a favourite walk?"

She said: "Esme used not to like walking. But she's done more walking during the last few months than ever before. I've seen her going along the cliffs towards Gara quite often. Sometimes in the evening."

Callaghan asked: "Do you think she'd be going to Gara? Or would she be going to some place between Gara and Margraud?"

"I don't see why she should go to Gara," said Audrey. She began to stack the patience cards. "There's only the hotel at Gara and the golf course on the other side of the hill. Besides, between here and Gara is a deep cleft in the cliff—a along one. It's quite wide where it runs into the sea and you have to walk right round the far end. That means climbing. I can't visualise Esme taking the trouble to walk uphill round the cleft, when, if she wanted to go to Gara, she could so easily go by road."

"Thanks," said Callaghan. "That's what I wanted to know."

She got up. She said:

"What's happening? Has Esme gone out? What is in your mind, please?"

Callaghan took out his cigarette-case. He offered her a cigarette, lit it, and his own. She stood quite close to him, holding the cigarette limply between her fingers, watching his eyes.

"Esme's ditched us," he said. "I knew she had a date with someone to-night at eleven-thirty. I particularly wanted to be present because I've an idea in my head that unless the person that Esme intended to meet is dealt with in rather a tough way he's going to make a whole lot of trouble. I imagined that she'd either take her car, in which case I'd arranged for Nikolls to go after her, or else, if the meeting-place was somewhere in the locality, she'd go out through the grounds. I've been waiting to see which thing she'd do. She got round the problem by taking out her car, driving like the devil for a couple of miles and leaving the empty car on the roadside for Nikolls to catch up with."

She said: "It's quite awful . . . isn't it? I wish I knew what to do. I'm scared about her. And I don't know why. Can *you* tell me?"

Callaghan grinned.

"I'll tell you what to do," he said. "You go to bed. Take three Veganin tablets and count sheep going through a gate. They tell me it works very well. Good-night."

He went out of the room.

She stood for a moment looking at the door after it had closed behind him. Then she went back to the table and took up the pack of cards. She began to play patience.

Nikolls was drinking whisky out of a hip flask when Callaghan came into his room. He said:

"Would you like a drink?"

He held up the flask.

Callaghan said: "I don't want a drink. I want a little action. Go down to the garage and get that car of yours. Drive over to the Yard Arm and see what's going on there. There's just a chance that Blaize hasn't gone yet. Even if he has there must be someone looking after the Yard Arm. See what you can find out. And look out for Esme."

Nikolls said: "O.K."

Callaghan went to his own room and got a hat. He went downstairs out of the side entrance, down the terrace steps, across the lawn at the bottom and out of the gate on the west side. He began to walk across the fields towards the footpath that ran along the cliffs.

It was a fine night. The moon was up and walking was not unpleasant. Callaghan stepped out briskly. After a while he came to the path that led along the cliff edge towards Gara. He walked for ten minutes, then stopped and looked at his watch. It was nearly twelve o'clock.

He lit a cigarette and continued along the narrow path. A few feet away on his left was the cliff edge. Below he could hear the sea breaking against the rocks. He thought, with a sardonic grin, that the cliffs and beaches in these parts had been wreckers' grounds in the old days and that even if there weren't any more wreckers the technique had merely altered with the passing of time.

On his right the ground sloped upwards towards the hills. He began to curve round the cliff. Except for the crying of the gulls as they hovered over the sea the night was still. Callaghan began to think about gulls and concluded that the feathered specimens were perhaps the luckiest.

He walked for another ten minutes before he saw Esme. She was sitting on a piece of cliff rock off the pathway on the hillside. Even before he was able to recognise her he knew it would be Esme.

She looked at him as he approached. Her face was pallid, terribly strained. Her large eyes peered at him questioningly. There were black circles beneath them, and in one hand he could see the screw-up ball of handkerchief.

He stopped walking and stood on the narrow footpath, looking at her. He produced his cigarette-case, took out two cigarettes. He handed one to her. She took the cigarette mechanically and put it into her mouth. Her hand was trembling almost violently.

Callaghan lit her cigarette and his own, shading the flame of the lighter from the sea with his hand. He said:

"Well . . . what sort of a show-down was it? Tough, very tough, or just normal?"

She said in shaky voice: "I don't know what you mean. I don't want to talk to you. I'm tired of you. I feel that most of the time you're watching me trying to find things out. Why don't you leave me alone? You won't do any good."

Callaghan grinned. He sat down on the grass by her side. He was careful to look out to sea. It was quite obvious to him that the last thing that Esme desired was to be looked at.

He said: "I'm sure you're tired of me, but it's a feeling that you'll have to get over. As for not wanting to talk to me, that's all right with me. If you don't want to talk—don't. What I want you to realise is that, having kept your nerve for so long, it's a damned silly proposition to lose it now. Even you must realise that there are other people to be considered. Besides your blackmailing friend—I mean."

Esme drew on her cigarette. He could see the end glowing. She said: "What other people should I consider?"

Callaghan grinned.

"You and I ought to stop fencing," he said. "It won't do you any good and it doesn't even amuse me. By 'other' people I mean your father. You knew that anyway. It must be obvious to you that he's got enough trouble as it is at the moment without you going out of your way to make things worse."

She laughed. It was a small hard laugh meant to indicate complete indifference. Then she said in a voice that was steadier:

"I don't care about anything else or any one else. I suppose it's fearfully selfish and cowardly, but I'm going to kill myself. After I've done that people can think what they like and blame me for everything. It's obviously the easiest way out of a difficult and quite ridiculous situation."

Callaghan grinned at her. He said coolly:

"Ridiculous is good! But that's all right by me. If you want to kill yourself, you go ahead and do it. But killing yourself won't do any good to anybody except you, and it mightn't even do you any good. Being dead is a lousy proposition and you'd probably go on worrying afterwards."

He inhaled a mouthful of cigarette smoke with obvious pleasure. He allowed the smoke to trickle slowly out of pursed lips. There was quite a pause before he went on:

"And even if you do kill yourself and everybody is quite prepared to blame you for everything . . . well, you might get some sort of a kick out of that, but it wouldn't alter the fact that the jewellery Blaize got was fake. There'd still have to be *post-mortems* on that angle. It wouldn't make your passing out any easier to realise that the police would probably have to arrest your father in any event. Even if they thought that you were responsible for the burglary, they'd know damned well that he must have been the person who switched the jewellery . . ."

She said: "Oh, my God . . . I never thought of that . . ."

She made a hoarse sobbing noise.

Callaghan said softly: "That's the trouble with you. You never think of anything or anybody except yourself. You're a selfish little fool. Because you were short-circuited over making a first-class damned fool of yourself with a good-looking fisherman from Beesands you have to get yourself in a mess, right up to the neck, with a cheap four-flusher like Blaize."

He inhaled some more smoke. He went on:

"Take a pull at yourself, Esme, and don't behave like a spoiled child. After all it must have been obvious to you when Blaize told you—as I imagine he has done and not so long ago—that the jewellery was fake—that he wasn't going to let the matter end there. That boy's going to talk even if he sinks himself in doing it. He's annoyed. I'll bet he's very annoyed."

"He *was*," said Esme. Her voice was almost shrill. "God . . . was he angry! But he won't talk. He won't ever talk . . ."

Callaghan made a grimace.

"Don't you believe it," he said. "He'll talk all right. He'll have to."

"He can't," said Esme. "He's dead . . . I killed him."

Callaghan looked at her quickly. She was looking out towards the sea. Her face was like a death mask.

He said quietly: "Hell . . . that was a damned silly thing to do. What did you do it for?"

"I didn't mean to," said Esme. "He brought one of the bracelets to show me. Apparently he'd kept that one. He'd sent the rest of the jewellery away. He hadn't discovered that it was all fake until the people who were supposed to cut up the stones wrote and told him so. Then he examined the bracelet and found it was true. He brought it to show me. I thought—quite insanely—that if I could get the bracelet—if he hadn't got any more of the jewels—he couldn't prove what he said. So I snatched it away from him and tried to run away."

She ran her tongue over her lips.

"We met by the cleft on the Gara side. We've always met there. It's been the place of some marvellous scenes—horrible, beastly scenes. When he came after me I ran towards the edge. I intended to throw myself over with the bracelet. At that moment the process seemed the obvious way out. As I reached the edge of the cleft—about ten or fifteen yards from the sea—he caught hold of me. I struggled and fought. I pushed him over. I stood there for a minute and then I heard him cry out."

Callaghan said: "What did you do then?"

"I ran away," said Esme. "I began to run towards Gara. I still had the bracelet, but I was so frightened, so *mad* that I dropped it. Presently I stopped and tried to think. I came back and tried to find the bracelet. I searched for a long time but I couldn't find it. Then I began to walk home. I stopped here because I was tired."

She began to cry bitterly.

He shrugged his shoulders. After a minute he said:

"I wish you'd stop crying. It doesn't help. I'm trying to think. Why the hell don't you stop being sorry for yourself and try to pull yourself together. You make me feel sick."

She stopped crying. She said:

"You're a nice sympathetic sort of person, aren't you?"

"I don't believe in sympathy at the wrong time," said Callaghan. "And this is the wrong time. There's no need to panic. There might still be a way out of this, but whoever finds it has got to be damned *good*. Tell me something . . ." he turned towards her. ". . . .If you were running towards Gara, you dropped that bracelet on the far side of the cleft, fairly near to it. Is that right?"

"I imagine so," said Esme. "But I don't *know*. I don't *know* anything. And what does it matter, anyhow?"

Callaghan said: "You listen to me. You're a damned selfish bit of work and I don't like you a bit. Even so, with a bit of luck you can get away with this. Not because you particularly deserve to but because it happens to suit my book."

Esme said: "What do you mean?"

There was a small note of interest in her voice.

"Listen to me," said Callaghan. "And listen hard. When you leave here and go home—which is what you're going to do in a minute—go straight to your room and don't talk to any one. You understand? Just go to your room and lie on the bed and relax, and then tell yourself this:

"You went to keep your appointment with Blaize tonight. You were frightened sick. You knew he was going to be tough. You knew he was going to be tough because you knew weeks ago when you let him into the house and he stole that jewellery it was fake. That's your story. *The only reason that you let him into Margraud to steal the jewellery was because you knew it was worthless.*"

"But I didn't . . ." she muttered. "I didn't . . . I . . ."

"Of course you didn't," said Callaghan cynically. "You intended to let Blaize steal the real stuff. That was his price, wasn't it, and you were prepared to pay for it . . . with somebody else's jewels? *All right.* Well, we don't have to tell 'em that. We tell 'em my story. So listen and don't talk.

"To-night when you went to meet Blaize you knew there was going to be one hell of a show-down. You knew that he would have found out the jewellery was false. And you were prepared to stand for what happened. But when you got there and Blaize lost his temper and began to get tough you ran away. You had met him at the top of the cleft and you began to run round the edge, towards Margraud. You got round the edge all right and you could hear him coming after you. You looked over your shoulder. Just as he was rounding the edge of the cleft he slipped. The grass is wet and slippery. You saw him fall. You heard him yell. You fell down in a faint. When you came to you walked along here and sat down trying to recover your nerve."

He got up. He stood looking down at her.

"That's your story. You stick to it and you'll be all right. There's no one can break it down because there's no one who saw. You've got to have the benefit of the doubt and all the facts leading up to the meeting in your favour. Well . . . are you going to do it?"

She said: "Very well. I'll do what you say. I'll remember that. It's near enough to the truth anyway . . . except for the bracelet."

"Don't worry about that," said Callaghan. "Nobody's going to visualize you struggling with Blaize for a worthless bit of goods like that bracelet. Anyhow I hope to find it. I'm going to look for it . . . Now pull yourself together. Get up and go home. When you get there be careful to give Audrey a miss. She'll probably be hanging about the place waiting to talk to you. Go straight to your room and get that story set in your mind."

Esme got up. She said:

"Very well. I'll do what you say." She smiled suddenly. A quick curious smile. "You're a funny man, aren't you?" she said. "Why are you taking all this trouble anyhow? What does it matter to you?"

Callaghan said roughly: "You mind your own damned business and get out of here. I'll see you when I get back, or to-morrow. Remember you've been a pretty fatuous sort of little idiot up to date. Try and square off the account by behaving yourself and doing what you're told."

She nodded her head. She began to walk unsteadily along the footpath towards Margraud.

Callaghan sat down on the stone and watched until she was out of sight.

After a while he took out his cigarette-case and lit his last cigarette. He smoked it slowly. It lasted twenty minutes. He stubbed the end out on the rock and began to curse fluently. He used some very curious and definite words about Esme.

Then he got up, stretched himself and began to walk back towards Margraud.

## CHAPTER ELEVEN
## BEDROOM SCENE

CALLAGHAN walked quietly along the corridor until he came to the door of Nikoll's bedroom. He turned the handle quietly and went in. Inside the door he found the light switch, turned it on. He closed the door gently.

Nikolls was lying on his back. He was sleeping soundly. An almost angelic smile wreathed his plump countenance. His mouth was wide open.

Callaghan went over to the bed. He shook Nikolls's shoulder. He said:

"Wake up, Windy. And I wonder if any one has ever told you how awful you look when you're asleep."

Nikolls gave a grunt and awoke. He sat up in bed, rubbing his eyes, trying to come back to earth.

He said: "Ain't it my luck? Ever since I been down here I been sleepin' bad. To-night I get a good sleep. I get around to dreamin' of a dame with the swellest hips I ever saw in my life an' I have ta get woke up. It ain't human. I wish you coulda waited another five minutes. Things was just gettin' interestin' with that dream dame. . . ."

Callaghan said: "Get up and get dressed as quickly as you can, Windy. Then go round to the garage and see if you can find a rope—a fairly long one."

"O.K.," said Nikolls. "What are we gonna do? Hang somebody?"

"No," said Callaghan. He grinned cynically. "The execution has already taken place," he said.

Nikolls got out of bed. He was wearing pale blue pyjamas with red spots on them. He looked like a gigantic and ponderous insect. He went over to the chest of drawers, found his whisky flask and took a long pull, sighed and began looking for his clothes.

Callaghan sat on the bed. He said:

"Did you find anything interesting at the Yard Arm? What about Ropey?"

Nikolls sat down on a chair and began to pull on his socks.

"Ropey's gone," he said. "Blaize ain't there either. I reckon you was right about those two babies. They both took a quick run-out powder. Blaize had fixed the sale of the Yard Arm an' the cottage to some guy days ago—a guy named Wallers. Not a bad sort of palooka."

He fixed a bright blue sock suspender round a calf that looked like a young tree trunk. Then he looked at Callaghan. He was grinning.

"This is where the story gets interestin'," he went on. "The Wallers guy tells me that Blaize has got out—to-day—an' that he reckons he's goin' abroad if he can get a boat to take him. He tells me that somebody else has been hangin' around tryin' to see Blaize an' that this somebody else come down in a car that was parked just inside the Yard Arm cottage orchard.

Wallers had told this bozo that he reckoned that Blaize was gone but that he didn't sorta think he'd been gone long because Blaize's stuff had only been taken outa the cottage a few hours ago. So the guy with the car says he'll take a look around."

Nikolls got to his feet and took another pull at the flask.

He said: "I thought I'd take a look in at the cottage orchard just to make certain, an' sure enough this guy's car was still there. He'd parked it under the trees—a big tourin' car—switched the lights off an' taken the ignition key away. There was a leather pocket in the side of the door on the drivin' side an' I took a look inside. I found a drivin' licence an' did I laugh or did I. The drivin' licence was in the name of Gabriel Ventura. Does that add up to anythin'?"

Callaghan nodded. He said:

"It's working out. Having got Ropey out of the way, Gabby just had to make sure that Blaize was gone. He had to make sure that he was gone, or if he wasn't Gabby was going to try and do a deal with him.

I bet he was disappointed when he found that Blaize had only left an hour or so before."

He lit a cigarette.

"Did Blaize leave any message with Wallers before he left?" he asked. "Any instructions about forwarding mail?"

Nikolls shook his head.

"Nope," he said. "The only thing he said was that he was goin' an' that he might look back to see if anythin' came for him by the late post. Well, he didn't go back, an' I'd like to know why."

Callaghan blew two or three smoke-rings. He said:

"Blaize has been having a busy day. He went out to-night—after he'd left the Yard Arm—to meet Esme. They had the devil of a rough house. Blaize fell over the edge of a cleft between here and Gara. That's why he didn't go back to collect that mail. He's probably lying down at the bottom somewhere. We'd better take a look at him."

"I see," said Nikolls. "Me . . . I don't want to beef or anythin' but I do think it's a bit tough to come out of a dream like I was havin' an' then haveta go an' look at what's left of fellas who have fell over cliffs. Life's a scream, ain't it?"

He struggled into his trousers.

Callaghan went on: "You get that rope and go out the back way over the far lawn and through the west gate. It's a fine night and you can see easily. Take the path that runs along the cliff edge towards Gara. When you get to the cleft you'll have to go uphill and work round it. Don't try and find Blaize until I get there."

"Oke!" said Nikolls. "What do I amuse myself doin' until you *do* get there?"

"When you're on the Gara side of the cleft," said Callaghan, "you start a search for a bracelet. I don't know what sort of a bracelet it is, but I should think you could find it if you look hard enough. It will be fairly near the edge of the cleft on the side farthest from the sea. Concentrate on that job, Windy. I want that bracelet."

"If it's findable I'll find it," said Nikolls. "An' supposin' I've found it. What do I do then?"

"Just take a rest and smoke until I get along there," said Callaghan. "Then we'll go into this business of discovering what's left of Blaize."

"That suits me," said Nikolls.

He began to put on his waistcoat. He said ruminatively:

"It's funny Blaize fallin' over the cliff like that . . . hey? Would that be convenient or inconvenient?"

Callaghan said: "It might be convenient."

"Yeah," said Nikolls. "It ain't often that somethin' happens at a time you want it to, is it?" He lit a cigarette. "It would be a yell if Esme had pushed that mug over, wouldn't it? An' I wouldn't put it above her."

"I wouldn't worry about it," said Callaghan easily. "We don't have to worry about how things happen. The fact that they happen is good enough. Besides we're working for the Vendayne family—not Blaize."

"I got that," said Nikolls. He grinned amiably at Callaghan. "I hope the Vendayne family appreciates the fact. Maybe those mugs don't know how lucky they are."

He went out quietly.

Callaghan walked down the corridor past Clarissa's door, past the next door—which was Audrey's—and stood listening outside the third door.

He could hear Esme crying quietly. Callaghan tapped gently on the door, pushed it open and went in.

She was lying face downwards on the bed. Her shoulders were shaking. She did not move when Callaghan closed the door.

He went over to the bedside and stood looking down at her. His expression was almost contented. He said:

"Cut it out, Esme, and quieten down. I want to talk to you. And what are you crying for? Don't tell me that your heart's broken because you've lost your lord and master. If it's not that, it's self-pity."

She moved her face away from the pillow and looked at him sideways. Her eyes were red-rimmed. Callaghan thought she looked rather ugly.

She turned over on her back and swung her legs off the bed. She sat on the side of the bed looking at Callaghan. She said in a dull voice:

"Did you find the bracelet?"

"I haven't looked for it yet," said Callaghan. "I'm going back there presently. Nikolls is on his way now. Also I want to have a look at Blaize. But the bracelet doesn't particularly matter at the moment."

"I see," said Esme. "What *does* matter?"

Callaghan said: "The story I told you to get into your head is the main thing. Have you done that?"

"Yes," said Esme. "I've got *that* in my head all right."

She got up and walked over to the dressing-table. She switched on a light and began to do her face. The process seemed to interest her. After a moment she drew up a chair and sat down before the mirror, using a lipstick with steady fingers.

Callaghan walked over to the corner of the room and picked up a chair. He carried it to the side of the dressing-table and sat down. He said:

"I suppose after you married Blaize in Malmesbury you realised that you'd made a fool of yourself. I suppose when you discovered just what sort of person he was you wanted to get rid of him."

"How did you know that?" said Esme.

She looked at him closely. Callaghan saw antagonism in her eyes.

"I knew you'd been to the Cape," he said. "I happen to remember Malmesbury. I wondered why Blaize's cottage should be called *Malmesbury*. I suppose you'd call it a good guess on my part, but then you see I know quite a lot about you."

"How nice for you," said Esme. Her voice was very nearly insolent. "And just *what* do you know."

Callaghan said coolly: "When a girl in your position is damned fool enough and cheap enough to go chasing a young fisherman and has to be sent off while the scandal blows over she's not likely to develop intelligence quickly. I should imagine that one man is very like another so far as you're concerned. You were just unlucky to pick on Blaize. He was too good for you. For once, instead of being the boss, you had to do what you were told—and like it."

She nodded.

"I'm not very lucky about men," she said. "I certainly wasn't very lucky about *him*. He thought I had more money than I had. He wasn't very pleased with that."

Callaghan went on: "He followed you over here and took the Yard Arm. I suppose he wanted to be in the neighborhood. I imagine he's had most of your money."

She finished with the lipstick. She put it into a drawer and shut the drawer with a click.

"He's had all the money I had—and could get," she said. "I was trying to buy him off. He said he'd let me divorce him quietly if . . ."

"If you could find enough money," said Callaghan. "And you couldn't. So then the idea of his taking the Vendayne jewels suggested itself to someone. Was that your idea or his?"

Esme looked at him. She was smiling faintly.

"That was my idea," she said. "And in point of fact it wasn't quite so selfish as it might appear on the face of it. I thought it might be a very good thing for my father if the jewellery were stolen. I imagined he'd have the insurance money—or some of it. I knew he wanted money."

Callaghan grinned.

"Killing two birds with one stone," he said. "The Major would have a fit if he had heard you say that."

She shrugged her shoulders.

"I had no reason to believe he would ever know about it," she murmured.

Callaghan lit a cigarette. He drew in a mouthful of smoke. He was watching her carefully.

"Before the idea of Blaize stealing the jewels suggested itself to you," he said, "you had been giving him such money as you had. I should think that wasn't very much. I imagine you tried to raise more . . . didn't you?"

"Yes," she said. "I tried everything I knew. But it wasn't any use. I couldn't get any."

Callaghan grinned.

"Not even from Lancelot?" he queried.

She looked at him sharply.

"How did you know I'd asked Lancelot?" she demanded.

"Just a guess," said Callaghan. "By the way, when you asked Lancelot if he could lend you some money to give to Blaize, you didn't by any chance tell him what the position was between you and Blaize? You didn't tell him that you were married to Blaize?"

Esme nodded.

"Yes, I did," she said. "I had to tell him something. He swore he'd never tell any one. He said he'd do anything he could to raise some money for me. He tried, but he couldn't manage it."

Callaghan said nothing for a moment. Then he began to grin happily.

"That suits me very well," he said. He got up. "Just stick to the story I told you, Esme," he said. "Maybe you won't ever have to tell it. But there's just a chance that a Detective-Inspector Walperton, who's in charge of the burglary, might want to ask some questions. I don't think he will but he *might*."

He walked to the door.

"If I were you I'd go to bed and get a really good sleep," he said.

She looked at him over her shoulder.

"You're very funny, aren't you?" she murmured. "As if I could sleep to-night."

Callaghan smiled at her.

"Why not?" he asked. "You don't mean to tell me that a little thing like a dead husband is going to keep *you* awake!"

He closed the door gently behind him.


It was two o'clock when Callaghan reached the cleft. He worked up the hill and round the end of the cleft. He found Nikolls seated behind a grassy mound, smoking a cigarette.

Callaghan said: "How about the bracelet?"

"Search me," replied Nikolls. "I've been over every bit of the ground with a tooth-comb—as the old lady said—but if there's a bracelet around here it's hidin'."

"All right," said Callaghan. "Relax. When you've finished that cigarette you can start looking some more. That bracelet has to be round here."

"Supposin' it is," said Nikolls. "It's no good—is it? It won't do any mug who finds it any good."

Callaghan grinned.

"I wouldn't want Walperton to find it," he said. "Esme was running away from Blaize with that bracelet in her hand when he fell over the edge—that's our story anyhow."

"I see," said Nikolls. "An' you won't need that rope. If you start climbin' down the cleft from the hill end it's easy. It's only the part around here that's steep. An' if Blaize was runnin' after Esme he'd have to be runnin' round the cleft edge up the hill, an' so he'd have to fall an' bounce a bit an' he'll be at the bottom at *that* end. That's logic, ain't it?"

"It's reasonable," said Callaghan.

He began to walk up the rising ground towards the end of the cleft.

The moon was full. On the hillside it was almost as light as day. Callaghan, after a long look over the cleft edge, began to climb down the incline of rocks and earth that led down to the beach below. As he progressed the way grew less steep, and after a while the climb became almost easy. Callaghan began to think about Esme. He began to wonder.

At last he arrived at the bottom. The walls of the cleft rising on each side of the thirty-foot space in which Callaghan stood, cast black shadows over the sandy rock-strewn ground. Callaghan looked about him in the half-darkness. There was no sign of Blaize.

After a moment Callaghan stopped looking. He lit a cigarette and began to walk towards the sea. As he walked the cleft widened and visibility became more easy.

Twenty feet or so from the end of the cleft, on the Gara side, Callaghan found Blaize. He was lying across a rock that was half-submerged in the sand. His face, white and distorted, with eyes wide open, showed plainly against the dark background of the shadows. His body, twisted peculiarly, told of a broken back.

Callaghan knelt down. He opened the dead man's coat and began to search through the pockets. He found nothing until he put his fingers into the inside jacket pocket.

He smiled and withdrew his hand. In it was the bracelet.

Callaghan, walking carefully over the rocky edges at the cleft-side, so as to leave no unnecessary foot-marks, made his way to the top of the beach. He looked at the bracelet in the moonlight. It consisted of twenty peculiarly cut rubies, mounted in antique gold settings, joined by tiny diamond clasps. He realised, after a moment's examination, that the diamonds—which were of the "splinter" type and of little intrinsic value—were real, that the rubies were merely excellent imitations.

He stood, looking at the sea, twisting the bracelet in his fingers, thinking. Then he threw away his cigarette, returned to the spot where Blaize lay and replaced the bracelet in the breast pocket of the dead man's jacket. Then he walked back to the end of the cleft and began to climb up the incline.

He climbed carefully, looking about him. Halfway up, on the Gara side of the cleft, separated from the incline which Callaghan was climbing by some fifty feet, and situated about fifteen feet from the top of the cleft, was a ledge. Callaghan noted its position carefully. He resumed his climb.

Arrived at the top, he found Nikolls gloomily considering a pair of gulls.

"I've been over the ground again, Slim," he said, "an' I'm tellin' you there ain't any bracelet around here. Either that or I'm losin' my eyesight."

Callaghan said: "Your eyesight's all right, Windy. The bracelet was below. I found it."

"How come?" said Nikolls. "Bracelets can't walk."

Callaghan grinned.

"You've said something, Windy," he said. "They can't."

Nikolls fumbled in his coat pocket for a cigarette.

"You got it, Slim?" he asked.

Callaghan shook his head.

"I left it where it was," he said. "In Blaize's pocket. His back's broken. He must have died right away. He won't worry any one any more . . . not so they'll notice it, anyhow."

"That's O.K.," said Nikolls. "But I thought that Esme had to have that bracelet. I thought it was bad evidence if the cops found it."

"I've changed my opinion about that," said Callaghan. "I think I'd rather like 'em to find it. In fact I'm going to take damned good care they do find it. Come on, Windy, let's get back."

They began their walk back to Margraud. When they were crossing the lawn at the back of the house Callaghan said:

"I'm leaving for London in an hour or two—about five o'clock. The roads will be clear and I can get a move on. I'll probably stop at Exeter and have a talk with the Major. It's time someone talked to the old boy. Anyhow, he'll have to come back into circulation fairly soon."

Nikolls grinned.

"Yeah?" he said. "If you talk to him an' tell him about Esme an' that stiff Blaize an' a few other things that've been happenin' around here he'll probably blow up altogether and hand in his dinner pail. I reckon he won't be so pleased to hear about little Esme havin' moonlight meetin's with the boy friend along the cliffs. Maybe it won't sound so moral to the old guy."

"It was moral enough," said Callaghan. "Esme was Blaize's wife."

Nikoll's eyebrows went up.

"You don't say?" he said. "It just shows you, don't it? Maybe they'd better've let little Esme have her fun an' games with the blue-eyed cod trapper from Beesands. Is that baby a mug or is she? I s'pose Blaize told her a bunch of fairy stories, an' bounced her into a quick seance at the register office with one eye on the family plate. Nice work if you can get it."

Callaghan said: "It didn't work out so well for him."

He stopped on the terrace to light a cigarette. He went on:

"I shan't be in London for long, Windy. And here's *your* end. First thing in the morning you take a walk along the cliffs and you *discover* Blaize's body. I said *discover*. Then you get right over to Kingsbridge and report to the police that you've found it. You don't know anything about it at all. You don't know who Blaize is or what he was doing. All right. It's going to take the Kingsbridge police a couple of days to get a post-mortem done and identification. Have you got that?"

"I got it," said Nikolls.

"Then the day afterwards you go dashing over to Kingsbridge again. You tell 'em that Esme has told you all about it and what happened. She knows her story and she'll stick to it for her own sake. They'll probably send an officer over to Margraud to see her. I say probably because maybe, in the meantime, I can fix something in London that will short-circuit police inquiries down here."

"Supposin' Walperton comes kickin' around in the meantime?" asked Nikolls. "Or suppose he sends some other guy down to check on Blaize over at the Yard Arm?"

"That's all right," said Callaghan. "What can they find out? Ropey's gone. If Walperton's sent someone down they'll have to get in touch with him for further instructions."

"An' in the meantime you're gonna pull another one on that sucker," said Nikolls. "This guy Walperton is gonna just love you before you're through on this job."

Callaghan grinned.

"The joke is he probably will," he said. "We'll see."

"O.K.," said Nikolls. "An' what about the bracelet? Wasn't that important?"

"Leave the bracelet out of it," said Callaghan. "Esme can tell the truth about it if she likes. The bracelet is all right. I've got an idea about that."

They had reached the house. Callaghan said:

"You can go fishing at Slapton all the rest of the time if you like. This case is almost over—bar the shouting."

Nikolls sighed.

"That's all right by me," he said. "I never did think much of this case. I wonder . . ."

"What do you wonder?" asked Callaghan.

Nikolls said: "Last night an' the night before I didn't take an indigestion tablet and I had two lousy nights. To-night I took one an' I had one helluva dream about that baby with the swell hips. I got a big idea."

"I'll buy it," said Callaghan.

Nikolls grinned at him. "I'm gonna take *two* of them tablets when I get upstairs," he said. "Maybe I'll dream about two honeys. Would that be a scream or would it? So long, Slim. I'll be seein' you. . . ."

He went swiftly up the staircase like a plump cat.

Callaghan switched on the torch he found in the hallway and investigated the lower regions of Margraud. He found the kitchen, the range, a kettle, crockery and a teapot. It took five minutes to unearth the tea.

He put the kettle on the gas range, arranged the teacups on the table and went upstairs. He walked softly along the bedroom corridor and listened outside Esme's door. He heard nothing. He moved along to the next door. A gleam of light showed beneath it. Callaghan tapped softly.

A moment passed and the door opened. Audrey stood framed in the lighted doorway. She wore a tailored dressing robe of white spotted red silk with a red sash. Her dark hair, tied with a ribbon, accentuated the whiteness of her face.

Callaghan smiled at her. He said very softly:

"You look marvellous. Most of the women I've seen in dressing-gowns look like sacks with a string round the middle. When I'm an old gentleman I shall remember how you looked to-night."

She smiled in spite of herself. She said as quietly:

"Did you come here to tell me that?"

"Not exactly," said Callaghan. "You and I have got to talk. It's important. I'm leaving in an hour or so and we've got to arrange things first. I've put the kettle on in the kitchen. I had an idea that you're going to need some tea."

She said: "So it's going to be as bad as that?"

"Yes," said Callaghan. "But *only* as bad as that. It could be a lot worse. In fact"—he smiled again—"with a little fan-dangling—as Nikolls would say—I think we can fix things. If we play it *my* way. D'you think you'd like to do that?"

"I've got to," said Audrey. "Candidly, I don't quite know just what I *ought* to do about anything. I don't know enough. If you mean do I trust you or not, I can only say I don't know. But I've got to trust some-body, so I might as well *try* and trust you . . . mightn't I?"

"That'll do," said Callaghan. "It's a start anyway. Let's go and get tea."

Callaghan put his cup down and produced his cigarette-case. He took out two cigarettes, handed one to Audrey, lit them both. He got up and leaned against the dresser.

She sat on the other side of the kitchen table. Her eyes, a little sleepy but curious, watched him. Callaghan thought: "I wonder is she thinking about what I'm going to tell her or wondering about me—or both. I hope she feels as curious about me as I do about her."

He said: "This is where you bite on the bullet, Audrey, because some of it isn't going to be quite so good. First of all, let me tell you one or two things about the Vendayne family."

He blew a smoke-ring with care; watched it until it dissolved. He went on:

"Clarissa is rather sweet. A trifle wild but straight. You're a dear. You're a little stuck up, a little too proud, but you're quite honest and I'm terribly taken with the way your mouth curls up at the end when you smile and the way that your clothes fit you. Esme is a damned little fool who is naturally dishonest. She's as selfish as the devil and quite reckless. Your father is a dear old boy who ought to be spanked and stood in the corner. If he wasn't your father I'd say he was a damned fool. I think you'll agree with that anyway.

"Lancelot, your cousin, is just a plain ordinary sonofabitch. He hasn't enough guts to be crooked—even to get something he wants—but he has enough brains to create—or help create—situations. So much for the family."

He blew another smoke-ring. Audrey watched him; her eyes, wider and less sleepy now, never left his face. Callaghan realised that she was one of those women who can look at you without blinking.

"I don't know how much or how little you know about Esme," said Callaghan. "But I do know that both you and Clarissa were a bit worried about Esme and this fellow Blaize. I suppose you thought it might be a repetition of the Beesands fisherman business; but in any event Clarissa tried to do her best to stop any eventualities by tagging along and playing gooseberry when she could. It was a good effort, but she might have saved herself the trouble. People like you and Clarissa will never be quite as clever, or smart, as people like Esme and Blaize. That's because you two girls are essentially honest and Esme and Blaize essentially dishonest.

"When I went over and saw the two girls at Blaize's cottage the first night I got down here, I noticed the place was called "Malmesbury." I remembered that there was a little place called Malmesbury near Cape Town. It struck me as a coincidence. I cabled an associate of mine over there and got a check up on Blaize. Esme married him in Malmesbury the day before she sailed for England. He came over three weeks afterwards."

She said: "My God . . how terrible. What is Blaize?"

"Blaize was a nasty bit of work," said Callaghan. "He was a specialist in women. He was attractive to people like Esme. His line was to make love to a woman and then collect what he could from her and clear out.

"Esme was just what Blaize was looking for. He married her because he thought that was the best way to make a really good clean-up and because the Cape was getting too hot to hold him. I believe the police want him on two or three charges for which they've been trying to get evidence for years. It's always damned difficult to get evidence against people like Blaize. You never get a prosecutor willing to go through with it, mainly because the prosecutors are usually women and they can't bear the idea of standing in a witness-box and practically telling the world that they've been foolish enough to be mistress to the marcelled, patent-haired cheat in the dock. That's why people like Blaize usually get away with it.

"He thought that she had a lot of money. Esme probably allowed him to think what he liked. She wanted to marry somebody. She couldn't marry the fisherman so she bounced back on to Blaize. He was masculine and virile and attractive. He belonged to that peculiar type that's obviously lousy and yet manages to get quite nice women to fall for it."

Audrey nodded. She said slowly:

"I can visualize Esme doing all that. It's what she would do. She's like that."

Callaghan said: "I'm not going into details because I haven't got time. I want to be in London as soon as I can manage it. Very well. Blaize has been getting such money as he could from Esme. She paid, first of all because she'd discovered what sort of a man he was and she didn't want her family to know what an utter fool she'd made of herself, and secondly because he'd told her that if she paid he'd allow her to divorce him. Naturally, he wanted more money than she had.

"Eventually," continued Callaghan, "things came to a head. Blaize was getting tough about money. Esme tried to raise money where she could. She even tried Lancelot. She told Lancelot the truth about herself and Blaize. Lancelot, naturally, didn't supply any money. He hadn't got it. Lancelot's broke.

"So Esme made a bargain with Blaize. She was to let him into Margraud, give him the combination of the safe and allow him to steal the jewellery. I must say she thought that the robbery might be of help to your father. She thought the mortgage on Margraud wasn't paid and she thought that it could be paid with the money he'd get from the Insurance Company.

"When Lancelot heard about the burglary he put two and two together and came to the right conclusion. He guessed that Esme was behind the steal. But it didn't matter to him. He was quite content to take three-quarters of the insurance money, leave your father with the odd twenty-five thousand and call it a day. But he wanted the claim paid. That's why he forced your father to bring me into the case. I was the fellow who was to put the screw on the company."

Audrey said softly: "This is all quite terrible . . . quite awful. . . ."

Callaghan said: "This is nothing. Just wait a minute."

"But," she said, "I didn't know the mortgage was paid off. Clarissa didn't know. How was that done? Who paid it off? My father couldn't. . ."

Callaghan said: "Let's leave that for the moment. We haven't got time for all that."

He lit another cigarette.

"Blaize and Esme had a meeting to-night," Callaghan went on. "There was a quarrel and Blaize fell over the edge of the cleft between here and Gara. His back's broken. He's dead, which is a damned good thing in one way because it simplifies matters."

She seemed stupefied. She put her hands over her face. Callaghan could see her fingers trembling.

"Take it easy, Audrey," he said. "Worse things happen at sea."

She took her hands away from her face.

"Go on," she said. "I'm all right . . . but . . . but . . . d'you think that Esme . . . ?"

"Do I think that Esme pushed Blaize over?" said Callaghan. "Candidly I did think so . . . but I'm not worrying about *that* now. I don't think the point matters. Anyway, Blaize got what was coming to him.

"Don't worry about Esme and Blaize," Callaghan continued. "Nikolls will look after that end. I've had a talk with Esme to-night and she knows just what she has to do. I don't think you'll be worried with the police. I've fixed things so that I get a day or two to do what I want to do. When I come back I hope we can clean up the mess. I've got an idea we can."

She smiled suddenly.

"You mean you have an idea *you* can," she said. "I haven't been very much use up to date, have I? You and I seem to have spent our time quarrelling."

"That doesn't matter," said Callaghan. "I hope we'll have an opportunity to quarrel again one day . . . a really nice quarrel."

"What am I to do?" she asked. "When are you coming back? What do you want me to do?"

Callaghan looked at his watch.

"Believe it or not," he said, "it's nearly five o'clock. I'm going to have a shower, change my clothes and get out of here. I shall be at Exeter by eight. You've got to get through to the nursing home and arrange for me to see your father at eight-thirty—that gives me time for breakfast. I've got to see him, otherwise he may find himself in a bad spot. Also I want to know where the nursing home is."

She told him. Callaghan said:

"All right. Now you go back to bed and get three hours' sleep. Telephone through at eight and tell 'em I shall be there at eight-thirty. And don't worry."

She got up. She said:

"I'm terribly grateful to you. I *do* trust you. I even believe that you'll manage to straighten out all this beastly business. God knows why you should take all this trouble."

Callaghan grinned. He said:

"I've three reasons. The first, you didn't like private detectives. You practically said so in that club in Conduit Street. D'you remember? I wanted you to change your opinion. Secondly, I was paid two hundred and fifty pounds by Layne to do this job."

She said: "You've forgotten the third reason?"

Callaghan said: "No, I haven't. And I don't have to tell you what it is. You know."

She blushed.

She said: "You're an extraordinary person, Mr. Callaghan. One might get used to you in time. I wonder if you know what I mean?"

"No," said Callaghan. "Do you?"

She smiled.

"Strangely enough I believe I do," she said.

Callaghan grinned.

"Go to bed. I'll be back in a day or two. Good-night."

She got up.

"Good-night," she said. "And thank you. Once again I'm very grateful."

"Don't be silly," said Callaghan. "You know you don't have to be grateful. You know it because you know I'd do any damned thing for you and you're beginning to realise that you like knowing it."

He went out.

Upstairs in her room, she waited until she heard the car leave the garage.

Then she sat on the edge of her bed and tried to think clearly, to sort things out. After a few minutes she gave up the process.

She discovered that logical thought was not possible. No matter what line of thought came to her she found Callaghan's face, his sardonic smile, his absolute *certainty* of the shape of events obtruded.

She decided to think about Callaghan and found that much easier.

## CHAPTER TWELVE
## CONFIDENTIAL STUFF

CALLAGHAN came into the bedroom and put his hat on a chair. He looked cheerful. He leaned up against the mantelpiece grinning at Major Vendayne, who regarded him with unhappy and curious eyes.

Callaghan said: "I suppose Audrey has been through on the telephone. Did you speak to her?"

Vendayne nodded.

"What did she tell you?" Callaghan demanded.

"Not very much, Mr. Callaghan," said the invalid. "She said you were coming here. She said that she'd decided you were a trustworthy person."

Callaghan's grin broadened.

"Well, that's something," he said. "Now listen, Major. The doctor tells me that you're not to be worried, so I'm going to make this as short and sweet as I can. Just believe what I say and don't argue. Not that you've anything to argue about."

Vendayne said: "Very well, I understand. I wonder if you know what a fool I've been."

Callaghan said: "I can make a good guess, but I don't know that it matters an awful lot."

He lit a cigarette.

"When I started on this case," he said, "I was very interested in that mortgage on Margraud. I was even more interested by the fact that you'd been able to pay it off, and within a few months. I had to make some guesses—I couldn't ask you; you were here and things were moving too quickly for me to come over. Also I didn't think you'd be inclined to tell me the truth at that time."

The Major looked up at the ceiling. After a moment he said:

"Why do you think that I shall be prepared to tell you the truth *now?*"

"You've got to," said Callaghan. "You're in a jam and you know it." He inhaled cigarette smoke. "The funny thing about this case is that there are two points of view that can be taken about the actions of practically every one concerned. I'm rather keen on getting over the points of view I want. If by some chance Scotland Yard succeeds in proving the other points of view it isn't going to be too good for you, for Lancelot, for Esme and for the Vendayne family generally. So let's get down to brass tacks.

"I believe," Callaghan went on, "that you put most of your available capital into some wild-cat scheme of Lancelot Vendayne's. Both you and he were certain that that share scheme—whatever it was— was going to come off. You wanted to spend money on Margraud, and you were so certain the Lancelot business was going to come off that you mortgaged the place. You imagined you'd be worth a lot of money within a few months.

"Well, it didn't come off. You were in a jam. Quite a large lump of your income which had been produced by your original capital was gone and you were faced with a £20,000 mortgage plus six per cent interest. Right?"

Vendayne nodded gloomily.

"That's right," he said.

"You were in a bad spot," Callaghan went on. "You didn't know what to do, but I've an idea that someone made a suggestion. I've an idea that somebody got in touch with you—somebody from London—and suggested that they might be prepared to give you a hand out of your difficulties. The reason this person probably gave was that he too had been taken in by the Lancelot scheme. He'd lost his money but he wasn't in such difficulties as *you* were. He rather sympathised with you.

"Of course you were pretty fed up with Lancelot, but you didn't say anything to Audrey because you had an idea that she might be going to marry Lancelot. Afterwards—when she decided she wasn't going to marry him—you were too worried and scared of the situation to want to discuss it with any one.

"Anyhow," Callaghan went on, "your benefactor lent you the twenty thousand. You had no security to offer him, so he had an idea. He suggested to you that you hand over to him the Vendayne jewellery—that he'd keep it until you'd repaid the twenty thousand. He suggested that, in the meantime, just for the benefit of those people who came to see the collection in glass cases when it was on view, he would replace the original jewellery with first-class replicas.

"Well, you accepted the proposition, and why not? You weren't doing anybody any harm. So long as you could pay that twenty thousand back in your lifetime you thought you'd be able to get the jewellery back again. To your mind the deal was not dishonest because in fact it was at the moment hurting no one. What you didn't realise was that the individual who lent you that £20,000 was quite prepared to kiss the money good-bye, *because he never intended to return the jewellery.*"

The Major said nothing. He looked at Callaghan in amazement.

"The trouble with people like you, Major," said Callaghan, "is that you trust people. You believe—because life has never taught you anything different—that people are as honest as you are. When you were told that the jewellery would be returned when you repaid the twenty thousand, plus whatever rate of interest was agreed on, you believed that.

"But you *didn't* realise that your benefactor had you where he wanted you immediately he lent you the money and took over the jewellery. Even if you'd gone along with the twenty thousand in your hand you wouldn't have got the jewellery. And then what could you have done? You couldn't have gone to the police and complained. You'd made yourself an accessory to an illegal transaction."

Vendayne said grimly: "What a fool I've been."

"The point is," Callaghan went on, "that the individual who lent you the twenty thousand never expected to be repaid. He believed that you were not long for this earth and that you'd probably die before you had a chance to repay the money. Then Lancelot would have gone rushing around trying to get his hands on £100,000 worth of jewellery to which he was entitled under the original deed and which he was also entitled to sell—if he wanted to sell it.

"But there wouldn't be any jewellery and Lancelot wouldn't get it until he'd done what your benefactor had made up his mind he was going to do. I doubt," said Callaghan with a grin, "if Lancelot would have got it even then."

He stubbed out the end of his cigarette, lit a fresh one. He said:

"Well, then, things went from bad to worse. Somebody stole the Vendayne jewellery. At least they stole the imitations. You can take it from me that Lancelot wasn't particularly surprised to hear about that burglary—he was rather expecting it. He could have made one guess as to who was really responsible and been right. But the situation was perfect so far as he was concerned. So he dashed down to Margraud and made a deal with you that seemed, on the face of it, generous. When the Insurance Company paid, you were to get £25,000, and he was to take the balance of £75,000. The devil of it was that the Insurance Company didn't pay. They didn't like the burglary or anything about it. So they stalled.

"You would probably never have put that claim in. Lancelot was the person who forced that issue, and you had to stand for it. You couldn't tell Lancelot or anybody else what you'd done.

"All right," said Callaghan. "Now the situation's not half as bad as it seems. There are three or four points that we have to worry about. But you and I at this moment are only concerned with two of those points. The first concerns the Insurance Company. Well, I think I ought to tell you that we don't have to worry about them because your solicitor has withdrawn the claim on the grounds that I have a very good idea where that jewellery is and that we feel we may get it back. The Insurance Company aren't worrying for another reason. Before I went down to Margraud in the first place I saw the Sphere & International arranged to represent them too. They know me—I've worked for associates of theirs before. So that situation is all right.

"The second point concerns the police. As you know, Scotland Yard have been brought in on this job. Things have happened since you've been in this nursing home which are going to interest Scotland Yard a great deal. With luck they won't disturb you, but if you're *not* lucky it's on the cards that a police officer is coming over here to ask questions. I think he'll only have one question to ask you and I'm going to tell you the answer.

"The only thing he'll want to know," said Callaghan, "is what is the reason that you removed the original—the real—Vendayne jewellery and had it replaced by imitations. Remember this: in his mind will be the idea that you might possibly have sold the original jewellery and that when the imitations were stolen you thought you could collect from the Insurance Company. We can answer the second half of this question because the claim against the Insurance Company has been withdrawn.

"In regard to the first half, the reason that you had the jewellery replaced by imitations is this: you knew that your daughter Esme was mixed up somehow with a nefarious character by the name of Blaize who had come to live somewhere in the neighbourhood of Margraud. You were afraid for that jewellery. So you had it replaced by imitations.

"It doesn't matter," said Callaghan with a grin, "whether they believe you or not. That's your story, and you stick to it and everything will be all right."

He picked up his hat.

"So long, Major," he said. "Don't worry. You probably won't even be worried at all. I think there's a good possibility that nobody will even want to ask you *any* questions."

He went out. Five minutes later the Jaguar was speeding along the Exeter-London road. Behind the wheel, the inevitable cigarette in his mouth, Callaghan pondered on possibilities.

But in the main he was satisfied.

Callaghan parked the car in Berkeley Square, walked to Hatchett's Restaurant in Piccadilly and ordered a chicken salad and a double whisky and soda. When he had finished his lunch he lit a cigarette and began to think. His thoughts were, in the main, concerned with personalities. He began to think about Lancelot and Gabby Ventura, both individually and as a possibly unwilling corporation of two. He thought about Esme and Blaize. Ropey Felliner was dismissed as being unworthy of consideration.

Having concluded this series of thoughts, Callaghan turned his mental attention to Detective-Inspector Walperton. He spent quite five minutes thinking about that keen and efficient police officer, but he was concerned with the *nuances* of Walperton's private character rather than with his abilities as a policeman.

Walperton was antagonistic and sure of himself and inclined to be what is generally known as "cocky." Walperton was *too* antagonistic, *too* sure of himself and, in effect, *too* cocky. But Callaghan realised that, after his last interview at Scotland Yard with the police officer, Walperton would, in all probability, take a more cautious view of Callaghan. He would be very careful not to walk into any traps. But he would certainly *not* give Callaghan the benefit of any doubt that arose.

Against all this Walperton was ambitious. And it was with this facet in his character that Callaghan was concerned. Walperton wanted to "get on." He would do anything that was legitimate and possible in order to get on. Callaghan made up his mind that Detective-Inspector Walperton *should* get on even if he, Callaghan, had to help him.

He paid his bill and walked out into the sunshine. Piccadilly was quiet and orderly and cheerful. There were fewer people on the streets, fewer cars. But in spite of the grimness of the war situation people were cheerful and more inclined to smile than to be serious.

Callaghan walked to Berkeley Square, got into the Jaguar and drove to the building in which his offices and flat were situated. He parked the car round the corner, went up in the lift to his own apartment, washed, rubbed *eau-de-Cologne* into his hair, then descended to the office floor.

Effie Thompson, immersed in the latest "romance" novel, with a box of chocolates open on the desk in front of her, sat relaxed in her chair. She straightened up as the door opened and Callaghan came in.

He stood behind her looking at the title of the novel. He said: "Any good, Effie?"

"Not too bad, Mr. Callaghan," she replied. "The book moves fast and my only objection to it is that none of the characters are alive."

Callaghan sat down in a chair on the other side of her desk.

"So the characters aren't alive," he said cheerfully. "What do they do that they ought not to do or what is it they don't do that should be done?"

She said: "The men are sticks. The hero never gets a move on. He is supposed to be a man of definite character and he's also supposed to be madly in love with the girl Germaine; yet when they have to make a forced landing in a deserted spot in the country, he leaves her with the aeroplane at two o'clock in the morning and goes off to look for help."

Callaghan nodded.

"Too bad," he said. "What ought he to have done?"

She looked at him coldly.

"I should have thought *you* could have answered that, Mr. Callaghan," she said, pursing her lips primly. "If I loved a woman—to that extent—and found myself in a deserted part of the countryside at two in the morning with an aeroplane *I* should do something about it."

Callaghan grinned.

"I gathered that, Effie," he said. "But what I wanted to know was *what* you would have done."

Effie looked out of the window. After a moment she said:

"You take a fiendish delight in embarrassing me, Mr. Callaghan, don't you? You know perfectly well what I meant. . . ."

Callaghan said: "I don't and you don't either."

"You'll excuse me, Mr. Callaghan, but I *do,*" she retorted.

"All right," said Callaghan cheerfully. "If you know you tell me. I want to know what you would have done."

She said: "You know perfectly well that it's impossible for me to answer that question, Mr. Callaghan." She looked out of the window again. "The English language doesn't lend itself to a description of that sort. What I mean is . . ."

"I know what you mean," said Callaghan. "You mean that if you'd been the hero in your book and—for the sake of argument—I'd been Germaine, the beautiful heroine, and we made a forced landing in a deserted part of the countryside you'd have taken advantage of me. That's what you mean, and you know it, Effie. . . . I'm surprised at you."

She blushed furiously. She said:

"Mr. Callaghan, you always put words into my mouth that weren't there. I mean to say, you always make me appear to say or think something that I didn't intend to say or wasn't thinking. It's too bad."

"I know," said Callaghan. "But even if I do pull your leg sometimes, Effie, you can always congratulate yourself that you've got a nice leg."

She said primly: "That, from you, Mr. Callaghan, is indeed a compliment. I'm sure you're an authority on the subject. Did you want to dictate something?"

"No," said Callaghan. "Just put your typewriter on my desk. I want to type a letter personally. Then look up the telephone number of Miss Paula Rochette—it's somewhere in Courtfield Gardens, after which you can take a couple of hours off. Just look in in time to close the office."

"Thank you," said Effie. "That is rather nice. I saw some sunbronze silk stockings that I thought I'd be able to buy if I had that rise you said you'd consider three months ago."

Callaghan grinned.

"This is no time for rises," he said. "Take up the question of a rise with me in three months' time, Effie. In the meantime Callaghan Investigations will stand you some silk stockings as a bonus." He laid three one-pound notes on her table. "The only thing is," he went on, "they should be beige—not sunbronze. Your type of leg needs a beige stocking."

She picked up the notes.

"Thank you, Mr. Callaghan," she said, "but I prefer sunbronze."

He shrugged his shoulders.

"That's all right with me, Effie," he said. "But I knew a woman once who used to wear sunbronze stockings and all of a sudden she went bow-legged. But don't let me put you off."

She did not reply.

She carried her typewriter into Callaghan's office, put it on the desk, found the Rochette telephone number, wrote it down on his desk pad, put on her hat and jacket and went out.

She walked to Bond Street and examined the sunbronze stockings. She came to the conclusion that they were just what she needed.

After which she bought half a dozen pairs in beige.


Callaghan sat at his desk with the typewriter before him.

He lit a cigarette and indulged in a little quiet consideration of the qualities, virtues, and possible failings of Detective-Inspector Walperton. He began to grin sardonically.

He put a sheet of notepaper into the machine and began to type a letter:

*To Detective-Inspector Walperton,*
*Criminal Investigation Department,*
*New Scotland Yard.*

*Personal.*

*My Dear Walperton,*

*I don't know you very well, because, as you know, my association at the Yard, over different cases that have come up, has always been with Chief Detective-Inspector Gringall, whose opinion I have found to be of great use to me whenever I have had occasion to ask for it.*

*Candidly, since I saw you last, and since my return this morning from Devonshire, I have been very worried. I am in a rather unpleasant jam. I have got to choose between my duty as a private investigator, employed by the Vendayne family and the Sphere & International Insurance, and my duty as a private citizen with its responsibilities of giving information to the police which I think they should have.*

*So I have decided to put myself absolutely and entirely in your hands. In spite of the fact that you have a reputation for not liking private detectives a great deal, I am of opinion that you are keen—as a police officer—to see that your duty is done and that a case which you are handling is brought to its official and proper conclusion. In this connection I know that you are as keen on protecting the innocent—even from their own foolish actions—as you are in seeing that the guilty person or persons are brought to book.*

*This is where I am in a jam. I want to talk to you and to put my cards on the table. When I have done this I think you will be able to go right ahead and close this case. But—and this is a big "but"—I have got to sort out my ideas and marshal my facts so that there is no possibility of innocent people being involved in a bad case. I know that you will agree with this.*

*So, with your permission, I propose to call and see you tomorrow and give you every bit of information which I have collected. The fact that I have (possibly) more information than has been available to the police, both in Devonshire and at Headquarters, is, of course, merely due to my personal contacts with members of the Vendayne family and others.*

*In the meantime, because things may be happening which will merit your professional attention, I would like to tell you that when*

*I returned to Devonshire after our last meeting I discovered the following facts:*

*1. Ropey Felliner has cleared out. I think I know the reason for this. Felliner was employed by Gabriel Ventura of the Ventura Club, near Shepherd Market, to keep an eye on Blaize. I have an idea that I can guess the motive for the necessity for this and will discuss this with you to-morrow.*

*2. Blaize has also disappeared. It seems that he was in the neighbourhood until some time last evening, and your own information has probably told you that he had arranged the sale of the Yard Arm Road House and the cottage behind it to a man named Wallers (who, I think, is entirely unconnected with this case) some days ago. Quite obviously Blaize has been preparing to make a quick getaway. I am not certain of his reasons for wanting to do this but I feel that they must, in someway, be connected with either (a) a member of the Vendayne family, or (b) Ventura.*

*3. Now I must make an admission. You will remember that when I saw you last I said that I was fairly certain that the Vendayne robbery was an "outside" job. I knew at the time that you thought I was wrong, and that the steal bore all the hall-marks of an "inside" job. You were right and I was wrong. The job was an inside one and yet the obviously guilty person is quite guiltless. Believe it or not, this is a fact!*

*I think that after we have had our conversation to-morrow—I will telephone you when I am coming along to see you—you will agree that, as always, I have tried to do my duty and given the fullest possible co-operation and information to the authorities.*

*Looking forward to seeing you,*

*I am, sincerely yours,*

*S. Callaghan,*
*Callaghan Investigations.*

Callaghan addressed an envelope, sealed it down, rang down to the porter's lodge for a page-boy. When the boy appeared Callaghan instructed him to take a cab and deliver the letter at Scotland Yard.

He replaced the typewriter on Effie Thompson's desk, returned to his office, sat down, put his feet on the desk and lit a cigarette.

When the cigarette was finished he looked at his watch. It was half-past four. Callaghan got up, walked into the outer office. He walked over to Effie Thompson's desk. He took up her note-pad, wrote on it: *"I bet you bought beige stockings."*

He closed and locked the office door and took the lift up to his apartment. He undressed quickly, dropping his clothes as usual on the floor, set the small alarm clock for six-thirty, lay down on the bed.

In two minutes he was asleep.

The afternoon sunshine, gilding the Berkeley Square roofs, came in at the open window and illuminated one half of the beige and blue carpet, over which Callaghan's clothes were strewn, with streaks of gold.

The small alarm clock on the bed-table, set for six-thirty, began to jangle. Callaghan grunted, awoke, looked at the ceiling as if he hadn't seen it before, and then, with a sudden movement, swung his legs off the bed and sat, running his fingers through his dishevelled hair, thinking.

This time it was Audrey.

After a few moments he got up, went to the compactum, got out fresh underwear, shirt and suit. He went into the bathroom, took a cold shower, dressed. He returned to the bedroom, drank four fingers of rye whisky out of the bottle in the cupboard and called the Rochette number on the telephone.

He was lucky. He grinned as the rather metallic voice of that lady came on the line. Callaghan said softly: "Is that you, Paula? This is Slim Callaghan speaking."

She said: "Oh, is it?" Her voice became very "county." She went on: "I'm a little bit surprised that you should have the sauce to ring me up, Mr. Callaghan."

Callaghan said: "I know, Paula, I know just what you're thinking, and believe me you're wrong. You think I ought to have set about Gabby Ventura when he was rude to you the other night."

"Well," said Paula, "what do you think? You tell me something, Mr. Callaghan . . . do you consider me to be a perfect lady or not?"

Callaghan said: "There can't be any question about that, Paula. I'll tell the whole world that you come out of the top drawer."

His mouth was twisted cynically.

"All right," said Miss Rochette. "If you think I'm a perfect lady, and if you consider you're a gentleman, Mr. Callaghan, all I want to know is why didn't you smack the ears off that lousy slob Gabby when he said he'd have me pinched?"

Her voice rose at least three tones.

Callaghan said very quietly: "That's just it, Paula—that's what you don't understand. Look here, my dear," he said, "you don't like Gabby, do you?"

"Like him!" shrilled Miss Rochette. "I know just what I'd like to do with him—I'd like to . . ."

She told Callaghan what she would like to do to Gabby. Callaghan listened appreciatively. When she had finished, he said:

"I feel like that too, but there's more ways than one of killing a cat. I didn't do anything to Gabby that night, Paula, because I've got something worse for him up my sleeve, and how do you like that?"

"I like it all right," she said. "I'd do anything to even up with that fat bladder of lard."

Callaghan said: "There's another thing, my dear, last time I saw you you did me the favour of accepting a little gift from me—that brooch—remember? Well, I've been thinking things over and I don't think it was good enough for you."

"Oh, yes?" said Miss Rochette suspiciously. "What's the idea? I suppose you want it back?"

"Nothing like that," said Callaghan. "I told you I thought it wasn't good enough for you. I thought perhaps you'd like to give it to a friend or get rid of it. I thought you'd like something better, but I didn't want to make a mistake about buying anything, so I thought we might meet to-night and have dinner, and I'd give you the fifty pounds to buy something really decent with."

Miss Rochette began to coo. She said:

"Mr. Callaghan—or perhaps I ought to call you Slim—I always felt underneath everything that you were a gentleman, and if you've got anything that you want put over on Gabby Ventura, I'm with you the whole way."

Callaghan said: "All right. Let's meet at the Jewel Club at eight o'clock tonight. We'll have dinner and I'll tell you my idea. So long, Paula."

He hung up the receiver.

His grin was more sardonic than ever.

# CHAPTER THIRTEEN
## NIGHT OUT

IT WAS seven o'clock when Callaghan, having finished his second whisky and soda, came out of the Berkeley Buttery.

He walked slowly down to the telephone box on the corner of Hay Hill and dialled the number of Grant's Hotel. He asked for Mr. Lancelot Vendayne.

He was told to hold the line. With his free hand he took his cigarette-case from his hip pocket, extracted a cigarette, lit it. He began to blow smoke-rings.

Callaghan was thinking of the number of times he had used this particular call box in regard to different business with which Messrs. Callaghan Investigations had been concerned in the past. He remembered that most of these investigations had been brought to a conclusion that was—if only from the point of view of Callaghan Investigations—successful. He remembered also that when you spin a penny although it may come down heads twelve times in succession it is all the tea in China to a bad egg that on the thirteenth spin it will come down tails.

He hoped that the Vendayne case was not going to come down "tails."

He drew on his cigarette appreciatively. He realised, quite definitely, that the results of the Vendayne case depended on the interviews he was hoping to arrange for the night that lay before him. In any event he had burned his boats so far as Walperton was concerned. He had done that when he had written and despatched the letter which, by now, had been read and re-read by the efficient police officer with—the detective thought—a certain relish. Callaghan had to present a cut-and-dried story to Walperton next day—a story that matched up. He *had* to. He had been forced to burn his boats by despatching that letter, because it was on the cards that the news of Blaize's death might have, by now, come through to Walperton. With Callaghan's letter in front of him Walperton could do nothing definite. He must and would wait. He must hear what Callaghan had to say before making a definite move.

Without the letter Walperton would, in all probability, be, at that moment, on his way to Devonshire, and once arrived might, by luck—or sheer ability—discover many things that Callaghan desired should not be discovered.

Lancelot Vendayne's voice came on the line. He said:

"Who is that?"

He sounded acid and unhappy.

Callaghan said: "This is Callaghan. How are you? Are you feeling well, Lancelot? Do you feel that you can stand up to life? Or do you feel that life is too much for you and that you just can't take it?"

"Look here . . ." Lancelot began.

Callaghan interrupted.

"I once said that you were a sonofabitch, Lancelot," he said amiably. "I was wrong. It would be complimenting you to call you that. You're something much worse. I'll probably think up just what you are and tell you when I see you at Grant's Hotel at eleven-thirty."

"I shan't be here at eleven-thirty," said Lancelot. "So you can save yourself the trouble of coming round. If I were here I shouldn't see you. You rather fancy yourself, don't you, Callaghan? To hell with you."

"All right," said Callaghan. "To hell with me. But even that isn't going to help you. Let me tell you something, you two-by-four love-child, and you listen to it and like it!"

Callaghan's voice took on a quality that was metallic and tough. He spoke almost softly but the words possessed a peculiar resonance that positively impinged, through the telephone receiver, on to Lancelot's ear-drum.

"I'm coming round at eleven-thirty," said Callaghan grimly. "You're going to be in your apartment, and you'll have a bottle of whisky and a siphon of soda waiting for me. If you're not there I'm going out to find you. When I've found you I'm going to knock about seventeen different kinds of hell out of you, and when you come out of hospital I'm going to have you arrested and slung into gaol like any other cheap crook who's caught breaking the law. Understand?"

"Oh, really . . ." Lancelot sneered. "And may I ask what the charge would be?"

Callaghan began to lie. His voice held the honest vibrancy of truth which invariably accompanied his best-thought-out and most blatant falsehoods. He said:

"I've got all I want on you . . . you nit-wit. I'm in possession of evidence which shows clearly that you were concerned with an individual named Blaize and your cousin Esme Vendayne in a plot to steal the jewellery at Margraud. Unluckily for you, the Major was too clever for you, and secondly, Esme has decided that it is better for her to tell the truth. I've got enough on you to put you inside for five years, you cheap four-flushing wash-out. And how do you like that?"

"My God," said Lancelot. "This is rubbish. This is . . ."

"Like hell it is," said Callaghan. "But if I were you I wouldn't take any chances on it being rubbish. You be at that hotel at eleven-thirty or I'll kick your teeth down your throat."

He hung up the receiver and stepped out on to Hay Hill. It was a quarter-past seven. He began to walk in the direction of Albemarle Street, towards the Jewel Club.

He thought that Lancelot would not have a very pleasant evening. He thought that Lancelot would spend two or three hours running round in circles and trying to think out just what Callaghan was planning to do to him. He grinned happily.

Miss Paula Rochette regarded Callaghan across the table, set discreetly in the corner of the Jewel Club, with an amiability that bordered on affection.

She had eaten an excellent dinner. She had, by now, accounted for three cocktails and the greater part of two bottles of champagne with appreciation. Her long, thin fingers were set daintily—with the little finger stuck well out in the manner of the best people—round the stem of a balloon glass that carried an adequate measure of *fine maison*.

Miss Rochette was—very nearly—at peace with the world. Wars may come and wars may go, thought Paula, but I'm here and so what. She considered that she was looking her best—a process which necessitated her squeezing a pair of hips that were beginning to show the first signs of spreading into a "wrap around" quite two sizes too small for her. Her bosom was encased in a new brassière which, invented by a lady with an eye for "uplift," was doing its stuff one hundred per cent.

Paula felt that she was uplifted in all the places that needed uplift and controlled in the places that needed control. Her complexion, after a three-quarters of an hour death struggle before the mirror in her bedroom, bore a peach-like bloom that was not more than one-sixteenth of an inch thick. Her eye-brows, plucked into the slimmest possible lines, were to her own eyes superb—even if to the impersonal gaze they resembled nothing so much as the track of an unintelligent and feeble centipede whose legs had been dipped in Indian ink. Her eyelids, shaded with a middle blue that, while suggesting to the most casual observer that Paula had not been to bed for about three years, to her own, favoured vision showed a delicate tiredness and an inclination for love—in the best possible manner *of course*.

She said: "Me . . . I've always been one for *dignity*—that's what I say, 'dignity,' and I don't mean anything else. My landlady—well, I call her that, but she's more of a lady's maid to me, so to speak—said to me the other day: 'Miss Rochette,' she says, 'what about these Germans, that's what's worryin' me. What do we do if they come 'ere?'

"I turned on her," said Paula. "I said: 'If they come heah, Mrs. Carroway . . . if such a process obtains, then what we need is fighting spirit and dignity—especially dignity."

"She says: 'Oh,' she says, 'an' what good's that goin' to do? They don't need dignity—what they need is a couple of Mills bombs.' So I turned on her again an' I said: 'Mrs. Carroway, the Mills bomb is for the soldier, but what a woman—a lady—needs is *dignity*. If I was to find myself confronted by a German officer of high rank, I should merely shrug my shoulders at him and say: "Herr Kapitan, I wish you to understand that you can't go on like that around here. Not with Paula Rochette anyway." I should freeze him with a look.'

"'Oh, yes,' she says. 'An' supposin' he wasn't goin' to be froze with a look? What about it then, Miss Rochette?'

"'Then an' only then,' I told 'er, 'I should use other means. I should probably set about him, but in a ladylike manner,' I said to her, I said. 'If the worst comes to the worst there's always the flat-iron . . . but dignity first. Let's be ladies while we can an' if we can't go on bein' ladies then, *of course*, we've just got to set about 'em.'"

Paula absorbed a large gulp of brandy. She leaned towards Callaghan.

"You've heard about Helen of Troy?" she said mysteriously.

Callaghan said: "No, Paula. Tell me about her."

*"There* was a woman," said Paula. "She'd got something all right. Look what she done to Marc Antony. When things was goin' bad an' this Marc Antony was ravagin' around the countryside like a human grass'opper, what does she do? Tell me that. What does she do?"

"Well, what did she do?" asked Callaghan.

Miss Rochette's lips set in a firm line.

"She lured 'im into 'er tent an' cut off 'is retreat," she confided. "An' the next day they gave 'er a golden apple. If you go down to Chelsea you can see the Chelsea 'Ospital that they built as a memento. What I've always said is the moment produces the woman. Every big moment produces a big woman. Boadicea, Joan of Arc, Nell Gwyn, Mae West and Mademoiselle from Armentières . . . history's full of 'em."

Callaghan nodded. "You're right, Paula," he said. "These were women who knew when and how to take their revenge. You're that sort of woman. A modern Boadicea with a touch of Mae West. That's why I wanted to talk to you about Gabby."

"*Gabby* . . ." She almost hissed the word. "*There's* somebody I'm waitin' for . . ."

Callaghan interrupted. His voice was soft and intriguing.

"Tell me something, Paula," he said. "Did Gabby try and get in touch with you after he was rude to you at the Ventura Club the other night? Did he try to apologise?"

"Apologise nothin'," said Paula. "But he got in touch all right. He 'ad the nerve to ring me up an' ask me what I'd been doin' with you . . . what we'd been talkin' about. He said he wanted to know an' that if I didn't tell him he'd fix it so that I never got another job in any club in the West End."

"Ah," said Callaghan. "And did you tell him?"

Paula made a grimace intended to denote deep disdain.

"I wish you could have heard what I told him," she said. "I was as cold as ice. I said: 'Mr. Ventura,' I said: 'there's no need for you to ring through to me an' ask me questions because I don't want to talk to you. Another thing,' I said, 'as for workin' at your club or any other club, any time you feel like tryin' to put the bar up to me, you go right ahead.' I said: 'I don't want to lose my temper or my dignity with you, Mr. Ventura, but if you try any funny business with me I'm comin' round to that lousy dump of yours that you call a club, an' I'm goin' to tear your bled-in' ears off. So now you know!' An' with that I hung up."

Callaghan nodded appreciatively.

"That's the spirit, Paula," he said. "It's time someone put Gabby in his place, and . . ." He leaned towards her, smiling. "I think you and I can do it."

Paula finished her brandy. She said vaguely:

"Anything you want, dear. I always liked you. I always know a gentleman when I see one. . . ."

Callaghan looked at his wrist-watch. It was a quarter to eleven. He put his fingers into his waist-coat pocket and extracted five new ten-pound notes. He folded them carefully and laid them beside Paula's empty brandy glass.

"Buy yourself something with that, Paula," he said. "Something worthy of you. I hate giving you *money,* but it's better than buying something that doesn't match up with your particular personality."

Her fingers closed over the notes. Callaghan went on:

"Gabby's met his Waterloo. And I don't mean the railway station. If I don't get him pulled in within two or three days, my name's not Callaghan. How d'you like that, Paula?"

"Marvellous," she said, with a suggestion of a hiccough. "I'd give a couple of toes to see that fat son of a so-and-so wearin' broad arrows. It 'ud suit his complexion."

Callaghan said: "Would you like to help in the process, Paula?"

His voice was almost like the cooing of a dove.

"You watch me, darlin'," said Paula with feeling. "I'd swim through fifty feet of snow to even up with that lousy false alarm—even if I am a lady."

She paused while Callaghan poured a generous measure of brandy into her glass.

He took out his pocket-book and extracted a card. He wrote something on it, handed it to Paula.

"At twelve o'clock to-night," he said, "I want you to telephone through to Gabby at the Ventura Club. When you get through say it's a matter of life and death. That you must speak to *him.* When he comes on the line say your piece. Tell him what I've written on that card. Only you needn't be polite about it."

Paula read the card. Her eyes popped.

"Lovely," she said. "This is where I get a real thrill. I'm goin' to love tellin' 'im that. . . ."

Callaghan signalled the waiter and paid the bill. He said:

"I've got to be getting along, Paula. One of these days, maybe sooner than you think, we'll meet again."

She gulped down the brandy. She said:

"Anytime you want to get in touch, dear, just ring me. There's something about you that sort of appeals to me." She looked wildly round the room. She believed she was being dramatic. She went on: "I've always been lookin' for somebody like you. Somebody who was a real gentleman with money no object. I wonder is my search at an end. . . ."

The effect of this speech was spoiled by another hiccough.

Callaghan said: "Let's leave future meetings in the hands of Fate, Paula. All you've got to remember is to get through to Gabby at twelve o'clock and give him that message. You won't forget?"

"Never," said Paula. "Never . . . while I can stand on my feet I always keep my word."

"Fine," said Callaghan. "I knew I'd picked the right woman. I'll put you in a cab, Paula. You'd better go home."

Miss Rochette got up with dignity. She said:

"Maybe you're right, sweet'eart. I think I *will* lie down for a bit, because I've got a feeling if I don't lie down, I'll fall down."

Outside, as Callaghan put her into the taxicab, she said:

"So long, Slim. I shall always remember you as the perfect gent. Only next time we meet you'd better come round and have a drink at *my* place. I think it does everybody good to relax sometimes. . . ."

The cab drove away. Callaghan heaved a sigh. He walked quickly back to Berkeley Square. Let himself into the office, sat down before Effie Thompson's typewriter, inserted a quarto sheet of plain typing paper and began to type . . . *"Grant's Hotel, Clarges Street . . ."*

At eleven-thirty precisely Callaghan walked into Grant's Hotel in Clarges Street. He went to the reception desk. He said:

"I've come to see Mr. Vendayne. He's waiting for me. Where's his room?"

The clerk told him. Callaghan walked up the stairs to the first floor. When he came to Lancelot's door he pushed it open and went in.

He found himself in a well-furnished sitting-room. To the left was an open door leading off, he imagined, to a bedroom. In the centre of the sitting-room was a table and on the other side of it sat Lancelot. Callaghan noted with appreciation that there was a bottle of whisky, a siphon and glasses on the sideboard.

Lancelot said: "You've got a hell of a nerve, Callaghan. I really don't know why I stayed here to talk to you. If I did the right thing I'd call the police."

Callaghan walked round the table past Lancelot and went to the sideboard. He poured himself out four fingers of whisky, drank it, followed it with a chaser of soda-water. He walked back to the table and stood looking down at Lancelot.

Callaghan said: "You're just a big air balloon, Lancelot. You're tall, you're good-looking, you look like a man ought to look, but inside you're all air. You make me feel sick."

Lancelot jumped up. He aimed a wild blow at Callaghan's face. Callaghan caught the punch easily with his left hand, then he stepped back and hit Lancelot fairly between the eyes.

Lancelot went over the back of his chair. He lay on the floor for a minute, then began to scramble up. When he was fairly set on his feet Callaghan knocked him down again. He said:

"That's that. Now let's finish with this idea of rough stuff; you're no good at it. You're no good at anything. Just sit down and relax. I'm going to talk to you."

Vendayne wiped the blood from his mouth. He said:

"All right, but I'm going to even up with you for this. You wait."

His voice was almost petulant, like that of an angry woman.

Callaghan said: "I'll chance that."

He went to the sideboard, mixed a stiff whisky and soda, brought it back, put it on the table before Lancelot.

"Drink that," he said. "You need it. I told you you couldn't take it."

He returned to the sideboard and got himself another drink. Then he moved to the fireplace and stood, his back to the empty grate, the whisky glass in his hand, looking at Lancelot.

"If you're wise," he said, "if you have any brains at all, you're going to listen to me very carefully. I'm going to tell you two stories. One of them is the truth. The second one is a little variation on the truth evolved by me. When you've heard it, you'll realise that the second story sounds as if it's the true one, and that the first story, which is in effect the truth, sounds as if it were false. Now here's the first story:

"Last year you got your uncle, Major Vendayne, to put a large lump of his capital into some wild-cat share scheme of yours. It must have been a good-sounding scheme because, not only did you get Major Vendayne to put his money into it, but you got Gabby Ventura to put money in too. Well, it didn't come off. Both Major Vendayne and Gabby lost their money, but whereas the Major probably considered that it was just bad luck that the deal didn't come off, Gabby wasn't prepared to be so accommodating. He had the idea that you anyhow had made *something* out of it. He didn't like that. I imagine he got rather tough with you about it, and in trying to excuse yourself you told him that he wasn't the only person who'd lost his money; that your own uncle had gone down too.

"At this time there was an idea about that you might marry Audrey Vendayne. Because of this the Major said nothing to Audrey about the share deal. Afterwards, when she decided she didn't like you very much—and I don't blame her either—he couldn't tell her. The reasons don't matter.

"Anyhow in those days you were hanging about Margraud, probably trying to get Audrey to change her mind, and you were hanging about there when Esme came back from Cape Town.

"Esme wasn't feeling so good. She was worried. She had to confide in someone and she wanted money. She wanted money to keep Blaize quiet. She tried everything she knew, but eventually she could do nothing more and as a last resort she came to you. She told you the story. She told you how she'd married Blaize in Cape Town, how Blaize was blackmailing her. She told you how he had come over and taken the Yard Arm so as to be in the vicinity. She told you how he'd promised, if he got sufficient money, he'd allow her to divorce him quietly without the news of the marriage coming to the ears of her father or family.

"I expect you were interested—possibly you were amused," Callaghan went on. "But you didn't do anything about it. When you came back to town I've no doubt that you told Gabby Ventura the news as an amusing tit-bit. You were trying to make friends with Gabby. You'd never been particularly happy since that business of the share deal. You were rather afraid of him.

"All right. The next thing is that you hear that the Vendayne jewellery has been stolen. You know that both the local police and Scotland Yard believe it to be an inside job. Well, it didn't take very much intelligence for you to put two and two together. You guessed that Esme had found a way of paying off Blaize. You guessed that she'd let him into the house, given him the combination of the safe. You didn't even guess, you *knew*. You knew Blaize had that jewellery.

"Well, that suited your book. What did it matter to you? In the normal course of events you would neither have had the jewellery nor the proceeds from the sale of it until after the Major's death. The burglary was all right for you provided the Insurance Company paid up. You just stood around and watched points. You noticed that the Major didn't seem in any hurry to put in a claim to the Insurance

Company. You practically forced him to. Incidentally, I expect you wondered why he hadn't done it earlier.

"But even after the claim had gone in, the Insurance Company weren't keen to pay, so you thought you'd use another lever. You got me brought in on this job, the idea being that when I went down to Margraud, Esme would get the wind up, tell her father the truth, and in order to save his daughter's reputation he'd come in on your side. He would insist on an immediate payment of the claim, and when he'd got it I imagine you'd have wanted all the money.

"When Audrey Vendayne heard the scheme for putting in a private detective on this case, she didn't like it—her reasons don't matter—I know and understand them. She came up to town. Her idea was to keep me *out* of this case. She thought she'd need some money to do it with, so she asked you to lend her £300. You lent it to her, not know-ing what she wanted it for, because you thought you might make a come-back with her, but you didn't lend her your own money—you hadn't got £300. You borrowed it from Ventura, and Ventura lent it to you because at that moment it suited his book.

"Naturally," Callaghan went on cheerfully, "you weren't very pleased when I told you that I'd got Layne to withdraw the claim against the Insurance Company. You went snooping around and found that I'd arranged to represent them too, so you rang through to Audrey and tried to make things tough for me. Well, it just didn't come off.

"In fact," said Callaghan, looking more amiable than ever, "I have for once done my complete duty. I've not only represented the Vendayne family fairly adequately, but it looks to me as if I've also saved the Insurance Company a whole lot of money. That," said Callaghan with a grin, "makes me feel very good."

Lancelot said nothing. Callaghan lit a cigarette, drank a little whisky and soda.

"Now, Lancelot," he said, "that's the truth—the whole truth and nothing but the truth. That's the story which, if I tell it to the police, they won't believe. You'll agree that to any normal policeman such a story would sound impossible.

"So," Callaghan continued, "I've another story, a story which isn't true, but which matches up with the facts. I'm going to tell it to you. When I've told it to you, you're either going to agree to do what I want, or I'm going to tell this second story to the police. I think it'll put you inside. Listen to it."

Lancelot sat back in his chair. He had finished dabbing his mouth with his handkerchief. He took a gulp of whisky and soda. His eyes were interested.

Callaghan said: "This Vendayne case is a scream. It's one of the funniest stories I've ever heard in my life. I'm going to give you laugh number one: when Blaize got into Margraud and stole that jewellery, he didn't get the real stuff. He got imitation jewels—fakes that the Major had had made in place of the originals. Esme didn't know that, and you didn't know it, at the time. But my story is going to be that you did know it. My story is that when Esme came to you and said she needed money, you suggested to her that Blaize should steal the Vendayne jewellery, knowing it to be imitation, so that the Major should be forced to put in what was in effect a fake claim on the Insurance Company, of which you would take £75,000 and out of which you promised you'd settle up with Blaize. If you examine the situation you'll find that the evidence points to that being the actual case, although, as you and I know, it isn't.

"Blaize knew about you," Callaghan went on. "Esme had probably told him that she was trying to get money from you. He also knew that when the Major died the jewellery came to you. When Blaize discovered that it was fake, that all his trouble and risk had been for nothing, he was naturally annoyed, so he tried to make things hot for Esme. He sent you an anonymous note—you showed it to me yourself— saying that the jewellery wasn't worth £40. You didn't do anything about that note," said Callaghan, "because you hoped the Insurance Company would still pay. That makes you out to be a crook, because you knew *then* that the jewellery that had been stolen was fake. But you told one person—I believe you told Ventura."

Lancelot said: "What's all this stuff about Ventura? How does he come into this?"

"That's no business of yours," said Callaghan. "When I want you to ask questions I'll tell you."

Callaghan finished his whisky and soda.

"I've got an appointment at Scotland Yard to-morrow," he went on. "I've got to tell something to this policeman Walperton, who's in charge of this job. Walperton is keen. He's thirsting for somebody's blood. Well, I'm going to give him somebody—I'll give him *you*, Lancelot."

Lancelot said bitterly: "I see. So I'm to be the one to suffer. But if you do that, tell me one thing: what explanation will you give to the police about the switch over of the jewellery? My uncle must have been responsible for that. Well, what will you tell them about that?"

Callaghan smiled. His smile was beatific.

"That's easy, Lancelot," he said. "The Major will tell them that he suspected an attempt, was going to be made on the jewellery, so he had it replaced by imitations—a most praiseworthy thing to do."

"I see," said Lancelot. "So that's the story. But at the same time you've got to admit one thing. He allowed that claim to be put in on the Insurance Company, knowing that the jewellery was fake."

"All right," said Callaghan. "Didn't *you* do the same thing? When Blaize wrote you that note and told you the jewellery was fake, did *you* go down to the Insurance Company and tell 'em about it?"

Callaghan's grin was broader than ever.

"You're beat, Lancelot, and you know it. If you've got any sense you'll play things my way. That way you'll get something."

Lancelot looked at the table. After a minute he said:

"Well, what's your way?"

Callaghan put his hand in his pocket. He produced the quarto sheet of notepaper. He said:

"I have typed out a little document here. You're going to sign it. I'll tell you what this document says. It says that as final and last owner of the Vendayne jewellery *after* your uncle's death, you're entitled to sell that jewellery. It says that you're prepared, with his consent, to sell it now, and that you're prepared and wish to divide the proceeds of approximately £100,000 with him.

"That means," said Callaghan, "that you'll get £50,000 and no accusation from me. Well, that's fair enough, isn't it, Lancelot?"

Lancelot said: "That's all right so long as I get some money. But how can we sell the jewellery? We haven't got it."

Callaghan said: "Don't you worry about that, Lancelot. I'm going to get it."

He walked over to the table and put the sheet of notepaper in front of Lancelot. He handed Lancelot his pen. He said:

"Of course you could say this document was obtained from you under duress. You could say a lot of things, Lancelot, but you won't, because if you do you know exactly what I'll do to you. I'll get you a sentence as an accessory before and after the Vendayne burglary. If Esme is brought into this, you're going to be brought into it too, and whatever she gets you'll get too. Remember that."

Lancelot said impatiently: "Very well, I've got no choice. I agree to sign the document."

As he laid down the pen he said: "And what about Blaize?"

Callaghan said: "You don't have to worry about Blaize. Nobody has to worry about him." He picked up the sheet of notepaper, his pen and his hat. "He hasn't even got to worry about himself," he said.

"Good-night, Lancelot."

Callaghan stood outside the entrance of Grant's Hotel in Clarges Street. He looked at his watch. It was twelve o'clock. He began to walk towards Berkeley Square.

Miss Rochette's alarm clock, which she had set carefully for midnight, exploded with a jangle. Paula, who, dressed in her cami-knickers, was lying full length on her bed, indulging in a little quite lady-like snoring, awoke with a start. She yawned, stretched, sat on the edge of the bed, ran her fingers through her hair. After a moment she got up. She went to a cupboard and extracted a bottle of gin, poured out a full measure, drank it. She went to the dressing-table and picked up the card which Callaghan had given to her. She walked a little unsteadily to the telephone, sat down by it, took off the receiver and dialled the Ventura Club. She said:

"I want to speak to Mr. Ventura . . . Never mind who I am, you can tell him it's urgent. It's a matter of life and death."

Her voice was dramatic. Paula was enjoying herself. After a moment Ventura's voice came on the line. Paula said:

"Is that you, you fat slob? This is Paula Rochette. So you're the feller who's going to have me barred from working in the West End clubs, are you? All right. Did anybody ever tell you that 'hell hath no fury like a woman scorned'? Well, you listen to this: I've been dining with a friend of yours tonight. Maybe he's not such a friend as you think. His name's Callaghan. He told me something in confidence, and I ought not to tell you. But I'm going to. You get those big fat ears of yours open and listen to this:

"Callaghan's got you. He's going to slam you inside. He knows all about the Vendayne jewellery. He knows all about you. You big fat false alarm, you haven't got a leg to stand on, and when they get you stuck behind the bars I'm coming down every day just to make faces at you. Good-night, sweetheart."

Miss Rochette slammed down the receiver. She looked at herself in the glass. The mascara from one eyebrow had run into her eye. She was not pleased with the effect. She sighed, drank a little more gin, saw Callaghan's five ten-pound notes folded on her dressing-table, sighed contentedly and went back to bed.

## CHAPTER FOURTEEN
## ONE FOR THE ROAD

IT WAS exactly twelve o'clock when Detective-Inspector Walperton braked his well-polished two-seater to a standstill outside a block of apartments in Chelsea.

He went inside, got into the lift and ascended to the second floor. He walked along to the flat at the end of the corridor and rang the bell. Then he lit a cigarette and waited.

Three minutes afterwards Chief Detective-Inspector Gringall, in a blue dressing-gown and with a surprised expression, opened the door. He stood for a moment looking at Walperton. Then he began to smile. It was a nice, sympathetic smile. It was the smile of a parent who has experienced certain difficulties in life and who realises that someone not so experienced as himself is beginning to discover them too.

Gringall raised one eyebrow quizzically.

He said: "Callaghan?"

Walperton nodded.

"Yes, Mr. Gringall," he replied. "Callaghan . . . you've *said* it."

Gringall said: "Come in. I rather thought you'd have something to get off your chest about the Vendayne business."

He led the way into his study, closed the door, got out a bottle of whisky, a siphon of soda and two glasses. He began to mix the drinks. Walperton sat in one of the big leather armchairs.

"Go ahead," said Gringall. "What's our friend Callaghan been up to now?"

Walperton took the glass from his superior's hand.

"I got a letter from Callaghan this afternoon," he said. "It was sent round by hand. It was a funny sort of letter. Perhaps you'd like to read it."

He brought the letter from his pocket, handed it to Gringall. Gringall read the letter. When he had finished, he said:

"I've had letters like this from Callaghan too. They tell you nothing. They suggest that Callaghan knows a lot and that in due course, if you're good and wait around, you'll know it too."

"It's like his damned insolence," said Walperton.

Gringall smiled.

"Quite," he said. "He is an insolent fellow, isn't he? But he's damned clever. What's the position, Walperton?" he went on. "Is there anything fresh in the Vendayne case?"

"Plenty," Walperton replied grimly. "When I got the letter from Callaghan this afternoon I wasn't worried. Things were more or less as they had been. There's only one point of interest since I last talked with you about this business and that was that Layne—Major Vendayne's solicitor—had withdrawn the claim against the Insurance Company, on the grounds that Callaghan had got a line on where that jewellery was. He thought he was going to get it back. That intrigued me, but there was no reason why I should do anything about it.

"Very well," Walperton went on. "At ten o'clock Gridley came through to me from Devonshire. I sent him down there last night to investigate a feller named Blaize who's been living in the neighbourhood. You notice Callaghan says in his letter that Blaize had disappeared. Well, they've found Blaize's body lying at the bottom of a sort of ravine in the cliff between Margraud and the place where Blaize lived."

Gringall raised his eyebrows.

"What do you think about that?" he asked.

"Work it out for yourself, sir," said Walperton. "Callaghan admits in that letter that his opinion about the burglary was the same as mine—that it was an inside job. That means it was some member of the family. That member of the family was probably working with Blaize.

"I see," said Gringall. "That makes it serious, doesn't it? And what did you do then?"

"I didn't do anything," said Walperton.

He paused for a moment because he noticed the faint smile which had reappeared on Gringall's face. Then he went on:

"I didn't do anything because I was a little worried. I thought it would be foolish for me to go down there or to give Gridley some definite instructions before I'd heard what Callaghan had got to say to-morrow."

"Quite," said Gringall. "Callaghan knew you'd do that. That's why he sent you that letter. He's playing for time."

He took a pipe from one pocket of his dressing-gown, a pouch from the other. He began to fill the pipe.

Walperton said: "If Callaghan obstructs me I'm going to arrest him, sir. I'm getting a little bored with Callaghan."

Gringall said: "Walperton, I've been bored with Callaghan. I've been angry with him. There have been moments when I could cheerfully have killed him, but I have never been such a fool as to consider arresting him."

Walperton raised his eyebrows.

He said: "No?"

"No," said Gringall. "Now let me tell you something. You've heard of the motto of Callaghan Investigations: 'We get there somehow and who the hell cares how'? The joke is he *does* get there somehow."

Gringall sat down in the other armchair. He drew contentedly on his pipe.

"My advice to you, Walperton," he said, "is just sit tight and hear what Callaghan's got to say to-morrow, because my bet is that you'll hear as much of the truth as he wants to tell you."

Walperton raised his eyebrows again.

"As much as *he* wants to tell me," he said.

"Precisely," said Gringall. "If Callaghan doesn't tell you any part of the story it's because he knows that the part he doesn't tell you is so vague, so ambiguous and so impossible for you to check, that he's safe in not telling it to you. I know the Callaghan system. To-morrow he'll give you just as many facts as he wants to give you." He smiled sympathetically. "I'll take a little bet with you, Walperton," he said. "Callaghan's got this case in the bag. Whatever he's planned to do has been carried to a more or less successful conclusion."

Walperton said: "Well, I hope it'll be successful in my opinion, Mr. Gringall."

"I don't see why it shouldn't be," said Gringall. "Work it out for yourself. Callaghan's been representing two parties in this case—two parties whose interests at first seemed to be at opposite ends of the stick—the Insurance Company and the Vendayne family. Well, he's done the right thing by the Insurance Company, hasn't he?"

Walperton nodded glumly.

"You mean they're happy because the claim's withdrawn?"

"Precisely," said Gringall. "And the second thing that Callaghan's got to do is to keep the Vendayne family happy, and I imagine he's taken steps to ensure that. Then there's a third thing—he's got to keep Detective-Inspector Walperton happy. I imagine," said Gringall, smiling broadly, "that he'll start making you happy to-morrow."

Walperton got up. He said:

"Thank you very much, sir. I'll wait and see what happens."

"That's right," said Gringall. "When in doubt don't do anything. I've always found that a very good rule for a police officer . . ." He led the way to the door. "Especially in dealing with Slim Callaghan."

Callaghan lay on his bed, looking at the ceiling. He was thinking about Audrey Vendayne and, at the same time, telling himself that he spent too much time on the process. He turned his mind to other matters.

Being a private investigator was an odd business, thought Callaghan. People came to you because they were in some sort of a jam; because they didn't want to go to the police, because for some reason they were afraid of the police.

Sometimes they told you the truth; usually they told you half or a quarter of the truth. Then you began to fill in the blanks for yourself and if you could you started something, sat back, watched things begin to happen.

You planned a definite scheme based on the personalities in your investigation. Once you had started the scheme you couldn't stop. You hoped for the best. But you could be certain of one thing. Either it came off or it didn't.

And up to the moment, Callaghan ruminated with a half smile, it had come off.

He hoped it would continue to come off.

He turned over on his side and reached for the whisky bottle which stood on the bed-table. He put the neck of the bottle in his mouth and took a long pull.

The telephone on the table began to jangle.

Callaghan, with the neck of the bottle still in his mouth, grinned. He finished drinking, replaced the bottle, picked up the receiver.

It was Gabby Ventura. He said:

"Hallo, Slim. Listen . . . I want to talk to you."

Callaghan said: "There's no law against it. Won't to-morrow do?"

He was still grinning. He looked almost satanic.

There was a pause. Then Ventura said:

"No. This is urgent, Slim. It's urgent for you an' me. I've got to talk to you now. What about coming over? I've got a bottle of champagne that's asking for you to drink it."

"I never drink champagne," said Callaghan. "Only whisky—at this time of night anyway."

He turned his wrist over and looked at his watch. It was twelve-forty.

Ventura said, in a voice that was intended to be facetious: "Well . . . I've got a lot of whisky. Come on over, Slim."

"Why don't you come over here . . . to the office?" said Callaghan. "*I've* got some whisky too."

There was another pause. Then:

"Look, Slim . . . don't be difficut. I want you to come over here. I've got somethin' I want to hand over to you."

Callaghan said: "Ah . . . Now you're talking, Gabby. Do I take it you're going to hand over the Vendayne jewellery—the *real* stuff?"

"That's right," said Gabby in a near-cheerful voice. "I know when I'm beat, Slim."

Callaghan swung his legs off the bed. He said:

"All right, Gabby. I'll come over now. I'll meet you in the club."

"No," said Ventura. "Don't do that. There's not many people there. They'll be closing down in a little while. Come around to the back door and up to the flat. I'll be waiting downstairs for you."

"All right," said Callaghan. "I'll be with you in fifteen minutes. I'll come straight round."

He hung up. He got up, put on his hat, walked along the corridor, took the lift down to the office. He opened the outer door, went into his own room, sat down in front of the desk and opened the lowest drawer in the right pedestal.

The drawer contained a Luger pistol, a .32 automatic and a bottle of Canadian Bourbon. Callaghan picked up the Luger, looked at it, examined the cartridge clip, pushed it back into the butt, pulled back the recoil action, thereby pushing a cartridge into the breech, put on the safety catch and put the pistol in the pocket specially inserted under his left arm.

He took a long swig at the Canadian rye, replaced the bottle, closed the door, went out of the office and took the lift down to the street level.

He closed the lift gates behind him and walked along the passage to the porter's lodge. Wilkie—the night porter—was sitting in his glass box smoking, reading *The Evening News*.

Callaghan said: "Wilkie . . . Listen to this, and no mistakes now. I'm going to see a gentleman named Mr. Ventura. You'd better write down his telephone number"—Callaghan gave him the number. "At ten past one precisely," he went on, "I want you to telephone through to that number. When you get through ask for Mr. Ventura. When he asks who you are, you say: 'This is Detective-Inspector Walperton, Scotland Yard. I want to talk to Mr. Callaghan, please.'"

Callaghan paused to light a cigarette.

"Have you got that, Wilkie?"

Wilkie said he had got it.

"Then," Callaghan continued, "I'll come on the line. I'll probably talk a lot of nonsense but you don't have to take any notice. See?"

Wilkie said that was O.K. Callaghan laid a pound note on the little desk in front of the night porter and went out.

He began to walk towards Shepherd Market. He skirted the market, turned into the Mews, turned right and found himself in the passage that led to the rear of the Ventura Club. Twenty yards away the passage was bisected by a narrow cross-road that ran down by the side of the club.

He walked slowly down the passage. When he had walked five or six steps he stopped and listened. He took out his cigarette-case and lighter and lit a cigarette. All the time he was listening.

He snapped out the lighter, put it back into his pocket and continued on his way down the passage. He was whistling softly.

He came to the place where the narrow roadway ran across the passage. Callaghan, his nerves alert, stepped into the roadway, made as if to take another step, stopped, jumped backwards.

A touring car screeched past, missing Callaghan by a good twelve inches.

Callaghan crossed the road. He moved into the shadows of the passage on the other side. He stood there waiting. Five minutes afterwards he heard the quiet throb of the motor.

He came out of the passage and turned up by the side of the Ventura Club. He walked twenty paces and turned right. He stopped in front of the dark entrance of the club. The driver of the touring car was turning the car, backing it towards the mews opposite.

Callaghan slipped his hand inside his coat for the Luger. He took three very quick, quiet strides. He put his hand over the side of the car and caught the driver by the front of his collar.

"Switch off, Ropey," said Callaghan. "You can leave the car here. And get out."

Felliner grunted. He switched off, put on the hand-brake and got out. He said:

"Look . . . what the 'ell . . .?"

Callaghan dug the Luger barrel into Ropey's soft oversized belly. He said:

"Just walk in front of me round to the back entrance. Gabby's waiting there."

Felliner obeyed. They walked back to the passage, turned left. Fifteen yards away Callaghan could see the dim glow of Gabby's shaded flash-lamp.

Gabby said: "What's goin' on, Slim? What the hell! Why . . . it's Ropey! Why . . .?"

Callaghan said: "Cut it out, Gabby. It didn't come off, that's all. Now we can have our little talk. But excuse me for just a minute."

He pushed Ropey against the wall. He said in a very soft and pleasant voice:

"I'm a bit fed up with you, Ropey. I don't like you. I never liked you anyway, but since two or three minutes ago I positively *dislike* you. You get out of here, Ropey, and keep going. In the meantime let me give you a little memento to keep with you."

Callaghan threw up the Luger and caught it by the barrel. He hit Ropey fairly across the face with the pistol butt. Ropey emitted a shrill whine. He slipped down against the wall until he was sitting on the stone pavement. His hands were pressed to his face.

Callaghan said: "Get up and get out. The next time I see you I'll tear you open, you cheap has-been."

Ropey got up. He was still whining softly. He kept his hands pressed to his face. He began to walk unsteadily down the passage.

Callaghan said: "Come on, Gabby. Let's have our talk. It's too bad for you that: Ropey missed me with that car." He paused to light a cigarette. "I've been waiting for you to telephone me," he went on. "I knew you'd try something directly Paula Rochette came through to you with that stuff I told her to hand out. I guessed you'd try something with a car. All Ropey had to do was to knock me down and then run over me again and finish me. Just another accident in the blackout."

He sighed.

"Nice work if you can get it," he said.

Gabby said nothing. He turned and began to walk up the stairs. Callaghan closed the door behind him and followed. When they got to the flat above he put the Luger back in his pocket.

It was five minutes past one. Callaghan, seated in the armchair by the side of the empty fireplace, watched Gabby as he mixed two whiskies and sodas at the sideboard. Gabby turned and brought the drinks to the table. He handed one to Callaghan. He said:

"Look, Slim, you know me. I'm one for letting bygones be bygones. It's no good me telling you that I wasn't behind this idea of Ropey's— this car business—because you wouldn't believe me. But I wasn't. I think maybe Ropey was a little bit annoyed with you on his own account, see?"

Callaghan said: "I see." He took a long drink. "Don't you think it's time you stopped telling lies, Gabby?" he said. "You know you're in a jam. There's only one way out of it."

Gabby sat down in the armchair opposite. He took a small but expensive cigar out of his waistcoat pocket and lit it. The diamond pin in his tie was twinkling. Callaghan noticed that Gabby's mouth was almost relaxed, apparently contented. He thought that there was nothing wrong with Ventura's nerve.

Gabby said pleasantly: "All right. For the sake of argument I'm in a jam and I can get out of it. Well, I never mind listening to you talk, Slim. You're always interestin'. How am I in a jam and how do I get out?"

Callaghan said: "Listen, Gabby. I know the story, so do you. Let me give you an outline of how you're mixed up in this thing. First of all you weren't very pleased with Lancelot Vendayne. He got you in that share deal. You put money into it. It didn't come off and you lost your dough. You began to dislike Lancelot. Well, Lancelot had a respect for you—he wanted to be on the right side of you. He was careful to explain that you weren't the only person who'd lost money. He told you that Major Vendayne had lost his too; that he was in a worse jam than you were—you still had *some* left anyway, probably plenty. Lancelot probably enlarged on that argument. He told you what a tough spot old man Vendayne was in. He probably told you about the mortgage.

"You got an idea, Gabby—quite a sound idea. Lancelot had pointed out that when Major Vendayne died he'd have the jewellery, that he was legally entitled to sell it; that he'd be worth £100,000. He promised you that he'd repay the money he owed you if you'd finance him some more.

"You probably agreed, but you wanted to keep an eye on Lancelot, so you introduced him to Paula Rochette, who was working in your club. You instructed her to let you know what he was doing.

"Well, the next thing that happened was that Lancelot told you that Esme Vendayne was married to Blaize. I'll take another shade of odds that he also told you that Blaize had come over to this country and was blackmailing Esme, that she'd asked him—Lancelot—for money, but that he couldn't put it up. I should think that he suggested to you that Esme might find a way out of her difficulties by letting Blaize steal the Vendayne jewellery. Lancelot wouldn't have worried about that anyway. If the jewellery was stolen he'd get the major portion of the insurance."

Callaghan paused. He drank a little more whisky.

He said: "How am I doing, Gabby?"

Ventura grinned at him quite amiably through the cigar smoke.

"You're not doing so badly. Go on, Slim. I told you you're always interestin'."

Callaghan went on: "The position wasn't good enough for you, Gabby," he said. "You've always been a one for taking chances, and you thought out a little scheme by which you could get on the right end of this deal. You made an appointment to see Major Vendayne. You pointed out to him that his position was fairly desperate, that if he didn't pay off that £20,000 mortgage, the mortgagees would foreclose on Margraud, and that would have broken his heart. You offered to lend him £20,000 to pay off that mortgage, provided he would hand over the Vendayne jewellery to you."

Callaghan lit a fresh cigarette. He went on:

"The old boy was quite desperate. He would have done anything to save Margraud, but he probably put up a couple of objections. You smoothed them over. You said that there'd be plenty of time for him to pay back the money, in which case you'd give him back the jewellery, and that if he died the jewellery would go to Lancelot Vendayne. You then told him how Lancelot had taken you both in over the share deal. You told the old man that you would simply hold the jewellery as a security, in the event of his death, until Lancelot arranged to pay you back what he owed you.

"The Major's next objection was what was going to happen on the occasions when the jewellery was supposed to be shown. You said you'd look after that," Callaghan grinned. "You know a lot of people in the fake jewellery business, don't you, Gabby?" he said. "Well, one of them did a nice job for you. He made you a complete replica of the Vendayne jewels and you handed them over to the Major. Even when they were sent back to the bank vault nobody would open the cases to look at them. It wasn't their business, and anyway nobody would distrust the Major." Callaghan paused. He said: "Am I still doing pretty well, Gabby?"

Ventura nodded. "Nice work. Slim," he said. His voice was almost patronising.

"Well," said Callaghan, "everything was all right. You'd got the Vendayne jewellery. You knew that the Major would never be able to repay the debt during his lifetime. You thought he'd die pretty quickly. You'd have stuck to that jewellery. You wouldn't have worried about the money that Lancelot owed you. The jewellery was worth much more.

"Unfortunately," Callaghan went on, "things began to happen. The fake jewellery was stolen. Then you began to get a little worried. Lancelot, I think, was rather pleased. He probably told you that this was the time to collect the insurance, that when he'd got the money he'd pay you back. That suited you all right, but you were worried in case Blaize discovered the jewels he'd stolen were fake, so when you got the opportunity you sent Ropey Felliner down to Devonshire to keep an eye on Blaize.

"I imagine Blaize is not much of an expert on jewels. Anyway, he probably sent that stuff away to be re-cut, only keeping one bracelet. It took quite a little time before his friends in the jewellery business told him that the stuff was fake. Then Blaize got tough with Esme. Not only did he get tough with Esme, but he sent an anonymous note to Lancelot, telling him the stuff was fake. Lancelot knew where that note came from. He showed it to me, and I'll bet he also showed it to you.

"Now look, Gabby," Callaghan went on, "you hand over that jewellery and as far as the Vendayne burglary is concerned, the claim on the Insurance Company and all the rest of that stuff, you're going to be all right."

He stopped talking as the telephone began to ring. Ventura lifted the receiver and spoke. After a minute he turned to Callaghan and said:

"There's a policeman—Walperton—wants to talk to you."

"Oh, yes," said Callaghan. "I fixed for him to ring through just in case anything happened to me around here."

He walked over to the telephone, picked up the receiver. He said: "Is that you, Walperton?"

At the other end of the line, Wilkie said softly: "O.K., Mr. Callaghan."

"I think everything's all right," said Callaghan. "I'm with Ventura now. I don't think there'll be any need for any prosecutions. The whole job's straightened out all right. Thanks a lot. Good-night, Walperton."

He hung up. Gabby was standing in front of the fireplace, one hand on the mantelpiece, looking down into the empty grate. He said:

"O.K., Slim. I know when I'm licked. This is the first time in my life I've been taken for a sucker. And I don't mean *you,*" he went on, "I mean that Lancelot bastard."

His face flushed. Gabby was very angry.

Callaghan said: "Don't worry, Gabby. I've seen Lancelot to-night." He produced the sheet of notepaper from his breast pocket. "You're going to be all right, Gabby," he said, *"now that you're going to play ball.* Lancelot and Major Vendayne have agreed that the jewellery shall be sold. Lancelot is going to get £50,000." Callaghan grinned at Gabby. "So all you've got to do," he said pleasantly, "immediately the sale is completed, is to keep after Lancelot for the money he owes you."

Gabby grinned. He said:

"That's pretty decent of you, Slim, to tell me that. I won't forget it."

Callaghan said, just as pleasantly: "I think it's decent of me, too, Gabby, especially after what Ropey tried to pull on me to-night."

Gabby shrugged.

"What's a little thing like that between friends?" he said. "It didn't come off—so what . . . When Lancelot settles up with me I'll look after you, Slim."

He went to the sideboard, poured out two more drinks. He said, raising his glass:

"Here's to you, Slim. You're a clever devil."

Callaghan finished his drink.

"That's fine," he said. "Now what about that jewellery?"

Gabby grinned.

"I've got it here," he said. "I'll get it for you."

Callaghan lit another cigarette. He watched Gabby as he took down a picture from the wall and opened the wall safe.

Callaghan stood in the open doorway at the bottom of the stairs leading to Ventura's flat. In his left hand he held one of Gabby's suit-cases. It was heavy with the Vendayne jewellery.

Ventura said: "Good-night, Slim. It looks as if everything's going to be fine for all of us. There's only one point that's worrying me now."

"I'm sorry to hear that, Gabby," said Callaghan. "What is it? Is there anything I can do?"

Gabby said: "About my getting that money from Lancelot. He can still do me down if he wants to. After he's got his £50,000 he doesn't *have* to pay me what he owes me—the money I lost was in a share deal. I've got no *legal* claim on him."

Callaghan said: "I wondered when you were going to think about that, Gabby. I've got an idea. You've played the game with me, and I'm going to do the right thing by you." Callaghan smiled in the dark-ness. "You be here to-morrow night," he said, "after the club's closed, about twelve o'clock. I'll bring Lancelot round. I've got him where I want him anyway. I'll make him sign a new document, admitting that he legally owes you the money, agreeing to pay it immediately the jewellery's sold. How's that?"

"Fine," said Gabby. "I'll be waiting for you, Slim. You're a good guy. I'll see you don't lose anything over this."

"Thanks, Gabby," said Callaghan.

He walked away into the darkness. Ventura stood in the doorway for a moment drawing on his cigar. He was smiling. After a moment he closed the door, went upstairs, gave himself a large drink.

Callaghan came out of the lift, walked along the passage, went into his apartment. He threw his hat on the table in the drawing-room, put the suitcase on a chair. He went into his bedroom, dialled "Trunks." He asked for the Margraud number. Twenty minutes afterwards, Stevens' tired voice came on the telephone.

"Hallo, Stevens," said Callaghan. "Sorry to worry you, but this is urgent. Ask Miss Vendayne to come to the telephone, will you?"

Stevens said he would.

Callaghan reached for the whisky bottle. He put the neck in his mouth, took a long pull. He put the bottle back on the table.

Audrey Vendayne came on the line. Callaghan said:

"Hallo, Audrey. Were you asleep?"

She said: "No. I was awake. I was thinking."

Callaghan said: "Are you wearing that white-spotted red silk dressing-gown?"

She said: "Yes. Why?"

"And have you got that ribbon in your hair?" queried Callaghan.

"My hair is tied with a ribbon too," said Audrey.

"All right," said Callaghan. "I wanted to know what you were wearing. The last time I saw you, you were wearing that dressing-gown. I thought you looked charming. I told you so. Do you remember?"

She said: "Yes, I remember. Did you want something?"

Callaghan grinned.

"I wanted to tell you that everything's pretty well all right," he said. "When I had that talk with you just before I came away—when I told you about Esme and Blaize and all the rest of it—there was just one little thing I didn't tell you. I thought you'd better not know it then, but you can know it now. The jewellery that Blaize stole from Margraud was fake—the Major had switched it over. He'd pawned the real jewels for £20,000 to pay off that mortgage."

He heard her catch her breath. She said:

"My God. . . ."

"It's all right," said Callaghan. "I've got the real stuff in an attaché-case here, and I don't think you need worry very much about the police. I don't think Esme need worry. If by any chance anybody asks her any questions to-morrow about what happened at her meeting with Blaize, tell her to tell 'em the truth, the whole truth and nothing but the truth. You understand?"

"I understand," said Audrey. "Is everything really going to be all right?"

"You bet it is," said Callaghan. He went on: "Let's change the subject. I want to ask you a question. Do you remember that night when we first met and you gave me £300 to stay out of this case because you yourself suspected that Esme had something to do with that robbery? Do you remember when I bought you that drink in the little club in Conduit Street—which you left, by the way? I've got an idea that that was the evening you told me you didn't like private detectives."

She said: "Yes, that's right. I didn't."

Callaghan said: "How do you feel about 'em now?"

She laughed. It was the first time he had ever heard her laugh.

"I don't think I want to discuss that with you on the telephone," she said. "When are you coming to Margraud?"

Callaghan grinned.

"Probably in the middle of to-morrow night," he said, "if I can get down there. If not, the next day."

"All right, Mr. Callaghan," she said. "When you arrive I'll tell you what I think about private detectives."

"Right," said Callaghan. "That's a bet."

He hung up.

## CHAPTER FIFTEEN
## YOU CAN'T KEEP THE CHANGE

DETECTIVE-Inspector Walperton, whose features expressed the most extreme and incredulous surprise, looked at Callaghan with his mouth slightly open. For the moment he was unable to speak.

Sergeant Gridley, lately arrived back at Scotland Yard from Devonshire, looked at his superior officer with an expression which, if anything, expressed more amazement than that of the detective-inspector.

Callaghan, an amiable smile wreathing his countenance, smiled at them both. He looked at his wrist-watch, noted that the time was eight o'clock.

Walperton said: "Callaghan, we've been listening to you talking since six o'clock. After I read your letter yesterday I thought that you were going to tell me something, give me some sort of information that might enable me to move in this case."

He sighed heavily.

"It seems," he continued, "that the sum total of your information adds up to the amazing fact that it is not possible for the police to arrest anyone at all in connection with the Vendayne burglary, that all they can do is to mark the case closed."

He got up and walked over to the window. He stood for a moment looking out on to the Embankment. Then he turned and walked back to his desk. He sat down, picked up a pen and began to stab the blotter viciously.

"I've never heard such damned impertinence in my whole experience as a police officer," Walperton continued. "Never."

He looked at Gridley. Gridley shrugged his shoulders. Walperton's eyes went back to Callaghan, who was busily engaged in lighting a cigarette.

"Just listen to his, Gridley," said Walperton. His voice was sarcastic. "I'm going to summarise what Mr. Callaghan has told us. I'm not going to embellish that summary with any opinions of my own. I'm merely going to state facts. When I've finished I want you to tell me quite candidly whether I'm stark, staring, raving mad, or whether I've misunderstood Mr. Callaghan."

He threw the pen down on the desk.

"First of all," he continued, "I would like to state the opening facts of the case. It seems that a burglary is committed at Margraud Manor. Valuable jewels, heirlooms of the Vendayne family, are stolen. They are worth somewhere in the region of £100,000 and are insured for that sum. The County Police are called in, and then, some time afterwards, we are asked to assist and take the case over. Everything about the burglary indicates that it was an inside job.

"Major Vendayne, the owner, in his lifetime, of the jewellery, does not, for reasons best known to himself, make a claim against the Insurance Company for some time, and even then *he* doesn't actually do it. His lawyer, Layne, does it, apparently at the request of Mr. Lancelot Vendayne, who has an interest in the jewellery after the Major's death."

Walperton stopped speaking and looked at Callaghan. "Do you agree with all that up to the moment?" he asked.

Callaghan nodded. He was smiling pleasantly.

"You're doing very well, Walperton," he murmured.

Walperton continued: "Then, when the claim does go in, the Insurance Company don't pay. I don't blame them. So Mr. Lancelot Vendayne insists that a private detective be brought in on the case in order to prove to the insurance people that the family are doing everything in their power to discover the whereabouts of the stolen jewellery.

"Mr. Callaghan begins to investigate, and I must say"—the sarcasm began to disappear from Walperton's voice—"that he discovered a great deal more than we were able to do. First of all, he discovers that the jewels that were stolen were not the Vendayne jewels but imitations, supplied by Gabriel Ventura, who had taken over the real ones as security for a temporary loan of £20,000 which he had made to Major Vendayne.

"Mr. Callaghan informs us that there is nothing illegal in the action on the Major's part. He points out that the original Vendayne Trust lays down that the jewels *must be kept in a safe place.* He says that the fact that the Major handed them over to Ventura as security for the loan does not break that rule in the original trust deed. Because, says Mr. Callaghan, Ventura kept the jewels in a safe place as agent for the Major, and his willingness to return them on demand has been proved by the fact that he has already handed them over to Mr. Callaghan."

Walperton sighed again. He continued:

"Mr. Callaghan tells us that there was nothing illegal in the claim against the Insurance Company. He says that the claim was made by Layne, the Vendayne solicitor, at the instigation of Mr. Lancelot Vendayne. He says that at the time the claim was made both these gentlemen believed that the actual Vendayne jewels had been stolen. He says that their complete innocence of any illegal motive is proved by the fact that immediately he informed Layne that the stolen jewels were fakes, Layne *withdrew* the claim against the Insurance Company."

Walperton drew a deep breath. Sergeant Gridley's face had assumed an expression intended to denote that he felt a great and unhappy sympathy for his superior.

The detective-inspector went on: "Now we come to the actual burglary. Mr. Callaghan admits that this burglary was a co-operative affair between Blaize, who is now dead, and Miss Esme Vendayne, who was his wife and whom he had, for some time, blackmailed into supplying him with money and, eventually, into assisting him in the burglary.

"Miss Esme Vendayne is responsible for supplying Blaize with the combination of the Vendayne safe, and for letting Blaize into the house on the night of the burglary. But Mr. Callaghan informs us that no police action is possible against either of these two people, because (a) Blaize is dead, and no action can be taken against him for that reason, and (b) that Miss Esme Vendayne is innocent because at the time she supplied Blaize with the combination and at the time she let him into her father's house *she knew that the jewellery was fake and therefore worthless,* and she knew that the real jewellery was in a safe place. Her reason in making herself a party to the business with Blaize was so that she might be in a position to prefer an actual charge against him and so rid herself of him once and for all."

A deep breath escaped from Gridley. It sounded almost like a groan of despair.

Walperton said: "Now we come to Ventura. Mr. Callaghan informs us that we cannot prefer any charge against Ventura, because Ventura has done nothing illegal. Mr. Callaghan says that Ventura generously advanced a sum of £20,000 to the Major and agreed to keep the real jewels as security in a safe place as joint custodian with the Major. Mr. Callaghan says that Ventura has never attempted to dispose of the jewellery and, as I have already said, has handed it back on demand."

Walperton banged his fist down on the desk. His face was scarlet.

"My God!" he said. "What a mess! The devil of it is I believe that Callaghan is right. I don't believe we've got a charge against anybody. I believe from first to last everybody in this case has been playing their own hand, doing what they want, making fools of the County Police, making fools of Scotland Yard."

He paused for breath.

"Hell!" he said bitterly. "Here we've got the one person that we could have charged and he's dead. . . . He had to fall over a cliff and kill himself!" Walperton gulped with rage. "Perhaps it's lucky for us he *is* dead," he spluttered. "If we'd pulled him in his defence would probably have been that *he* knew the jewellery was false as well . . . that he just stole it for fun. . . . !"

Callaghan blew a smoke-ring. He said:

"I'm damn sorry for you, Walperton. From your point of view this case has been a lot of trouble about nothing. However . . . let's get down to the thing that matters. . . ."

Walperton pricked up his ears.

"So there *is* something that matters?" he said. "Amazing." His eyes narrowed. He shot a sharp look at Callaghan. He said: "Callaghan, I believe you've got something up your sleeve. Mr. Gringall said . . ."

"That I always keep something up my sleeve," said Callaghan with a grin. "Well . . . why not?"

He got up.

"Listen, Walperton," he said. "I told you that if I could do anything for you I'd do it. You've played ball with me. You've practically admitted that there's no police charge lying against my client, Major Vendayne, or any member of the Vendayne family. You *have* admitted that, haven't you?"

Walperton said: "Well . . . supposing I have? All right, for the sake of argument, I *have.*"

Callaghan walked over to Walperton's desk. He stood looking at the police officer. He was smiling pleasantly.

"I'm going to give you a damned good case, Walperton," he said. "But you've got to do something for me first. . . ."

"What?" demanded Walperton. "What do I have to do first?" His voice was suspicious.

"Nothing much," said Callaghan. "But I've an appointment to-night. I want to talk to you before I keep it. I'm going to suggest that you pick me up at my office in Berkeley Square at eleven-thirty. I think I can promise you an interesting evening."

Walperton said nothing for a moment. He was thinking about Gringall, remembering what Gringall had said about Callaghan.

Eventually: "All right," he said. "What can *I* lose? I'll pick you up at your office at eleven-thirty. But remember this . . ."

Callaghan put up his hand.

"Don't worry, Walperton," he said amiably. "You come round at eleven-thirty. I'm going to make you a promise. *I'm still going to give you the Vendayne case on a plate!*"

He nodded to Gridley and went out.

Callaghan lit a cigarette, tilted his office chair back and put his feet on the desk. He sat there for five minutes, pondering on possibilities, assessing chances. Then he took his feet off the desk and looked at his wrist-watch.

It was twenty-five minutes past eleven.

He picked up the telephone and rang down to Wilkie, the night porter. He said: "I'm expecting Mr. Walperton. When he comes bring him up to my office, put him in my room and give him a cigarette. I'm going up to my flat. I'll be down in a few minutes."

He went out of the office, up the stairway to his apartment. He went into his bedroom and opened the wardrobe. He took out a dark grey felt hat.

Inside the hat, fixed on a leather base, just underneath the fold in the hat, was a wire spring. Callaghan went to the chest of drawers, unlocked one of them and produced a .22 automatic. He slipped the automatic into the spring inside the felt hat and put the hat on his head. The butt of the automatic rested on the top of his head, taking the weight off the inside of the hat.

He went to the corner cupboard and took out a fresh bottle of Canadian Bourbon. He unscrewed the cap, put the neck of the bottle in his mouth, took a long pull.

He went downstairs to the office. Walperton was sitting in a chair, smoking. He said:

"I've got to admit I'm very curious about all this."

Callaghan sat down behind his desk. He grinned at Walperton.

"I've got to admit that you're entitled to a lot of explanation, Walperton," he said. "But not now."

He inhaled a mouthful of cigarette smoke.

"I take it," he said, "that you meant what you said earlier this evening, that so far as the police are concerned they're not interested in any members of the Vendayne family from the point of view of *any* sort of proceedings?"

"You can take that as official," said Walperton. "I've seen my chief about it. He agrees that there's no point in a prosecution against anybody as regards the robbery. But there's one point I've got to make."

Callaghan said: "Don't try and make it. I know what it is. Let it alone for the moment."

He got up and stood leaning against the mantelpiece looking at Walperton. He said:

"Gabby Ventura is expecting me to call round and see him with Lancelot Vendayne. Lancelot owes Gabby money. Gabby thinks that now the Vendayne jewellery is in the market legally Lancelot will have some money. Gabby wants to make certain of getting it."

Walperton said: "I thought Lancelot was your client?"

"You've thought a lot of things that have been a bit wide of the mark," said Callaghan cheerfully. "Let's go."

Walperton got up.

"You're a damned funny fellow, Callaghan," he said. "But I believe you know what you're doing."

Callaghan walked towards the door.

"You'd be surprised," he said.

It was just after twelve. Callaghan and Walperton stood at the back door of the Ventura Club. Callaghan put his hand into his pocket and produced his "spider" key. Walperton's eyebrows went up in the darkness.

"So we're going in *that* way," he said. "Illegal entry?"

Callaghan started work on the door lock, fiddling the "spider" until it found the wards of the lock.

"We should worry about that," he said.

He pushed the door open.

They began to walk up the stairs, Callaghan in front. They walked very quietly. At the top, Callaghan pushed open the door and stepped into Gabby's sitting-room.

Ventura was sitting at his desk. He spun round as they entered. He said, with a grin:

"How the devil did you get in, Slim? I was waiting to hear you ring."

Callaghan said: "I had a key. This is Detective-Inspector Walperton, Gabby. He wanted to have a little talk with you. He's rather interested in one or two aspects of the Vendayne case. Mind you . . . there's nothing to worry about. Everything about the burglary and all that is quite in order, but there are one or two little points. . . . So I brought him along. I thought Lancelot could wait until to-morrow."

Ventura got up.

"Surely," he said. "I'm glad to be of any help to anybody, any time."

He walked over to the sideboard and produced whisky, a siphon and glasses.

He mixed three drinks. Callaghan and Walperton sat down on one side of the table. Ventura, his drink in his hand, stood in front of the fireplace.

Walperton put his hat on the table. Callaghan kept his on his knee.

Ventura drank some whisky. He put the glass down on the mantelpiece behind him. He said cheerfully:

"Well . . . what can I tell you, Mr. Walperton?"

He was at ease, expansive.

Callaghan said: "I'll do the talking, Gabby." He paused for a moment, then continued: "Let's get down to brass tacks. The position is a little bit difficult. You see, Mr. Walperton isn't satisfied with just one aspect of the Vendayne case. He's not satisfied about Blaize."

Ventura looked at Callaghan. His eyes were very bright, very intelligent. Walperton, his hands clasped easily on his knee, was watching Callaghan.

Ventura said: "Well . . . what about Blaize?"

Callaghan went on almost casually.

"The devil of it is, Gabby," he said, "something serious has turned up. Just at the time when I thought I'd got everything very nicely cleaned up; just at the time when I believed we could call the Vendayne case closed and all go home and be happy, this thing has to turn up. It's the very devil. . . ."

Ventura said impatiently: "Well . . . what is it?"

Callaghan said smoothly: "Don't be impatient, Gabby. Getting impatient won't get you anywhere."

He took out his cigarette-case and lit a cigarette. He took a lot of time about lighting the cigarette.

Walperton was sitting very still. He was thinking. "My God . . . I wonder . . . ?"

Callaghan said: "Mr. Walperton isn't satisfied with the obvious explanation for Blaize's death. He believes that Blaize was murdered. He doesn't believe that Blaize fell over the edge of the cleft accidentally. He believes that possibly someone *pushed* him over."

Ventura smiled. He felt in his waistcoat pocket and produced a small cigar. He bit the end off and lit it with a gold lighter. He said:

"Well . . . if you ask me, I think he might be right. After all, Esme Vendayne didn't like him very much, did she? When she met him. . . ."

He looked at Walperton and Callaghan. He shrugged his shoulders expressively.

Callaghan said: *"How did you know that Blaize had met Esme Vendayne on that night? How did you know? There's only one person could have told you. And that person was Blaize!"*

Ventura's jaw dropped. His mouth opened. Walperton caught his breath.

Callaghan went on: "Why don't you stop stalling, Gabby? You know damned well you killed Blaize. We've got a cut and dried case."

Ventura laughed. It was a peculiar laugh. He said:

"You think you're damn' clever, don't you, Callaghan? Well . . . perhaps you'll tell me how and when and where I killed Blaize. You must be nutty. You ought to take more water with it or see a doctor or something. . . ."

Callaghan said: "On the night that Esme Vendayne went to meet Blaize I knew all about it. I'd had the telephone wire tapped by Clarissa, Esme's sister. After Esme had gone off to meet Blaize I sent Nikolls over to the Yard Arm. Then I went after Esme.

"When I found her she'd seen Blaize. She had tried to run away from him with the fake bracelet that he had brought to show her, to prove to her that she'd made a fool of him. She was running round the hillside edge of the cleft and he came after her. He fell over the edge. She went on running, and dropped the bracelet. She tried to find it but she couldn't.

"I sent her home. I followed her and saw Nikolls. Nikolls had been over to the Yard Arm. He saw the man Wallers who'd bought the place from Blaize. He was told by Wallers that Blaize had said he would be back to see if any letters for him arrived by the late post. Wallers had told you that too. Nikolls found a car parked near the cottage. It was your car. Your driving licence was in the pocket. *You were waiting somewhere in the neighbourhood for Blaize to come back for his post.*

"After I'd seen Nikolls I sent him back to the cleft to look for the bracelet. I had a talk with Esme and then I went and joined him. I climbed down the cleft and found Blaize's body *a good fifty feet from the place where it ought to have been.*

"Blaize's body ought to have been at the bottom of the incline. And the bracelet ought to have been lying about somewhere on the cliff top, near the far edge of the cleft. It wasn't. It was in Blaize's pocket.

"I got it at once. When Blaize went over the edge of the cleft he fell on to the ledge fifteen feet below. He lay there for a little while and then climbed back to the top. Esme had gone. Blaize searched until he found the bracelet and put it in his pocket. Then he went and picked up his car, which he had parked somewhere in the vicinity, and drove back to the Yard Arm Cottage. He went back to collect his post.

"You were waiting for him. You stopped him before he arrived at the cottage. I imagine that Blaize was rather interested to meet you. You probably first of all offered him money to keep his mouth shut about the jewellery being fake, but Blaize wasn't having any. He was going to tell the world the truth just to get back on Esme and ruin her once and for all.

"That didn't suit your book. Did it, Gabby? You wanted to keep the Vendayne jewellery, and if once Blaize publicly stated that the stuff he'd stolen was fake then the game was up so far as you were concerned. The Major would have to tell the truth about his deal with you and you'd have to hand over the jewellery.

"Blaize played into your hands. He told you about the row he'd had with Esme. He told you how he'd fallen over the cleft edge and climbed back again. So it was easy, wasn't it, Gabby? You hit Blaize over the head and knocked him out. You drove back with him in his own car to the nearest point to the cleft. You carried him down there and you threw him over—unfortunately you threw him over in the wrong place. Also, unfortunately for you, he had said nothing to you about the bracelet. You didn't know that he had it in his pocket.

"And you've just given yourself away absolutely and entirely by telling us that Blaize had had a row with Esme, that he had met her, when the only person who could have told you that was Blaize himself.

"It's too bad for you, Gabby," said Callaghan. "You were in a hell of a hurry to return the real Vendayne jewellery to me because you wanted to save your own skin. You knew that I would do everything I could to keep the Vendaynes out of this. You thought that Wallers was the only person who'd seen you in Devonshire and that he would never connect you with Blaize's death—why should he? Once the jewellery was returned to me you'd be out of the case. No one would worry about you. Well . . . how am I doing, Gabby?"

Ventura said: "Very nice . . . very nice indeed . . . Callaghan. There's only one point you've missed. Let me show you something. . . ."

He walked over to the roll-top desk and pulled the top up. He spun round suddenly. Walperton saw the automatic in his hand and stiffened.

Ventura said: "All right. Well, I've still got a chance. Maybe with all this black-out I can still make a break. But I'm going to fix you first, Mister bloody Callaghan. I'm going to . . ."

"Like hell you are," said Callaghan.

He fired through the hat on his knee.

Ventura looked surprised. The automatic pistol slipped from his fingers. He sagged at the knees, flopped on to the floor.

Walperton said: "Nice work, Callaghan . . . phew . . . I didn't like that a bit. This boy's nasty."

He went to the telephone.

Callaghan kneeled down beside Ventura. Gabby was bleeding from the mouth.

Callaghan said: "Well . . . it's better this way, Gabby. Better than a six-foot drop."

Ventura said hoarsely: "You bastard . . . you . . ."

His head turned over as he died.

Walperton was saying: "Whitehall 1212? O.K. This is Walperton. Get me an ambulance round to the back of the Ventura Club. Yes . . . all right . . . make it snappy."

He hung up

Callaghan said: "Well, Walperton, I promised you the Vendayne case on a plate. You've got it and I hope you like it."

Walperton grinned.

"By God, you're a marvel."

He sat down and produced a packet of cigarettes. He handed one to Callaghan. He said, still grinning:

"Gringall told me the motto of Callaghan Investigations—'We get there somehow and who the hell cares how' . . ."

He began to laugh.

"You're telling *me,*" he said.

Effie Thompson looked quickly at Callaghan when he came into the office. He was wearing a blue suit with a faint chalk-stripe, a pale blue silk shirt and collar and a navy blue tie. His dark brown shoes shone as the sun caught them.

She said: "Good-morning, Mr. Callaghan. I've seen the papers this morning. It seems that you're quite a hero."

"Thank you, Effie," said Callaghan. "So long as I'm not like the hero in that book you were reading. . . ."

He went into his office.

Through the open doorway Effie Thompson could see the day porter struggling along the passage with a Callaghan suitcase in each hand. She sighed heavily.

Callaghan came out of his office. He said:

"Effie, I'm going to Devonshire. I shall probably be away for two or three weeks. I'll keep in touch. Nikolls will be back here to-morrow. He can take over."

"Very good, Mr. Callaghan," said Effie.

Callaghan went on: "You might get through at once to Miss Audrey Vendayne at Margraud. Tell her I'm on my way and that I'm not telephoning personally so as to save time. Tell her I hope to arrive about three o'clock this afternoon."

He put on his hat, walked towards the door. He was almost outside when she said:

"Mr. Callaghan . . . when I said you were a hero I certainly did *not* mean that you were like the hero in the book I was reading—the one who left the girl in the aeroplane while he went off to seek aid. . . ."

Callaghan grinned.

"I'm glad about that," he said.

She went on: "I've a message for you. Miss Audrey Vendayne telephoned through at nine o'clock this morning. She gave me definite instructions that you were not to be disturbed. She asked me to tell you that she received the telegram you phoned through to Kingsbridge last night. I was also to tell you that she and her family are eternally grateful to you and she expects to be able to thank you personally shortly. The rest of her message was a little cryptic, Mr. Callaghan. She said that when she did see you she hoped to be able to continue with a conversation which she once had with you in a summer-house somewhere."

She shut her notebook with a snap.

"Thank you, Effie," said Callaghan. "The message isn't at all cryptic. You'd better get through to Miss Vendayne and tell her I'm coming right away."

Effie Thompson looked at Callaghan primly.

"I hope it keeps *very* fine for you, Mr. Callaghan," she said.

THE END

# DECAD

# Black Sabbath

## in the 1970s

Chris Sutton

sonicbondpublishing.com

Sonicbond Publishing Limited
www.sonicbondpublishing.co.uk
Email: info@sonicbondpublishing.co.uk

First Published in the United Kingdom 2022
First Published in the United States 2022

British Library Cataloguing in Publication Data:
A Catalogue record for this book is available from the British Library

ISBN 978-1-78952-171-9

Typeset in ITC Garamond & ITC Avant Garde
Printed and bound in England

Graphic design and typesetting: Full Moon Media

# DECADES

# Black Sabbath

## in the 1970s

Chris Sutton

sonicbondpublishing.com

Dedicated to Tara, Richard and Nuala Sutton,
Henry Wan and Sam Pillay


## Thanks to ...

Special thanks to Russ Brown, Chris Heard and Mike Butcher
for their massive support and interest

# DECADES | Black Sabbath in the 1970s

## Contents

# Introduction

Black Sabbath were undoubtedly one of the biggest rock bands to come out of Britain in the late '60s/early '70s, but, despite their success, they never received the same acclaim and respect from the music press as their peers. It didn't seem to bother them so much in the early years, but by the time of *Sabbath Bloody Sabbath* onwards, it became a growing issue. The diversity and quality of that record, from the songs to the sleeve design and the copious instrumentation credits, all showed a band hungry for, and deserving of, respect. It never came and the band's path descended after the last hurrah of *Sabotage*. During the period of the last two albums, Ozzy claimed that they were trying to emulate other bands, and no longer doing what they did best.

When Sabbath were at their best they were as good as any of their peers. Musically they did in fact move on to new ground, in at least a small way, from album to album, but there are certain tropes that are generally true in their work:-

• The riff-driven songs dominate the albums and generally consist of an intro, three verses (with no chorus), a middle eight where they go off on a tangent, and an outro.
• For added diversity, there will usually be at least one track that has a different sound-scape to the riff-driven tracks. These rarely make the setlists live.
• Tony will usually get in a whimsical guitar piece, sometimes as a separate track and sometimes as an intro, somewhere on the album.

These tropes served them well through their first six albums but none of them really work quite as well on their last two albums, if they are used at all.

## Source notes

In 2016 Sheffield Auction Gallery announced it would be selling a collection of Black Sabbath memorabilia that had been rescued in the '80s from a London Docklands building due for demolition. The items were owned at one time by the Osbourne family, and it was no surprise when they were removed from sale, apparently purchased by Ozzy. Fortunately, the Gallery listed some items in the pre-sale blurb and they provide fascinating insights into the early years. They are referenced in the text as SAG-2016.

## Interviews

In the absence of new interviews with Black Sabbath, I used quotes from older sources. Few are from the 1970s because interviews with the band then are rarely insightful. Tony Iommi is quoted at times from his autobiography *Iron Man* and Ozzy Osbourne from his, *I Am Ozzy*.

Those who did contribute their thoughts for this book are: Robin Black, Mike Butcher, Ernie Cefalu, John Garbutt, Richard Digby Smith, Colin Elgie, Richard Jones, Mike Lewis, Andy Pearce, Alan Perry and Rick Wakeman. Jones's thoughts first appeared in the *Rock Around The Hills* project in Malvern.

# Back To Earth

All four of the band were born and raised in Birmingham. Anthony Frank Iommi was born 19 February 1948, the son of Anthony Iommi and Maria Sylvia (nee Baciocchi, and always known as Sylvia). William Thomas Ward was born 5 May 1948, the son of William Ward and Beatrice (nee Lane). John Michael Osbourne was born 3 December 1948, the son of John Osbourne and Lilian (nee Unitt). Terence Michael Joseph Butler was born 17 July 1949, the son of James Butler and Mary (nee Fennell). Osbourne is always known as Ozzy and Butler as Geezer, so for consistency, this book will refer to Iommi and Ward by their forenames as well. Incidentally, Butler became known as Geezer during his primary school days when he used to call all males a 'geezer' (meaning a man). Eventually, friends started calling him Geezer and the name stuck!

The work backgrounds of their parents give an indication of the working class industrial demographic that the band members grew up in. The 1939 Register reveals that William Ward was a Corporation Ashman (Dustman) John Osbourne was a Tool-room Planing and Shaping Machinist, while his wife Lilian was an Automatic Feeding Machinist. James Butler was a Steel Tube Bundler. The one that doesn't quite fit is Frank Iommi, who was an ice-cream vendor.

Circa 1958, Tony's family moved to 67 Park Lane in Aston, where his mother ran a general stores, which later became something of an operational base for Earth/Black Sabbath. By day Tony was an apprentice sheet metal worker; by night, he gigged with local bands getting a reputation as a fine guitarist. His first electric guitar of note was a Watkins, which he played through a small tubed Watkins amplifier. The accident at work in 1965, which saw Tony lose the tips of two fingers, was something he was still trying to find a workable solution for when he left The Rockin' Chevrolets and joined The Rest in 1966/67. The drummer in The Rest was Bill, whose home address in the early years was at 15 Witton Lodge Road in the Erdington district.

The ambitious Tony left The Rest to join Mythology, who had a strong reputation in Cumbria, where they gigged a lot. Two months after joining Mythology, Tony got Bill in as their drummer. Mythology's progress was halted by a drug bust at their flat in Compton House, Carlisle, in 1968 which led to heavy fines. News of the bust was picked up by the Birmingham Evening Mail, whose midday edition of 8 July 1968 carried the story on their front page. Mythology split under the ensuing pressure, leaving Tony and Bill with no option but to return to Birmingham, where they set about starting a new band. A new band and a new name meant that the drug bust stigma could be avoided.

Better news in the meantime was that Tony had solved the problem of how to fret the guitar strings with two missing fingertips. He discovered that melting down a Fairy Liquid washing-up bottle to make prosthetic substitutes did the trick. Some leather glued on the tips stopped his fingers from slipping on the strings. A further far-reaching improvement would come by the time of the third Black Sabbath album.

Ozzy's home address is always stated as 14 Lodge Road in Aston, but his earliest years were spent elsewhere. He was born in Marston Green Maternity Hospital in Coleshill, while at the time, his parents were living at 5 Swains Grove in Kingstanding, Birmingham. They must have moved fairly soon to Aston because Ozzy never mentions living anywhere else other than Lodge Road.

In adulthood, he worked at Lucas's factory as a car horn tuner, and then in a slaughterhouse for eighteen months. On leaving there, he resorted to burglary as a means to get by, but it was a short-lived solution. He broke into a shop behind his home and got caught trying to pass the goods on (valued at £25, said his charge sheet). Unable to pay the £40 fine and unable to persuade his father to pay it, he was sentenced to 90 days in Birmingham's Winson Green Prison. He was inside for six weeks before being released on account of good behaviour. That good behaviour didn't last on the outside, where there was nearly a second spell in prison (claims Joel McIver in *The Complete History Of Black Sabbath*) after Ozzy got into a drunken fight at a local pub and punched a policeman in the face. This time the fine was paid and more jail time averted.

Taking stock in winter 1966, Ozzy's first thought was to join the army, which seemed to him to be the only option left, but they turned him down. What was left was music. He loved music, especially his beloved Beatles, and that pulled him through, especially the idea of being a singer. Why couldn't he be a singer?

To help him pursue a career in music, his dad bought him a £250 PA (amplifier and two speakers) from George Clay Music on Broad Street, Birmingham. Local band The Music Machine took him on as their singer, partly attracted by that astute PA purchase. Struggling to get gigs, they changed their name to The Approach, but found they were still faltering. A restless Ozzy then placed his legendary advert at Ringway Music in the

Bull Ring, Birmingham City Centre – 'Ozzy Zig needs gig, got own PA'. The first response came from Geezer, who called to see Ozzy and offered him the job singing with his band Rare Breed.

Geezer was still at this time a rhythm guitarist, living with his parents at 88 Victoria Road in Aston. His possible first gig with Ozzy was at the Central Birmingham Fire Station Christmas party, playing to what Ozzy claims was two firemen, a bucket and a ladder! Rare Breed split in 1968. Geezer recalled to Rick Nicholson (for *Bassplayer* magazine in 2013) that, 'Ozzy and I wanted to do music full time, but the other guys in the band didn't'. The duo kept in touch while looking for another band, and Ozzy placed his advert again at Ringway Music. This time it was Tony and Bill who came calling. Tony was surprised to find it was the John Osbourne who he had had little time for at school, but despite reservations, decided to take a chance on him. Ozzy suggested Geezer for the band as well. 'I still had my Fender Telecaster', Geezer told Nicholson, 'but Tony said, 'I don't want to play with a rhythm guitarist — you'll have to switch to bass.' So Geezer switched to bass in what was a six-piece band, the foursome being accompanied by two other local musicians – Alan Clarke on saxophone and Jimmy Phillips (who had played with Ozzy before) on slide guitar.

At Ozzy's suggestion, they named themselves The Polka Tulk Blues Band, either after a brand of talcum powder used by Ozzy's mum, or after a local business. It was possibly a combination of the two – Polka talcum powder and P.R.H. Tulk building contractors in Birmingham. Also joining the entourage, at Geezer and Ozzy's suggestion, came former Rare Breed roadie/road manager Geoff 'Luke' Lucas.

The basement of Geezer's parents' house provided an ideal rehearsal space. It was free to use and did the job until the band found somewhere more suitable. Once they got round to playing live, it quickly became apparent that things were not working out. After their third gig, it was decided that Jimmy Phillips and Alan Clarke were surplus to requirements. The sax wasn't working in the mix and Tony's playing left little room for slide guitar. The classic four-piece line-up was now in place, and wisely they ditched the hopeless name for something better. This time it was Bill's suggestion, originally as the Earth Blues Band, but quickly and wisely abbreviated to just Earth on 1 September 1968. Even with these changes, things were still not quite right. Tony recalled in *Iron Man* that 'This band was not nearly as good as Mythology, but I said give it time and it will be alright. I could see that there was some potential.'

Geezer, meanwhile, was still adapting to the bass, telling Nicholson that:

I had never played bass before, so I started really listening to what Jack Bruce was doing. I couldn't afford a bass, so I'd tune my Telecaster down. Eventually, I bought a Top Twenty bass and played it through a Selmer amplifier. I borrowed a friend's Höfner 'Beatle' bass on the way to one of our gigs, which was the first time I had ever played bass on stage.

Geezer added that the reason he decided against using a pick to play with was because: 'I saw Jack Bruce (of Cream) play with his fingers, and I said *that*'s the way you play bass. After we got the first gigs out of the way, I swapped my Telecaster for my first Fender Precision bass'.

The early years proved difficult financially. Ozzy recalls in *I Am Ozzy* that the band struggled to get by and were always broke. Had it not been for Tony's mum supporting them with bits and pieces from her shop, as well as petrol money from time to time, he feels they couldn't have kept going. One prudent purchase the band made was a decommissioned police van to take them and their gear to gigs.

All four of Earth were regular attendees at the Henry's Blues House nights, held in the upstairs room of the Crown pub on Station Street in Birmingham City Centre. One night Ozzy and Tony asked the club manager, Jim Simpson, if they could play a support gig there. Simpson got the band to audition for him, liked their potential, and offered them a slot supporting Ten Years After on 16 September. The band went down well and Simpson offered to take on their management via his Big Bear management stable. He booked them in as the opening act at his second Henry's Blues House nights, which he started on 30 September at the Station Hotel in Brownhills. As well as playing at Henry's, Simpson sent them on a UK tour, called Big Bear Follies, with four other bands he managed.

On 24 November, the band played their fateful support to Jethro Tull at Mothers Club in Erdington, Birmingham. Tull were playing their final dates with guitarist Mick Abrahams, and Tull's Ian Anderson saw enough in Tony to offer him an audition. With the full support of his band-mates Tony went to the auditions, where his flair and mix of jazz and blues influences got him the job. However, it proved to be not what he wanted. His stay with Tull lasted a week (from Sunday 1 December to Friday 6 December), which he spent going through ideas and rehearsing arrangements for their forthcoming album, *Stand Up*. Interestingly Tony says that he contributed a couple of the riffs that were later used for the track 'Nothing Is Easy'. Ian Anderson felt that 'musical differences' were part of the reason for Tony leaving, telling *Ultimate Classic Rock* in 2021 that if Tony had stayed:

It would have radically changed the way Jethro Tull's music had gone. It would have changed the way I wrote songs – the batch of songs that became our second album, Stand Up, in 1969. I ran through a couple of things with Tony and it seems it was not his cup of tea, the shape of those songs that I was working on.

Another issue that would have cropped up sooner or later was Anderson's dominance of Tull's songwriting. Steve Howe (later of Yes) turned down the gig for that reason, and Tony could well have had the same misgivings. Tony left at the end of the week but returned to appear with Tull on The Rolling Stones *Rock And Roll Circus* show on Monday 9 December (rehearsals) and then the full recording on Wednesday 11 December. It was a helpful gesture to make that final commitment, but the truth is that they could have got anyone to do it because only Anderson performed live. The other three, Tony, Glenn Cornick and Clive Bunker, mimed to the backing track of 'Song For Jeffrey', featuring Tony's predecessor.

While things hadn't worked out for him with Tull, it gave Tony an insight into how a professional band worked, and he brought back a more disciplined approach to implement with Earth. Rehearsals were scheduled for the Burlington Suite in Newtown Community Centre at Six Ways, Aston, starting at nine in the morning. To ensure that everyone got there on time, Tony made sure to pick Ozzy and Bill up, Geezer being trusted to walk the short distance from his house.

# 1969: Find out I'm the chosen one

The year started well with Earth's most prestigious gig to date, a support slot to Colosseum at London's legendary Marquee Club. What the audience thought seems lost in the mists of time, but Marquee manager John Gee was unimpressed with their volume and allegedly scruffy appearance. He banned them from ever appearing there again but later relented after intervention by mutual friends Alvin Lee and Ric Lee of Ten Years After.

Earth gigged anywhere they could, but their two strongholds in the UK were Birmingham and Cumbria. The latter still had high regard for Mythology, and Earth – with two former members in Tony and Bill – picked up the audiences who had loved them. In February, Jim Simpson got them some gigs in Denmark, at the Pop Klub in Brondby and the Gladsaxe Teen Club and Revolution in Copenhagen. These were their first European dates and meant the band could see progress under Simpson's guidance. They were back in Europe again in April, this time for a residency at the legendary Star Club in Hamburg, where The Beatles had honed their act. It proved similarly useful for Earth, who spent a week there playing several sets a night. That Beatles connection was in Ozzy's mind when he wrote a postcard (SAG-2016) home to his parents:

> We arrived here on time for once. The nightlife here is really great, it never stops. There are thousands of strip clubs all over the place. I have met a rather nice German girl, her name is Sylvia. We are going down rather well at the Star Club. Incidentally, it is the same club that The Beatles first made D BIG TIME.

In the meantime, the band were busy putting together new material and the first two songs to emerge were 'Wicked World' and 'Black Sabbath'. The ABC cinema, across the road from their rehearsal studio, was showing the film version of Dennis Wheatley's novel *The Devil Rides Out*, and inspired by this, the band set about writing 'scary music', as Ozzy put it. The still-unnamed 'Black Sabbath' was tried out live the same day they came up with it, because they knew they had something special. The Pokey Hole Blues Club moved around to different venues, but on that night (possibly 11 July 1969) it was in an upstairs room at the Robin Hood Pub in Lichfield, Staffordshire. Geezer told *Metal Hammer* in August 2020 that, 'The whole pub went mental. That's when we realised we were onto something good'. That extreme crowd reaction sealed the band's future direction.

After turning up for a gig in Manchester on 3 August, where the management found they had booked the 'wrong' Earth, the band decided a name change was due, something that suited their new direction.

Geezer had the strongest interest in the occult, and it was he who came up with the name. They were travelling on a cross channel ferry on 9 August, heading for a residency at the Star Club (beginning on 10 August). 'Black Sabbath', suggested Geezer, who had got the name from a 1963 horror film starring Boris Karloff. Another source could have been the début album by American band Coven, which included a song called 'Black Sabbath'. The name worked well with the current vogue for colourful names – Pink Floyd, Deep Purple, King Crimson – and it sounded right to all four of the band, so Black Sabbath it was.

On their final night in Hamburg, Earth played a version of John Lennon's recent hit 'Give Peace A Chance'. The following week's bands, The Tremors and Junior's Eyes, joined them on stage for a rousing performance. Junior's Eyes' name obviously struck a chord with Sabbath as it popped up again in 1978.

When they got back to Birmingham, they told Simpson of the name change. Although unimpressed, he went along with it and told them he would arrange studio time to record demos to attract record company interest. The two recorded were a Simpson choice, 'The Rebel', and a band choice, 'Song For Jim'. 'The Rebel' was written by Norman Haines, who played with Simpson in his band Locomotive. Both were recorded on 22 August at Trident Studios in London, with Gus Dudgeon overseeing the production, although it was his assistant, Rodger Bain, who was credited as the actual producer. The idea to release a single of 'The Rebel' and 'Song For Jim' was subsequently shelved, probably to the band's relief.

The first announcement of the new name came on 26 August at Banklands Youth Club in Workington, Ozzy telling the audience that they were now to be known as Black Sabbath. Their first gig officially as Black Sabbath, however, was booked by Severn Promotions at Malvern Winter Gardens four days later on 30 August, although they were booked originally under the name Earth. To further signify the name change Luke Lucas used black tape to make up the new name on Bill's bass drum. In *Iron Man* Tony says that he regards Malvern as Black Sabbath's first gig.

Shortly after that, on 4 September, the band played their most important gig to date, at Wolverhampton's Lafayette Club. The DJ John Peel had a residency at the club and was well known for his influential radio show *Top Gear*. Sabbath played there for expenses only, the goal being to impress Peel enough to get a slot on his show. Peel was impressed and agreed to put them on later in the year. In sharp contrast to that success, they had the ignominy five days later in Hanley, Stoke-On-Trent of being jeered and booed by a gang of skinheads who wanted music more to their taste. A disgusted Sabbath obliged them with a version of the soul standard 'Knock On Wood' before leaving the stage.

Better fortune came at their Birmingham haunt, Henry's Blues House. There to see them was Tony Hall, who ran an independent promotions company called Tony Hall Enterprises. Earth signed a deal with them, with Hall agreeing to put up the money to record an album. The band also signed a publishing contract with Essex Music, run by David Platz. This contract, it later transpired, signed away their publishing rights in perpetuity.

On 19 September, Sabbath returned to Trident Studios again, this time with Rodger Bain producing, and recorded demos of 'Black Sabbath', 'Behind The Wall Of Sleep' and 'Wicked World'. Sadly none of these three demos have seen the light of day officially or unofficially.

On 7 October, Sabbath entered Ladbrooke Sound Studios (upstairs from Vincent Ladbrooke's piano dealers) at 32 Bristol Street in Birmingham to record more demos, This time, they recorded the first version of 'The Wizard' and another Norman Haines song, 'When I Came Down'.

While the deal to record the album was being finalised, Simpson arranged for the band to return to the studio yet again to record two songs for a single, to be released by Fontana. So on 10 November, it was back to Trident Studios with Rodger Bain again producing (and Barry Sheffield engineering). The A-side, 'Evil Woman', had been a hit in America for Crow and you can understand why this was thought to be a good choice. Sabbath hated it, but they were fast coming to the end of the period in their career when they would have to take on board suggestions of songs to cover. The success of their forthcoming album put paid to all of that. The B-side was a band original called 'Wicked World'.

The following day, 11 November, the band recorded a set for John Peel's Top Gear radio show, featuring 'Behind The Wall Of Sleep', 'N.I.B.', 'Black Sabbath' and 'Devil's Island'. The last track was re-titled for the album as 'Sleeping Village'. Any musical differences between the four tracks and the album versions are unknown as there appear to be no recordings in circulation.

On 17 November, the band entered Regent Sounds Studio in London to record the remaining tracks needed to make up their first album. Rodger Bain was back again to produce, having got on well with the band at the Trident sessions for the single. The album session costs were paid for, as agreed, by Tony Hall. Having a completed, mixed and produced album would give the band significant leverage to get a record deal.

Following their day in the studio, Sabbath left for Europe - back to Denmark, and then to Zurich, where they played at The Hirschen Club. Ozzy, in a postcard he sent home to his parents (SAG-2016) felt Zurich had not quite been ready for Black Sabbath:

Arrived here safely but it is not a very nice place. I don't think the people like long hair. We start playing tomorrow afternoon at 3 o'clock until 7 o'clock on the night. But apart from that, I am still in one peace (sic). By the way, don't forget we are on the radio next Saturday.

The band made the most of their time in Zurich, using the gigs to try out ideas. Tony recalled in *Iron Man* that:

The place was as dead as a doornail. Our audience was a couple of hookers and some lunatic who used to come in and do handstands in front of the stage while his change fell out of his pocket. But it gave us the opportunity to jam and write because we had so long to play. That's where 'War Pigs' came from.

The Saturday appearance Ozzy alluded to was the John Peel session. The first three tracks were broadcast on Saturday 29 November and then all four were broadcast on 21 March 1970. The radio sessions got a great response and did a lot to spread the word back home about Black Sabbath. Meanwhile, in Switzerland things seemed to be going from bad to worse. Another card from Ozzy mentions that the band had found local restaurants were unimpressed with their hair and appearance, 'Everywhere we went they refused to serve us', he complained.

A few days after his earlier cards Ozzy sent another from Switzerland (SAG-2016), handily dated 27-11-69, this time from St. Gallen. Things, it seemed, were looking up:

We are now in a very quaint place and it is thick with snow. There's some really great sights. I can say that I have never seen anything (like) it before in my life. It really is great. I have met a great chick here, name is Marianne. She is a really nice person (she is coming to England in January). By the way, Jim phoned us the other day and he said he has got us a TV show in Germany next month, so we don't know if we will be coming home in three weeks. We might be over here for Xmas but I don't really know yet... PS. I hope you herd (sic) us on the radio.

By the time it arrived, his parents would have heard that all-important *Top Gear* radio session, but that German TV show would take till May 1970 before coming to fruition.

In December, the band signed, via Tony Hall, with the Phillips record label (owned by Phonogram), who initially placed them on their subsidiary label Fontana. Each of the band got an advance payment of £105, more money than they had ever seen in their lives. Soon after signing with Phillips, Ozzy and Tony went on a night out together at the Rum Runner Club on Broad Street in Birmingham. It was there that Ozzy saw Thelma Riley (nee Rees, born in Birmingham in 1948) for the first time. Thelma was a divorcee with a son named Elliott from her first marriage and worked at the club on the cloakroom counter. She and Ozzy hit it off immediately.

If 1969 had been a great year, with the band expanding their following and getting to record a radio session, single and album, then 1970 was set to be bigger beyond their wildest dreams.

## *The 1969 Demo Recordings*: Trident Studios, London – 22 August

An acetate of 'The Rebel' and 'Song For Jim' allegedly has the band name down as Black Sabbath, which would make it the first 'official' mention on record of them using the name. 'The Rebel' is easy to find online, while 'Song For Jim' has yet to appear in the demo form.

### 'The Rebel' (Norman Haines)

Haines played with Simpson in his band Locomotive and added piano and organ to this song.

Simpson's plan was to add Haines to the line-up and that might have worked if the band had stuck to songs like this. The band, though, were having none of it. Although Haines was used again, the band didn't want anyone else in the line-up.

There must have been some problems with getting the song down as it took 19 takes, a luxury they wouldn't even have when they recorded their first album! 'The Rebel' has emerged on the internet, and what we get is a charmingly naïve song. Haines's piano part opens it with a cheery pub sing-along vibe. Strangely he doesn't appear again other than to add backing vocals throughout. The band put in a credible performance all round and there are hints of what is to come with some searing lead guitar lines and inventive percussion.

## 'Song For Jim'
It was presumably written by the band and was dedicated to their manager, who would have enjoyed the jazz tones in the song. The demo has not yet got out, although one live recording exists, recorded at Rugman's Youth Club in Dumfries. If the demo is broadly similar, then it is an instrumental with a strong Jethro Tull vibe. Tony only plays flute on the live version, but you can hear how easily he could have worked in a jazz guitar part. The live version tops and tails an extended drum solo. What we get of the actual song is tantalisingly promising.

## *The 1969 Demo Recordings*: Ladbrooke Sound Studios, Birmingham – 7 October
Simpson has said that the band recorded other songs along with the two which appeared on an acetate. One he has mentioned is a cover version of a song by Jimmy Rushing called 'Evenin'. The acetate of 'When I Came Down'/'The Wizard', was marked up as produced by Zella Promotions. This recording of 'The Wizard' has not surfaced, but the owner (Joe D'Agostino) was reported on *Blabbermouth* in 2003 as saying that, 'You can hardly hear the guitar on 'The Wizard', the vocals and harmonica come through well, though.'

### 'When I Came Down' (Haines)
It has surfaced on the internet, albeit in an edited form. It's apparent from the little there is that their sound had by now got closer to that of their debut album. Tony gets in a decent riff, which Geezer closely follows, and Ozzy is on commanding form. Bill is a little indistinct, but you can make out his busy percussion work. It sounds like the band are enjoying playing it.

# 1970: We sail through endless skies

On 9 January 'Evil Woman' was released on Fontana as the band's first single, a great step forward for Sabbath, but sadly it didn't trouble the charts. While the single failed to register, fortune smiled when Vertigo Records had an album drop out of the release schedule. With a gap to fill they remembered they had an album waiting, completely mixed and mastered – *Black Sabbath*. Vertigo were owned by Phillips as an imprint for their more non-mainstream signings. The album seemed a good fit for the label, so Phillips decided to take another stab on Sabbath, with nothing to lose as the outlay was so low. Aptly the album was released on Friday 13 February in Britain.

It was a massive shock to the label, as well as Sabbath when the album reached the heady heights of number eight in the charts. A truly astonishing success for a largely unknown band, but a testament to the responses they were getting live. As the band went back out to gig on the back of the album, it was apparent that the success came at a price, and that price was the fees charged for the gigs. Sabbath had plenty of bookings made before the album was released and these were priced accordingly for a band without a record. Now they were a top ten act; the fees, which were fixed, were a bargain in hindsight for promoters. Jim Simpson, who had negotiated those fees, took the view that you had to be fair to promoters who had booked in advance prior to Sabbath's success. That was, he said, the right thing to do, but it caused friction with a band working hard and eager to see commensurate financial rewards.

Sabbath played on the first day of the week-long Atomic Sunrise Festival at The Roundhouse in London on 9 March. Four days later, they returned to the Marquee Club for a triumphant show. Then it was back to Birmingham where they embarked on two residencies – playing at Henry's Blues House for several weeks on a Tuesday night and four Wednesday night gigs at the legendary Mothers Club in Erdington.

The punishing schedule saw them back over to Germany for just one date, playing the Pop and Blues Festival in Hamburg on 30 March. Ozzy managed to connect with a girl named Erika Beskow at this show and gave her his address, hoping she would get in touch again.

The success of the album prompted Vertigo to try their luck re-releasing the 'Evil Woman' single. It didn't do any better this time in spite of the non-album (in the UK) B-side of 'Wicked World'.

The press quickly latched on to the occult connotations in the band's name, songs and album cover. The continual linking of Sabbath to black magic prompted an exasperated Tony to speak to *New Musical Express (NME)* on 4 April. 'Everybody thinks we're a black magic group, but we just picked the name because we like it', he complained. Aware that their material might suggest there was a little more to it, he added that 'I agree that some of the numbers on the LP are about supernatural things, but that's as far as it goes'.

Determined to draw a line under any black magic links, they turned down an invitation to play at a Walpurgis celebration on 30 April at Stonehenge. This, too, came at a price, with the band being told they were now 'cursed' as a consequence. At the time, the band played this down publicly, but since then have admitted they took it rather more seriously. They took to wearing aluminium crosses, which were fashioned for them by Jack Osbourne, Ozzy's father.

Better news, on the musical front, was a live gig, recorded for John Peel's Sunday Show on 26 April, which got a discrete release years later.

Possibly to Ozzy's immense surprise, Erika Bescow from Hamburg got in touch saying she was in London at the Brompton House Hotel, along with her friend Brigitte! It's a sweet postcard and clear that they are hoping to see the band again.

By May, the band were still honouring gig contracts at places that were small and/or off the usual gig circuit. Some had been pre-booked before the album breakthrough, but to their annoyance, they found themselves playing new bookings at such venues. One place was Jephson Gardens Pavilion on 17 May in Leamington Spa. The gig was controversial for being booked on a Sunday (the Sabbath day, ironically) and local legend has it that rats ran over the stage, disturbed by the volume! Geezer, for one, didn't notice as he had overdosed on acid. He told *Classic Rock*'s Paul Elliott in 2016 that: 'As we were driving into the park, I thought the flowers were trying to get into the car to strangle me. It ended up with me playing on stage thinking I was on a boat and the buildings were waves, and I thought my hand was a big spider running up and down my guitar.'

On 24 May, the band played on the third day of the Hollywood Music Festival in Newcastle-Under-Lyme. Also appearing at the festival were Free and The Grateful Dead, but the band who went down best were apparently Mungo Jerry, who released their smash hit single 'In the Summertime' shortly after. Sabbath would gleefully recall this when making *Sabotage* in 1975.

The following day, the band jetted off to Germany, where they recorded 'Black Sabbath' and 'Blue Suede Shoes' live at Radio Bremen studios in Bremen. Soon afterwards, these tracks were aired on the German music show *The Beat Club*.

Sabbath made a return to Malvern Winter Gardens on 30 May. Their fortunes had changed dramatically in the year since they were last there. Richard Jones and John Garbutt (on behalf of Lansdowe Methodist Youth Club) were among many promoters who found the booking fee had become an issue. Jones recalled:

> When they were booked, they were relatively unknown. The fee was fifty pounds, which for a Methodist youth club was quite a substantial sum back then. But they came back and said, 'We're not coming for fifty pounds, £250 please.' So that was a bit of a dilemma as to whether we just cancelled the whole thing or whether we took a risk and went with £250, which is what we decided in the end.

Helping the promoters balance the books was by increasing the audience capacity. Jones and Garbutt were there when Sabbath arrived and there when they left too. 'We helped them load in and out', says Garbutt, who has happy memories of the gig:

> Officially the capacity was 1200, but we had some in over that. It wasn't like these days when that kind of thing is very tight. Some nights we'd sold out of tickets but still sold admittance on the door, For Sabbath, the Winter Gardens were full, so everyone came out a winner. They went down a storm and got a real connection with the crowd. They played a lot of songs off their forthcoming album. Ozzy had had a bit too much of something and at the end of the night, they had to carry him out. They were a down to earth bunch and easy to get on with off-stage. We didn't book them again because most bands we got were on the way up. They would get too expensive for us, and they were looking for bigger venues too.

In early June, Sabbath went to Rockfield Studios in Wales for a week to work on writing and rehearsing material for their next album. Back on the road again before going into the studio, the band ran into problems in Weston-Super-Mare on 13 June. A now routinely predictable argument over their fee led to Geezer going in search of a phone box to call Simpson. Once inside the box, Geezer realised he was surrounded by skinheads who were in the mood to give him a good kicking. Geezer got hit but managed to get away and back to the venue, where Tony and Ozzy, in particular, were in the mood to hit back if needed. A fight broke out, which saw the skinheads take a battering, as to some extent did the band who managed to escape in their car.

The same day as the fight, they had appeared in the *NME,* with Tony complaining about the lack of good reviews for their debut. He told Roy Carr that, 'We want to excite our audiences, but only with our music, which is mainly based on simple riffs and a heavy beat. Some people have put us down for this, but we like what we play, and it seems that everyone else does, so that's it'. The lack of respect and praise from the press was something that would gnaw at Tony each time they returned to the studio. The increasing sophistication, diversity and eventual dilution of the Sabbath sound are testimony to his attempts to get the acclaim he felt they were due.

Sabbath returned to Regent's Sound Studio on 16 June to record what they still thought would be titled *War Pigs.* Tony recorded the album still nursing a black eye from the fight in Weston, but at least they got a song out of the fracas.

Late June saw the band back in Europe for five dates in West Germany and an additional one in Belgium on the drive back to the ferry. The German dates included West Berlin on 26 June, which was a problematic gig to get to, with intense scrutiny from the border guards. The gig proved to be a huge success, which was hardly surprising given the strong attendance by American forces personnel based in the city.

A first American tour had been planned for July. The first album had sold well there and *Paranoid* was set to do even better, but the tour was cancelled. The reasons are cloudy; one view is that their alleged occult connections were too raw for American promoters nervous about any links being made to the Charles Manson killings. More down to earth, and credible, is that it had not been possible to get contracts sorted in time for the tour.

'Paranoid' was released on 17 July as a single. The band promoted it with their first appearance on *Top Of The Pops* on 22 August. The single's success led to Sabbath attracting younger fans, whose exposure to the band was based on their *Top Of The Pops* appearance with the catchy hit single. For a time, the gigs attracted an element who were there entirely because of that song. It annoyed the group intensely, who took to opening their shows with it to get it out of the way.

A successful provincial band looking to get ahead always attracted the interest of big management companies, and Sabbath, disgruntled at their income, were wide open to offers. The band were courted by Don Arden (who had managed The Move and Small Faces), but when it came to signing, they chose to think things over. Arden's assistant, Wilf Pine, who had driven them to the meeting with Arden, decided to step in. He formed his own management company, World Wide Artists (WWA), with Patrick Meehan, senior and junior, who were also connected to Arden.

Jim Simpson was sacked as the band's manager on 4 September. He received a letter from lawyers acting on behalf of WWA telling him not to contact the band and that he had been dismissed. Sabbath had signed with WWA, with Pine and Meehan claiming they could indemnify the band against any legal action by Simpson (they couldn't) and promising to take the band to the next level of success. Sabbath consequently would leave Birmingham to a base in London. It's unlikely Simpson could have taken Sabbath to worldwide success, so in spite of the manner of his dismissal it was the correct one to part ways with him.

Sabbath set out on a brief tour of the UK in support of *Paranoid* on 11 September, starting off in Swansea. This was the last tour where their fees were still set at the agreed rates Simpson had got for them. With *Paranoid* looking set to be even bigger than their début, this was cause for grumbling and reaffirmed to the band why they had changed management.

*Paranoid* was released in the UK on 18 September, while the band were busy preparing for a European tour, with Bill taking delivery of a second bass drum to add to his kit. The first date was on 20 September at L' Olympia in Paris. During these dates, the band recorded a second performance for *Top Of The Pops*, which was transmitted on 24 September. Appearing on *Top Of The Pops* was a major barometer of success in Britain. To your family, it meant you were a success, as a telegram from Ozzy's sister Jean made clear. 'Thrilled with the group's success, John, shall be watching you all on *Top Of The Pops* tonight' (SAG-2016).

During the Dutch dates, the band recorded 'Paranoid' for *TopPop*, a new music show in Holland along the lines of *Beat Club*. The footage survives and is the excellent, commonly seen black and white film. The band also appeared on *Beat Club* again in September, performing 'Iron Man' and 'Paranoid'.

They finished their European dates on 10 October. The band were in Brussels at the time and eager to learn the latest chart position for

*Paranoid*, which had leapt to number three the previous week. They rang home from a phone box at the railway station to learn that *Paranoid* had officially reached number one on the UK album charts, an amazing achievement given the uncompromising nature of the music. It stayed there for one week before being replaced by the more soothing tones of Simon & Garfunkel's *Bridge Over Troubled Water*, which *Paranoid* itself had replaced at number one!

Sabbath returned for more UK dates, commencing at the Marquee Club in London on 13 October.

There were still nights when things didn't work out well. The Newcastle Mayfair gig on 23 October being a perfect storm of things going wrong. A long journey from Birmingham to find that amongst the audience were youngsters there just for 'the single', and a large number of others who were drunk. Difficulties getting their correct fee paid by the promoter didn't help matters, but things took a turn for the worse when the stage was invaded. Sabbath ended up playing with a number of the audience on stage for the whole set. Their only option to stop things from getting out of hand was to grit their teeth, play and get through it. By the end of the gig, they were left with some smashed equipment, stolen drumsticks and the long drive back home.

The following night's appearance at Newark was cancelled because, they said, of Tony being injured in the Newcastle chaos. As it was Tony who drove them half of the way back, it feels more likely they just needed a day's break. Fortunately, Bournemouth on 25 October was better, and that was followed the night after with a prestigious support slot to Emerson, Lake & Palmer at the Royal Festival Hall in London. It proved to be a rapturous night; The *NME* reported that the stewards had been unable to keep the audience in their seats and that the encore saw Sabbath return for 'Fairies Wear Boots' amidst 'unprecedented scenes' in the auditorium.

One consequence of their astounding success was the loss of John Peel's support. It niggled at Tony, who complained to the *NME* in October 1970 that, 'He helped us a lot, but he seems to be against us now. I don't know what we've done. He keeps having digs at us'.

Sabbath finally flew out in October for their first American tour, arriving in New York for press and sightseeing on 28 October. Tony says they played their first American gig for the Warner Bros management, promoters and media on 1 November, the first of two nights, at a club called Ungano's Ritz on Staten Island. The first night didn't start well.

When they plugged in the equipment, all the fuses blew because Sabbath had taken their own PA, which was wired differently!

*Paranoid* had been delayed until January 1971 for its American release due to the continued steady sales there of *Black Sabbath*. It left Sabbath to some extent effectively promoting an album they had moved past, although the *Paranoid* single was released to coincide with the tour.

At The Fillmore East in New York on 10 November, they supported The Faces and went down so well that the audience didn't want The Faces to come on! The band played five nights from 11 – 15 November at the Whiskey A Go Go in Los Angeles. Each night they did two sets, and the headline act were Alice Cooper, who had just broken through with their huge hit single 'I'm Eighteen'. By the last few dates of the tour, Sabbath were headlining, two rapturous nights at the Easttown Theater in Detroit being the pick of the bunch,

Sabbath returned to Europe for further dates, finishing their 1970 touring schedule back in Paris, again at L' Olympia, on 19 December. While the band were playing those December dates, their thoughts were already on recording their third album, and sessions were due to start in early 1971.

## Black Sabbath *(Vertigo/Warners)*

Personnel:
Ozzy Osbourne: vocals, harmonica on 'The Wizard'
Tony Iommi: guitars, flute on 'Evil Woman'
Geezer Butler: bass
Bill Ward: drums
and:
Rodger Bain: jaw harp on 'Sleeping Village'
Produced at Trident Studios, London, 10 November 1969 and Regent Sounds Studio, London, 17 and 18 November 1969 by Rodger Bain
UK release date: 13 February 1970. USA release date: 1 June 1970.
Highest chart places: UK: 8, USA: 23
Running time: 38:12
All songs by Black Sabbath, except where noted.

Rob Halford says in the liner notes of the 2016 reissue that the album was the 'blueprint for metal'. It's actually one of a few records that did that – the first two Led Zeppelin albums, 'Deep Purple In Rock' and Uriah Heep's début, for example, all fall into this category. Where Sabbath have the edge is in Tony's use of a Laney amplifier on the record. The Birmingham based company had a close relationship with Sabbath. The owner, Lyndon Laney, used to play with the Band Of Joy (with Robert Plant and John Bonham) and they knew each from the local gig circuit. The Laney amplifier gave Tony the crunching sound that came to typify metal, his opening riff to 'N.I.B.' being the obvious example. Another key facet of the sound was Geezer's bass part mirroring Tony's guitar. Geezer told Rob 'Blasko' Nicholson, for *Bassplayer* in 2013, that, 'Practically always I'm following Tony's riffs, unless it's something that I've written, like 'N.I.B' or 'Behind the Wall of Sleep'.

Tuning-wise, the band play in standard E on the record, which was the norm, but they soon started making changes on-stage where they dropped to Eb, a subtle difference at first.

Overseeing the production was Rodger Bain, with Tom Allom engineering the bulk of the tracks. Allom found the Sabbath sound a completely new experience, telling *Metal Hammer* in 2020 that, 'I hadn't heard anything like it before. I was completely mystified by it. But Rodger Bain completely understood what they were doing'.

Stories about the speed of recording the album have smoke-screened the facts. As well as Allom, the album also credits Barry Sheffield as an engineer. Given that he co-owned and worked at Trident, it affirms that 'Evil Woman' and 'Wicked World' were from the recording sessions on 10 November. That left Sabbath only needing to work on six more tracks. All six were recorded on 17 November (in allegedly just 12 hours from 10 am to 10 pm) with the band playing live together in a studio about the size of a small living room. Tony and Geezer stood in one area, separated from Bill by a partition, with Ozzy in a booth in the corner.

Essentially this was a live recording with the only overdubs being Tony's lead guitar solos and the jaw harp. While the band initially felt some luxury in having so much time to go through their live set, the pressure started to tell later on. There was little time for retakes and 'Warning' was a long track, so it had to be got right quickly. When Bain professed the first take to be 'the one', it took some effort from Tony to get him to allow them to try it again.

The second day at Regents (18 November) was reserved for edits and final mixes by Rodger Bain and Tom Allom – the band having driven off to Europe for gigs. A final addition before the album was mastered was the rainstorm that opens 'Black Sabbath'. The first time the band heard it was at Jim Simpson's house when he played them the album!

The end result was an astonishingly successful album which hit the UK top ten pretty much by word of mouth sales from the fan base they had built up with their heavy gigging schedule. There was no media campaign or gushing reviews to push the record.

For the cover design, Vertigo gave the brief to Keith Macmillan (aka Marcus Keef). Macmillan listened to the album to get ideas, telling *Rolling Stone* in 2020 that, 'Obviously, the lyrics go in the back of your mind, but it was more just the overall vibe that struck me. Sorry to talk like an old hippie, but you have to go with a kind of overall feel for the art.'

For the location, Macmillan decided on a place he knew well – Mapledurham Watermill in Oxfordshire. It is now a spruced-up tourist destination, but back in 1969, it was, 'A run-down and quite spooky place. The undergrowth was quite thick and quite tangled, and it just had a kind of eerie feel to it', recalled Macmillan. Inspired by the location, he created an unsettling scene. The mill in the background looks spooky enough, but the foreground figure in black demands your attention, looking directly at you. A cloaked, strangely serene looking, lady stroking a cat. It's an eerie, unnerving image.

The model was Louisa Livingstone and she was faced with an early start as Macmillan wanted the shoot to be done early in the day to get more atmosphere. She told *Rolling Stone* in 2020 that:

I had to get up at about four o'clock in the morning, or something as ridiculously early as that. It was absolutely freezing. I remember Keith rushing around with dry ice, throwing that into the pond nearby, and that didn't seem to be working very well, so he was using a smoke machine.

The rear of the cover is a continuation of the scene and your eyes are drawn to the sinister crow sat on the stump. This was Yorick, stuffed and thus able to cope with the cold, and usually found in Macmillan's studio.

It's worth noting that the sleeve doesn't carry any pictures of the band, which is odd considering that Sabbath had no involvement in the packaging. Vertigo/Warners had promo shots they could have used, but they didn't, and no photo session with the band was planned for the cover. Continuing the foreboding feel of the front cover, the black inside cover featured an upside-down cross with a poem inside it. It was written by Macmillan's assistant, Roger Brown, who uncannily captures the vibe of the cover and the title track perfectly. It's way over the top and ladles on doom by the word. The speed in getting the package out meant some typos got through in the poem, but it doesn't distract from the overall effect. The cross and the poem upset the band (although they liked the front cover). They pointed out that their lyrics concerning Satanism were a warning to the curious. Those typo problems extended to the credits, too, as both Rodger Bain and Ozzy Osbourne's names are spelt wrong!

When they returned from Switzerland, they went to Jim Simpson's house, and he showed them the cover and played the album. 'It had a gatefold sleeve and started with all this thunder and lightning – it just blew my mind!', Ozzy recalled to *Uncut* in July 2014.

Black Sabbath is a stunning début, especially given the rushed circumstances. Three tracks clearly show the way forward for the band. 'Black Sabbath' remained a big number for them, 'N.I.B.' was the first of the big riff songs, and the first part of 'Sleeping Village' showed their intentions to keep light and shade an integral part of their records.

## 'Black Sabbath'

The second original song the band came up with started off with Geezer playing the riff from Gustav Holst's 'Mars'. Tony joined in and played around with it, the familiar ominous guitar riff soon emerging. The story behind the lyrics came from Geezer, who told Amit Sharma (*Kerrang,* 2019) what had happened:

I'd moved out of my mum's house and got a flat with my girlfriend. I was really interested in black magic and painted my entire room black, with inverted crucifixes all over the place. It was back when we were called Polka Tulk and Ozzy had brought me this black magic book in Latin or something. We had a few joints and he left me with it. Later that night, I put the book in the airing cupboard outside on the landing, and I went to bed. I woke up scared to death; there was this big black shape looking in at me. Whether it was a dream or not, who knows, but it was very real at the time. I got really frightened by it all. I immediately got up and associated it with the book Ozzy had given me, but the book had vanished! I told Ozzy the next day and that's how he came up with the lyrics for 'Black Sabbath'.

You wonder if the 'big black shape' at the foot of the bed and the vanishing book had more than a little to do with Ozzy, but the story is a good one either way. The lyrics are surprisingly a joint effort from Ozzy and Bill (not Geezer) and the song serves as a warning, as Bill told

*Melody Maker* in July 1970, 'Against black magic and all its implications'. Tony felt (in his book) that Ozzy got the melody first and came up with the opening lines based on Geezer's story. The title itself is never mentioned in the lyrics.

Early live versions inserted a short refrain of the outro riff and an extra verse after verse two ('Big black shape with eyes of fire'). The extra verse runs: 'Child cries out for its mother, mother's screaming in the fire. Satan points at me again, opens the door to push me in.'

Tony recorded a guitar intro piece for the song, the same one he always used for 'Black Sabbath' live circa 1970/71. Two takes were done of what the tape boxes note as 'Guitar Link Remake', but neither were used. That he recorded this intro piece suggests that it was not originally planned to open the album with 'Black Sabbath'. Opening the album with it meant they had to get to the riff quicker to grab attention, although they still made an 'atmospheric' tweak.

'Guitar Link Remake' was not included in the deluxe edition of the album, but you can hear the best quality version of it on the Brussels 1970 recording that comes with the *Paranoid* super deluxe set. There is also a nod to it in the studio version of 'Wicked World'.

The church bell was already part of the track before Sabbath finished recording, so only the thunderstorm was added at the mixing stage to enhance the mood. To open the first track on their début album with these effects was a piece of genius on the part of Rodger Bain. The storm is shattered by Tony's simple scary riff. There's nothing to it – just three ominous notes – but it's one of the greatest intro riffs of all time. Bill's tom-toms weave around the tolling bell, adding to the sense of unease with the unpredictable nature of what he plays.

The next clever part of the arrangement comes at 1:07 when they drop the levels, Tony's guitar backing off from the heavy riff to a softer take on it. The atmosphere is charged and changing – ready for Ozzy's entrance on the first verse. He intones the words giving them full weight, while Bill's tom-toms patter around him. Geezer's bass is a little indistinct at times on the verses, you kind of feel him more than hear him with the odd notes popping through.

They turn the apocalypse back on full between the first and second verse and then again after the second verse. There is a held note at 4:30, the signal for what would normally be the middle eight/ bridge. In this case, it's effectively a long second half/ outro sequence because they never return to the main riff/ verse format. At 4:35, the galloping guitar riff comes in, giving that sense of something, or someone, in pursuit. Ozzy sings the final verse over this riff, ending with an agonised, 'No, no, please no'.

As soon as Ozzy finishes, Tony's terrific overdubbed solo kicks in over the driving backing track. The nice final touch is the Bolero ending and full stop.

'Black Sabbath' is one of their all-time classic songs that, in effect, kick-started their career. If there is a fault with it, it's that the lyrics could have done with more work. Geezer told Amit Sharma that, in particular, he didn't care for the line, 'Satan's coming round the bend'. The lack of the middle eight is an interesting touch and certainly allows the song to grow and pick up pace.

On a trivia note, Sabbath road manager/sound engineer Richard 'Spock' Wall recorded a tribute song to Black Sabbath entitled 'The Mill'. It's on Youtube and is as much a homage to the 'Black Sabbath' song as it is to the band. It's well worth a listen; all instruments and vocals are by Spock.

## 'The Wizard'

At an Earth gig, Ozzy and Geezer were amused by the antics of a guy outside the venue. Looking to them like an elf, they soon changed it to a wizard. The lyrics describe the man they saw that night. The track was actually originally entitled, far more fancifully, as 'Sign Of The Sorcerer'. A surviving lyric sheet by Geezer (SAG-2016) has this as the title, along with some different lyrics. The original title is crossed out on it, replaced by the snappier new one. Geezer told Neil Jeffries, for the 2005 *Q Classic – Ozzy,* that, '*Lord Of The Rings* was *the* hippy book. That was where the lyrics to 'The Wizard' came from'.

It opens with a repeated harmonica phrase by Ozzy that suggests a strange character going about his business. The band crash in at the twenty-second mark with Ozzy still on harmonica but now wailing away at the same melody they are playing. Tony hits the jagged riff at 1:06, but it's Bill you can't ignore. He is superb; his drum fills throughout are pure joy, giving the track movement and life. Ozzy is on great form with the vocals, with no trace yet of the slight hoarseness that crept in as the album session went on.

An interesting feature is that the chorus, 'Never talking, he just keeps walking,' is not overly different to the structure and melody of the verses. The instrumental break is also the same with Ozzy's harmonica taking the lead spotlight.

It's a good track which is raised higher by the powerful performances, particularly of Ozzy and Bill.

On a final trivia note that old lyric sheet for 'The Wizard' has a running order for the album at the top which includes 'Fairies Wear Boots' on side two, some months before it was known to have started to appear via live jams and rehearsals.

## 'Behind The Wall Of Sleep'

Geezer's inspiration for the lyrics came from the H.P. Lovecraft story *Beyond the Wall of Sleep,* which is about an otherworld entity who communicates through a dying inmate in a mental hospital. After the inmate dies, a large bright star is seen in the sky. This is referenced directly in the last verse: 'Now from darkness, there springs light, Wall of sleep is cool and bright, Wall of sleep is lying broken, Sun shines in, you have awoken'.

Tony's tumbling intro riff waltzes in on the intro, over which he dubs some lead fills. Under that is typically melodic bass from Geezer. It's a clever intro that leads into one of the recurring motifs in the Sabbath catalogue, with the song taking a different turn just 32 seconds in. Everything drops away except for Bill's bass drum, snare and hi-hat work. Throughout the song, Bill keeps the jazz tones going.

Tony/Geezer and Ozzy handle the verses as a call and response, with Ozzy's voice given added effect with what sounds like a compressed double-tracked vocal. Amusingly they even swap Ozzy's vocal from speaker to speaker, so he is singing the call and response line by line with himself!

At 1:29, we get a change of mood with the middle eight. Geezer's bass is more prominent on this part of the track, which is brightened by a lively guitar solo from Tony. There is a clue after this section that the band were still sometimes struggling to find a way to extend a song in a meaningful way because at 2:30, we go straight back into the identical opening part of the track. In comes that tumbling riff again, followed again by Bill's solo drum pattern and then the final verses. You can forgive them this repetition because it's a great piece of work and finishes off, quite rightly, with more of Bill's busy percussion, which gradually fades away.

This has remained a well-received fan favourite that got elevated in stature due to its presence in the live sets in the reunion years. It was easy to adjust it to Ozzy's reduced range and its exuberant qualities always went down well with the crowd.

## 'N.I.B.'

This is the one that showcases the first appearance of the patented Iommi big riff that is a hallmark of so many great Sabbath songs. There is also the riff on 'Black Sabbath', but that's a tad more subtle than this beast.

While the lyrics are about the devil taking human form and falling in love, the title refers to Bill's beard, which at that time was shaped like a pen nib! On the *Black Sabbath Story Volume One* Geezer admitted that: 'I couldn't think of a title for the song, so I just called it Nib, after Bill's beard. To make it more intriguing, I put punctuation marks in there to make it N.I.B. By the time it got to America, they translated it to Nativity In Black.' There have been two compilations since then called Nativity In Black and that interpretation resonated with Ozzy's replacement Ronnie James Dio who would refer to the 'alternative' title onstage. The song came out of a jam, started by Geezer, who came up with the bass riff.

It cross-fades in from 'Behind The Wall Of Sleep' with Geezer's wah-wah bass solo intro, 40 seconds of pure magic, a melodic chaser for the main course. At 0:40, Geezer audibly turns up his volume and a second later, Tony, who is mixed way up front, crashes in with THAT riff that drives this song along. Geezer doubles him for added effect.

At 51 seconds, the sound changes very noticeably – less close and more distant. While Tony and Geezer keep the riff going, in comes Bill and Ozzy, but this sounds like a different take or edit piece that has been patched in.

On the verses, Ozzy sings the riff while Bill keeps things simple, everything is hanging on that monstrous riff. Unusually for Sabbath, there is something approaching a chorus. The 'Your love for me has just got to be real' section comes in after the second verse and has a relaxed reflective melody to it. Bill adds tambourine for effect here and this 'chorus' does the job of cueing things back up for the third verse.

The middle eight follows at 2:52, with the band stretching out from the well-drilled discipline of the verses. Tony gets in an exciting solo over the now pacier backing track, and double tracks a second solo guitar which you can hear coming in from the 3:11 mark, adding sweetening to the sound. The middle eight segues stunningly and abruptly back into the main riff at 3:37 and that surely must be an edit there!

Ozzy repeats verse two again for the fourth verse, so lyrically, things are running on empty, but they get away with it because it's just so glorious hearing that melody and riff. The chorus that isn't a chorus returns after it, and this time it acts as the tonal change before the final verse, which, with the lyrical well still dry, is a repeat of verse three.

The final rush to the end comes at 5:01 and is an extended repeat of the middle eight section. Tony's solo is longer because of this and he gets off some of those fluttering/trilling runs that will become one of his trademarks. A big crescendo ending finishes off one of the best songs in their back catalogue that always remained a huge crowd pleaser live.

## 'Evil Woman (Don't Play Your Games With Me)' (Larry Wiegand/Dick Wiegand/David Wagner)

The Trident session logs reveal that there were four completed instrumental backing tracks of 'Evil Woman' (out of thirteen takes) comprising of guitar, bass and drums. Take thirteen was deemed the best take and master, over which Ozzy's vocals, Tony's flute and a four-piece brass section were overdubbed. The flute and brass are mixed in a low to inaudible state on the released take.

Also added was a second drum track. There is no audible second drum track in the final mix, so this new track, if it was used in the mix, must have replaced Bill's original. The horns are mixed down extremely low but are very audible on the different mix that emerged as a bonus track for the deluxe edition of *Black Sabbath*.

Side two in the UK opened with this song, originally recorded by Crow. It was suggested by Jim Simpson, who felt they needed a commercial track for the single. The band put in a creditable performance, especially Geezer, whose supple bass lines dominate the melody. His bass is by far the best thing about this track. Ozzy's admonishing tone suits the lyrics well, but Tony and Bill have little chance to impress. Tony's solo reveals his low interest, a half-hearted affair that comes in at 1:39.

All in all, this song is not as bad as it has been made out to be, it's not a great Sabbath track, but it's an enjoyable one. What it does do, though, is to considerably skew the dynamics of side two, making for a much lighter tone that sits at odds with the rest of side two. The American version, with 'Wicked World' in its place instead, makes more sense.

The unsuccessful UK/Europe single of the song had 'Wicked World' as the B-side.

## 'Sleeping Village'

The title was changed to 'Sleeping Village' from 'Devil's Island' quite late in the day. On the outtakes, Ozzy can be heard still calling the track 'Devil's Island' while they were in the studio making the album.

In its own way, this track is as spooky as 'Black Sabbath', if not more so. There is a similar sense of the supernatural – something coming, something about to happen – that the seemingly peaceful lyrics do nothing to dispel. The live version (reviewed later) adds a second verse that firmly shatters any illusions of serenity.

It opens with Tony playing one of his acoustic pieces that will crop up repeatedly on future albums. He gently picks an attractive insistent melody, backed only by soft bass work from Geezer, Bill's delicate cymbal strokes and the odd but effective jaw harp plucked by Rodger Bain. It sets a bucolic cosy scene interrupted by Ozzy, who here sings just one verse – 'Red sun rising in the sky, Sleeping village, cockerels cry. Soft breeze blowing in the trees, Peace of mind, feel at ease.' He gets real resonance in his phrasing, although his voice sounds hoarse – probably due to the song being recorded at the end of the sessions. The lyrics affirm the tranquillity in the music, but the peace is soon shattered after just 53 seconds of this surreal lullaby.

It's the most startling edit in the Sabbath catalogue because the incoming second part of this track, in tone and feel, is more akin to 'Warning', which it segues into. The opening riff of part two is functional rather than spectacular, although Bill keeps it lively with some castanets work. After that riff comes a slow section where it sounds like the track is going to stumble to a stop. But on it lurches with an intensity and purpose they will later revisit in a similar style on 'Iron Man'. It barely lasts any time at all before they hurtle off into a fast shuffling jazz section, with Bill and Geezer setting the pace. Tony overdubs two lead parts, which are almost a prequel to what is coming next. The effect is rather busy and It doesn't work as well as it could. With more time, they could have come up with something inventive here. This is illustrated by the ending. Bill plays a turnaround at 3:05 and they return to the lurching slow riff sequence. This time it finishes with sustain and vibrato from Tony, which segues into 'Warning'.

'Sleeping Village' is a tale of two halves, and the first half is excellent, setting a compelling mood, while the second half seems less thought out and somewhat aimless.

### 'Warning' (Aynsley Dunbar/Alex Dmochowski/Victor Hickling/John Moorshead)

This cover version was a song they had jammed on during live sets for a year or so. The original (just 3:24 long) was by The Aynsley Dunbar Retaliation, which Sabbath used as a basis for their extended jam.

The second and final take is the one you hear on the album. It ran for fifteen minutes and Rodger Bain edited it down to the 10:28 we have on the record, the cuts coming out of Tony's solo section.

Effectively 'Warning' is split into two sections. The first half being the song as such, and the second half an extended jam for Tony to solo over.

The inclusion of 'Warning', and its extension, does suggest a lack of decent material for the album. Certainly, there is nothing else that has been rumoured to have been a possible for inclusion. Though if they wanted to, they could have included both 'Evil Woman' AND 'Wicked World' by editing 'Warning' down further.

The song part of the track is done well and is equally as good, if not better, than the original. The band attack it with verve and Geezer and Bill get a groove going that the original lacks.

The second part of the track, the jam, comes in at about 3:20 with Bill's rolling drums. Although both he and Geezer play on this section, it is really Tony's showcase, and he is given full opportunity to shine. After a minute of heavy riffing, there is a swinging section at 4:30 with great bass from Geezer as Tony wails away, until at 5:14, the mood changes again with a shuffle rhythm. Geezer and Bill fade away by 6:15, leaving Tony alone. He solos away, but in all honesty, it isn't as interesting as it could be, although he does his best to inject colour and variation. There is a particularly bright sequence at 7:50 when he wanders off into one of his 'medieval' toned passages. The roots of 'Embryo' are here to be heard at this point.

What sounds like an edit breaks the medieval spell at 8:09 as Tony hammers out yet another riff with plenty of tremolo and vibrato. That, too is replaced at 9:03 by a full band attack that glides back into the reprise of the 'Warning' song with Ozzy popping up again at the end for his closing words.

The bravery of 'Warning' comes with that extended instrumental second part. Among their peers and those who came after, I cannot think of any other band that allowed their guitarist to play such a long solo piece on a studio album. That they pretty much pull it off speaks volumes for their confidence.

## 'Wicked World'

It was recorded at the same Trident sessions as 'Evil Woman'. America got this song opening side two, although CD reissues have gone with the trend of putting 'Evil Woman' in the running order and featuring 'Wicked

World' almost as a bonus track. If you sequence 'Wicked World' at the top of side two, it makes for a more cohesive sequence of songs.

It was the first track recorded and the only track from the sessions that Tony recorded with his white Fender Stratocaster. The pick-up broke after they finished getting the track down and Tony swapped to his backup guitar, the Gibson SG. From then on, it became his guitar of choice.

The song came out of Tony's guitar riff, which he had been playing around with for a while. All of the lyrics are by Ozzy, with Geezer at that time yet to establish main responsibility for the job.

It opens with Bill's sizzling hi-hat cymbals, which follow a similar pattern to that played by 'Legs' Larry Smith on the Bonzo Dog Doo-Dah Band's 'The Intro And The Outro'. He is swiftly joined by Tony and Geezer for the opening riff sequence. A nice drum full from Bill at 0:34 changes the pace slightly as Tony and Geezer again join in with unison riffs.

At 0:53, we head into the song proper as Tony pulls out a great riff. There's a definite blues feel here as the others join him. Ozzy finally comes in at 1:05, using his lowest register. It simmers along nicely, but the production is thinner than on the other album tracks. Ozzy's voice sounds harsher too.

At 2:06, the band change the tempo. Over Geezer's rumbling bass, Tony plays some beautiful arpeggios, which he uniquely doubles with the same part played backwards. It's the most creative idea they explored at these sessions and it's terrific. It sounds much like the intro Tony used for live versions of 'Black Sabbath'. Here it cues up Tony's guitar at 2:56, where he pulls off a piercing blues-based solo that is in a similar vein to his style on 'Warning'.

Ozzy returns for the outro, which (at 3:51) briefly features the melody that will later be used prior to the main riff on 'Fairies Wear Boots'. It all ends with howling sustained notes from Tony over Bill's distant drum rumbles.

The song's jazz overtones are particularly noticeable in Bill's work. It was the oldest song recorded for the sessions and the one that marks the transition from Earth to Black Sabbath. However, it sounds unfinished, save that impeccable guitar interlude, and the production lets it down. It's a hard track to get overly excited about; good but not great.

For many years it had a semi-mythical status as a great lost track in the UK because it was impossible to find unless you picked up a copy of the 'Evil Woman' single, where it was the B-side. That changed when it was featured on the compilation *We Sold Our Soul For Rock 'N' Roll* and it became apparent that the song didn't exactly live up to the myth. Oddly it was later released as a single in some parts of the world backed with 'Iron Man'!

Even odder was that Black Sabbath continued to believe in the song for much of their '70s touring years, where it was over extended on-stage.

## USA edition notes

The album came out on Warner Bros. in America with changes to the running order. 'Evil Woman' was dropped in favour of its B-side 'Wicked World', and three extra tracks seemed to be added. The reason for these additions was because the band needed a minimum of ten songs per album to satisfy the requirements of their American publishing agreement. Every album up till *Sabbath Bloody Sabbath* had extra tracks 'created' to meet that requirement. Of course, more songs on an album also meant more publishing income.

Tape box details in the UK confirm these extra track names were not used during recording sessions. The additions to *Black Sabbath*, confirmed by the notation in the Hal Leonard Publishing songbook for the album are:-

'Wasp', which is actually the first 32 seconds of 'Behind The Wall Of Sleep', up until it drops down to Bill's drums.

'Bassically', which is Geezer's solo bass intro to 'N.I.B.'

'A Bit Of Finger', which is the 53-second acoustic intro to 'Sleeping Village'. This makes sense given the fact it is listed before that song, but some sources erroneously claim it to be Tony's guitar solo in 'Warning'.

## Black Sabbath – deluxe edition

A two-disc deluxe edition was released in 2009, which included alternative session takes on disc two as follows:

### 'Black Sabbath' (outtake)

A fascinating take featuring an intro of studio patter making it clear how 'live' this album was recorded. The tolling bell is present, too, acting almost as a count-in or cue. It re-appears one extra time over the released version, coming in quietly at 2:55. The bell is mixed much higher on this version and dominates the intro. The decision for the final released version to add the rainstorm and mix the bell down, so it sounded more distant was a good one.

Bill's drums already have the echo on them, so that was obviously not added later. Ozzy's vocal isn't as assured; at times, he audibly struggles and sounds hoarse.

### 'Black Sabbath' (instrumental)

A straight run-through of the track, complete with the bell mixed too loud on the intro. The real benefit of this take is that you can clearly hear the inventive percussion parts played by Bill.

### 'The Wizard' (outtake)

Not much different to the released take, but hardly surprising given the time constraints and how well-rehearsed the band were! This is a complete run-through of take one. The only real difference is Ozzy's harmonica which is less crisp than the released version. You can hear him breathing after the long notes on the intro. Musically it sounds the same; even Bill's solitary cowbell strike is in place!

### 'Behind The Wall Of Sleep' (outtake)

Ozzy is less authoritative than on the album version. As it's his voice that gives the song a lot of the power, it's no wonder that this take was shelved. Musically it's pretty much the same as the released take.

### 'N.I.B.' (outtake)

This is close to the released take. The sleeve labels this as an instrumental version, but Ozzy is present and correct. The only major difference seems to be that the tambourine part that comes in at 4:04 on the released take is missing here.

### 'Evil Woman' (alternative version)

The most interesting out-take from the album. The brass section is placed higher in the mix and Tony adds a somewhat superfluous flute part. It makes for a different sound, but they wisely decided that these touches took away from the bouncing melody and catchy vocals.

### 'Sleeping Village' (outtake)

There are differences on the intro section. Bill's cymbals and Geezer's bass are higher in the mix, giving it more of a band feel. There is not as much reverb used on Ozzy's voice, so the effect is that he sounds right up close in the room with you. A very worthwhile version.

### 'Warning' (part one)

As per the released version, they segue straight in from 'Sleeping Village' (but this time from the outtake above). This establishes that these two tracks were performed in one run-through for the album and that they weren't segued by Rodger Bain later. This must be take one, as Tony says in *Iron Man* that there were only two takes and they only did take two because he wasn't happy with take one, specifically his solo. Therefore it's understandable that it's the bulk of his solo that is cut in this edit of take one.

## *Paranoid (Vertigo/ Warners)*

Personnel:
Ozzy Osbourne: vocals
Tony Iommi: guitars, flute on 'Planet Caravan'
Geezer Butler: bass
Bill Ward: drums, congas on 'Planet Caravan'
and:
Tom Allom: piano on 'Planet Caravan'
Rodger Bain: tone generator on 'Planet Caravan'
Produced at Regent Sounds Studio, London, 16 to 17 June 1970 and Island Studios, London, 18 to 21 June 1970 by Rodger Bain
UK release date: 18 September 1970, USA release date: 1 January 1971.
Highest chart places: UK: 1, USA: 12
Running time: 41:51
All songs by Black Sabbath

The pressure was on to maintain and even improve, on the high standard they had set themselves with their debut. Second albums are a notorious stumbling block for artists, but songs such as 'War Pigs', 'Rat Salad' and 'Fairies Wear Boots' had been in development for months. 'War Pigs' even pre-dates the first album. Sabbath used their live sets to try out the arrangements, which gave them a good foundation for the album.

In spite of the intense live schedule, the band found time to book into Rockfield Studios at Monmouth in Wales for a week to finesse the new songs. Accompanying them to Rockfield was Rodger Bain, back again as producer. Sabbath set up and played through the songs in the newly built Coach House Studios while Bain chipped in with advice.

'We were very loud and Rockfield allowed us the freedom because no one would allow us to play as loud as that – the roof tiles were rattling', Ozzy recalled in the film *Rockfield: The Studio On The Farm.* 'Rockfield will always be a part of me. I can go and live in Beverly Hills, but for some reason, I end up back in Rockfield. It's just magic.'

The intention was to go back into Regent Sounds Studios and Island Studios to record, but Ozzy, for one, was mystified. 'Why don't we record here?', he asked Bain, and he had a point. Bill told the *NME* in October 1970 that 'Iron Man' and 'Electric Funeral' had got as far as being roughly completed takes at Rockfield.

They moved to Regent Sounds on 16 June for two days to get the backing tracks down. After that, they decamped to Island Studios (which was in a converted church on Basing Street) to take advantage of their sixteen track mixing desk (Regents only had four-track) for overdubs and mixes. As with *Black Sabbath,* they stayed with standard E tuning (albeit slightly sharp) for the album.

Keith Macmillan's work for the cover of *Black Sabbath* was superb, so he was an obvious call to do *Paranoid.* His brief was to create a cover for an album called *War Pigs.* Without any music to listen to in advance this time, he was left with the evocative title to give him ideas. A visit to a props shop resulted in a sword, shield and, most importantly, a pig mask to create the war pig.

Macmillan and his assistant Roger Brown went after dark to Black Park by Pinewood Studios. Macmillan told Kory Grow (*Rolling Stone,* February 2020) that: 'We used ultraviolet light and an ultraviolet flash, so everything was fluorescing.' Brown ran from behind the tree many times as Macmillan experimented with the settings. When Macmillan was happy, Brown then did the trickier runs wearing the pig mask, his visibility significantly reduced!

The problems came when Vertigo, alarmed by the proposed title of *War Pigs,* changed the title of the album to *Paranoid,* thus making the cover look completely out of sorts. Macmillan says they used a test shot (without the pig mask) in error, but my guess is they deliberately picked it to further downplay the *War Pigs* links. So the end result is odd. It doesn't work as a cover for anything called *Paranoid,* but it somehow has an impact in spite of itself! Macmillan also took the inside sleeve photograph of the band, a relaxed black and white image in complete contrast to what you might expect from the music.

*Paranoid* saw the band defining and refining their sound. The arrangements are tighter than on *Black Sabbath* and the sound is better for the use of Island Studios. A slight negative is that the album sounds too well drilled and dry at times, lacking a little warmth and life. The songs would have benefited from the live feel of their debut.

Lyrically there is also a change, with Geezer now commenting on social issues. If you wanted to know what was wrong with the world,

Black Sabbath told you and they stood alone among the bands they were starting to be compared to in that respect. It's their most successful album from the '70s, featuring several of their 'big hitters'. The importance of the album in Sabbath world is reflected in the number of deluxe editions and a 'making of' documentary. The reunion live sets, in particular, featured this album heavily.

It remains one of the highest regarded albums in Black Sabbath's catalogue. Rick Wakeman, who later sessioned for Sabbath, enthuses that: '*Paranoid* is an absolute classic and always will be. 'War Pigs' is a stand-out for me as a Sabbath track, but I'd probably select a different track tomorrow!'

## 'War Pigs'

'War Pigs' is one of the all-time great Black Sabbath tracks. It was originally entitled 'Walpurgis' and had been a work in progress for many months. The title came from the annual celebration (known as Walpurgis Night) on 30 April/1 May. The night was a kind of early Halloween, a warning that dark forces may lie in wait in the shadows. Central to this was the memory of Saint Walpurga, an abbess who was born in Devon in 710 A.D. Walpurga was a missionary in France and Germany, working to alleviate diseases and counter the effects of witchcraft.

So the original lyrics were anti-witchcraft, which seems to be lost in translation in most accounts.

Tony says in *Iron Man* that he wasn't aware why Geezer changed the lyrics, but when he was interviewed by *NME* back in March 1970 (before they recorded the album) he said that 'We might change some of the words of the songs so that we don't have any trouble.' The 'trouble' coming from their increasing association with black magic, which seems to have been based on two songs on their first album and the cover.

Getting back to the lyrics for 'Walpurgis'/'War Pigs', they alter a lot over the course of 1970. Even after recording the song as 'War Pigs', Ozzy would still, for some time, throw in lines or verses from the original version. The change in title intrigues because phonetically, it's not such a big stretch from 'Walpurgis' to 'War Pigs'. Lyrically it was now a completely different story, with Geezer railing against the horrors of war, specifically the plight of American soldiers in Vietnam. He then expanded on their experiences in 'Hand Of Doom'.

The air-raid sirens, used to brilliant effect on the intro, immediately conjure up images of WW2 instead of Vietnam. A shift in emphasis that the band might not have been happy about at first. They were added by Rodger Bain in the final mix and it's possible that the band (as with the rainstorm on 'Black Sabbath') never heard them till they got the album! The ominous crunching opening riffs are accompanied by something unexpected from the rhythm section. Bill explained his thinking to *Drum!* In 2012:

> I put the whole thing in waltz time and Geezer went there, and he fitted it perfectly with what Tony was doing. So that's what it is. I think the song would've been a train wreck had I played straight drums to it. I went into waltz time and I made broad strokes and huge cymbal crashes – that's what made the whole thing 'pop'.

Bill's insistent hi-hat work has prompted an Ozzy-led clap-along live ever since they first played it.

Tony, meanwhile, adds nervy guitar fills on the verses, keeping things edgy. Ozzy uses a rising sing-song vocal melody ('generals gathered in their masses') for most of the verses.

Bill plays a turnaround after the second verse and the band break into a secondary riff sequence that leads into the song's first major melodic change. This comes in at 2:07, signalled by a stuttering riff from Tony! Cleverly this new riff pattern forms the backing track for verse three ('Politicians hide themselves away') and verse four ('Time will tell on their power minds'). It's also on verses three and four where Ozzy changes to an accusing tone, pointing the finger at those responsible for the devastation.

The middle eight comes in at 3:30 and the band opt for a melodic alternative to the staccato riffing of the verses. It's built around Tony's wandering solo, one guitar at first but he adds a second harmony part later.

Verse five ('Now in darkness') along with verse six ('Day of judgement'), uses the same backing track pattern as the first two verses. Ozzy also reverts to that sing-song vocal style.  Lyrically it's impressive because we have six different verses to drive the anti-war message home, making almost a small essay!

The outro comes in at 5:44 on the back of yet another riff. This is one of the best outros in the Sabbath catalogue. Tony's fuzz-toned chiming riff descends until another Bill turnaround (at 6:30) surprisingly leads into a grande finale, a final flourish with a dramatic solo from Tony. Two lead parts as usual, but they add thickness more than contrast. The sped up ending is a surprise, including to the band, who had never intended it to be that way. The production team added it during the mixing stages and it's clear the band never liked it because it was not used on the later quad mix, which band roadie Spock Wall helped to oversee.

## 'Paranoid'

This is the song that has transcended the rock fan base to become recognisable by many who 'don't know' the band's music. This last-minute add-on to the album brims with attitude right from the powerfully charged opening riff. The song's relative brevity, and the catchy riff and melody, heighten the impact.

It was the only track that was recorded entirely at Island Studios, and then only because Rodger Bain said they needed one more track for the album. It's worth noting that had they not decided to cut 'Planet Caravan' short, it would have meant there was no need for another track.

It was towards the end of the second day of recording at Island (17 June) that Bain asked them to come up with something else, something short. The fact that Warners (their American company) immediately jumped on 'Paranoid' as a single is suggestive. Had they in fact, asked for something more commercial (and short)? It certainly looked that way from the master tape boxes, on which 'Paranoid' was identified only as 'single'.

While the others went to the pub, Tony stayed behind and came up with the famous riff. On returning, the band got into it right away, despite Geezer's initial reservations that the chugging riff was not dissimilar to Led Zeppelin's 'Communication Breakdown'. Overcoming his reservations, Geezer duly came up with lyrics for 'The Paranoid', the title soon shortened and never mentioned in the song itself. Geezer told Joel McIver (*The Complete History Of Black Sabbath*) that the inspiration came from his own personal experience. 'I suffered with depression on and off over the years. People used to think I was just being miserable, but it was actual depression. Originally, and unknown to me, that was what 'Paranoid' was about, the way I was feeling at the time'.

The recording session has been said by the band to have been a speedy affair. Bill recalled in the Super Deluxe Edition booklet that: 'It was about 1:30 in the afternoon, Tony had the riffs, and by two o'clock we had 'Paranoid' exactly as you hear it on the record.' An earlier take featured Ozzy's guide vocal, but it seems they nailed the track as soon as Geezer had his lyrics done.

The need for speed in recording the song comes over in the urgency of the backing track. Tony's raucous opening riff sets the scene (doubled by Geezer) before he drops down into the chugging second riff, which he plays throughout the rest of the song. He doubles that riff with a second rhythm part, while Geezer follows suit and Bill keeps things tight and simple. It all gives the sound a satisfying mid-tone crunch that hits home hard. Full credit to Ozzy for his vocal, which melodically stays close to the riff, but he gets in enough inflections to keep his vocal sounding lively. Another nice touch are the notes Geezer throws in on the end of the riff when his bass rises up in the mix.

Tony's solo comes in at 1:22 and is a mildly controversial affair because he has professed, in *Iron Man* and on other occasions, that he didn't care for Rodger Bain's decision to put it through a ring modulator. It gives his solo a heavy fuzz tone, and in spite of Tony's concerns, it comes across perfectly for the song and its theme. It is a great economical solo.

Familiarity has dulled the song's impact, but when it catches you unawares it still has that capacity to excite. It remains one of Sabbath's best songs and earned its place as a live set staple, and, for most of its existence, was the obvious encore.

'Paranoid' was released as a single backed with 'The Wizard' and reached the dizzy heights of number 4 in the UK chart and number 61 in America. It has been released countless times as a single since then and has regularly turned up on rock compilation albums.

Finally, on a trivia note, the intro riff had been recorded before in a quite similar version. A song called 'Get Down' by Detroit garage band Half-Life sounds incredibly similar to 'Paranoid' on the intro. They apparently recorded it in July 1969, and it didn't get wide exposure, meaning Sabbath couldn't have heard it. However, the looser feel of the Half-Life track reveals that the intro has some common DNA with the Stones' 'Jumping Jack Flash'.

## 'Planet Caravan'

A hazy dreamy beautiful song that is one of the best tracks they ever recorded. Musically it evokes the journeys of the original caravans – a group of merchants or traders travelling across Persia. Geezer expanded on that concept and lyrically made it a journey through the galaxy from planet to planet with the one you love. Ozzy told the *NME* in September 1970 that, 'It's a smoky-jazz-club number', and those elements are certainly there in the arrangement.

The tone is set from the delicate intro. Tony's haunting guitar melody is matched by a slow undulating bass pattern from Geezer and Bill's closely miked congas, which give the song a relaxed swaying movement. Ozzy sings through a Leslie speaker, which gives his voice an ethereal quality that fits the song's mood. Producer Rodger Bain also contributes to the track. It's him rotating the tone generator, making the flute-like noises that can heard throughout.

Tony's solo comes in at 2:30 and is an absolute joy and a marathon as he keeps going all the way to the end of the song. A touch of echo effect on his guitar and he stretches out on a homage to the jazz guitarists (such as Django Reinhardt) who were a huge influence on his sound. The travelling at the heart of the song's subject matter is reflected in his solo as his fingers wander around the fretboard. It is a masterful piece of work. The solo marks the end of Ozzy's vocals, meaning he appears on less than half of the song, but you don't miss him because this instrumental second half is so enthralling.

While Tony is still soloing, Tom Allom's piano accompaniment joins the backing track at 3:10, some basic notes for added emphasis, which he plays all the way to the slow fade outro.

The earlier alternative lyrics take is a minute and a half longer, featuring even more of the jazz backing track and melody line, while the quad mix is 14 seconds longer.

It was never played live in concert, but they did play it at least once at a sound-check in recent years, but without vocals.

## 'Iron Man'

The subject of the song is a time traveller who, knowing the future of the world, comes back to warn people of the consequences of their actions. On entering Earth's atmosphere, he is caught in a magnetic storm and turned into iron. Unable to speak, save his opening salvo, he is ignored and reviled. The song was inspired by Ted Hughes' book *The Iron Man,* which was published in 1968. Geezer must have read this because there are close parallels with his lyrics.

'Iron Man' has been embraced in popular culture, turning up in several TV shows and over the end credits of the Marvel *Iron Man* film.

Ozzy didn't come up with a vocal melody, so he sings along in perfect synch with Tony and Geezer's riffs. By accident or design, this gives the vocals even more weight. Speaking of 'weight', Bill was never happy with the somewhat muffled drum sound, and he has a point because it always sounded much bigger live. 'It was a 22" Ludwig, quite beaten up,' Bill recalled to *Drum!* In 2012, 'You know, just trying to do its best to emulate something walking menacingly towards you – some kind of a giant.'

Bill's pounding drums open the track, not sounding anywhere near heavy enough to be the foot stomps of the iron man, but it works for an attention-grabbing intro in spite of that. Joining the footsteps comes Tony's painful sounding string bends, adding to the sense of horror, broken by the immortal words, 'I am iron man', intoned by Ozzy with a ring modulator effect. Just 27 seconds in, Tony cracks out the immortal main riff from the song, it sounds big, dumb and sassy all at the same time and it's an absolute monster. Tony thought so, too, telling Greg Prato of *Songfacts* (March 2021) how he came up with the riff:

Bill started playing this boom, boom, boom. He started doing it, and I just went (sings bending string bit before the song's riff) and came up with this thing and thought, that's cool. Bill kept playing it, and I just went to this riff.

Most of the riffs I've done I've come up with on the spot, and that was one of them – it just came up. It went with the drum, what Bill was playing. I just saw this thing in my mind of someone creeping up on you, and it just sounded like the riff. In my head, I could hear it as a monster, so I came up with that riff there and then.

Bill plays a great fill after Tony's first pass at the riff and then he, Geezer and Ozzy add their own dynamics to that riff. Tony breaks it up at 1:14 with a new riff before Bill plays the turnaround at 1:31 back into the main riff, with Ozzy continuing the story.

Tony leads the way as they change tempo at 3:11 for what becomes a frantic middle eight featuring a jazz toned solo that harks back to 'Warning'. Listen out for Geezer, too, as he plays an equally breathless bass run. The middle eight breaks down and they change tempo in a heartbeat back into the main riff.

For the final mix, Bain added a spiralling effect on Ozzy's voice at the end of his last line (4:19), 'Iron man lives again'. As Ozzy bows out, it's the surge to the finish as Tony solos away with two lead guitar parts playing in harmony.

'Iron Man' is one of Sabbath's classic tracks, especially popular in in America, where it was regularly their best-received song in the live set. Its apparent simplicity hides some complex work in the middle eight and outro.

It was released as the follow-up single to 'Paranoid' in America (backed with 'Electric Funeral') and got to number 52.

## 'Electric Funeral'

Geezer's lyrics take us deeper into contemporary issues, looking at the after-effects of a nuclear war. The mood is set from the intro by Tony's psychedelic wah-wah conjuring up a sickening nightmarish feel. The slow, deliberate pace of the rhythm is picked up by Ozzy as he emphasises the words with an equally deliberate diction. It's another example of Ozzy singing the riff, which makes the song simpler, more direct, and works well to get the message across. There's a nice touch from Geezer as his bass rises up in contrast on the last notes of the first part of the guitar riff.

The middle eight change of tempo comes in at 1:49 with Bill's pounding toms. Tony adds a new riff, which he pauses at 2:16 for an 'electric' faster riff, joined in unison by Geezer and Bill. The pace is furious now, with Ozzy almost unintelligible trying to keep up. Geezer's bass is fabulously busy all over this section, which winds down with Ozzy's cry of ''Lectric funeral' – the first 'E' is dropped – which he doubles with his deeper backing vocal.

Bill plays the turnaround at 3:05, which gear changes back into the familiar main riff and backing track to accompany the final verses. The mix drops lower at 4:09, slightly subdued, as the extended outro mirrors the quiet after this particular storm. There's nothing new added to the outro, just the fading tones of that malevolent riff and backing track.

It never made the live set during the *Paranoid* era, and in truth, it's one of the less notable tracks on the album. The riff and the tone of the track are fine, but the middle eight lacks the ingenuity and wow factor of their best work. So not a top drawer track, but a good one.

## 'Hand Of Doom'

Geezer came up with the lyrics after speaking to servicemen at gigs at two U.S. army bases (one in Germany and one in Britain) in 1970. Before returning home, servicemen had a cooling down period and the band were shocked at what they saw. These were battle-scarred young men, with post-traumatic stress issues, having used drugs, including heroin, to cope with the pressure. In the *Classic Albums: Paranoid* documentary, Geezer recalled that: 'There was nothing on the news about this. There was no programs telling you that the U.S. troops in Vietnam, to get through that horrible war, were like fixing up and all this kinda thing. It just stuck in me head and when we got to 'Hand of Doom', that's what I wrote about'.

'It's almost like a day in the park', Bill enthused to *Drum!*, 'It's just real funky, it's really jazz-like to me. I can do a lot of nice hi-hat work, a lot of stick work. I play on the rim, live, like a rimshot. I can put in nice big bass drums.' Bill's work on this track is amongst his best with Black Sabbath.

It's the darkest track on the album, filling a similar role and vibe to 'Black Sabbath' on their debut. Geezer's ominous bass riff opens it, complemented by Bill's busy percussion work. Unusually for Sabbath, Tony holds back here, quietly accompanying Geezer's bass with delicate rhythm playing. The first verse comes in and Ozzy adopts a warning tone for the lyrics. In spite of his delivery, the lyrics have been often misunderstood. He is clearly and obviously warning against using heroin and not extolling the virtues.

Tony enters big style just before verse two, his slabs of guitar doubling Geezer's bass riff pattern, the song really coming to life now. While Tony and Geezer grind out the riffs, it's Bill yet again who catches the ear with his always inventive percussion fills. They drop back down to Geezer's dominant bass riff after verse two, an intelligent move as it gives verse three more space for the lyrics. This is the definitive verse that links directly off to 'War Pigs' – 'First it was the bomb, Vietnam napalm, disillusioning, you push the needle in.'

For the crashing fourth verse, they repeat the trick they worked on verse two of Tony coming in to double Geezer. It sounds for all the world like the song is fading out to a stop on Geezer's bass, but after a pause, there is a sudden rush of sound at 2:05, a change of pace suggestive of the rush from the heroin injection. The boogie style rhythm keeps things chugging through verses five and six.

The middle eight change to a staccato pounding rhythm comes in at 3:27, which lasts through verses seven to eight – 'You're having a good time baby, but that won't last' – concentrating on the short-lived euphoria of the drug.

Tony takes a brief solo at 4:24, understated and neither showy or flashy. After some filling riffs, it's back to Geezer and Bill for the intro section again. 'Now you know the scene, your skin starts turning green', observes Ozzy in verse nine. It all builds to a crescendo on the final verse with Ozzy's final, 'Now you're gonna die!'

Things slowly die down musically, just Geezers bass left, not quite a heartbeat but fading nonetheless. This is one of the most effective uses

Sabbath make of returning to the intro. In this case, it gives the song a horrific circular effect of the addicted soldier rising out of his lethargy and depression for drug-induced relief and euphoria before finally succumbing to what seems inevitable.

Perhaps its roots in the suffering of the then still happening Vietnam War made it too controversial and uncomfortable a listen, but it is a great track.

## 'Rat Salad'

It comes over as a riposte to Led Zeppelin's 'Moby Dick' – a drum solo sandwiched in a riff-heavy instrumental. Zeppelin were a favourite band of Sabbath's. Robert Plant and John Bonham were friends of theirs, going back years on the Birmingham music scene.

Bill opens with snare, bass drums and cymbals, getting in some great fills as Tony and Geezer weave around him with tight guitar and bass. The three-part instrumental they play until 1:16 sounds like something that could easily have been used as the basis for a song with Tony getting in some effective wailing guitar.

Bill's solo comes in at 1:16, with him adding the toms to the mix. It's a short solo by the standards of the time, which is partly why it never loses your interest, but respect to Bill here too, because he is always an interesting and thoughtful percussionist. The briefest of pauses at 2:06 and we are back to the opening riffs again, with Bill getting in more terrific fills. Then it's all finally over after a mere two and a half minutes.

You can imagine how this track could have been extended in the way that 'Warning' was. One option to make up the album time would have been to extend this and restore 'Planet Caravan', rather than come up with a whole new song. Because of its brevity and invention and the terrific wraparound full band backing track, this holds up as a good solid piece of work.

## 'Fairies Wear Boots'

The fight with the skinheads in Weston-Super-Mare partly inspired the song. It's the only track on *Paranoid* that has a positive 'up' feel to it, the band kicking out in style. The swinging riff that dominates the song owes a debt to a Blodwyn Pig song from 1969 called 'Aint Ya Coming Home Babe'.

It opens with Tony's fuzz-toned guitar duelling, with a second lead part and Geezer and Bill adding flourishes in the background. At just thirteen seconds in, Tony cracks out his first riff as the others lock in with him. Geezer plays some great melodic bass that really enhances the riff. Still, only a mere 38 seconds in, there's the cool call and response between Tony and Bill that leads into Tony's first solo. Again Geezer and Bill do so much to add colour and dynamics behind Tony.

At 1:15, the swinging riff comes in, that really defines this track. It is just brilliant, up there with Tony's very best. This is the musicality that is the mark of their best work. It heralds the first verse, in which Ozzy sets the scene, 'Going home late last night, suddenly I got a fright'.

The instrumental break between the first and second verse hangs onto the swinging riff, which remains in place for verse two. Lyrically it's weak stuff with little more than Ozzy declaring that fairies wear boots and you gotta believe him!

The expected middle eight comes in at 2:40, a less bombastic section livened up by Tony's shrieking bluesy solo. It sounds like that will be it, and back to the riff, but instead, they switch tempo at 3:28 with a stuttering riff and driving drums and bass, which leads back into the intro riff sequence again. This is a straight reprise that dovetails into the swinging riff and verse three. It's here that things take a lazy turn as verse three is exactly the same as verse two. Surely they could have come up with something better than repeating what was a fairly poor verse in the first place?

Verse four is little better with the trip to the doctors and his advice, but at least we get some fresh lyrics. The outro adds late interest, an intriguing chiming riff at 5:42, accompanied by Geezer and Bill, which slowly fades out.

While the intro and main riff are Sabbath at their best, the verses are, in honesty, sub-par save for the first one. Fortunately, there is still more than enough to enjoy.

## USA edition notes

The tracks 'created' for the American edition are:

'Luke's Wall', which is the two-minute section that closes 'War Pigs'. It starts at 5:43 with Tony's ringing notes and carries on till the sped up outro. The name is a nod to the band's faithful roadies of the time – Luke Lucas and Richard 'Spock' Wall.

'Jack The Stripper', which is the intro to 'Fairies Wear Boots' up until Tony hits the riff at 1:15.

## Paranoid – deluxe editions

A three-disc CD deluxe edition was released in 2009, which included a remaster of the original album on disc one, a quad mix on disc two and alternative session takes on disc three.

A super-deluxe edition CD box-set came out on Rhino in 2016. This featured a new 2012 remaster on disc one, a stereo 'fold-down' of the quad mix on disc two, and two live concerts on discs three and four. That same super-deluxe edition was re-released in 2020 as a vinyl box set (plus a reissue of the CD set).

The live concerts are reviewed in the chapter *Killing Yourself To Live*, while the alternative takes and quad mix reviews follow here:

## Paranoid – Alternative Takes
### 'War Pigs' (instrumental)
No sirens on the intro as these were added in the final mix. Ozzy is technically missing, but if you turn your speakers up, you can hear him quietly bleeding through on the instrumental track.

### 'Paranoid' (alternative lyrics)
The first complete backing track of the song, complete with Ozzy's guide vocal and thus different lyrics. This establishes that the song took a little longer to record than legend has it. The main thing missing is Tony's overdubbed guitar solo.

### 'Planet Caravan' (alternative lyrics)
What we get musically is the full extended backing track, which makes it the most worthwhile addition to the selection of bonus tracks. The album version fades out and finishes at 4:34, while here, the track carries on until 6:04. You can't argue with the quality of the extended Tony solo over that sublime backing track. A longer version of this is most welcome!

The second major point of interest is Ozzy's untreated voice singing a guide vocal. All of the words he apparently made up on the spot, but none of them made it through to Geezer's final lyrics.

### 'Iron Man' (instrumental)
This backing track sounds slightly different. Tony's guitar, for example, sounds to have less chorus pedal on the intro on this version. More likely is that the final released version was remixed.

The principal interest is in being able to clearly hear what is going on in the music, the chief beneficiary being Geezer, whose melodic bass runs are more apparent. It also reveals that there is no overdubbed guitar. When Tony plays the lead parts, there is no rhythm guitar picking up the slack, just Geezer and Bill.

### 'Electric Funeral' (instrumental)

A chance to hear the musical backing on its own. It's the same length as the released backing track, too, although nine seconds of silence are added.

### 'Hand Of Doom' (instrumental)

The same as the released version, minus vocals.

### 'Rat Salad' (alternate mix)

More bass-heavy than the album version, Geezer is way higher in the mix and Bill's drums thunder along with more impact. Tony's guitar sounds more muted and it's that which is the main loss in this mix. Play the album take right after this one, and you can hear immediately how brighter and more trebly that version is.

### 'Fairies Wear Boots' (instrumental)

This seems to be the same take as the released version backing track. It's a different mix, though, an obvious change being no panning from speaker to speaker on Tony's guitars on the intro.

### The Quad Mix

The vogue for quadraphonic equipment led to Mike Butcher and Spock Wall remixing the album in 1975 at Morgan Studios, Brussels, after they had finished recording *Sabotage*. There are several differences to the original stereo mix. The sirens come in five seconds earlier on 'War Pigs' and last longer before they fade out. The sped up ending is ditched in favour of a final big chord. On 'Paranoid' the ring modulator effect on the guitar solo is dialled down. 'Planet Caravan' seems to have more bass and extra tone generator swirls, and it's a longer version. The bass on 'Hand Of Doom' is lower in the mix, which is a mistake. The opening guitars on 'Fairies Wear Boots' are swapped so they are on different speakers. It fades out ten seconds earlier than the standard stereo version too.

Overall what we get is a denser sounding version of the album, particularly on the stereo fold-down of the quad mix.

### Classic Albums: Paranoid (DVD and Blu Ray)

The fortieth anniversary of the album's release was commemorated by this 2010 film, which was part of a series on classic albums. All of the band, plus Tom Allom, are interviewed extensively about the making of the album and there is deep analysis of each track. The track analysis is where things get really engrossing as Allom digs into the master tapes, while Geezer, Bill and Tony run through their parts and riffs, showing how the songs were constructed. It's utterly fascinating to watch, though a shame that 'Rat Salad' is relegated to being part of the bonus features.

The package is nicely rounded out with film of the band on TV and live in 1970. Nothing new here, but nice that it's all from the right era. This is an essential purchase for your Sabbath collection.

# 1971: My life is free now, my life is clear

A year of personal changes for the band. Ozzy and Thelma got married, close to where they first met, at Birmingham Register Office in June. The couple, along with Thelma's son Elliott, had set up their first home in a flat above a launderette at the shopping precinct in Wheeleys Road, Edgbaston, Birmingham.

Later in the year, Geezer married Georgina Pugh in Birmingham. Bill's marriage details are uncertain, but what is certain is that Tony didn't follow his band-mates down the aisle. Instead, he refined his image with shorter hair and snappier clothes. His Italian roots now shone through in his appearance, and with these changes came an even bigger one. At some point in 1971, he moved to the centre stage position, ostensibly so he could hear the sound better. But it also put himself in the spotlight as the band's focal point, with Ozzy taking his place at the side of the stage. The only exceptions to this were for studio TV performances.

The likely start of the new stage configuration would be the beginning of the *Master Of Reality* tour in July. It was an odd move and one that never looked right. For all Tony's ability, he was not a front man, and in Ozzy they had one of the best in the business but in the wrong place.

For the band, the year started with the release of *Paranoid* on 1 January in America. The same day Sabbath went into Island Studios in London and put down the bones of at least three tracks for *Master Of Reality*.

Meanwhile, the band headlined a UK tour running from 7 January at Hull City Hall through till 23 January at Leeds University. Support on the tour was from Freedom and Curved Air. Following those dates, they headed off for their first concerts in Australia and New Zealand. They were supposed to follow these gigs with a tour of Japan, but the drug convictions of Tony and Bill while with Mythology, plus Ozzy's spell in Winson Green prison, put paid to that. Their visa applications were refused, so the opportunity was taken instead to get on with the third album.

Early February saw them back in Island Studios to continue recording. The bulk of the work must have been completed inside the first couple of weeks as the band embarked on an American tour from mid-February. On 17 February, they began that tour with a date at The Sunshine in Asbury Park, New Jersey. A barometer of their rapid progress in becoming one of the hottest live acts were their sell-out headlining shows on the East coast at New York's Fillmore East on 10 and 20 February. These were followed by equally sold-out shows on the West coast at the Los Angeles Forum on 23 and 24 February. A recording survives of the first night at the Forum, which tantalisingly has the band returning for an encore that opens with The Beatles' 'Day Tripper'. Sadly we only get ten seconds or so before it cuts out.

The tour ended on 2 April at The Spectrum in Philadelphia. The band were middle of the bill that night between Mountain (who headlined) and Humble Pie. Geezer reflected on the punishing tour/album/tour treadmill to *Metal Hammer* in May 2021: 'With such a gruelling schedule, we were taking more and more substances to keep us going, instead of taking time out to breathe. We wore ourselves out in the end, and the dream became nightmarish at times'.

The recording of *Master Of Reality* is said to have been from February to April, but realistically it looks hard for them to have popped back home to record during the tour. There is hardly a spare day in the schedule. Any remaining work that needed doing, overdubs perhaps, must have been done in the ten-day or so gap after the American tour. 'After Forever' and 'Spanish Sid'/'Into The Void' were tried out live to give the band chance to work out the arrangements and lyrics.

After that touring gap, they went back to Europe again, opening in Copenhagen on 14 April. The final show of the *Paranoid* tour came at the Royal Albert Hall on 26 April. The show started late due to Sabbath being presented with gold discs for UK sales of *Black Sabbath*, *Paranoid* and the advance sales of *Master Of Reality*. Ozzy told Geoff Barton for *Metal Hammer* in 2017:

That was a big show. I couldn't believe it. One minute I was playing the Marquee club with a pyjama shirt on, no shoes, with my knees hanging out of my jeans, and the next I was on stage at the Albert Hall. All our parents were in the audience. I thought: 'I'm going to fucking die as soon as we start playing'. I can't remember much about it, to be honest. One day I was a nobody, the next day I've got an album in the charts and I'm playing the Albert Hall. It was weird.

They spent three days back at Island from 25 to 27 May, putting the finishing touches to *Master Of Reality*. Incredibly two songs were only worked up for the first time on 25 May.

Sometime in the June/July period, Sabbath decamped to Rockfield Studios for six weeks, which they spent working on material for their next album, which would eventually come out as *Black Sabbath Vol. 4*.

*Master Of Reality* was released on 1 July in Britain. The following day, the band opened their third American tour with a date at the Public Auditorium in Cleveland. On 10 July, they played Tampa in Florida, and Ozzy sent a postcard (SAG-2016) home from The Manger Motor Inn, where the band were staying: 'Going down well at gigs. Whether (sic) is great and everybody is suntanned. We have sold a few crosses and everyone who has seen them thinks they are great. We are getting two gold discs at the end of the tour.'

The band had started selling the crosses at gigs as merchandise, perhaps the finest early concert merchandise tie-in item ever sold. The band's own aluminium crosses were upgraded for gold ones later on, supplied by their manager, Patrick Meehan.

*Master Of Reality* got its American release during the U.S. tour on 21 July. Following a show in Miami at the end of August, Sabbath got a break of sorts when they flew to Europe for nine days. During that time, they played three festivals – Speyer in Germany on 4 September, Vienna in Austria the following night, and finally Palermo in Sicily on 7 September. Ozzy wrote to his parents (SAG-2016) that they had: 'Travelled through Germany, Austria and Italy to here, Sicily. The weather here is gorgeous. Travelling has been a bit tiring, but it's been enjoyable on the whole. Both missing Elliot but will be home Thursday or Friday. Love John & Thelma.'

Palermo would have been extra special for Tony as his mother was born there on 5 July 1920. Thelma's presence on the dates hints that there was anticipated downtime in the sun. But if they hoped to be back home soon, they were wrong. After Palermo (7 September), two shows back in America at Syracuse on Friday 10 September and Rochester on Saturday 11 September were listed at short notice. They were booked to support Led Zeppelin and they weren't about to miss out on that! The rest of the American dates resumed on 18 September at Pittsburgh, ending on 28 October back at the War Memorial Auditorium in Rochester, New York.

The success of Sabbath's albums and their sold-out gigs led to major income for WWA, their management company. They had been listed on the London Stock Exchange at the tail end of 1970 and they merged with Hemdale Ltd (co-founded by the actor David Hemmings and his partner John Daley). The merged company now moved to deluxe new offices at South Street in the Mayfair district of London. Rick Wakeman, who joined Yes in August, recalled that: 'I met them (Sabbath) for the first time in the offices of Hemdale in South Street in London where both our managements were in-house'. He would be seeing a lot more of Black Sabbath in 1972.

## *Master Of Reality* *(Vertigo/Warners)*
Personnel:
Ozzy Osbourne: vocals
Tony Iommi: guitars, synthesizer on 'After Forever', flute on 'Solitude'
Geezer Butler: bass
Bill Ward: drums, timbales on 'Children of the Grave', sleigh bells on
'Solitude'
and:
Tom Allom: organ on 'Children Of The Grave', piano on 'Solitude'
Produced at Island Studios, London, January to May 1971 by Rodger Bain
UK release date: 1 July 1971, USA release date: 21 July 1971.
Highest chart places: UK: 5, USA: 8
Running time: 34:29
All songs by Black Sabbath, except as noted.

The album title comes from Geezer. The lyrics, largely written by him, are
observations on reality and he saw the final product recorded on a master
tape as a master of reality. He told *Metal Hammer* in May 2021 that:

> Sabbath was all about the dark reality of life. At the time, Vietnam was
> raging, the Cold War was at its coldest, the Troubles in Northern Ireland
> were close to home. A few others were singing about the underside of
> life, but we had the heaviness to hammer the subjects home.

A common complaint is that the album is too short, which it is. Tony's
comment to *Uncut* (July 2014) that, 'We'd been touring so much on the
*Paranoid* album, by the time we'd got to the studio we'd not had much
time to come up with stuff', tells exactly how it was. Writing and rehearsal
sessions were grabbed when possible between gigs. By the time they got
down to recording, they were still short of songs and this is largely how
the two short guitar pieces came to be added to the running order. Both
were composed by Tony in the studio to flesh things out and add to the
light and shade that was becoming a trademark. As well as the guitar
pieces, 'Solitude' was something of a resurrected song, leaving only five
completely new band tracks.

The one known out-take, 'Weevil Woman', could have been made to
fit, although it probably would have been extended longer than the
three minutes it lasts. If it had been included, then 'Orchid' would
likely have had to go, and the balance of the album would have been

affected. It's a shame that Rodger Bain seemingly didn't insist on another track, as per *Paranoid*, but what we do have, in spite of that, is a perfectly formed album.

In all they spent a luxurious (by their previous standards) ten days in total recording the album. The first session was on 1 January 1971 at Island, with further sessions put in when possible until the final studio dates from 25 to 27 May.

While *Paranoid* certainly had its dark moments, the band take it several notches further this time. Tony recalled in *Iron Man* that, 'We tuned down to get more power and a fatter sound. Of course, Ozzy started singing higher. He'd go, 'Oh, I can reach that note now.' However, when we got on stage he couldn't do it.' This explains why several classic Sabbath songs never, or rarely, made the setlist.

The decision to drop the tuning to C# on 'Children Of The Grave', 'Lord Of This World' and 'Into The Void' gave those songs a heaviness the like of which had not been heard before, along with a pervasive gloomy atmosphere. The other big tracks, 'After Forever' and 'Solitude', are in standard D.

While the previous two albums had many great songs, there is a directness and purpose here that is very pleasing. There was social commentary on the *Paranoid* album, but there is an air of distance in the communication. *Master Of Reality* feels more personal, as though Ozzy is talking directly to the listener.

Tony's immense riffs are such a huge part of Sabbath's sound, and on this album, his guitar is dominant like never before. As well as unintentionally inventing grunge, the dropped tuning meant his strings were less tightly wound, so Tony could play in more comfort. That accident in the sheet metal works had unexpectedly led to a new sound, which somehow pervades the tracks which aren't in C#. Tony's solo acoustic piece, 'Orchid' has an unsettling quality, while 'Solitude's' morose lyrics are barely lifted by his lilting guitar.

It's not just the dropped tuning that Tony, and also Geezer, adopted that gives the album such a startling sound - it's Bill's drums too. They have far more power in the Island Studios set-up than he got at Regent Sounds. There his drums had all been close-miked, but this time use was made of ambient miking and boom mikes giving the drums more presence. Bill recalled how he felt his kit sounded on the first two albums to Andrew Lentz of *Drum!*: 'A lot of our drum sounds were very clicky. They were very boomy or blatty. I listen back and I still go, 'Ooh'. It's pretty painful.'

The sheer presence of the music is stunning. It's hard to think of anything else from that time that matches this album in terms of in-your-face dynamics. Ozzy is on imperious form; he seems practically in front of you – almost a live performance. Behind him, the band rock hard and swing like their lives depend on it. The energy levels just crackle with life.

Geezer told *Uncut* (July 2014) that the success of the 'Paranoid' single had left them concerned they could be labelled as a pop band. 'So we deliberately said, 'No more singles'. Although, to be fair, the one thing nobody at the record label heard on this album was a single. The subject matter in any of the contenders would have been problematic, but in truth, nothing had that catchiness of 'Paranoid'. It also would have made a short album look even less value with a single pulled off it!

It was while recording this album that the band spent an hour and a half with engineer Tom Allom marching up and downstairs singing 'Hi Ho' from *Snow White*. It was supposed to end with a door shutting, followed by the intro riff of 'Into The Void'. The idea never worked out and was abandoned.

Keith Macmillan returned to do the cover. He came up with a stark, simple design of bold lettering on a black background. The production of the sleeve was handled by The Bloomsbury Group, and to make it stand out, they embossed the lettering for the UK release. It also had a flap style closure to the sleeve. On the back were Geezer's lyrics, featured for their thought-provoking content and also to help them (hopefully) from being misconstrued. Inside, along with the record, was a poster of a group photograph taken by Macmillan in Black Park. The muted tones and dark look of the image capture the mood of the record perfectly.

## 'Sweet Leaf'

One of the last songs put together for the record, with work on it only starting on 25 May, two days before sessions ended. Geezer recalled the lyrical inspiration in a 2001 interview with *Guitar World:*

I'd just come back from Dublin, and they'd had these cigarettes called Sweet Afton, which you could only get in Ireland. I took out this cigarette packet, and, as you opened it, it's got on the lid: 'It's the sweetest leaf that gives you the taste'. I was like: 'Ah, Sweet Leaf!'

It opens with Tony's cough, recorded after he took a drag on a reefer handed to him by Ozzy, while he was recording 'Orchid'. It's crazy, but it's an appropriate, attention-grabbing intro. As soon as the band come in, there's a real sense of them being unleashed. The primal power of this song just hits you from the off.

The interplay between Ozzy's vocal and the riff is clever, the vocal pauses allowing the riff to 'pop up' at you. The audible string squeaks as Tony frets the notes also work, even though there would have been no intention for them to be part of the recording. The fuzzy molten tones that he gets are complemented by Geezer's bubbling bass and a steady rhythm from Bill, to which he adds some great fills between verses. The second verse (which comes in at 1:17) sees Tony adding a high harmony rhythm part for variation.

The middle eight at 2:27 marks a change of tempo as the band switch up through the gears for a breathless instrumental break. Bill's gong shimmers as they lock into a tight groove. Tony's rhythm guitar drops out of the mix just as his trilling lead guitar comes in for his solo spot. It's a brief solo, with Geezer and Bill keeping up the relentless rhythms until they pull off one of those lightning tempo changes. A split-second pause and then an almighty crash back into the main riff (complete with the harmonic lead).

Ozzy comes back for a final verse, which sees him exuding even more passion than he did on the earlier verses, imploring the listener to, 'Come on now, try it out'. After the final verse, they swing on that big riff all the way to the outro as Ozzy improvises a vocal line.

It's one of their biggest opening tracks and is justifiably held up as a Sabbath classic.

## 'After Forever' (Iommi)

Tony's solo credit for writing it has to be an error, given that Geezer wrote the lyrics, which Tony acknowledges in his autobiography. The track was one of those they worked on at the first session on 1 January.

It opens with what sounds like cymbals recorded backwards and put through a flanger. Tony's chiming guitar comes in next, with bubbling bass from Geezer. Along with Bill's drum track, there is also some tambourine added for effect.

The verses feature a chugging riff as Ozzy declaims the often misunderstood lyrics. The line 'Would you like to see the Pope on the end of a rope' was picked up as another example of Sabbath being controversial. But the lyrics are questioning that perspective rather than supporting it.

Between the first and second verses, they go back into the intro riff, but after the second verse we get the middle eight with the main song variation. Tony comes in with a slow riff with Geezer and Bill in unison as Ozzy sings, 'Could it be you're afraid of what your friends might say if they knew you believe in God above'. You expect the solo to come in next, but instead, they switch back to the intro riff (at 2:36).

The expected solo still doesn't come as they head back into another verse. The surprise is that they have another variation to pull out. In comes a new riff at 3:26, which is kind of a more agile and spritely version of the one in the middle eight. This time we also get the long-awaited solo from Tony. It comes in at 3:37 and you can clearly hear the sound change as Tony's rhythm part is faded down so as to give his overdubbed lead guitar space to shine. As his solo picks up, it is panned increasingly faster from speaker to speaker until the intro riff comes back in again.

The track could have been faded out after the 4:10 mark and it would have worked well, but there is still over a minute to go. Given the album's abbreviated running time, it sounds like it was extended to make up the minutes. So we get another verse at 4:15, which is good but feels like one too many. The ending is better as they lock back into the intro riff with the effects stepped up, climaxing with a repeat of the intro backwards cymbal sounds.

The song has been somewhat overlooked due to the top drawer quality of the several bigger hitters on the album, and also it never being a live set staple (at least in the 70s). There is a rushed feel to it and it could have benefited from a stronger middle eight, but it's an enjoyable piece of work.

## 'Embryo' (Iommi)

Tony plays it on a detuned electric, cleverly playing the melody on the top strings while leaving the bottom two to reverberate. The track's almost medieval feel has uneasy, even sinister, overtones that hint at the menace to come. There's not much to it in its own right, it's a mere 38 seconds long, but it perfectly sets up and puts you in the mood for 'Children Of The Grave'.

## 'Children Of The Grave'

Lyrically this is a warning and a prequel to 'Electric Funeral'. This is the fate that awaits, opined Geezer if the warnings in 'Children Of The Grave' are ignored. 'Must the world live in the shadow of atomic fear, will they win the fight for peace, or will they disappear', he asks.

It's another one of the last songs to be worked on for the album, first run through on 25 May. It is an outstanding classic Sabbath track and a contender for being the best song they ever recorded.

The unease from 'Embryo' is maintained in the intro, a low rumbling rhythm in which you can hear the staccato picking of Tony's plectrum. The riff that comes in is a killer, alternating between a smooth chord progression that switches to a staccato riff, underpinned by Geezer's bass doubling it. The recording of the guitar and bass rhythm parts is superb, with great presence and clarity, in no way compromised by the dropped tuning. However, it's Bill's clattering overdubbed timbales work that is the memorable extra ingredient. As well as that, he uses double bass drums to power the galloping rhythm track along. Ozzy handles the vocals with his usual aplomb, while Tony adds a squeal of guitar at the end of each of Ozzy's lines to add emphasis. The squeals sound like they might be overdubbed, and it certainly would have been easier to add them in that way.

The middle eight comes at 2:08 and it's one of the best tempo changes Sabbath came up with. A quick linking riff played in unison by Tony, Geezer and Bill makes way for a monumental riff that defines this track as much as the more familiar main riff on the intro and verses. It's an evil beast of a riff with Bill playing an almost military beat on his toms behind the huge sweeping riff. In the background, there is an organ part doubling Tony's riff, presumably played by Tom Allom.

The switch out of the middle eight is staggeringly smooth. It leads back into the main riff and a final verse, capped off with Tony's solo at 3:43. He double tracks a second lead part onto it, the two parts duelling from different speakers. The thicker melodic sound he gets from this works well over the riff, which still features his rhythm guitar.

The outro comes in at 4:17 with Tony's repeated squealing riff (doubled by Geezer) that is not dissimilar to the punctuations he used on the verses. Rumbling timpani from Bill fades up louder, getting more ominous, but there is no crashing final chord as you might expect. Instead, a sinister noise comes in, which sounds like Tony's guitar with an effect used on it. It pans from speaker to speaker as Ozzy's whispered voice spectrally intones 'Children Of The Grave'. It's a truly disturbing ending, which, it has since transpired, could have been even more unsettling if they hadn't faded it out. The full-length version is on the instrumental out-take.

It was released in Portugal and Mexico as a single, backed with 'Solitude'. There was a DJ promo issued in the UK, backed with Status Quo's version of The Doors' 'Roadhouse Blues'.

## 'Orchid' (Iommi)

Not the side two opener you would expect. Only Tony features on this and he uses a dropped tuning to get the quietly still quality. He plays a steel-strung acoustic guitar in a fluid Spanish style. The muted tones are heightened by the reverberating bottom strings that comes and goes. It's another admirable piece of work that bears repeated listening, as well as doing the job of softening us up before 'Lord Of This World'.

## 'Lord Of This World'

Lyrically it's a simple but thought-provoking tale. Geezer has said, on occasion, that it is the devil speaking in the first person, but that is not overtly clear in the lyrics. He observes that mankind has turned away from their creator, 'You made me master of the world where you exist' and questions who you will turn to 'when it's your turn to die'.

The intro is a twisting, subtle riff with Tony and Geezer in unison, while Bill's drum fills add contrast. The main riff comes 28 seconds in, another one of Tony's best, melodic and catchy but still heavy due to the dropped tuning. At 30 seconds, you can just about hear the piano part (by Tom Allom) that wasn't used on the final take but survives as a couple of clear notes. It sounds to be there in the background throughout the track, so it may be a bleed through on the rhythm guitar parts. The verses have an edginess with Ozzy's precise emphasised diction, singing along with the guitar riff. He gives the song real power and it's his performance that is the stand-out.

The usual switch comes at 2:03 without any real tempo change this time. Tony plays a variant on the main riff and Bill taps out the same riff on his percussion. The guitar solo comes in at 2:17, with Geezer adding a brilliant complementary bass part. At 2:35, Tony adds a second lead part to harmonise with his solo. Ozzy sings a middle eight section at 2:59, which sees the only mention of the title.

There's time for one final verse, which sets the seal on things before the big finish. First up is a repeat of the instrumental section from 2:03, complete with Bill's tapped percussion. The section that follows this with the two harmony lead guitar parts also repeats as before.

The surprise on the outro is a new riff, coming in at 4:58. It might have been something they could have built a whole new song around, but as a final surge of energy, it does the job just fine.

This popular song didn't get to be a live staple in the '70s, but in the down-tuned reunion era, it, at last, found a place in the set and always went down well.

## 'Solitude'

The lyrics were originally written by Geezer and Ozzy way back during the Earth days. The surviving lyric sheet (SAG-2016) has the song titled as 'Changing Phases'. The new single-word title, 'Solitude', is a much more effective and empathic summary of the effects of depression on the mind.

It takes its place on the album in the same way that 'Planet Caravan' did on *Paranoid* – a chance for the band to show another side to their music. The despair and futility in the lyrics are accompanied paradoxically by a beautiful swing feel and lilting quality to the music, with Tony's guitar and Geezer's bass holding down different but complementary melody lines. A delay is used on Ozzy's voice to enhance the distant wistful feel of the song.

Great care was taken with the instrumental details, which add so much to the effect. Tony's flute part is simple but effective and the tinkling sleigh bells, courtesy of Bill, are mesmerising once your ears lock into them. It's his only contribution and he plays them on most of the song.

They play the intro instrumental section again after the first verse and also after the second verse. The second verse (which comes in at 1:40) features a snatch of piano, which sounds like it had been treated with reverse reverb, giving the effect of the piano whooshing in. The piano is kept in the mix for the remainder of the song, making the sound thicker, and was probably played by Tom Allom.

Tony's solo comes in at 2:32 and he opts to play a slight variation on the melody line, which maintains the feel of the song. At the end of the third verse (at 3:53), Tony's flute features more prominently on what is an extended fade-out, finishing off with just those tinkling sleigh bells, which leave your ears straining to hear them.

It's a wonderful, touching song that deserves to be better known. Sabbath never played it live, but It has been covered by Opeth in concert, who delivered a great version of it.

## 'Into The Void'

Lyrically it's about what is left of mankind escaping an earth ruined by nuclear war, something of a sequel in effect to 'Electric Funeral'.

Tony recalled, in *Iron Man*, that it was a problematic song to get down:

We tried recording 'Into The Void' in a couple of different studios because Bill couldn't get it right. Whenever that happened, he would start believing that he wasn't capable of playing the song. He'd say, 'To hell with it – I'm not doing this'!

The intro is a scene-setting device, establishing the mood and feel of the track. Tony's glissando down the frets is followed with a slow insistent riff, joined by Geezer and Bill. Geezer's top notes bubble out of the stew, which continues, with a brief variation, until 1:13, when Tony switches things around with THAT riff, the one that you wait for. It's one of his finest riffs and he knows it. The stuttering attack of it is joined by Geezer and Bill, anchoring the song superbly; Geezer's bass is the pulsing heart of things here. Ozzy finally steps up at 1:39. The lyrics are among the hardest he ever had to perform with Sabbath – a stream of consciousness with scarcely a chance to pause for breath.

At 3:03, they switch and up the tempo with the interlude riff, where Ozzy sings the 'Freedom fighters set out to the sun' verse. Listen out for Bill as he contributes a blistering drum part. It all stops and changes in a split second as the main riff comes back in at 3:32 for a repeat of the opening part of the song but with different verse lyrics. Tony takes his first solo at 4:46, surprisingly late, and adds a barely audible second solo part underneath it. It's not one of his best solos by any means, but it's good enough.

There's a brilliant call and response at 5:15 between the rhythm section and a shivery fuzz-toned guitar lick from Tony. Listen out for an over-dubbed lead guitar part that sounds like it was recorded much later, the squeals cutting right through. Tony then slides down into some bluesy notes before locking back in with Geezer and Bill for the outro riff, which ends on an echo of Tony's guitar.

'Into The Void' is a classic Sabbath song with one of Tony's top riffs. Like 'Lord Of This World' it surprisingly never really got into the setlists back in the '70s but secured its place in the live set in the reunion era, where the riff was always greeted with frenzied delight.

## USA edition notes

The tracks 'created' for the American edition are:-

'The Elegy', which is the intro to 'After Forever' up until the heavy riff comes in at 34 seconds.

'The Haunting', which is the spooky end vocal section to 'Children Of The Grave'.

'Step Up', which is the 27-second intro riff to 'Lord Of This World'. This is repeated later in the song.

'Death Mask', which is the first part of 'Into The Void' up until 1:14, when Tony cracks out the main riff.

## Master Of Reality – deluxe edition

A two-disc deluxe edition was released in 2009, the second disc featuring the following tracks, including alternative takes and, best of all, a previously unreleased song!

## 'Weevil Woman 71'

The Holy Grail is this previously unknown and unreleased song, recorded at the first album session on 1 January but subsequently abandoned. The title obviously refers back to 'Evil Woman', but otherwise has nothing in common. It's typical of the heavier tracks on the album, driving along on a choppy, crunching guitar riff. Ozzy's guide vocal line would have changed in time, and the arrangement refined and honed if they had continued with the song, but it was not to be. The band obviously felt they had better material coming through and it wasn't worth persevering with 'Weevil Woman', but, given the album's brevity, that seems a mistake.

## 'Sweet Leaf' (alternative lyrics)

Recorded on 25 May, this features Ozzy's guide vocal and lyrics. The date is important because Ozzy clearly has future plans on his mind as he sings, 'I want you baby to be my wife, to love and cherish for the rest of my life, you want me too to be your man'. Thelma was very much on his mind and no wonder as they were married the following month.

## 'After Forever' (instrumental)

Sounds like the same take used for the final mix, minus Ozzy. Tony's panned solo is present and correct.

## 'Children Of The Grave' (alternative lyrics)

An early run-through minus the overdubbed timbales, guitar solo and outro 'Haunting' section. Ozzy performs a guide vocal spouting whatever came into his head; annoyingly, this includes him shouting 'save me' a lot. An interesting work-in-progress, but is not one you want to come back to often.

## 'Children Of The Grave' (instrumental)

Bill's percussion overdubs are present, so all that's missing is Ozzy. It's 46 seconds longer than the album version, which in essence means more of the 'Haunting' outro. Added to the background is an organ playing a familiar fairground/circus tune – 'Sobre Las Olas' ('Over The Waves') by

Juventino Rosas. The incongruity of the piece works incredibly well and they should have left it in for the final master take. After all, they had the space for it.

### 'Orchid' (alternative take)
A cough from Tony (could it be THE cough) opens this take, which is a brighter mix than the album version. It still has a beautiful pastoral feel to it.

### 'Lord of This World' (alternative take)
Take one was set to be 'the one' for the album but was replaced. It's worthy of note because it features overdubbed slide guitar parts by Tony, which the album version does not have.
There is also a piano adding support to the riff all the way through. This suggests Tom Allom making his first uncredited appearance on the sessions. It can't be Tony on piano as he hadn't started playing one at this stage of his career. The piano and slide parts were rightly deemed superfluous to requirements. That being said, the extra parts make it one of the most interesting of the outtakes to have emerged.

### 'Solitude' (alternative take)
No Leslie speaker effect is used on Ozzy's voice and Tony plays in a different tuning with no chorus pedal. The overall effect is to put Ozzy and Tony 'closer' in the mix. Geezer plays pretty much the same melodic bass part, but there is no flute overdub weaving around him. Bill is completely missing on this version, which is a minute or so shorter.
    The spectral quality of the released version and the beautiful tinkling percussion is missing but had they stuck with this treatment, it would still have been an interesting diversion.

### 'Spanish Sid'
This early version of 'Into The Void' was tracked at the first recording session for the album on 1 January. Tony's guitar intro hasn't got the deep, playful dirty feel of the album version. That remains the same when he hits the riff too. The reason for this is it's not played in the dropped tuning used on the album, proving they got the decision to do so spot on!
    Ozzy performs his guide vocal as usual. Tony does get in a solo that is broadly similar to what he did for the released take, but they knew they could do a lot better with this track and the fabulous riff that drives it.

# 1972: The snowflakes glisten on the trees

At some time in 1972, Tony recorded lead guitar for the LP *Funkist* by former Procol Harum drummer Bobby Harrison. Tony did his parts at Morgan Studios and can be heard on the track 'King Of The Night'. Its release seems to have been delayed for three years.

The working year began with three days booked at The Marquee Recording Studios, located behind the famous club. They laid down two tracks for the next album, 'Snowblind' and 'FX' as well as two unnamed backing tracks. Some final work was also done at Island Studios and another track was worked on at De Lane Lea Studios, also in London. How much of these recordings made it to the final mixes is unstated, but the varying sound palette on *Volume Four* suggests that some of these recordings made it into the final mixes.

Ozzy and Thelma's first child, Jessica Starshine Osbourne, was born on 20 January in Birmingham. There wasn't much time for the family to acclimatise to the new arrival as Ozzy was due out on a 20 date UK tour. This started on 24 January at Birmingham Town Hall (the first of two nights there), supported by Wild Turkey, who featured Tony's week-long band-mate from Jethro Tull, Glenn Cornick. Wild Turkey got the support slot because they were managed by Patrick Meehan (of Sabbath's management) and Brian Lane. Lane's main client was Yes, which is how they ended up supporting Sabbath (along With Wild Turkey on some dates) on the American tour that followed on from the UK leg. As well as those two crazy hometown Birmingham gigs, there was also a special return to Carlisle on 30 January. There they played a charity gig in the Market Hall as a thank you to the city and surrounding areas which had been such a partisan fan base.

There was a week's break after the final date in Bradford on 24 February before they left for America. On 1 March, they started a month of engagements with an appearance at Fayetteville, South Carolina. It was during this tour, dubbed the 'Iron Man Tour', that the band started travelling between gigs by plane, to cut down on travelling times. Following an incident in which Ozzy 'had a go' at piloting the plane, Bill (always a nervous flyer) got his brother Jim to drive him between gigs in a mobile home.

The shared gigs with Wild Turkey and Yes went down a storm, the audiences having no problem accepting the musical diversity between Black Sabbath and Yes. It was on this tour that Sabbath struck a close friendship with Rick Wakeman, Yes's keyboard wizard. Wakeman recalled those days:

Rock audiences had a huge variety of rock variations that they liked, or would be happy to be introduced to. Back in the early '70s, there were often three, and sometimes four, bands on the bill. The Eagles supported Yes on two tours and people loved it. I enjoyed being part of the Sabbath/ Yes touring as I loved Sabbath, so it was win/win for me. I spent a lot of time with the band. I travelled in their plane sometimes (which upset the Yes guys), but we had fun, and drank quite a lot too! It was proper old fashioned touring – lots of travel, short stays in hotels, plenty of alcohol. Then there was the usual backstage shenanigans which I certainly will not go into!

An unexpected catastrophe came when the band passed through the border between Canada and the USA in March. Geezer told *Bassplayer* (2013) that:

We were on tour in America, somewhere between Detroit and Toronto. Someone had opened the case of my Fender bass and smashed it to pieces. You could see the hammer marks. It was a Sunday, and shops weren't open, so we got in touch with the promoter, who had a friend who ran a music shop. He opened it up for us, but it was mostly cheap stuff. The only reasonable bass they had was the Dan Armstrong.

Sabbath were up in the Detroit, Montreal area in late March. They had played in Montreal on 24 March and then Rochester on 25 March, which would leave the discovery of the shattered bass being at Salem, Virginia on Sunday 26 March. The Dan Armstrong bass is the clear plexiglass bass that Geezer continued to use up until the next American tour.

The American tour ended on 2 April at the Capitol Theater, Passaic, New Jersey. From there, Sabbath were booked to play at the The Mar Y Sol Festival in Vega Baja, Puerto Rico, and then onto Japan for dates in Osaka. The Japanese dates were cancelled as the band were still unable to get entry visas due to their criminal records. They reluctantly pulled out of Mar Y Sol, too, because they were unable to reach the festival site due to gridlock. So the band now got something approaching a rest period. A new album was due, but rather than write it on the road, they were given the luxury of working the material up in a rehearsal room again (as per

*Paranoid*). Where Sabbath were ensconced has not been stated, except that it was in Birmingham.

From there, they flew out to Los Angeles to further prepare material and record the album. Thanks to a postcard (SAG-2016) sent home by Thelma Osbourne, we know the band arrived in Los Angeles on 1 May 1972 or a day or so before. During their time in Los Angeles, Bill met Melinda 'Mysti' Strait at a gig in Hollywood. The couple hit it off right away, leaving Bill with the difficult decision to end his marriage to his wife.

Their next American tour (their sixth) started off in Wildwood, New Jersey, on 7 July, supported by Black Oak Arkansas. The following day they were at Pocono International Raceway at Long Pond, Pennsylvania. There they played on an incredible bill, including Humble Pie, The Faces, Emerson, Lake & Palmer and Edgar Winter. The strain of constant touring was now starting to show, with Ozzy's voice giving out on the night, resulting in the next few shows being cancelled.

Gentle Giant supported Sabbath on dates in August and September, but their brand of prog rock met a different response to that which Yes had received from American audiences earlier in the year. At the L.A. Forum, Gentle Giant found their compatibility on the bill was called into question. Lead singer Derek Shulman recalled to *Ultimate Classic Rock* in 2019 that:

When we'd finish the shows through North America, we got a good ovation. But at the L.A. Forum, we'd change into softer music with a violin and cello, which fans of Black Sabbath had never seen or heard. During the song 'Funny Ways', someone threw a cherry bomb on stage, and it exploded in front of me and my brother Phil.

The band decided to leave the stage, but as he walked past the microphones, a frustrated Phil Shulman (of Giant) shouted that 'You guys are a bunch of f*cking c*nts', prompting an even bigger reaction from the crowd.

The American tour ended abruptly on 15 September with a show at the legendary Hollywood Bowl in Los Angeles. Sabbath completed the prestigious show, but Tony passed out almost as soon as they came off stage. He was diagnosed with exhaustion and ordered to fly back to England and rest. He wasn't the only one who had reached the end of their tether. Geezer was suffering from kidney stones and had to be admitted to hospital, while Bill also went to hospital suffering from hepatitis. Ozzy, meanwhile, seemed to be indestructible. He arrived back in England and went straight to his new home, Bulrush Cottage on Butt Lane in Ranton, Staffordshire.

On the record front, 'Tomorrow's Dream' was released as the new single before the album, but the date is uncertain. What is sure is that ten days after the Hollywood Bowl show, *Black Sabbath Vol. Four* was released.

With the band still recovering from the strains of touring, it was decided to reduce their commitments. In October, they announced that they would not be undertaking further tours of America for the time being. With a break in their schedule Tony, Geezer and Bill followed Ozzy's lead and also moved house. Tony moved to The Moat House on Lower Penkridge Road in Acton Trussell, Staffordshire. Geezer bought a place in Cleobury Mortimer, Worcestershire and Bill rented Fields Farm at Bishampton near Worcester. Bill later moved to Summerville House in Bromyard, near Malvern, Worcestershire. Ozzy also persuaded his parents to leave Lodge Road in Aston for Northfield, in South Birmingham.

## *Black Sabbath Vol. Four* (Vertigo/Warners)

Personnel:
Ozzy Osbourne: vocals
Tony Iommi: guitars, piano on 'Changes'
Geezer Butler: bass, 12-string guitar on 'Wheels Of Confusion', mellotron on 'Changes'
Bill Ward: drums, percussion
Produced at The Record Plant, Los Angeles and Island Studios, London, May to June 1972 by Black Sabbath (and Patrick Meehan)
Release date: 25 September 1972
Highest chart places: UK: 5, USA: 13
Running time: 42:18
All songs by Black Sabbath.

Ozzy told *Metal Hammer* in 2017: 'We wanted to call it *Snowblind* because we did so much coke making that record, but the record company said no'. Warners firmly refused to put out an album called *Snowblind*, knowing full well what was behind the title. Instead, we got the dull *Black Sabbath Vol. Four* title which does nothing to inspire. Strangely Warners did commission a press advert with the *Snowblind* title. It's included as a poster in the Super Deluxe edition of *Volume Four,* and features a negative 'white-out' image of the band that would have made a great album cover.

For this album, Sabbath rang the changes. After three albums, Rodger Bain was not asked back to produce, the band feeling they now knew enough to do it themselves. They also decided to record abroad for the first time. The reasons behind this were down to reducing their tax burden and wanting to try a new studio. The band rented the philanthropist John Dupont's house at 773 Stradella Road in Bel Air, Los Angeles, to write and rehearse. Two mostly completed tracks ('Snowblind' and 'FX') and two backing tracks came with them from sessions at The Marquee Studios back in January.

As well as the business of writing new material the band indulged in (according to Ozzy in his autobiography) an epic bender of substance abuse at the mansion.

Somehow they got the material together to take to The Record Plant. In all, the process took from six to eight weeks – their longest time yet. Compare that to the fact that the three albums before it had been recorded in just under three weeks in total. While the rest of the band had their input in producing, and Patrick Meehan had himself listed as co-producer, this must surely be the album where Tony started to get his chops together as a producer. With the luxury of having more time to record, the band were able to splice parts from different takes together. This was something that is not mentioned as having taken place during the first three albums.

When the press asked Ozzy (quoted in the deluxe edition) what they could expect from the fourth album. He replied that it would be 'The Black Sabbath sound, but it's more melodic. I'm singing different melodic things and it's all building up'.

Most of the album is excellent. Sonically it's a brighter sound than on *Master Of Reality* until we get to side two, where the *Master Of Reality* vibe returns for 'Under The Sun' and 'Cornucopia'. The only below par tracks are 'FX' and 'St. Vitus Dance', but there is an inequality between the two sides. Side one is ('FX' apart) solidly great. But side two somehow doesn't work as well, despite opening with a solid classic in 'Snowblind'. Tuning-wise, they drop again to C# on all of the tracks, although 'Changes' kicks off in B major.

Geezer wasn't happy with his bass sound on the album. He used the Dan Armstrong bass you can see on the sleeve photographs and he complained to *Bassplayer* (2013) it had resulted in the album having, 'probably the worst bass sound of any Sabbath record'. Geezer soon changed his instrument, swapping to custom Jaydee and John Birch basses.

The album was finished off at Island Studios in London, which for the most part, was final mixing. The one exception was Bill's parts on 'Under The Sun', which they finally got down there after failing to do so at The Record Plant. Uncredited on the album is an unnamed orchestra who were used on two tracks, 'Snowblind' and 'Laguna Sunrise'. Where their parts were recorded is unstated too.

The cover was again shot by Keith Macmillan. It's a striking classic image of Ozzy on the front. Macmillan proudly told *Rolling Stone* in 2020 that, 'Sometimes you just catch one of those iconic images. It's been parodied to death, hasn't it?' Iconic, yes, but you wonder why the band went with it. Given their all for one philosophy, it seems strange to push their singer as the cover star. As if to compensate, Ozzy gets one solo picture on the inside booklet while the others get two. The double-page centre spread has a great full band shot that captures the relationship between Sabbath and their audience. The symbiosis between them and their fans is there to be seen. All of the pictures were taken at Birmingham Town Hall in January 1972. This is easily the most lavish package Black Sabbath ever had for an album, though *Sabbath Bloody Sabbath* runs it close.

## 'Wheels Of Confusion'

The working title was 'Illusion', which features in the last line of the first two verses. Instead, they went for part of the opening line of verse three as the title. The lyrics see Geezer ruminating on what life was like as a youngster and how things have panned out since, concluding that no matter what you do, 'The world will still be turning when you're gone.'

Tony's mournful twin guitars on the intro capture the philosophical mood, until, just 20 seconds in, he cracks out an insistent riff, joined by Geezer and Bill. Ozzy comes in for verse one and you are struck right away by just how great the sound and the mix are. It's brighter than we have heard before, but the sound is well-balanced and nicely crisp. While the others keep things simple, Bill provides the colour with a busy percussion track.

The middle eight comes in at 2:25 with the inevitable change of tempo, switching to a faster pace. It's a cleverly constructed section as, rather than chug along on the boogie rhythm and put a solo over the top, it switches again with Tony playing a slow melody line (coming in at 2:51) over the rhythm as a contrast. He then adds some swooping lead lines over that before signalling the end of the middle eight with some crunching chords, leading into verse three.

Verse four is a musical repeat of verses one and two, but Geezer has some fresh lyrics to conclude his musings on life. That would be it normally, but Sabbath on this occasion are not finished, and they have 'The Straightener' ready at 5:14, the instrumental coda that lasts for another two and a half minutes. Ozzy was credited (in the notes of the deluxe edition) with playing mellotron, and if he plays it anywhere on the track, then it's on the backing track here, but it's not audible if he did. Equally, this seems likely to be where Geezer plays 12 string guitar (as also credited in the deluxe edition).

Tony opens 'The Straightener' with a chiming riff through a Leslie speaker cabinet and it makes for a beautiful change of texture on this powerhouse outro. He adds a second harmony lead guitar part to the mix, doubling the riff. The guitar solo comes in at 5:58, picking up from the melody line and expanding on it, repeating the lead line, ascending the fretboard and punctuating the melody with elegant streams of notes. It is, in fact, two solo parts weaving together, making for a truly magnificent end to the track as it slowly fades out.

The song was played live but didn't become a live set regular. 'The Straightener' would have been an interesting addition as part of the jam sections in the live set.

## 'Tomorrow's Dream'

One of the first songs the band recorded at the Record Plant. Sabbath had been working on it since at least January 72, when it had been included in the set for the British tour, albeit with different lyrics. It's a transitional track from *Master Of Reality* and could have fitted seamlessly on that album.

It opens with a rolling lurching fuzzy riff which is kind of like a slower 'Supernaut'. Again you notice the clarity and punch of Bill's drums, which are much better recorded than on the previous three albums. In the liner notes for the deluxe edition, Bill noted that 'This was really the first time I'd ever felt the power of my bass drums when recording'. The first two verses are sung over the riff and the thrusting bulldozing rhythm.

The middle eight comes at 1:27, with Ozzy singing a different melody line. He reflects that 'When sadness fills my days, It's time to turn away. And let tomorrow's dreams become reality to me'. Ozzy had a great knack for knowing how best to handle Geezer's lyrics.

It's a typically effective middle eight from Sabbath, with the band keeping things powerful, before we switch back to the onslaught. Tony plays a short solo at 1:54 with a second sharply ascending guitar part behind it. The two parts work well in tandem before Tony drops back to the main riff and verse three. Rather than come up with a different outro, they stay with the riff, which fades out.

It is over and done by 3:04; one of the shortest songs in their catalogue but no less effective for that. It has always gone down well live, where it could be anything up to a minute longer.

Due to the catchy melody and convenient brevity, it was selected to be a single, backed with 'Laguna Sunrise'. Without airplay, it failed to trouble the charts anywhere. The better option for a single was the next track.

## 'Changes'

It was during their time at the Dupont house that Tony first started playing the piano. The first fruit of that was the piano melody for 'Changes', which Ozzy reinforces by singing the same melody. The overwhelming sense of loss in the lyrics obviously suggested a sensitive string arrangement. Rather than use a string section, Geezer added mellotron strings instead, their haunting quality suiting the lyrics perfectly. He uses the mellotron again on several later songs.

Rick Wakeman visited them in the Record Plant and it would have been perfectly understandable if they had asked him to re-record the piano part, but to their credit, they didn't. It would have sounded more polished, but there is a simple yearning quality to Tony's playing that works well for the song. The heartfelt, somewhat basic lyrics are by Geezer, who used Bill's marriage breakup as the catalyst. To his great credit, Ozzy gets far more mileage out of his delivery of the words than would seem possible when you read them.

It isn't a classic and it's not even the best of their atypical compositions, but the song's undoubted qualities stay with you. It made it onto the B-side of the 'Sabbath Bloody Sabbath' single, but nobody could ever have foreseen it hitting number one in the UK in 2003 as a duet between Ozzy and his daughter Kelly. It makes you wonder what it might have done if it had been an A-side in 1972. It is the kind of song that could have been a surprise hit in the UK in that era. But, if it had done well, it could have left Sabbath having to explain why they wouldn't perform it live and feeling burdened by it. That being said, it was hugely popular in Australia and New Zealand and the band decided to play it there for their 1973 dates.

## 'FX'

This is a long 1:44 of the band tapping anything they had to hand on Tony's plugged in guitar. In later years Tony has dismissed the results as a joke and admits in *Iron Man* that there had originally been no intention to put it on the album. It was only when the band heard a playback with a delay effect on it that they thought it had something. But it hasn't; it is a tedious listen, which most listeners surely skip if they can. What was so obviously needed instead was one of Tony's solo pieces for a different vibe before the glorious 'Supernaut'.

## 'Supernaut'

What exactly is a 'Supernaut', Greg Prato (*Songfacts*) asked Tony? 'Geezer came up with some great titles – really unusual titles, as he did with the lyrics. He was really good at that. I can't remember where he got that from, but it was his idea.' So no clues there. The lyrical message seems to be to live life your way. Perhaps that is the very essence of being a supernaut.

The main riff is just fabulous, with a funky edge coming through. Tony was pleased with it, telling Prato how the song had come to fruition. 'I had a wah-wah going and started playing this riff. Everybody liked it, and we made it into the song. That's how we always went about the Sabbath stuff.'

It opens with striking hi-hat cymbal work from Bill, who is on colossal form throughout the track. Tony's jubilant wah-wah intro riff comes in, matching Bill's percussive power. Geezer's bass adds to the power, doubling Tony. You know you are in for something special from that intro alone, but nothing prepares you for a second riff coming in after only 20 seconds have passed! This beast of a riff is huge with a coda to it where Geezer's bass hits new depths. The exciting feel is picked up in Ozzy's vocals.

Cleverly after the first verse, there is an interlude of the intro wah-wah riff back again, after which they switch again to that dive-bombing monster riff for the second verse. After that, it's back to the wah-wah, but this time it gives way to Tony's solo (at 1:40), in which he plays sharp trilling notes over the wah-wah rhythm. It's a flurry of sound that just gets better and better before the solo abruptly cuts off, leaving just the wah-wah.

It sounded completely left-field back then and still does today because nothing prepares you for what comes next (at 2:37). This is a middle eight break like no other in their catalogue. Bill's thunderous drums and cymbals lead into a samba rhythm that really shouldn't work at all. Yet it does so perfectly and is easily one of the most extraordinary passages in the Sabbath catalogue. It's an utterly magical irresistible vibe. Their decision to use it was possibly influenced by the rise in cultural popularity of the samba, which formed the musical backdrop to Brazil's World Cup-winning campaign of 1970.

The sheer cheek of this musical diversion can only be broken by one thing, and of course, it's the big riff back again for a final verse. The switch from the Samba to the riff is such an immense jolting contrast that it makes it sound even bigger than before! Ozzy signs off triumphantly with 'Don't try to reach me, 'cause I'll tear up your mind, I've seen the future and I've left it behind'. And off they go into the distance, a long fade out on the wah-wah rhythm.

'Supernaut' is such an exciting track, and it's a shame it never became a live staple. Even when it was featured live, it was only ever used in part. The joyous samba break looks like it might have been the stumbling block in the end.

## 'Snowblind'

Another song that had been worked on for some time prior to recording the album. It was part of the setlist for their March 1972 American dates and was listed as part of the set in a review of the Birmingham Town Hall January 1972 gigs. For me, this is the greatest ever Sabbath track, a triumphant masterpiece with everything I love about Black Sabbath, although the subject matter is highly provocative. It's a homage (if that is correct) to their drug of choice at the time, softly whispered by Ozzy at 0:39 but always ecstatically bellowed out on stage.

It opens with a brief stately crunching riff which gives way after a mere 16 seconds, replaced by the song's killer main riff. It's a real ear-worm, a melodic hook that stays in your head and forms the rhythmic basis of the verses.

Right from the first verse, it's clear that Ozzy is well on top of the lyrics, his delivery is masterful. At the end of each verse, there's a catchy descending coda just before Tony plays the killer riff again.

What in other people's songs would be a chorus, comes in at 1:22, but it's more of an early middle eight. The band change through the gears for the big sing-along section, with Ozzy at his very best,' My eyes are blind, but I can see, the snowflakes glisten on the trees' The backing from the other three is just glorious, the descending arpeggios from Tony, in particular, are a treat.

Tony's sublime solo follows next (at 2:20). He starts off with some high notes making his way down the fretboard before coming back up again for some final high notes. You just know we are going back into the riff again, but there's an additional clever engineering trick at 2:52 where the faders are pushed up. It's not so audible on the latest remaster but was very audible on older ones. That push just gives the riff more presence and raises the energy levels as Ozzy comes back in for the third verse – 'Let the winter sunshine on' The sound-scape has completely changed now; everything is clearer and louder and closer, including Ozzy's vocals.

Not content with giving us one great riff, Tony busts out another one at 3:26 for what is, in effect, another middle eight. This driving riff accompanies Ozzy's protests that 'Don't you think I know what I'm doing?'

Still not done, the band return to the riff for a fourth and final verse. The unexpected bonus is a string section, which comes in at 4:11. The strings add a sublime euphoric lift filling out the sound as the band riff out to the outro. Tony, for good measure, adds a sensational stinging final solo with those trilling fluttering notes just flying off.

'Snowblind' is a magnificent piece of work.

## 'Cornucopia'

In Greek mythology, the cornucopia was a symbol of abundance and nourishment. It's colloquially known as the Horn of Plenty, and was, not surprisingly, a horn-shaped vessel containing fruits, nuts or flowers. The song then is an observation about gluttony and greed. Among the possessions listed by Geezer are Matchbox toy cars, possibly their only mention in a song!

It opens with a compressed, slow lurching riff which is not far off from 'Tomorrow's Dream', picking up in pace as Tony changes the tempo to a galloping rhythm. They sustain this through the verses, but at 1:43, the familiar musical switch comes in. Fuzz guitar and a gong lead into a faster section, with Tony adding a second lead part to thicken the sound. This fast boogie rhythm is kept as the backing for the third verse, with a switch after that back to the original riff briefly, before returning to the galloping rhythm they used for verses one and two for the fourth and final verse.

This track could have been a lot better than it is, with careless production the main fault. Even in the latest remasters, the details are fuzzy and hard to pick out. The backing track is a little low in the mix compared to Ozzy, who is right out front. The intro and the riff are excellent and Ozzy gives it his best, but it doesn't really go anywhere. Poor Bill had all sorts of problems with the song, telling *Louder (Classic Rock)* in 2019 that: 'I hated the song 'Cornucopia'. There were patterns that were just horrible. I nailed it in the end, but I got the cold shoulder from everybody. I felt like I'd blown it, I was about to get fired.' In spite of these faults, the song is still a worthwhile listen because of the energy they put into it.

## 'Laguna Sunrise'

This was written by Tony while watching the sunrise over Laguna Beach in Los Angeles. Rather than leave it as an acoustic piece, Tony felt that an orchestral accompaniment would enhance the track. The use of an orchestra, as opposed to a mellotron part, is more evidence of the band's desire to develop their sound.

It has an attractive, easy laid back feel with Tony's guitars (two acoustic parts) meshing well with the strings when they come in. The string arrangement is stunning, but no arranger is credited. Tony told *Rolling Stone* in 2021 that he had come up with the arrangement, aided by Spock Wall, so it could be that he directed the string section himself.

In the same *Rolling Stone* interview, Ozzy implied that there had (from his point of view) been a thought to add a vocal track. 'Laguna Sunrise' was a beautiful piece of music,' he noted. 'I would have loved to try and put melodies to it. I couldn't beat what he'd already done with guitar, so we left it.'

While it is a beautiful piece, it goes on for too long with little variation. A similar problem will strike with 'Fluff' on the next album.

The latest master (by Andy Pearce and Matt Wortham) smooths out Tony's guitar sound on this track, so it sounds less brittle.

## 'St. Vitus Dance'

The title is the colloquial name for the medical condition known as Sydenham's Chorea. This is a rare neurological condition characterised by involuntary tremors or twitches. Lyrically there is no connection as the song is about a relationship breakup, sung in the third person giving advice to a lovelorn friend.

Getting back to the title of this track, the inspiration may have come from Tony's spasmodic riffs. The fuzzy intro riff is abrupt after the peaceful 'Laguna Sunrise'. It's a touch indistinct and slightly muffled, but Tony grabs the song by the scruff after only 13 seconds and pulls out one of his patented killer riffs before dropping back into the intro riff. It pretty much carries on alternating between the two riffs with little else happening. Even the four verses are as brief as possible, giving Ozzy little to do.

There is a middle eight (at 1:17), but the variation is not great, clearly, the inspiration was lacking to find something to lift the track. The lack of a solo from Tony is the final clue that this track did not have a lot of time lavished on it.

Really this is a filler track with a decent Tony riff to keep you listening. Not surprisingly, it was never played live.

## 'Under The Sun'

The working title apparently was 'Four X', maybe a reference to the Australian beer brewed by Castlemaine, or that it was a track being recorded for the fourth album, but with no title yet! Either way they changed it to the enigmatic 'Under The Sun, ' which doesn't obviously link to the lyrics. These see Geezer advising us to be careful who we listen to and follow, especially organised religion and exponents of the darker arts! 'Just believe in yourself', he urges.

It's another track that harks back to *Master Of Reality* with its dense subterranean sound. It's also another where Bill had problems getting the drum part down, much to his frustration. An unsympathetic Ozzy recalled in *I Am Ozzy* that by the time Bill nailed it they had thought of renaming the song 'Everywhere under the fucking sun'. Ozzy was credited (see deluxe edition book) with playing pinball machine on it, but likely it's a sarcastic joke about what he did while Bill was going through purgatory.

It opens with a monstrously heavy riff before a tempo change and a twisting new riff comes in at the 32-second mark leading into the first verse. Ozzy's vocal is not as distinct, mixed lower and part of the general miasma. Tony plays almost a Gaelic jig type fill before they plunge back into the riff and verse two.

Another Gaelic fill from Tony and next up, at 1:55, is the middle eight/ bridge section. This is the 'Everyday just comes and goes' section which features a riff that is exactly like Deep Purple's 1970 song 'Flight Of The Rat'. Sabbath up the tempo, with Ozzy having a real battle to get the words out in time. Bill gets a great extended fill before Ozzy returns for more break-neck vocals. Then Bill plays yet another fill before Tony takes his solo at 2:47, a squealing fluttering stream of notes that ends sharply and abruptly as the song's main riff comes back in at 3:10. If they did swap tempos here without an edit (something they have managed before), then this is even more impressive than the tempo change on 'Iron Man', for example.

Verse three is the final advice from Geezer, with Tony's guitar spiralling into the heavens as Bill's reversed cymbal or gong shimmers. That could have been the end of the track, but no, instead we get the best part of the song. A stunning instrumental coda (at 3:57) with a triumphant riff from Tony, to which he adds an equally uplifting pair of harmony lead guitar parts. It makes for a stirring end to the album. As one final surprise, Sabbath slow things down and down, the riff getting progressively more ponderous until the crescendo.

It's another song that is not among the best, but the riff is solid enough and the outro is superb. I have reservations about the middle eight mostly, which sounds a little jarring.

## USA edition notes

The tracks 'created' for the American edition are:-

'The Straightener', which is the end section of 'Wheels Of Confusion' from 5:14, There is a cross-fade effect on the intro, but it actually does sound like a bolted-on extra track. That supposition is substantiated by the deluxe edition out-takes, which credit 'The Straightener' as a separate track completely.

'Every Day Comes And Goes', which is the section from 1:55 to 3:09 in 'Under The Sun' when it speeds up. This also sounds like an extra track, particularly noticeable in the splice at the end of the section when the main riff comes back in. It's not smooth enough to disguise that the piece has been cut in.

## Volume Four – super-deluxe edition

This was released as two box sets in 2021 – A four-CD edition and a matching five LP edition. The original album was remastered by Andy Pearce and Matt Wortham. Pearce says that: 'We were asked specifically to do this in a different way, a more contemporary master because it had just been reissued not too long before. They liked what we had done on the previous masters and this time, we were given free rein. Imagining the band is in the studio right now recording it, so how would you interpret it. It's a lot cleaner, a bit brighter.'

Steven Wilson remixed the alternative takes and out-takes, unusual because Wilson normally works on remixing the actually released album. The final CD/pair of albums in the set is a dramatically remastered 'Live In The UK 1973', effectively a sonic upgrade of *Live At Last/Past Lives* (disc one) and reviewed in the 'Killing Yourself To Live' chapter.

## Volume Four out-takes and alternate takes

'Wheels Of Confusion / The Straightener'
The intro is different, with a more subdued guitar part from Tony, which kicks into the riff at the same time as the album version. Ozzy sings the original lyrics for the track, which have a stronger environmental crisis tone. The mix is less bright, as is clearly evident in the fast section that comes in at 2:25.

'The Straightener' outro section is 27 seconds longer and features a different guitar solo from Tony. It's not as bright as the released take, but it's more effective in the piece itself. He plays an absolute storm.

## 'Changes'

It is 1:30 shorter than the released take. The piano part is hesitant without the finesse of the released version, so it's likely an earlier take. Ozzy is also more hesitant and sings different lyrics on the verses. Given that these are not the final lyrics, it's understandable that his performance is not as commanding.

Geezer's mellotron part dominates this version and is much higher in the mix. As with the piano, this is also played with less aplomb and there are audible issues, such as at 1:27, where there is a jarring chord. Apart from Bill still sitting the track out, there is no bass either from Geezer on this take.

## 'Supernaut'

An early (shorter) run-through with guide vocal lyrics from Ozzy. This is the main interest as the instrumental backing is also not quite together yet. The guitar, in particular, is really out at times, with Tony getting a little lost here and there. He doesn't attempt a guitar solo because it wasn't needed yet. The break into the samba isn't there either, just that pounding drum rhythm that underpins it.

## 'Snowblind'

This sounds close to the released version. The main differences are some lyric changes, and a more pronounced chorus effect on Ozzy's voice which is mixed lower. Tony's solos are missing, but all the backing rhythm tracks are the same as the released take.

## 'Laguna Sunrise'

This is actually a series of run-throughs of the guitar part by Tony. In effect, we have a 'Laguna Sunrise' that is more in the vibe of 'Orchid'. It's got a lovely, hazy, summery quality to it and works better without the lush strings. In terms of musical progress, you can see why they would go for the strings, but this simpler version is more affecting and would have made a better choice.

## 'Under The Sun' (Instrumental)

The mix on this is monolithic, a quite different presentation of the soundscape to that used on the original album version. It fades out at 3:44, which is about where the cross-fade comes in on the album version for the 'Every Day Comes And Goes' coda.

## 'Wheels Of Confusion' (False Start with Studio Dialogue)

'What's it called, asks an engineer (Colin Caldwell or Vic Smith). 'Bollocks', replies a gleeful Ozzy. Primarily this is included for that amusing exchange because we only get a little over 16 seconds of the intro before things break down, with Ozzy exclaiming, 'That was a bit too fast Billy'.

## 'Wheels Of Confusion' (Alternative Take 1)

The earliest first run-through of the first half of the track, featuring that different set of environmental crisis lyrics again. Tony's guitar solo is missing, as are the sweeping accents he puts in on the section from 2:41 onwards. It breaks down suddenly, sounding like they go into what would be 'The Straightener' closing section by mistake a minute too early.

## 'Wheels Of Confusion' (Alternative Take 2)

A full run through this time of the first half of the track, again with the original lyrics. Still missing some of the extra touches and accents they subtly add to the released version.

## 'Wheels Of Confusion' (Alternative Take 3)

Yet another full run-through as per take 2. There is an error around 11 seconds in from Tony that sticks out, but otherwise, this has nothing extra to note.

## 'Wheels Of Confusion' (Alternative Take 4)

Called out by the engineer as being take five before the intro. This is the longest full run-through of the first part of the track and the tightest version yet. By the end, you can hear they have nailed the backing track, with just the lyrics and additional touches to add to the mix, plus that segue into 'The Straightener'.

## 'The Straightener' (Outtake)

The title is noted as such on the multi-track tapes, which means this is one of those 'extra' titles on the American editions of the albums that had some roots in actually being a separate piece of music. The engineer notes it as 'edit section one', so it was always intended to be added to 'Wheels Of Confusion'. Tony's guitar intro is cleaner and his solo seems brighter and higher in the mix; this is better than the released take/mix. Hearing the edited piece as a separate piece of music really showcases just how good it is.

## 'Supernaut' (Outtake)

This is a brave inclusion for the super deluxe edition, Sabbath feeling their way with a soon to be classic song. Because of the unfamiliarity, it is taken at a slower pace, but even so, it's loose and ragged. Tony, in particular, drifts all over the place with the riffs at times. You can imagine him shaking his head in amusement. At other times you can hear he is trying to find somewhere else to take things but hasn't quite worked it out. Bill, meanwhile, has already worked out how he is going to handle the drums; the basics are there. As usual, the lyrics are guide vocals from Ozzy at this point.

## 'Supernaut' (Alternative takes with false starts)

This thirteen and a half minutes compilation starts with take one of 'Supernaut'. This is the backing track with Ozzy's guide vocal, and considering it's take one, it's really excellent. It breaks down at 1:51 and is followed by take two, which ends on the intro at 2:14. Take three is next up and more successful, with Ozzy getting some vocals in before it stutters to a halt at 4:09.

Back to the beginning again for take four which fares better before coming adrift at 6:33 after some ragged guitar from Tony. Take five is doomed from the start with some wayward notes and looseness, but they persevere with it, presumably to try and make it to a problem part of the backing track, which is that guitar part.

At 9:37 of this compilation, we get what the engineer announces as 'intercut one'. After a pregnant pause, it kicks in at 10:07 but never gets going. Neither do intercuts two to six. Finally, intercut seven reveals what exactly it is they are working on in these cuts. It's the lead in from Tony to the guitar/drums samba section, the samba section itself, plus the section with Ozzy's vocals that follow it. It's still a little rudimentary but thrilling to be almost in the room with the band as they try to get it right.

### 'Snowblind' (Alternative Take 1 – Incomplete)

A spirited run through of the track, with Ozzy on especially vibrant form. There are minor lyric differences and Tony's solos are missing. It stops after three minutes, with Tony again trying that descending riff he plays during the 'My eyes are blind, but I can see' section.

### 'Under The Sun' (False start with studio dialogue)

It opens with Ozzy asking the engineer to turn up Tony's guitar in Geezer's cans. Some nice tentative strums through the intro chords from Tony and Geezer and they launch into a full sounding version of the backing track. It breaks down all too quickly, which is a shame as they had a great vibe going on this take.

### 'Under The Sun' (Alternative take with guide vocal)

A really fascinating take instrumentally, which has a brighter sound than the released version. Despite the talk of Bill having trouble with the drums on this track, he sounds just fine even at this early stage. Ozzy hasn't come up with any lyrics for the guide vocal, so he just hums and lah-lah's along with it. It stops short of the epic closing section, which was obviously an added on edit piece that could have been given a separate name as per other edit pieces.

DECADES | Black Sabbath in the 70s

# 1973: The race is run, the book is read

In January, Sabbath commenced their first tour of Australia and New Zealand. They opened the six-date run in Wellington on 5 January.

In the early part of 1973, Tony produced the debut album by his protégés Necromandus. The album, *Orexis Of Death*, was recorded at Morgan Studios, with Tony also contributing the guitar solo on the title track. The album is well worth hearing for any Sabbath fan, and it's a great shame its release was shelved for many years. For Mike Butcher, it was the start of his working relationship with Tony and Black Sabbath:

I was an in-house engineer at Morgan Studios in London. I started my career there. In the early '70s there was one week where six of the top twenty best-selling albums in the States had been recorded, or partially recorded, at Morgan. It was one of the leading studios in the world. Tony came in with a band called Necromandus which he produced and I was assigned to engineer the sessions. He didn't know me beforehand and we got on well together.

The long-overdue tour of Europe, commenced in Hamburg on 15 February, running through to L'Olympia in Paris on 3 March. Six days later they began the UK leg at Green's Playhouse in Glasgow. Support for the British dates was from Badger and Necromandus, with Badger dropping out halfway through the tour. Dates at Manchester and The Rainbow in London were recorded for a prospective live album, but the results were deemed unsatisfactory. They were eventually released years later as *Live At Last*. The final UK date was on 18 February at Newcastle City Hall, marking the end of the dates to support *Vol. Four.*

The plan had been for American dates, due to commence on 2 April in Chicago, but the tour was cancelled. Instead, band activity was given over to writing and recording *Sabbath Bloody Sabbath*. Initial sessions took place in Los Angeles, with the band renting the Dupont house again, but this time the muse was not with them. Sabbath thus returned home to find their inspiration at Clearwell Castle in Gloucestershire. Once they had the songs worked out the band decamped to Morgan Studios in London, where the album was recorded.

The band did play one gig over the summer – at Alexandra Palace in London on 2 August as part of the London Music Festival. The gig saw Sabbath play the as yet unrecorded 'A National Acrobat', 'Sabbath Bloody

Sabbath' and the new, but becoming familiar, 'Killing Yourself to Live' in an eleven song set.

Tony married his first wife, Susan Snowdon, on 3 November, with John Bonham as his best man. Tony had met Susan earlier that year via Patrick Meehan, and Tony had agreed to come up with material for her to sing. Her recording career never took off, but at least the romance did.

*Sabbath Bloody Sabbath* was released on 1 December, the same day as the title track was released as a single. As a bonus for UK fans, they played four dates: Newcastle (9), Bristol (11), Birmingham (14) and Leicester (17). The gaps between the shows are unusual for that era and hint at a need for rest days.

## Sabbath Bloody Sabbath *(WWA/Warners)*

Personnel:

Ozzy Osbourne: vocals, synthesiser on 'Killing Yourself To Live' and 'Who Are You'

Tony Iommi: guitars, flute, piano, synthesiser, harpsichord, organ, mellotron (instruments credited in track reviews)

Geezer Butler: bass, synthesiser and mellotron on 'Who Are You', nose flute on 'Spiral Architect'

Bill Ward: drums, bongos on 'Sabbath Bloody Sabbath', timpani on 'Who Are You' and 'Spiral Architect'

and:

Rick Wakeman: piano and mini-moog on 'Sabbra Cadabra' and possibly 'Who Are You'

Wil Malone: conductor/ arranger on 'Spiral Architect'

The Phantom Fiddlers: strings on 'Spiral Architect'

Produced at Morgan Studios, September 1973 by Tony Iommi

UK release date: 1 December 1973, USA release date: 1 January 1974

Highest chart places: UK: 4, USA: 11

Running time: 42:35

All songs by Black Sabbath.

The title is supposed to have been Bill's idea and is a reworking of a *Melody Maker* headline title which read, 'Bloody Hell, Black Sabbath'.

During the writing sessions before the album was recorded, the band were visited by some of Led Zeppelin. John Bonham was excited by 'Sabbra Cadabra' and wanted to have a go at that, but Sabbath persuaded the Zeppelin boys to jam on something else instead. It's not thought that any recordings exist of this supergroup jam session, affectionately recalled as Black Zeppelin.

To engineer the album, Tony was keen to use Mike Butcher, who he had got on so well with at the Necromandus sessions. Mike feels that there was a final test to see if he was the right man:

Tony came in to Morgan with Bill Ward because Bill wanted to do a solo track. I think it was to see if Bill liked my drum sound, so we recorded this one track. I don't know if anything ever happened to it, I don't think I even got as far as mixing it. Anyway, Bill liked the drum sound.

Having passed the test with Tony and Bill, Mike was given the good news when the whole band came to see him at Morgan.

They asked me to record the album in the States. I was a young engineer and I thought this was just fantastic, going off to California. They went over there a couple of months before I was due to join them so they could rehearse. Two days before I was supposed to fly out, I got a message from their management saying they had been back to see the studio and it had changed, and they didn't like it, so they were going to come back home. They decided to record the album at Morgan, London and a few weeks later, we started recording there.

There had indeed been problems in Los Angeles, with Tony experiencing difficulties in coming up with new material and the band unimpressed with changes at the Record Plant. So Sabbath returned to England for the rural and spooky atmosphere at Clearwell Castle. To help get his mojo going Tony spent time listening to the new Golden Earring album *Moontan* (featuring their hit single, 'Radar Love'). The castle environment also provided inspiration, initially leading to the riff for the title track when the band first set up their gear in the dungeon. The castle was supposed to be haunted, something the band took seriously when Tony and Ozzy followed a figure who allegedly walked into a room and vanished.

It wasn't just Tony who benefited from the location, as Clearwell had a restorative effect on the whole group. The band particularly enjoyed their downtime at the Wyndham Arms pub in Clearwell. Meanwhile, a walk through the Forest Of Dean got a lot of the footage used in the promo video for the title track.

More than one account says the band also used Rockfield Studios while they were stopping at Clearwell Castle and that the actual demos they worked on were recorded at Rockfield. Invigorated by the new material, the band played the aforementioned concert at Alexandra Palace in London on 2 August, showcasing the forthcoming opening pair of tracks plus the already road-tested 'Killing Yourself To Live'.

Clearwell, Rockfield and the triumphant gig at Alexandra Palace did the job. Now armed with enough material, the band decamped to Morgan Studios in London, where, accompanied by Mike Butcher, they set about committing the songs to tape. Mike enjoyed working with Sabbath:

> I liked them; they were very friendly people. To be honest, a lot of the time, it was a bit like schoolkids – playing jokes, jumping around – but when we worked, we really did work. I really did appreciate that about Sabbath, when they needed to concentrate, they put the time in. They were very well rehearsed so we would get the basic track down in two or three takes usually.

Rick Wakeman was also at Morgan:

> Yes were in the studio just across the road recording *Topographic Oceans* and Sabbath were in studio two, both part of Morgan Studios. As a bit of history, when Morgan was first built, it had one studio and that was what became the bar/cafe after they had built studio one upstairs, studio two downstairs, studio three across the road, and studio four around the corner!

The album was recorded with a dropped tuning, as was now their norm, to C#. By contrast, Ozzy sings higher on this album more consistently than ever before. His vocal performance is first class throughout but the trade-off was that little of the album made it into the live sets. Musically it expands on *Volume Four*, moving on from the likes of 'Wheels Of Confusion', 'Snowblind' and 'Supernaut'. It's a great album with more consistent production than *Volume Four*, with only three tracks preventing it from being a fully top-drawer set – 'Fluff', 'Looking For Today' and 'Who Are You' being the still very listenable make-weights.

Tony goes on record in his book that he was looking for the band to progress, and with that in mind, *Sabbath Bloody Sabbath* is their first sophisticated album. The production is lusher and fuller than on previous albums and the cover package is equally lavish. It all sounds and looks and feels like a top-flight rock band with no expense spared.

An interesting point about the sequencing comes from Mike Butcher, who recalled that, 'We did a running order, and then when we listened back to it, we didn't like it. I wish I could remember what that original order was'.

While it looked like Sabbath had signed to a new label, WWA, they were actually still signed to Phonogram, who took on the label. World Wide Artists (WWA) had been created by Patrick Meehan and was administrated by his father. The idea behind it being to give Sabbath a 'better' record deal with Phonogram. The label didn't last long but did manage to reissue all of the previous Sabbath albums plus some compilations.

The fabulous packaging was the first that the band had any real say in. The front and back cover scenes were created by Drew Struzan, who worked for Pacific Eye and Ear (noted for their work with Alice Cooper). The two scenes portray diametrically opposed versions of a man's death – on the front, he dies alone, tormented by demons, while on the back, he is comforted by his family and welcomed by angels. Ernie Cefalu, director and chief lettering designer of Pacific Eye and Ear, pointed out a last-minute change to the cover:

The 'bolt' lettering for the band name was put on after we submitted the final art (with my logo) and the change was unbeknownst to us. If you look closely at the skull area the curves of my logo were still left In the art!

Ernie's original logo was in a gothic script, something along the lines of the Judas Priest logo on their *Sin After Sin* album. The hurried replacement lettering was designed by Geoff Halpin.

The inner gatefold sleeve, photographed by Pacific Eye and Ear, is curious. The band are posing topless, their bodies as see-through as ghosts, inside a room which feels like it is supposed to be the one on the outer cover, except the bed is now a four-poster. The picture of Sabbath is superimposed on the background. In the 2005 magazine *Q Classic – Ozzy* Tony confirmed to Pete Makowski that the reason he and Geezer are covering their faces was that both had recently shaved off their moustaches and 'felt strange'.

The actual record bag had not only the lyrics to every track but also full musician and instrument credits.

## 'Sabbath Bloody Sabbath'

The first song that Tony came up with at Clearwell Castle, thanks to the spooky environment which invigorated him and helped him over the writer's block he had suffered in Los Angeles. The lyrics are all by Geezer and are thought to reflect how the band felt when they couldn't get things going in Los Angeles.

It opens with the seismic opening riff, a fuzz-toned monster that is doubled by Geezer and matched by Ozzy's astonishingly powerful vocals. The first verse rides on that riff, and then they shift into the chorus at 0:43, which is utterly different. This has a laid back Californian feel – 'Nobody will ever let you know' – and is a delightful contrast with some attractive guitar licks. It gives Ozzy some respite, too as he drops down his register.

Back to the big riff for verse three and Ozzy is back to the top of his register for more angst. I love the pause in the first line, 'The people who – have crippled you, you want to see them burn'. Geezer gets in another back catalogue reference later in the verse with, 'You're wishing that the hands of doom could take your mind away.' The easy listening chorus comes back at 1:54, but this time it features Ozzy's ad-libbed coda of 'You bastards!'

The middle eight comes next, which sees the band jamming on the riff while Tony overdubs a solo. A short melodic bridge and a turnaround from Bill finishes this off before Tony, and Geezer's deep and dirty fuzz bass, introduce the song's second riff at 3:18. 'Where can you run to?', sings an anguished Ozzy. They stick to the immense riff pattern for two verses before Ozzy signs off with 'Living just for dying, dying just for you, yeah'. The outro is another change of pace, a shuddering rhythm with descending shapes from Tony and a controlled wah-wah solo.

A promo video was made for the song, filmed near Clearwell Castle and also at sites around Birmingham. It's an engaging watch, filmed at a time when there was no clever editing or messages required in a video. Do your best to ignore the appallingly edited single version of this outstanding Sabbath song, backed with 'Changes'

Minor controversy arose when a song called 'What To Do' by Brazilian singer Vanusa got attention outside of her native country. It came out as part of her album, ironically called *Vanusa Volume Four*, in 1973. It was claimed that Tony got the riff from here, but it's nonsense. It's unlikely Tony would have heard her album for a start. And then 'What To Do' is the English language song on her album and sounds exactly like a song where the riff has been borrowed to fit. Although her album is supposed to have come out before *Sabbath Bloody Sabbath,* it just doesn't ring true.

## 'A National Acrobat'

Geezer: "A National Acrobat' was just me thinking about who selects what sperm gets through to the egg.' There is an interesting back reference in the lyrics. On 'Supernaut' Geezer wrote in verse two that, 'I've lived a thousand years, it never bothered me' and in verse two here, he writes that, 'I've lived a thousand times, I found out what it means to be believed.'

It's never picked up as one of their best songs, but it really is and deserves wider recognition. The main riff and tone of the piece are suggestive of *Master Of Reality* and the likes of 'Cornucopia' or 'Under the Sun' off *Volume Four*.

Tony credits Geezer as coming up with that intro riff. It's a catchy, utterly superb riff and one of Sabbath's best. It's played in unison by Tony and Geezer, with a flattish sound to it, but it works! Tony adds a second higher guitar part doubling his riff that gives it a lift as the first verse approaches. Bill, meanwhile, keeps things simple to give that twisting riff space.

Vocally it's well within Ozzy's range and he gives the somewhat obscure lyrics real passion. It's one of his best-ever performances with Sabbath, enhanced by the doubling of the vocal track. Bill gets to add some fills while Ozzy sings and, delightfully, that riff comes back in between each of his lines. For the second verse, which opens with 'I've lived a thousand times', Ozzy moves up his register for emphasis and overdubs a harmony backing vocal.

This sets a pattern, as the third verse ('When little worlds collide') returns to the format of verse one, while the fourth verse ('The name that scorns the face') repeats the format of verse two with the backing harmonies.

The middle eight is unusual for Sabbath in that it's not that big a stretch harmonically from the main riff. Tony's new riff comes in, making use of his wah-wah pedal with a stuttering hook on the end, while Ozzy exclaims, 'You gotta believe it, I'm talking to you'. Tony gets his solo at 3:34. For this he plays two lead parts, squealing and harmonically twisting around each other while the backing track remains the same as for the middle eight. There are additional droning guitar fills for effect in the mix, making four guitar parts during the solo section! That droning sound effect guitar is retained initially as Ozzy comes back in for more verses.

Ozzy's 'Ha ha' at 4:38 heralds the big change of tempo for the extended outro section. It starts with a slow build-up, but the tempo picks up for what could be described as a jaunty melody. This segues into a stunning hard rock finale featuring Tony letting fly with a fast stream of notes that cascade off into the distance and an abrupt stop. The end to an absolute Sabbath classic!

## 'Fluff'

Alan 'fluff' Freeman, Radio One DJ and fan of the band, got this track 'named' after him as a thanks for his strong support. It got an early airing at Tony's wedding when it was played as his bride, Susan Snowdon, walked down the aisle. It's easy to imagine it was intended for just that purpose.

The sequencing of 'Fluff' following 'A National Acrobat' is excellent. It opens with Tony's solo acoustic melody line, which he then harmonises with on a second acoustic. Mike Butcher: 'Because of his fingers, Tony played very light strings on his guitar. So on an acoustic guitar, it's difficult to get a nice recorded sound. It turned out really well'.

Delicate harpsichord, also by Tony, sweetens things up before he (now multi-tasking at an incredible rate) adds a piano part. At 1:03, his lead electric part comes in, which has overtones of Peter Green's work on Fleetwood Mac's 'Albatross'. It's a beautiful yearning sound that does Tony great credit.

It's also at the 1:03 mark that Geezer's bass enters, soft touches on the low notes. It's his bass that carries the melody line before the middle eight comes in at 1:42. Not much of a change of pace here as Tony picks out an attractive melody on steel guitar, with piano, harpsichord and bass backing. He also picks out counterpoint melodies on the electric. This is the loveliest section of the track. At 2:32, we go back again to the first part of the track, which is played through twice before Tony wraps it up with a three-note descending guitar coda.

While the track undeniably has a pleasant bucolic feel, there are niggles. Firstly it's too long by at least a minute, the second run-through of the intro section after the middle eight should have been chopped. Secondly, it could have done with more of the electric guitar, which is a highlight of the track. There's not enough going on otherwise to make it rise above being pleasant.

**Above:** A 1970 promo picture, probably taken in London. There are several pics of the band wearing the same clothes around the city. (*Author collection*)

**Above:** The Iommi family shop at 67 Park Lane in Aston (near right). (*Author collection*)

**Below:** The band honed their early material at Newtown Community Centre in Birmingham. (*Author collection*)

**Above:** *Black Sabbath* (1970). The full spooky gatefold sleeve of the self-titled debut. It captures the mood of the title track in particular. (*Vertigo/ Warners*)

**Below:** Sabbath in a garden, circa 1970. (*Author collection*)

**Left:** A Rarely seen colour photo from a 1970 shoot outside a church or possibly a mausoleum. (*Author collection*)

**Right:** Sabbath in 1970 on the verge of success and on the verge opposite Jim Simpson's house. (*Birmingham Mail*)

**Right:** *Paranoid* (1970). The second album is loaded with classics, housed in this curiously inappropriate yet somehow appealing cover. (*Vertigo/ Warners*)

**Left:** Hometown heroes. Black Sabbath at the Town Hall in Birmingham, 1971. (*Author collection*)

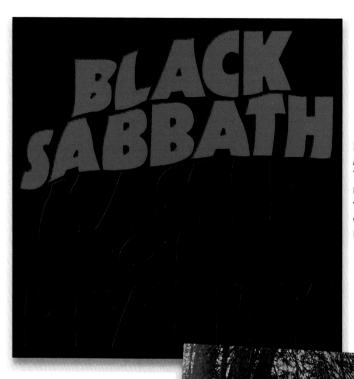

**Left:** *Master Of Reality* (1971). The down-tuned masterpiece with a starkly effective cover. (*Vertigo/ Warners*)

**Right:** The grainy poster from *Master Of Reality*. (*Vertigo/ Warners*)

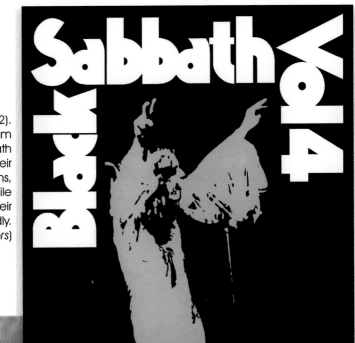

**Right:** *Vol. 4* (1972). The fourth album sees Sabbath expanding their musical ambitions, recorded while expanding their minds, supposedly. (*Vertigo/ Warners*)

**Left:** Time out in the USA during their crazy 1972 sojourn there. (*Kevin Goff*)

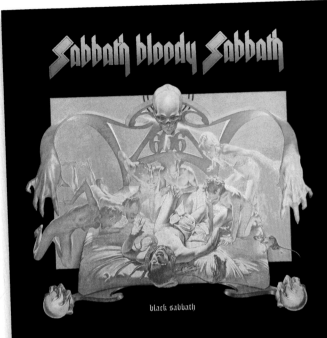

**Left:** *Sabbath Bloody Sabbath* (1973). A great album combined with Drew Struzan's stunning cover images. The increased complexity of the songs meant the album never got a fair showing live. (*WWA/ Warners*)

**Above:** The band pose for the inside sleeve of *Sabbath Bloody Sabbath*. This is what you would have seen if it had been a full-length shot! (*Pacific Eye & Ear*)

**Right:** *Sabotage* (1975). The last truly great album by the original band. The endearingly daft cover always raises a smile. (*NEMS/ Warners*)

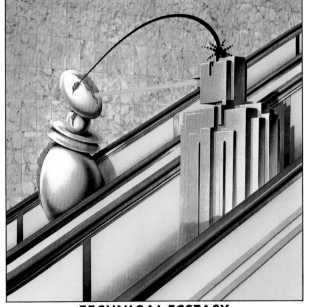

**Left:** *Technical Ecstasy* (1976). Over technical and somewhat sterile – both the songs and the cover. The bright spots are enough to keep you listening. (*NEMS/ Warners*)

**Left:** Ozzy at the California Jam in 1974, their biggest audience yet! (*Author collection*)

**Right:** Geezer happy to be back on stage again. California Jam, 1974 (*Author collection*)

**Left:** Bill, the engine room of the band, at the California Jam in 1974 (*Author collection*)

**Right:** Tony, without moustache, at California Jam in 1974. (*Author collection*)

**Left:** Jez Woodroffe handled the keys from the *Sabotage* dates through to the *Technical Ecstasy* album and tour. (*Author collection*)

**Right:** Receiving silver discs for *Technical Ecstasy*. (*Author collection*)

**Above:** Bill on stage at Long Beach Arena, 1975. (*Author collection*)

**Below:** Geezer rocks out at Long Beach Arena, 1975. (*Author collection*)

**Above:** Tony, very much in the zone at Long Beach Arena, 1975. (*Author collection*)

**Below:** Ozzy loves you all at Long Beach Arena, 1975. (*Author collection*)

**Left:** Bill on the *Technical Ecstasy* tour in 1976. (*Author collection*)

**Right:** Ozzy feeling the love and the music at Lewisham Odeon in 1978. (*Dick Wallis*)

**Left:** What is this that stands before me? Lewisham Odeon in 1978. (*Dick Wallis*)

**Right:** Geezer at Lewisham Odeon in 1978. (*Dick Wallis*)

**Left:** Van who? Tony gives it his all at Lewisham Odeon, 1978. (*Dick Wallis*)

**BLACK SABBATH**
*Never Say Die!*

**Left:** *Never Say Die* (1978). The final album by the original band. A mixed bag of a record that doesn't live up to its title. (*Vertigo/Warners*)

**Left:** A rare surviving Earth poster from 1969. (*Author collection*)

**Right:** Sabbath's first manager Jim Simpson in more recent years outside The Crown in Birmingham. This was where he set up the first Henry's Blues House. (*Birmingham Mail*)

## 'Sabbra Cadabra'

Despite the close proximity of Yes at Morgan Studios, the only member they saw much of was Rick Wakeman in the cafe. Wakeman feels that 'It was more a bar than a cafe if the truth be known'.

Rick recalls the invitation to come and see what he could add to the recordings: 'It was by both Tony and Ozzy. I was good friends with all of them and I think the fact that my personal lifestyle was more akin to Sabbath than Yes cemented our friendships!'

Sabbath asked Wakeman to play on the album. 'It was great fun to do but I remember very little as it was gone midnight when I did the sessions after I had finished with Yes over the road. It's always nice to be asked to perform on tracks by a band you are a fan of'. Rick adds synthesiser and piano to the track. Both parts, he says, were overdubbed.

Ozzy says they 'paid' Wakeman for his contributions with two pints of Directors Best Bitter, but Wakeman plays that down. 'It's a bit of a myth. I didn't ask to be paid, I did it because they were mates and I was a fan. I'm sure they bought me some drinks in the bar, but equally, I'm sure I bought them some as well!'

The lyrics are mostly by Ozzy, who, so he says in his book, came up with all the 'Lovely lady make love all night long' etc., references from the porn films the band were watching. The title is a pun on abracadabra, a word with origins in ancient texts which is used as a spell in magic tricks.

It opens with a catchy guitar riff, joined with a descending bass part from Geezer and a shuffle rhythm from Bill. Tony thickens things up just before the first verse by adding a rhythm guitar part to the mix. Ozzy is at the top end of his register and the track bounces along in a feel-good fashion, which, judging by the lyrics, it should! It's a different tone for Sabbath but doesn't jar in the way the later similarly feel-good 'Rock 'N' Roll Doctor' does.

Tony rings the changes for the middle eight at 1:59 with a change of tempo, but the big change is the arrival of Rick Wakeman to the song. He plays piano, keyboards and Moog synthesiser on his overdubbed parts, and he blends in perfectly with Sabbath, never overbalancing the sound. In fact, it works so well you could have made a good case for them taking on a keyboard player based on this track. But rarely on later albums do they come remotely as close to using keyboards as effectively as this. Ozzy's voice is treated on this section, distorted with an echo effect added.

Wakeman's piano is higher in the mix from 2:54 onwards, with Tony sticking to rhythm guitar to allow Wakeman space. His attractive piano lines are broken up by a cascading riff, which he himself joins in with on synth.

The long outro kicks in at about 3:53 after Ozzy declares, 'I'm never gonna leave you anymore, no more'. It's a spellbinding outro as Ozzy scats lyrics over the jammed ending, with Wakeman absolutely killing it on piano. Tony's rhythm part gets more urgent as the track winds down, while Ozzy gets unintelligible, thanks to Mike Butcher. The problem was that as the outro jam went on, Ozzy had taken it on himself to unleash a volley of words that were too offensive to go out on record. The long jam outro was otherwise great, so to keep it and use it, Butcher masked Ozzy's vocals. A great final ending, too, with Bill's drum fill and the last notes from Wakeman.

'Sabbra Cadabra' made it to the live set, a surprise really given the prominence of Wakeman, but the simpler arrangement worked well live.

## 'Killing Yourself To Live'
Mike Butcher singles this track out above all the others:

At the time of recording that was my favourite song. We mixed it twice. That big reverb on the guitar in the middle, I did it in the first mix and they didn't like it. Well, it was 'somebody' who didn't like it and they asked me not to do it. Then they asked me to remix the song. So I did a second mix, kept that reverb, and this time they said that's really good! They were acting like they had never heard it before.

It was the first track the band had for the album, appearing in live sets going back to February 1973. Geezer told *Q Classic – Ozzy*, in 2005, about the real-life inspiration behind the song:

We were touring and stuck in hotels on drugs all the time. We had to maintain such a heavy schedule of touring that we were, by then, constantly on coke, coming down, on smack or whatever. We were literally killing ourselves to live.

It's a great song and up there with their best work, becoming the main track from the album that they played live. It opens with a chugging riff, soon joined by Ozzy. In truth, not the most dynamic opening, but your ears prick up when an evil descending riff comes in at 0:53 that hammers home the resignation to their situation in the lyrics. The format is repeated with the next verse using the intro riff before falling back on the descending riff for the chorus. Second time around, it gets expanded on superbly with Tony overlaying two lead guitar parts, duelling with himself. With the pressure building up, Ozzy, too, raises his game with the 'I'm telling you, believe in me, nobody else will tell you' lines.

The switch to a different tune comes at 2:45. It's a new riff and a different feel with blasting synths coming through in the background, care of Ozzy or Tony. It's a more euphoric section than the first half of the song, inspired by the solution to their touring pressures. 'Smoke it' urges Ozzy, and then 'High!' There is a nice slow build-up by the band, which leads into the middle eight, after which they gallop into the closing section at 4:06. Bill's drums herald the assault. Tony throws in yet another riff that sounds like something Thin Lizzy would have got a whole song out of. As if that wasn't enough, he also overlays two more solos together while Bill pounds away and Geezer locks in with him. Tony finishes off with a breathtaking buzzing final riff that stops suddenly.

## 'Who Are You'

Mike Butcher: 'It was a bit like they let Ozzy do it, and then Tony and the others thought they had better fix it up and make it a little more interesting. They took rough mixes home and Tony and Geezer came up with that middle section'.

The lack of a question mark in the title is an oversight, though the lack of it does make for a more enigmatic title!

This track was written mostly by Ozzy, who came up with the main synth riff at home, pre-empting one-figured synth pop by six years or so. Both Ozzy and Geezer are credited with playing the synth part and there are two parts going on. The main riff is Ozzy, with Geezer adding the swirling sounds behind it. Despite the duelling synths, it sounds, for the most part, like it never got much beyond the demo stage, with little of interest going on, despite the efforts of Geezer and Bill to add heft to the bottom end. Ozzy's vocals are underplayed though he keeps the melody going nicely. To vary things a little, his voice is double-tracked for the second verse, which makes a big difference to the impact of the song.

At 2:01, the middle eight comes in, which is by far the best part of the song, and noticeably the section of the song that sounds like it had the most work done on it. The piano is credited to Tony (who plays no guitar on this track at all), while Geezer adds mellotron washes in the background. It's over all too quickly as Bill's drums cue us back into the main theme for an agonisingly long further minute and a half, livened only by cymbal effects and synth rumbles.

It is possible that Rick Wakeman also plays on this track. In his book, Ozzy talks about Wakeman improving on how he was playing the melody to 'Sabbra Cadabra' on an ARP synthesiser. The one-fingered riff that Ozzy mentions is clearly not 'Sabbra Cadabra' but 'Who Are You'. Wakeman's advice could be his only 'contribution', but Mike Butcher feels he also played on the released track. Rick Wakeman says that 'I always thought I did, but due to a long passage of time, plus undoubtedly a fair intake of whisky, I can't be sure. I'd like to think that Mike was right.' Fortunately, this experimental filler track has never been played live.

## 'Looking For Today'

Heavy reverb on the intro immediately makes this sound different to the other tracks. There's a thicker, soupy bottom end that makes it sound a little indistinct. Ozzy is also less clear in the mix than elsewhere on the album. The difference in the sound is explained by Mike Butcher. 'We didn't mix all the tracks in the same studio; we used all three of Morgan's studios. I think that one was mixed in studio three, which was the newer studio. I think it was the last song we recorded and mixed for the album'.

What we have here, in spite of the slight production woes, is a good track. It's nowhere near being great, but it's catchy enough. The riff that drives it along isn't one of Tony's best by his high standards, but for many bands, it would be a classic. He also adds a flute part that flutters up in the mix.

An example of the problems with the clarity comes at 1:34 when Ozzy comes back in for a verse. Bill sounds to be doing great work, but he and Geezer are muffled. The bass, in fact, is hard to pick out on much of the song.

Some clarity comes at 2:03 with the middle eight, which Ozzy opens with 'Everyone just gets on top of you'. Listen to the song closely and your ears feel like they have been syringed here; such is the change in dynamics. Suddenly the bass and drums are audible and the whole sound spectrum opens out. From there, at 2:35, it changes into a glorious section led by a new riff from Tony. Ozzy sings the title over some muscular riffing until 2:59, when we head back into a repeat of the intro section. Ozzy's ad-libbed plea to 'listen' lead us into the final verse. Needless to say, it's all got rather soupy again, except that Ozzy is much higher in the mix than he was on the intro.

The final section of the track comes in at 3:42, with that second riff kicking things off.

It was never played live, but you can see how it could have worked well with a heavier live vibe. This would have made a better choice for the single from the album.

## 'Spiral Architect'

Quite simply, this is one of the best songs Black Sabbath ever recorded. In the liner notes to the later *Reunion* album Geezer explained that: "Spiral Architect' was about life's experiences being added to a person's DNA to create a unique individual. I used to get very contemplative on certain substances.' Ozzy was amazed at the speed with which Geezer came up with the lyrics. He recalled in *I Am Ozzy* that he rang Geezer up from Morgan when he was having a day off, 'C'mon Geezer, I need some words for 'Spiral Architect''. An hour later, Ozzy rang him back and Geezer read all the lyrics out to an astonished Ozzy, who thought he must have got them out of a book! They are among his most profoundly thought out lyrics.

Tony did try to play the bagpipes on the track, but without success, so that was abandoned. We do, however, get a wonderful inventive string score, played by the mysterious Phantom Fiddlers and orchestrated by Wil Malone. Mike Butcher:

Wil was an in-house producer at Morgan. Morgan had a production company, so he was often around. When it came up to have a string arrangement, Wil was well into it – he was a great musician and arranger, but was also young enough to appreciate rock music. Geezer did a guide string arrangement with the mellotron to give some idea of what was wanted, but most of the arrangement is Wil.

The strings were recorded at Morgan in Studio 2. Wil booked the studio, but the band assumed it was in the afternoon. I was at home when I got a phone call saying the string players had turned up to the studio in the morning and the studio wasn't free. It was supposed to be Studio 1, but luckily the people in Studio 2 understood and let us have it. You can't cancel string players, you have to pay them whether they play or not. So I rushed to the studio in a taxi. When we recorded the strings, Sabbath weren't there. I think Spock Wall was there; we managed to contact him. So when the group turned up, the string players had already gone.

The track has a beautiful melodic feel to it with a similar vibe to early Yes. The structure is more traditional than is normal, with Black Sabbath having a recognisable chorus. It opens with a lovely arpeggio from Tony, which ends after 44 seconds to be replaced by the guitar riff backed by the huge rhythm track assault. Bill's cymbals sizzle while his drums go off like depth charge explosions. Geezer doubles the riff here, but throughout, he comes up with some beautifully worked out bass parts.

Ozzy is brilliant, a little reverb on his voice and sporadic use of double-tracking, giving his vocals extra lift. He gets the right amount of reflection and affirmation into his delivery to enhance the depth of the lyrics.

Malone's strings come in on the first chorus, 'Of all the things I value most of all'. It's a stunning dramatic arrangement that became a trademark of his on the countless arrangements he has done right up to recent times. They come back again for the two subsequent choruses.

The middle eight comes in at 3:17 with a subtle tempo change. It's a glorious blend of the strings and Black Sabbath dovetailing together. This part is so good they could have built it up into the ending, but instead, they come back for another verse and the final chorus. The strings stay with them throughout now, in perfect harmony.

The outro builds to a crescendo, broken by applause over a cool down refrain from Geezer and Bill. The applause was Mike Butcher's idea: 'We knew it was going to be the last track on the album so that's why the idea for the applause at the end was put forward'.

## USA edition notes

The tracks 'created' for the American edition of this album were never credited on any sleeve or label. They are, however, included in the songbook for the album:-

'You Think That I'm Crazy' is the section from 2:45 to 4:05 in 'Killing Yourself To Live' accompanied by a change of pace and yet another great riff from Tony.

'I Don't Know If I'm Up Or Down' is also in 'Killing Yourself To Live'. It comes in with Bill's turnaround right after 'You Think That I'm Crazy'. Tony's riff takes off for a fast section that goes right through to the outro.

'Prelude To A Project' is Tony's superb acoustic intro to 'Spiral Architect'.

# 1974: I don't know if I'm up or down

There are persistent rumours that Sabbath thought of bringing in a keyboard player, following on from their sessions with Rick Wakeman and their slowly increasing use of keyboards to add colour to their sound. Was Rick Wakeman asked to join? Rick:

I can only answer this with hearsay. I believe that Tony thought it would be a good move to invite me to join as he knew that although I was enjoying performing with Yes and loved the music, socially, we were chalk and cheese and we disagreed a lot. But the ask never came, so I can't really answer. I am sure I was told that Ozzy felt it wouldn't work as metal bands then were solely guitar-based and not really a keyboard in sight, and he was right, I think. I'm not sure fans would have accepted a change of direction and sound from them. Ironically, keyboards are now widely accepted in metal bands and my son Adam has played keyboards for Ozzy and Black Sabbath for close on twenty years now.

*Sabbath Bloody Sabbath* was released on 1 January in America. Sabbath started a European tour at Gothenburg on 11 January, ending in Stuttgart on 19 January. They then returned to America for another tour. This ran from 31 January in Hershey, Pennsylvania to 8 March at the Nassau Coliseum, Long Island. Support bands included Spooky Tooth, Bob Seger and, on most dates, Bedlam, who featured future Sabbath drummer Cozy Powell. Steve Rosen caught up with Tony for *Guitar Player* magazine during the American dates and found out that his live set-up onstage was different in America. In Britain, Tony was using a wah-wah and a mini guitar Moog, but in America, this caused a significant drop in amplifier power and sound due to the differing system of electrical grounding. So he had given up using pedals in the States while the search went on for a solution that would work with his beloved Laney amplifiers.

Nothing was originally scheduled from now till May, not even recording sessions as would usually be the norm. However, the band were made an offer to appear at the California Jam Festival at Ontario Raceway in California. This one-day festival, held on 6 April, also featured Deep Purple, The Eagles and Emerson, Lake & Palmer. There was little time for rehearsals, so Sabbath resorted to rehearsing their set, without amps, in a hotel room! An estimated 250,000 people saw them blow off the cobwebs for an epic performance (reviewed under live recordings).

The band, supported by Black Oak Arkansas, played a 14 date tour of the UK, beginning on 17 May in Bradford. Bill would have been happy for the time at home in 1974 as his first child, Aeron Russell Ward was born.

The band regrouped to rehearse at the sports centre in Birmingham's Cannon Hill Park prior to heading off for a return tour of Australia in November. There were no New Zealand dates this time around, and they played eight shows supported by an up and coming band called AC/DC.

On their return, Sabbath were served with a subpoena by Jim Simpson's lawyer, which prevented Sabbath from playing live until grievances over his dismissal were sorted. This took them off the road for eight months in total, through till July 1975. It left Sabbath with a month or so break while they considered their options. There was little choice other than to return to the studio.

# 1975: You bought and sold me with your lying words

January saw Sabbath begin rehearsing material for what was to be *Sabotage*. Instead of Rockfield, the sessions were held in an extension Ozzy had built onto the back of his home in Staffordshire. Rehearsals lasted two weeks before the band decamped to Weobley Studios in Herefordshire, a former vicarage that had been fitted out as a rehearsal studio. Happy times for the band, regrouping to do what they loved, but there were major difficulties in the background, with the band trying to put their management issues in order.

The first big clue that something was dreadfully wrong was the discovery that their fee for playing the California Jam had been circa $250,000, but the band had only received $1,000 each. Either they were being hoodwinked, or the expenses had gone off the charts! The second major clue came when the band found out that Patrick Meehan had not signed the management contracts, which all four of the band had signed. They fired WWA as their management company, but WWA owners Patrick Meehan and Wilf Pine could not be directly sacked due to contractual small-print. In the interim, the band attempted to manage themselves, aided by their lawyers, but this proved difficult. So Don Arden, who they had rejected in 1970, was invited to become their manager. Arden knew that earnings from their previous albums would likely be frozen while the legal case with WWA was happening, so he got the band an advance from Phonogram and Warners and told Sabbath to get back in the studio, and then on the road where they could earn money.

The legal issues over these changes affected the band all through the recording of *Sabotage* in February and March. While the band were involved in the case with Meehan, they still had the ongoing case with Jim Simpson, which had not been settled. As well as suing the band, Simpson had also sued Patrick Meehan. The final court hearing to judge a settlement would not take place till March 1976.

At some point in the year, Ozzy found time to make a guest appearance on a single for a close friend. Chris Sedgwick had put together a band called Birmingham Free Music and recorded a single which he distributed around pubs in Birmingham for their jukeboxes. The A-side was a cover of 'Don't Let Me Be Misunderstood', featuring Ozzy singing harmony vocals on the chorus. It's available online and great to hear Ozzy's unmistakable contribution.

Gerald 'Jez' Woodroffe joined the band in May, recruited back in Birmingham via his father's music shop – Woodroffe's. It was Bill who asked Jez to come over to Ozzy's house and have a jam to see how they got on. Woodroffe fitted in well, was taken on and spent a further six weeks rehearsing with Sabbath at Ozzy's house. Even so he wasn't brought in as a 'full' member, originally only for the stage line-up to recreate the keyboards parts. He first appeared on-stage with them for the two month-long American tour that kicked off on 14 July in Toledo, Ohio. *Sabotage* was released two weeks later on 28 July.

The band now had a summer break, handy particularly for Ozzy and Thelma as their second child was born, Louis Jon Osbourne. He can be seen with his dad on the cover of the *Diary Of A Madman* album.

Sabbath renewed activities with a UK/European tour, beginning at the Liverpool Empire on 9 October. Following the gig in Düsseldorf on 2 November, there was a break before the intended return to the UK for eight final dates. All eight were postponed due to Ozzy injuring himself in a motorbike accident. In the gap, NEMS released 'Am I Going Insane' as a single on 7 November.

The first of the rescheduled dates was at Cardiff Capitol Theatre on 22 November. Just over a week later, they were back on tour in America, this time for only seven dates, beginning at New York's Madison Square Garden on 3 December. Cashing in on the tour was their now nemesis Patrick Meehan who rushed out a double-album compilation called *We Sold Our Soul For Rock 'N' Roll*. The title dripped in irony, given the circumstances. It came out on 1 December in the UK on NEMS and included 'Wicked World', which was at that time still hard to find in the UK. It got to number 35 in the album charts.

## Sabotage *(NEMS/Warners)*

Personnel:
Ozzy Osbourne: vocals,
Tony Iommi: guitars, piano, synthesiser, organ, harpsichord on 'The Writ'
Geezer Butler: bass, mellotron on 'Megalomania'
Bill Ward: drums, vocals on 'Blow On A Jug'
and:
Wil Malone: arranger on 'Supertzar'
Skaila Kanga: harp on 'Supertzar'
English Chamber Choir: vocals on 'Supertzar'

Dave Tangye, Graham Tangye, Jim Ward: hand-claps on 'The Thrill Of It All'
Produced at Morgan Studios, London and Brussels, February to March 1975
by Tony Iommi and Mike Butcher
Release date: 28 July 1975
Highest chart places: UK: 7, USA: 28
Running time: 43:44
All songs by Black Sabbath.

Ironically *Sabotage* came out in the UK on NEMS, which WWA had bought. Similarly to *Sabbath Bloody Sabbath*, Phonogram retained the band's contract and did a deal for the album to come out on NEMS. Consequently all of Sabbath's previous albums were reissued on NEMS.

The immediate point of discussion is the cover, which has an engaging awfulness about it. The concept was inspired by the work of the surrealist Rene Magritte – in particular his 'La Reproduction Interdite', and ideas by band roadie Graham Wright, who was a graphic artist.

It was intended to be shot with a moody dark feel in a castle, the band appropriately dressed in black. Suitably impressed with the concept, the band turned up for the test shots, wearing the now legendary mix of stage costumes and everyday wear. Bill resorted to borrowing a pair of his wife Mysti's red tights and Ozzy's underpants, while Ozzy went for what he later wryly called his 'homo in the kimono' look. By contrast Tony and Geezer pretty much get away with their look. Those test shots somehow ended up being the actual cover shot and it has been ridiculed ever since. Despite that the character of the band comes through and curiously the cover kind of works.

The band stopped at the Swiss Cottage Holiday Inn in London from Monday to Friday while recording at Morgan Studios, returning to their homes for the weekend. The album was produced by Tony and engineer Mike Butcher, who was a big help to Tony in getting the production finished. Mike explains how he got that co-producer credit:

I think it was because I interfered a lot (he laughs). It was Bill who first said that they should credit me. I mixed it mostly all day by myself and then they would come in and make comments. I didn't actually get paid any extra money for being credited as co-producer, but it was nice to get the credit. And I think it was also because I stuck with them through a bad time. I did most of *Sabotage* and I mixed it. I had moved to Brussels already, so on the sessions I couldn't do Robin Black recorded.

**Black found Sabbath to be friendly, but a handful:**

> They were a tricky bunch to work with. I love them dearly, but it was
> always full on. Taking over from another engineer is always difficult
> because the other guy has already got a rapport and understanding with
> the band, the characters, and how they work. So to come in out of the
> cold is hard. They are also thinking perhaps, 'Why haven't we got the
> other guy?' So you just do your best. The important thing is to get to
> understand the psyche of the band. Now every member of that band was
> totally different.

While Black was on duty the band had a friend visit. 'John Bonham came
in. He sat down at the drum kit and he played so hard that he put the
pedal right through the skin of the bass drum'.

The music is a breathtaking rush from start to finish, with lyrics that
reflect their personal trauma at the time. The band use C# tuning again,
and there is a spectral quality to the sound, slightly distant but intense,
which suits the material well. Joining the engineering team was the
band's live sound engineer Spock Wall, who had been with them from the
beginning. His principal role was to get the best sound for Tony, and, song
after song, his guitar comes through with real bite and fire.

The band had more recording tracks available than when they recorded
*Sabbath Bloody Sabbath,* and thus more potential for overdubs. Mike
Butcher explained that this was due to Morgan upgrading the consoles.
'*Sabbath Bloody Sabbath* was recorded 16 track, and *Sabotage* was
recorded 24 track, so it gave more possibilities sound-wise and adding
stuff. We would work for, say, three weeks and then come back a month
later. So things would be added to songs sometimes weeks later after the
initial sessions'.

That wasn't the only change to the recording methods; part of
the album was recorded in Morgan Studios, Brussels. Mike Butcher
elaborates:

> *Sabotage* was recorded over the period of a year. We might do one or two
> tracks in a week and then they would come back again later, so it wasn't
> all done in one block. I had moved to Brussels in between *Sabbath
> Bloody Sabbath* and *Sabotage,* so I was travelling backwards and forwards
> between Morgan London and Morgan Brussels. We recorded *Sabotage*
> mostly in London, but there was a period of a few weeks when Morgan

London wasn't available, so they came across. We did about two or three weeks at Brussels, recording overdubs for guitar and percussion. I don't think we did any vocal overdubs. We had exactly the same console in Brussels as in London Morgan Studio 4, although, of course, the room acoustics were different.

**Butcher's dedication to the project was a major asset for Sabbath. Ozzy memorably failed to break his concentration one day at Morgan Brussels.**

I was doing a rough mix, so very concentrated at the console and all of a sudden, I heard them laughing. I stopped the tape and asked them why they were laughing. They said, 'Well while you were working Ozzy had his dick on your shoulder for about five minutes'. I am not particularly religious, but I thanked God I didn't notice.

**Another incident came with Morgan London's Steinway piano, a great asset that needed careful handling, as Butcher found out:**

It was the engineer's responsibility to make sure it wasn't damaged. One day in Studio Two, the piano lid was open and the strings were exposed. We had some take-away Chinese food and Bill was standing in front of the piano. Ozzy shouted, 'Hey Bill, catch this' and he threw an open packet of fried rice at Bill, who jumped out of the way. All of the rice fell into the piano. I remember the assistant tape op looking at me; he didn't say anything; we didn't have to speak. He rushed to get a vacuum cleaner. Luckily the rice hadn't managed to fall under the strings too much and we managed to get almost all of the rice out.

Tony says in *Iron Man* that there was a reaction in the band to the diversity of *Sabbath Bloody Sabbath* and that the intention now was to make a rock album. Ozzy, by contrast, has said many times that for him, it all went wrong after *Sabbath Bloody Sabbath*, but it must be the legal issues they had while recording *Sabotage* that colours his memory. It must be that because *Sabotage* is unequivocally magnificent.

The backs-to-the-wall scenario was one they could relate to and they dug deep and pulled it off, the last great album by the original band. Mike Butcher says that they worked out the running order almost immediately. Side one is a breath-taking four-track suite that's as good as anything they ever did elsewhere, a band at the top of their game. Side two is a different flavour altogether, 'Supertzar' and 'Am I Going Insane' attracting criticism. The first is an epic, refreshingly different track, although too long, while the latter is the album's weakest song, though it too has some good things going for it. Whatever the arguments about those two, side two opens and ends with 'The Thrill Of It All' and 'The Writ' – both great songs.

Mike Butcher tantalisingly adds that:

> There was one extra song recorded, but I don't think it got to the stage where Ozzy's vocals were put on. There was a sound effect on it of a Stuka dive bomber. This was added on a session that Robin did. I think the track was left off because it would have made the album too long. I don't know what happened to the multi-tracks.

Having completed two albums with Sabbath, Butcher gave his thoughts on them as musicians and their working relationship:

> Bill is an underrated drummer. For me, Sabbath is that band with Bill. I listened to the last album Sabbath did (13) and the drums are very good, but it's not Bill. Bill wasn't just a drummer, he had a distinct musical style and he played riffs on the drums. He was unusual for that style of music. I thought that back at the time we were recording those records. Without him, it wouldn't have been the same. Tony started the songs off and would bounce off Geezer because Geezer always had ideas. Whereas when Bill had ideas, it was more, 'Oh let Bill try it out'. Because of all the years since and what Ozzy has been through, there is a tendency for people to look back on those years in the wrong way. Ozzy could sing. Some of the melodies were not simple, and he was doing all that in the days before autotune.

## 'Hole In The Sky'

Mike Butcher got to kick the album off:

> That's me shouting 'attack' at the beginning. In those days, the talkback used to literally be a tannoy speaker in the studio. Ozzy had told me a story about a support band on one of their tours in the States. This band's manager was completely over the top, and while they were playing, he would be standing at the side of the stage screaming 'attack', to get them to give it more energy. This became a running joke between us in the studio, so when I was pushing on the talkback to tell them the

tape was rolling, I shouted 'attack'. When we came to the mix, it was still there on the tape, so we decided to leave it. It made an interesting start to the album.

There's an infectious powerful and melodic feel to this track. Tony's swinging yet crunching riff bounces along while Geezer and Bill get a similar swing feel going in the rhythm section. It's a real statement that they mean business opening with this track. Although it's heavy on the melody, it's still a balls-out track that sweeps you along. It sounds like Tony has doubled his rhythm guitar parts, the guitar sound is so thick!

Butcher: 'That's backwards cymbals that you can hear. We liked it. 'Hole In The Sky' was recorded in the newest studio (four), which had a different sound. The drum mics were placed differently and yeah, it came out nice'.

Ozzy's vocals on the verses are punctuated by Bill's cymbals. An interesting touch is that there is hardly any gap between the first and second verse, just a brief repeat of the intro riff. The middle eight switch comes in at 1:31 with Ozzy exclaiming what is effectively the song's chorus of 'Hole in the sky, gateway to heaven', as the band play a choppy riff behind him. Bill's turnaround on the drums leads back into the main riff again.

Verse three follows, the one with the oft-quoted lines, 'And even though I'm sitting waiting for Mars, I don't believe there's any future in cars', which nail home the eco-concerns at the root of the lyrics. The chorus crops up again after verse three. Bill plays another turnaround after it, this time leading into Tony's solo. It's double-tracked and he doesn't let rip as might be expected. What we get is richly melodic, with two interwoven guitars harmonising with the riff in the background. It's a great piece of work from Tony, with the urgency and power still carried by the riff.

Surprisingly, in what is only a four-minute song, we get a fourth verse after the solo. From there, it's a long outro that grooves out on the riff, brought to a shuddering halt by 'Don't Start, Too Late'.

This is a marvellous track that sets the tone for the album perfectly. It made it into the live set for the *Sabotage* tour but was dropped after that. It could have easily held down a place at the top, or near the top, of the set on subsequent tours, but probably got dropped because of the notes that Ozzy hits on the studio version.

## 'Don't Start (Too Late)'

Mike Butcher was the inspiration for the title, but the familiar story, as reported in the Super Deluxe Edition booklet, that it was the band starting to play before the tapes were rolling is incorrect. Mike recalled that, 'It was something I would say to them, 'Don't start'. It became a joke in the studio like they would say can we do this, Mike and I would say, don't start, meaning stop messing me about. It was just a fun reference'.

Tony sees the piece as directly connected to 'Symptom Of The Universe'. He told *News In 24* (June 2021) that it, 'Came to me spontaneously before I attacked the riff of 'Symptom'. The sound engineer was already recording, (so) we kept it.'

Tony plays double-tracked Spanish style acoustic guitars that delightfully weave in and around each other. It's another of the diversions that pepper the Sabbath albums and this is a little oasis of calm. In spite of the calmness in the guitar melodies, it also has the air of the classical piece 'Flight Of The Bumblebee', sounding for all the world like something rushing to escape an oncoming storm. Which, in a way, it is, as it's cut abruptly short by a deadly incoming riff.

## 'Symptom Of The Universe'

Mike Butcher: 'The basic track was done live, A lot of the work involved was fixing in the overdubs and changing guitar sounds'.

The first part of the track is a high octane assault. Tony's scything buzz-saw riff cuts in, destroying anything in its path. Geezer doubles it on bass, while high in the mix, you can hear Bill's ride cymbal furiously swishing away. It's a full-on assault of an intro. If it has any nagging familiarity, it's because it is basically the riff to 'Black Sabbath' excessively drawn out.

A brilliant aspect to the first half of the track are Bill's drum fills. He gets them in all over the place and they help keep the track exciting, as important to the track's success as THAT riff. Bill's first fill comes in at 21 seconds as Tony plays the descending sequence before going back into the riff. Bill is just outstanding throughout.

Ozzy enters at 0:43 for the first verse, an almost breathless stream of consciousness with no real pauses between the lines. His cries of 'Yeah' at the end of each verse do verge on the tiresome after repeated plays, but you get past it because of the urgency and pace of the song.

After the second verse, we get a switch with some speedy riffs from Tony punctuated by Geezer's low bass notes. Another frantic verse follows after that, and then the same speedy riffs before we hit the flashy middle eight. In it comes at 3:35, an almost boogie stun guitar riff from Tony, over which he adds his lightning-fast double-tracked solo. While you are vibing out on the solo, you don't see the complete change of style, key and tempo coming. It's brilliantly masked with a cross-fade edit of Tony's guitar fading out over Bill's drums as the second half of the track comes in at 4:12 seeing a switch to chilled out jazz.

This second half originally came out of a jazzy blues-based studio jam, started by Tony, which the band recorded AFTER finishing 'Symptom'. It has the mood of parts of *Sabbath Bloody Sabbath* (album) about it. Tony swaps to acoustic and Bill adds in percussion for a warm, happy vibe that's the complete antithesis of part one of the track. Geezer gets a chance to show off his chops, too, with his expressive bass playing.

Ozzy gets a break too after the 'sturm und drang' of part one as he doesn't have to push his voice; the comfortable range on part two, allowing him to modulate more than in part one. For extra colour Tony overdubs a lead part in his jazz picking style, and it's utterly delightful.

'Symptom' became a mainstay of the live set (well, part one at least – part two never made the setlist) and remains one of Sabbath's best-loved tracks, although part two deserves more acclaim.

## 'Megalomania'

Mike Butcher: 'The basic track was recorded by Robin Black. I came back for the overdubs and mixed it. Robin Black did 'Thrill Of It All' too, and some vocal overdubs which were done over a weekend'.

After the epic 'Spiral Architect', Sabbath upped the stakes with this one, the most adventurous diversion they had yet taken, or would ever take. It has been called 'prog metal' and you can see why as the track twists and turns. While the lyrics are obscure, it is thought that Geezer's muse was the torment and frustration the band were feeling at the ongoing lawsuit. The heavy riff section that comes in at 3:06 was one of the earliest parts they had worked out for the album, first appearing in the mid-1974 setlists.

It opens with an echoing mournful guitar riff over shimmering cymbal work and see-sawing bass notes. There is also a keyboard part thickening the backing track. Ozzy's voice with an echo repeat on it fades up in the mix, a trick repeated for every verse. Butcher is proud of the effect, but the idea was not his this time. 'Robin made that effect originally. I remember that I 'tweaked' it. I think the idea came from one of the band'. Ozzy sets the scene in the first verse, a conspiratorial tone to his voice. There is no real gap before the second verse, cued in by Bill's drum fill, but the band change tack with Tony using a heavier tone on the riff as well as an overdubbed shrill harmony part. The verse segues into what is effectively a chorus, the 'Why don't you just get out of my life' part.

From there, the pattern is set for a repeat of the structure of the song we have had so far. It's back to the breezy intro again, then a reflective verse in the style of the first verse. That is followed by a heavier verse section as before and a repeat of the chorus.

All really good so far. The now expected change of tempo and mood comes next (at 3:06). A fairly standard rock chord switch with prominent backing piano doubling Tony and Geezer's riff. Bill breaks it up with a cowbell cueing Tony to play a snapping riff that is not a million miles away from 'Symptom'. It's heads down, almost Status Quo like, as the tempo picks up with Ozzy practically shouting the lyrics – 'Well I feel something's taken me, I don't know where'. You can hear the huge effort he is putting into his performance.

Tony gets off a brief fuzz-toned solo at 5:42, which sounds like two guitar parts together. It barely breaks the insistent chugging riff pattern that dominates this half of the track. As it builds to the climactic ending, Geezer adds mellotron strings, coming in at 8:09, to build a wall of sound effect. It gives the track an icy feel that we will be hearing more of on 'Supertzar'. Tony's final short solo struggles to be heard above the backing track and the ending is rather abrupt. In his book, Tony says that the track was faded out, and that they kept playing the outro for much longer.

'Megalomania' was a real step forward for Sabbath, but the complexity of the arrangement, plus the effort required to deliver the vocals, meant it did not survive in the live set as long as it should have done. It's an engrossing piece of work.

## 'Thrill Of It All'

The working title was 'We Sell The Worst Chips In The Country', which clearly had to change! 'Thrill Of It All' is the perfect side two-track one and one of the great 'forgotten' tracks of the Black Sabbath catalogue.

A brooding intro opens the song, punctuated by a sharp busy solo from Tony at 0:32, which is then cut by the riff coming in at 1:02. He's soon joined by Geezer and Bill, making for a deliciously tight section with a swing in the rhythm section giving the music real movement. Bill's decision to coerce three spare bodies in the studio to put in the hand-claps was a good one. With this irresistible groove, it would be hard for Ozzy not to deliver a great vocal, and he nails it.

It's the riff that keeps it in the Sabbath style, but it's clear that they wouldn't be able to get a whole song out of it, so at 2:39, the band change things around and the piano (played by Tony)comes in, which takes us into part two. The pace picks up at 2:59, with Tony now adding Moog synthesiser to the mix. This is now upbeat Sabbath with Ozzy urging us to 'Forget your problems that don't even exist, and I'll show you a way to get high'. It does run out of inspiration a little in this half of the track with a lot of 'Oh yeah' interjections instead of lyrics, but it's delivered with such positive energy that they get away with it. Perhaps sensing things need a boost, Tony gets in another (brief) solo at 4:10 and again at 5:09, which goes on all the way to the fade.

Part one of the track is terrific and part two would be even better if they had edited it. There isn't enough in the second half to justify the length, which Tony's two solos do their best to cover up. All in all, it's still a great listen, though.

## 'Supertzar'

Tony defended the track to *News In 24* in June 2021 saying, 'We always played what we felt at the time. 'Supertzar', for example, is an experiment. We liked it; why wouldn't we have it included on the record?'

Mike Butcher enjoyed the different set-up for this track. 'Wil Malone was back and did the arrangement. Recording the strings and choir was different to recording a rock band but if you are a good engineer, it's not a problem. The strings and choir were recorded as overdubs'.

The piece was written at home by Tony, who experimented with the choir settings on a mellotron. After putting a guitar overdub on top, he knew he had something special. Taking it into the studio, he repeated his guitar part, but the mellotron choir part was replaced with the English Chamber Choir conducted by Malone. Mike Butcher says, 'It was Wil who came up with the idea of the choir and Tony and Geezer said go for it'. Also added into the mix was Skaila Kanga on harp, still one of the world's foremost players of the instrument.

In 'Supertzar', either deliberately or inadvertently, Tony came up with the perfect intro tape for Sabbath to use live. The Russian title was suggested by the glacial music, which (for me) conjures up a hoard of Cossacks riding over the permafrost into battle. A glockenspiel tinkles with added icy effect throughout the track.

There are two distinct aspects to the track. The band play their part quite subtly on the whole, with Bill adding distant drums, low bass notes from Geezer and Tony playing an acoustic rhythm part. There are two featured instruments – Skaila Kanga's harp, which is too low in the mix, and the prominent lead guitar part.

The English Chamber Choir (conducted by Wil Malone) dominate the track with an epic vocal performance. In his book, Ozzy says he doesn't appear on the track because he couldn't think of anything to sing. This is surely sarcastic humour because at no point does it sound like it was intended to have a lead vocal. Tony recalled it differently, telling *News In 24* that, 'In the middle of the session, Ozzy showed up at the studio. He saw the backing vocals, thought he had the wrong venue and he left! He returned a quarter of an hour later, asking 'What is this mess?''

'Supertzar' fills a similar role to 'Orchid' or 'Don't Start Too Late' as an instrumental change of atmosphere, but it is about a minute too long. For me, It's also in the wrong place in the running order, breaking the flow. If it had been sequenced opening side two, it would have worked better.

All this being said, its cinematic qualities make for an interesting diversion on the album and it's an enjoyable piece of work. The choir especially are fantastic.

## 'Am I Going Insane (Radio)'

The 'Radio' has nothing to do with prospective single mixes or airplay. It comes from Birmingham slang speak for someone said to be 'mad'. There was a chain of electrical retailers in the 1970s in Birmingham called Radio Rentals; thus someone who was 'mad' was said to have gone a bit 'radio rental' – mental.

This Ozzy-driven track lacks a Tony and Geezer inspired middle eight of the kind that saved 'Who Are You'. It opens with an upbeat keyboard riff, underpinned by the doom and gloom rhythm section. Geezer's throbbing bass and Bill's intuitive clattering percussion add most of the interest to the song. Tony, by contrast, is quite low in the mix. Mike Butcher comments that, 'Bill suddenly had this idea and said I think I can do something on this. Tony was low in the mix to make it sound different and keep it a more synthesiser piece'.

To get home the song's mental uncertainty, Ozzy uses his lower range to heighten the lyrics' ambiguous edgy quality. At times he comes over like a serial killer confessing all! A nice back- reference in the lyrics comes with the line, 'Feeling paranoid inside'.

Yet again, we have the problem that the song is too long to sustain the minimal content. It isn't helped by the fact that the choruses sound similar to the verses. One of the best aspects of Ozzy's vocals is the intelligent use of harmony parts (all by him).

At 2:09, with still two minutes to go, Tony pulls out a solo which is still rather low in the mix, until at 2:39, he shifts up a gear and it's the first real blast of something different we have heard yet. It's overall too soon and not surprisingly, we are back for more verse/chorus lack of variation till the outro when things get bizarre. Mike Butcher: 'There was a tape lying around in the studio from another session, and it was a baby crying. We found that if you played it back at half speed, it sounded like an old man screaming. Somebody had the idea to put that at the end of the track and have it cross-fade into 'The Writ''.

In conclusion, it's a listenable but less than impressive track. It was released in a well-edited version as a single backed with 'Hole In The Sky'.

## 'The Writ'

Mike Butcher's additional input was suggesting the title. 'I said to Tony, call it 'The Writ', because a few days before, somebody had come in and handed Tony a writ. He thought it was funny. In fact, the title has nothing to do with the song as such'.

The tone of the song is set by the vitriolic lyrics. Ozzy: 'I wrote most of the lyrics myself, which felt a bit like seeing a shrink. All the anger I felt towards (our manager Patrick) Meehan came pouring out.' Looking at the lyrics, it's easy to see the hand and mind of Geezer, too, at times, so he obviously made some revisions.

The song segues in from 'Am I Going Insane', Geezer's wah-wah bass rumbling ominously until Tony and Bill come crashing in with ferocity at 0:39. So too does Ozzy, and it's clear he means business. 'The way I feel is the way I am, I wish I'd walked before I started to run to you, just to you'. The backing track is one of the most intense Sabbath ever recorded, a monstrous wall of sound, though they still get a groove feel with Geezer's bass giving the music movement beyond the crashing chords. Pleasingly he sticks to the wah-wah pedal for all of the first part of the song.

There's respite from the intensity at 1:58 as everything drops back down to the wah-wah bass again, with backward cymbal effects for a little extra colour. From there, it's back to the increasingly personal verses, with Ozzy pointedly declaring that the subject (allegedly Meehan senior) is, 'A poisoned father who has poisoned his son, that's you. Yeah, that's you'.

The middle eight comes in at 3:36 with a sleazy new riff as Ozzy intones, 'Cats, rats'. The verse following it sees Ozzy changing his tone too, less obviously furious, but the lyrics are as scathing as ever. 'Probably dead, they don't feel a thing, To keep them living for another day'. Ozzy doubles his voice on this section with a deeper harmony vocal.

The following verse is one of those that has Geezer's hallmarks, based on the language and imagery. 'You are nonentity, you have no destiny, you are a victim of a thing unknown. A mantle picture of a stolen soul, a fornication of your golden throne'.

Time for a tempo change again at 4:23 with the return of that sleazy guitar riff and a turnaround from Bill. Meanwhile, Geezer's off the wah-wah pedal to give the bottom end more depth. Ozzy switches his delivery again at 4:45 and there's a suggestion here that there is hope for a brighter future. Cleverly they emphasise it musically with the warmer tones that kick in at 5:05, with Tony's harpsichord being a key feature. He also plays an acoustic rhythm guitar part here and the effect takes you back to 'Fluff'. It's an unexpected and welcome diversion, as Ozzy gets a firmer grip on his feelings, 'But everything is gonna work out fine'. Bill's percussion sparkles here, with some lovely xylophone notes catching the ear.

The outro comes in at 7:25, with Tony grinding out the sleazier riff. Bill sticks to a simple driving rhythm while Geezer chooses not to stick too close to Tony's riff, adding melodic variation on the end of his runs. Surprisingly there is no guitar solo on the outro, nor has there been one anywhere in the song.

'The Writ' has never been played live, and it's that sunny diversion at 5:05 that would have caused problems even if they had wanted to play it. The lack of the guitar solo is perplexing, but it remains a good solid, enjoyable end to the album. Well, nearly the end.

## 'Blow On A Jug'

Mike Butcher had the presence of mind to spot an alternative conclusion:

> They were standing around the piano and there was a microphone there, so I pushed on record. Bill was on piano and singing, with Ozzy standing next to him and singing along. They had no idea it was recorded and never heard it till they got the album. Looking back – yes, it was a brave thing to do to them.

This impromptu skit came about as the band recalled how Mungo Jerry got the crowd going at The Hollywood Music Festival in 1970. To their amusement, this had been aided by Mungo Jerry's Paul King blowing on a jug after he had drunk the cider in it!

Mike adds that: 'After the album came out, I was back in Morgan London for another session and they came in to say hello and thank you. I cannot say they were 100% happy about 'Blow On A Jug' being included at the time'.

It has never been listed on the album sleeve or label and was cut completely from some releases of the album. It raises a smile and shows the warm side to the band that understandably is absent from the rest of the album.

## Sabotage – super-deluxe edition

This was released in June 2021 and included a 2020 remaster of the original album by Andy Pearce and Matt Wortham. This is the best *Sabotage* has ever sounded with gloriously rich mid-tones. Geezer's bass definitely benefits most from the new master. While it all sounds fabulous, I have to single out the sound of the choir on 'Supertzar', which is revelatory.

Pearce explains the considerable work that goes into a mastering project: 'We research our work, I've got the master tape, or as close to it as possible, I will have an original vinyl issue, and I'll have any CD issues so I can see what's been going on with it'.

Also included was a single of 'Am I Going Insane (radio)'/ 'Hole In The Sky', notable for the amusing fact that the A-side IS actually a radio edit this time and rather well done as single edits go.

Missing from the package was the long rumoured quad mix or a possible 5.1 mix of the album. Mike Butcher told me that, 'I definitely didn't do a quad mix of *Sabotage* and I don't think anybody else did, either'.

The final musical addition was a double CD coyly named as *North American Tour Live '75*. The first clue as to the source came in the promo blurb, which said three tracks had been previously released. These being the three tracks from Asbury Park included on *Past Lives*. What we have here is the official release of that concert, reviewed in the *Killing Yourself To Live* chapter.

# 1976: I'm a back street rocker and I will be till the day I die

The year began with the rescheduled mini-tour of the UK covering venues that they had had to cancel (except for Manchester). This ran from Portsmouth on 8 January to Hammersmith Odeon on 13 January, marking the end of the *Sabotage* tour dates. The main activity in February was the release of *We Sold Our Soul For Rock 'N' Roll* in America.

Sabbath appeared in the High Court, London, on 16 March for the case brought against them by Jim Simpson. The hearing lasted five days and resulted in a 'victory' for Simpson. The band were ordered to pay him £7,500, and Patrick Meehan to pay him £27,500. Simpson said he had sued for the money he would have made if his contract had been honoured and that his award would be sunk into his Big Bear Records label. Ozzy suggests in his autobiography that Simpson didn't get that much in effect due to the costs of paying legal fees.

With the case now behind them, Sabbath turned to thoughts of a new album. Jez Woodroffe was invited to be a big part of the new sounds they were keen to try out. As usual, they decided to rehearse and try out ideas in a small studio. This time they decamped to Glaspant Manor in Wales, with further sessions at Ridge Farm Studios, Horsham. They then took a month off. During that downtime, Bill got his assistant Dave Tangye to make some wrought iron gates for his house with the riff to 'Paranoid' across them as per a music score. They are still there today!

Back to work and Sabbath headed to Miami in Florida to record *Technical Ecstasy*. They arrived in Miami on 28 May, two days after their crew, with sessions commencing the following day at Criteria Studios.

On his return to England, a frustrated Ozzy decided he wanted to have a play with other musicians. He had been seen around Miami in a t-shirt emblazoned with 'Blizzard Of Ozz', telling those who asked that it was what he would call his solo band if he ever had one. So something seems to have been stirring. He asked Barry Dunnery, Dennis McCarten, and Frank Hall of Necromandus to come to his house to try out some ideas. Frank Hall had regrets over the rehearsals, telling *Rock Arena* that shortly after rehearsals began, Phil Collins got in touch about the second drummer position with Genesis. Hall ruefully says that:

If I had the foresight to see what wasn't going to happen with John Osbourne, God bless him, I'd have jumped ship there and then, rather than hang on and put together this mish-mash of songs that weren't going to work anyway. We were thinking on different levels; Ozzy couldn't get his head around it, so we called it a day.

Also contributing to things fizzling out was the Sabbath machine switching back on for the coming *Technical Ecstasy* tour.

Interestingly *Technical Ecstasy* was released earlier in America than the UK, coming out on 25 September. The UK had to wait a little longer, till 8 October, to get it. After their sojourn on the NEMS offshoot label in the UK, they were now on Vertigo, where they belonged. Another sign of the band's growing status was their decision on the venue for the all-important pre-tour rehearsals. Rather than somewhere in the UK, they went for a soundstage at Columbia Studios in Los Angeles. Sabbath flew out there in advance of the tour, taking a Concorde flight. Accompanying them again was Jez Woodroffe.

Concern about the drop-off in album sales affecting attendance at the gigs led to the likes of Boston, Bob Seger and Ted Nugent being booked in as support acts. All three were breaking big in America and ensured the gigs would sell out. The first leg kicked off on 22 October in Tulsa, running through till 12 December in Syracuse. A high point, as always, was the date at Madison Square Garden in New York. They played there on 6 December and were 'introduced' by Frank Zappa, although plans for him to guest appear that night didn't come off. From there they jetted home for a break, with the knowledge that they would be returning in January 1977 for the second leg of the American tour.

## *Technical Ecstasy* (Vertigo/Warners)

Personnel:
Ozzy Osbourne: vocals
Tony Iommi: guitars, piano, synthesiser, organ
Geezer Butler: bass
Bill Ward: drums, vocals on 'It's Alright'
and:
Gerald Woodroffe: keyboards, synth, clavinet
Mike Lewis: string arrangements on 'She's Gone'
Produced at Criteria Studios, Miami, June 1976 by Tony Iommi
UK release date: 8 October 1976, USA release date: 25 September 1976

Highest chart places: UK: 13, USA: 51
Running time: 40:35
All songs by Black Sabbath.

Jez Woodroffe worked with Tony on the initial writing sessions at
Glaspant Manor in Wales before a further six weeks at Ridge Farm Studios,
Horsham. Woodroffe has said he should have had writing credits for his
input, which included working on the arrangements and the chords used
in the songs. The intention with the record was to expand on their sound
and use Woodroffe's keyboard as a feature. Another change to the sound
was the decision to tune back up to standard E. This was a major change
as they hadn't played as high as E since the first two albums. It meant
that some of the character of Black Sabbath was lost and they sound less
distinctive. The riffs often lack the visceral power they would have had in
a dropped tuning.

Once the material was ready, Sabbath headed to Miami to record
the album. String arranger Mike Lewis says that 'The entire album was
recorded and mixed in Miami, including the strings.' So contrary to
speculation elsewhere, there were no final mixes back in Britain. Sessions
started at four pm each day, with Sabbath then working on through
the night. This was the most comfortable time to work in Miami when
temperatures were at their coolest.

This time the production was solely down to Tony, a fact that Ozzy tartly
observed meant it was 'A Tony album'. Whether Tony would have welcomed
input from the others is debatable, but the facts seem to be that they never
gave him the option to refuse, instead taking more opportunity to revel in
the delights of the West Palm Beach area. The original intention was to take
Mike Butcher, but he says that, 'By then, I had gone off to live in Brussels.
They got in contact with Robin (Black), who they had also got on well with'.
But Robin feels that the contact was accidental more than deliberate:

I was on tour with Jethro Tull, mixing the sound, and during that tour,
we were stopping at a hotel and I walked past one of Black Sabbath's
roadies. He said, 'The band are here too, do you want to come and say
hello?' We went down and they were hanging out in a jacuzzi-type place.
They said that they were going to be doing an album and would I be
interested in working on it? I said yes but thought no more about it. But
then, back In England, I got the call officially asking me to do the album.
They wanted me because they knew I would get the job done.

Robin duly flew out to Miami from London with Sabbath and started his duties immediately on arrival:

We were staying at a place called The Thunderbird Hotel. When we got there, somebody said we're going to the hotel, but someone will take you to the studio to see if there are any problems. I went there and it seemed OK, the room looked big enough and there was going to be a guy there to show me over the desk. I asked this guy if he could take me to the hotel. Unbeknownst to me, he was on something, and as we were driving, he tried to turn right into the central barrier. Eventually, we got to the hotel safely and by now, it was getting dark. I saw this side entrance and as I walked towards it I saw movement on the floor. It was a carpet of about a thousand cockroaches. I leapt over them pushed the door open, exhausted and needing my bed. I walked up to reception to get my key and some woman walked up to me and said, 'Do you like oranges?' Stupidly I said, yeah of course I like oranges, to which she said, 'Oh are you English? I've got oranges in my room, would you like to come and see them.' I said that's kind of you, but I am really tired. I thought, oh crikey, this has only been my first couple of hours in Miami.

Once the band got into the studio to lay down the backing tracks, they found the neighbours were unimpressed. The Eagles were recording *Hotel California* in the next studio and found their sessions interrupted by the volume of the Sabs coming through the walls.

The cover art was put together by Hipgnosis, and while their artwork was a success for countless artists, their work here is underwhelming. It doesn't look like it should be a Black Sabbath cover at all, which may have been an idea of progress. Its futuristic and impersonal feel does capture the title, but in the end, Ozzy saw it as, 'Two robots screwing on an escalator'. It's hard to argue with that. Much better were the illustrations on the reissues and in the tour programme of the band with their faces revealing robotic origins showing through. Good or not, it gave Sabbath's artwork a popular feel as Hipgnosis were red-hot in the album sleeve market at that time.

The inner record bag had the album's lyrics overlaid on line drawings created by Colin Elgie. Elgie worked for Hipgnosis and is best known for his work designing the covers of *Trick Of The Tail* and *Wind And Wuthering* for Genesis, *Live Dates* for Wishbone Ash and *Year Of The Cat* for Al Stewart. Elgie explains the process for the *Technical Ecstasy* package:

I had nothing to do with establishing the concept, which came entirely from Hipgnosis having the title and possibly some lyrics. From that, they said OK, let's do something with robots having sex, but how would robots have sex? It was thought it would be cold, remotely and at a distance, perhaps even in passing on an escalator. That was the kind of thought process. I thought the cover was quite clever in its way. You had the male robot, all straight lines and the lady robot was different and they are having some kind of exchange.

The album cover was done by a whole bunch of people. The designer on it was George Hardie, he did the robots cover images. It was then heavily retouched by Richard Manning. We all worked together on it, but not at the same time.

I was aware that my design would be going underneath the lyrics. A guy called Richard Evans did the paste-ups, back in the days before computers. Sticking everything down onto art boards and so on. He would have got all the lyrics done and put on the overlay. The background I came up with was a stylised male and female shoe on the escalator. It was thinking about what lies unseen because you can't see the bottom halves on the cover. It was all done like a technical blueprint.

Although *Technical Ecstasy* was the most mainstream album the band had made yet, it saw a dropping off in sales which the band put down to new musical trends coming in. The problem with that is that the punk genre in Britain had barely taken root by *Technical Ecstasy*'s release date in October. More likely at fault was the material on the album, which featured several less than stellar tracks and the over use of keyboards which changes the band's dynamics. Geezer's lyrics are mostly underwhelming too. Little of what he comes up with is up to his usual standard, with only 'Back Street Kids' and 'All Moving Parts' really passing muster. Another factor in the lukewarm reaction to the album is the musical input from Geezer and Bill. Rarely do we get much of the inventiveness that characterises their best work.

While there had always been diversity on Sabbath albums with the likes of 'Planet Caravan' or 'Solitude', there is nothing on this album that hits those highs. 'It's Alright' and 'She's Gone' are just not in the same league. The best tracks are 'Back Street Kids', 'You Won't Change Me', 'All Moving Parts' and 'Dirty Women'. Some of the others have their moments, but on the whole, are not up to standard. Surprisingly only 'Gypsy' made it out as a single (Netherlands only). For all its faults, you could have seen 'Rock 'N' Roll Doctor', for example, getting an American release.

Noticeably missing is 'an Ozzy track', as per the previous two albums, to give a different tangent, but there is nothing of that nature from him here.

Robin Black says that making the album was, 'Quite hard work. There were times making the album that there was a lot of friction', although he adds that, 'The band worked hard'. The drop in the quality of the material along with the attempt to find a new direction and incorporating a keyboard player, presented significant challenges. Black agrees the keyboards were a sticky point:

I think they were experimenting a bit, trying to move on. I think they were looking around at the time to see who was doing what. It was a tricky one, suggesting how far keyboards should be pushed up in the mix. I wasn't sure if all the band were comfortable with having a keyboard player. I think there was a slight awkwardness about it.

Despite any difficulties, Black is adamant that the mood was positive when they had finished. 'I remember on the plane back, Tony Iommi said to me, 'You've become a friend to the band', which was nice to hear. We all flew home together, except Ozzy. I am pretty sure he left before the rest of us because he had done his vocals and he wasn't one to sit around for mixing.'

Four of the tracks were played live: 'All Moving Parts', 'Gypsy', 'Rock 'N' Roll Doctor' and 'Dirty Women'. Mike Butcher caught up with the band at Brussels for their date at Cirque Royal on 16 April. Ozzy asked him what he thought of *Technical Ecstasy*. Mike:

I told him I wasn't too keen on it and he said when they got to the studio in Miami, they didn't like it very much. Ozzy was not entirely happy about how it had gone. I think Tony was trying to do something, but I don't know if he was entirely happy with it.

A key problem with the album became more obvious with the release of the super deluxe edition in 2021 – the production.

## 'Back Street Kids'

The lyrics are clearly from the heart; you can take the boys out of Aston but never take Aston out of the boys. Nice references too by Geezer to two old songs in the lyrics, 'Writing about the stars, and thinking about the hand of doom'.

It opens with a powerful surging riff, with the band playing in unison. As well as the crunching rhythm guitar, Tony adds a melodic part over the top. Ozzy puts on his best-tortured artist voice, but gets that terrific melodic switch with, 'Nobody I know will ever take my rock and roll away from me'. A typical Sabbath switch comes at 1:46 with the middle eight, introduced by jarring brash keyboards and swirling synth from Woodroffe. 'Living life comes easy, if you know which way you're going', sings Ozzy, changing his tone for this section, sounding easier and less anguished than on the verses. Tony predictably ends the middle eight with a solo (at 2:44) before the main intro riff comes back in for a similar section to the first half up to the middle eight. The surprise sudden stop ending, 'Nobody I know will ever take my rock and roll away from me', is highly effective.

This track has enough in the dynamics and intent to keep Sabbath fans happy. In terms of Sabbath upgrading their sound from *Sabotage*, it still sounds like Sabbath, but there is a warmer presence already to be heard than on *Sabotage*, with the band sounding closer in the mix. Woodroffe's keyboards are OK but hardly essential, crossing over to being an annoying distraction on the middle eight.

## 'You Won't Change Me'

Lyrically this is a reflective part two to 'Back Street Kids'. It opens with spacey sound effects and a buzzing synth pattern before Tony comes in with a great doomy opening riff, one of his best on the album. If the tuning had been dropped, this would have been business as usual. It helps that Woodroffe's keyboards are sensitively done and don't overwhelm the sound palette. The intro could have been developed more with lead guitar and drum fills, but instead, the tempo switches at 1:02 with a keyboard motif leading into the first verse. There is a big production feel on the verses and Ozzy's voice is not as high in the mix as on 'Back Street Kids', recorded more distantly but double-tracked to give a choral effect. Sound-wise this has a feel of *Sabotage* about it. Bill's cymbal work adds interest to the keyboards riff that dominates the melody on the verses.

Tony's guitar solo comes in at 3:28 – stunning blues-based bursts of fire. He gets in and out quickly and it's back to the melancholic but grandiose verses before Tony unleashes another solo in the same idiom as his first. How to end the song was clearly something they never quite resolved, so we get a fading out of the keyboard melody, Woodroffe alone, and it feels an unsatisfying ending.

This is a candidate for the album's best track, comparing well with their past albums, albeit stretched out longer than it needed to be. It's one of two or three songs that show the band adapting to using Woodroffe's keyboards as part of the sound without sacrificing their essence. Sadly it never made it into the live set, where it could have worked out well as a vehicle for Tony.

## 'It's Alright'

This song had been around in one form or another since 1972 but had never been taken further.

Bill's debut as lead vocalist is better than alright; he's actually very good. It's effectively a pop song, although Bill gets off a ferocious drum fill 22 seconds in that breaks up the plaintive intro. From here, it picks up and there's a tasty rhythm part backing his voice, with nice piano accompaniment from Woodroffe. Tony takes his first solo at 1:38 but doesn't over embellish it.

The best part of the song comes next: Bill plays a turnaround and the song switches to a warmer vibe at 2:24 as Tony swaps to acoustic. His playing here is quite lovely and he comes up with a beautifully sensitive accompaniment that dovetails so well with Bill's reassuring words. In the background, someone (Geezer or Woodroffe) plays an effective mellotron strings part.

In 2005 Bill told James McNair for *Q Classic – Ozzy* that:

I felt a little uncomfortable at first because Ozzy was our singer and I didn't want to tread on his toes. But I'd written the song and Ozzy liked it and was very supportive about me singing it, so why not? I'd sang back in the church choir as a kid.

It's a very good song, but too left-field an inclusion for the album, which needed something more potent in the atypical tracks. Its potential as a 45 was spotted and it was released as a single backed with *Rock 'N' Roll Doctor,* though it didn't trouble the charts anywhere.

## 'Gypsy'

The song has three distinct sections to it. A bright intro with Bill's pounding drums promises a lot and Ozzy is on top form melodically for the opening verse. Woodroffe's keyboards sit well in the mix and there are some of those melodic fills that characterise Geezer at his best. Once we hit the chorus at 1:02, it gets a little disappointing. Without the dropped tuning, it sounds a little rock-by-numbers and could be anyone. This could have really crunched, but it's too light and the lyrics are dull.

The section where Ozzy visits the gypsy, which comes in at 1:50, is long and uninteresting, though Ozzy does deliver the line, 'She didn't like my thoughts at all' with conviction and feeling. The backing track on this section is clumsy, sounding like a poor horror film soundtrack. At 2:41, Tony cuts in with some dynamic lead guitar over a repeated chorus. It could have done with an ending tagged on here, but no, we get another verse that's as dull as the others. Ozzy signs off at 3:47 with a deadpan 'It's over', but of course, it isn't. It's the cue for Tony to solo away till the end of the track. In fairness, he gets in one of the best solos on the record and it's also by far the best thing about the song. We could have done with more of that spirit elsewhere.

It was released as a single in the Netherlands, backed with 'She's Gone', but didn't chart.

## 'All Moving Parts (Stand Still)'

The title seemed to be connected to the album cover, but Geezer revealed to Mick Wall that, 'It's about a female transvestite who becomes president of the United States because America was such a misogynistic society at the time'. The lyrics are intriguing and by far the best on the album. Geezer was clearly inspired when it came to this one, and you can hear that Ozzy relished singing it. Listen to his glee as he delivers, 'I like choking toys'. He almost talks his way through a lot of the lyrics to get the clear, deliberate delivery, but it works a treat.

Musically there's a quirky, fun feel to the song with a real groove in the rhythm section and hints of funk and ZZ Top style riffing. It's the first time Geezer and Bill have had a chance to stretch out and try something different on the album, and it's glorious to hear the obvious joy they had playing this.

The progression from the verses to the 'choking toys' part is well done. A good link and flow because they are at the top of their game with this track. But wait, at 2:58, we get a completely different section, a riff-heavy rhythm with tasteful synth fills that switch on the tightest of changes back into the song's main riff. It is a phenomenal switch of tempo to pull off.

We end with more verses and a Tony solo that gradually fades out. You are left feeling delighted by the invention and obvious pleasure the band have in playing the song. If only the whole album had had this spirit and passion to it. It remains one of the most enjoyable tracks.

It was tried out live where it worked well on the first half of the tour before being surprisingly dropped, so perhaps it wasn't getting a great audience reaction.

## 'Rock 'N' Roll Doctor'

This was likely the first song written for the album, as it crops up in setlists as far back as 1975. The intro is great, and you can cope with the cowbell, but the wheels come off as soon as the piano comes in. As befitting the title, Woodroffe goes for a rock 'n' roll style that sits at odds with the insistent rhythm playing of Tony, Geezer and Bill. It sounds for all the world like Woodroffe is playing a completely different song. It's not his fault because somebody else clearly felt it would work, but he's low in the mix rather than the dominant lead instrument. It just sounds distracting and wrong.

Apart from that, the song itself is dull and should never have made the final cut. It sounds exactly what it is – Sabbath trying to be somebody else. The rock 'n' roll shuffle rhythms being a leap into foreign territory for them and pointing to the likes of Foreigner. Full credit to Ozzy for doing his best to inject (excuse the pun) some excitement, but this was a terminal case.

The titular doctor was 'Doctor Max', who used to look after Elvis's needs. When the band needed a little extra to get them through it was Max they turned to.

## 'She's Gone'

Lyrically this is in a similar vein to 'Changes', but there the similarity ends. While that song adopted a minimal approach that worked, this one is dominated by Mike Lewis's strings. They are superb, no question, but the band are lost in the mix. Tony's acoustic guitar part works and later, we get some nice subtle bass, but Ozzy sounds plain wrong with the strings. This song would have benefited from the less is more approach. Mike Lewis:

I was hired by the producers, Ron and Howard Albert, brothers who worked at Criteria a lot in the 70's. Their production company was called Fat Albert. The studio was owned by Mac Emerman, who had built the original Criteria in 1956. At the time, they had five rooms. Studios A, B, C, D and E. We used A for Black Sabbath.

I was not familiar with them at that time, so I went into the gig without any pre-conceived ideas of what they would like. I had complete freedom to do what I thought was best. One could say I had a clean slate. Normally I ask clients if they have any musical ideas so I can start with some direction in mind. However, they said, 'Just do what you want', so, of course, I did.

I was given a rough mix of the band track and a rough vocal performance. The string section was my regular group of people. In those days, I used eight violins, four violas, and two cellos. We only used less players if the budget didn't allow the full fourteen players.

The rest is history. I have to confess when we did it, I was so busy at the time it was just another string chart in a long succession of string (and horn) charts. It's nice to look back and see that something I wrote made a difference.

Take away Mike's string arrangements and there is little left. He adds that, 'I'm not sure what the original concept of the tune was, but I didn't feel that any of the band were going to add more to it'. It's frustrating because you feel they could have made this into a better track and, as the super deluxe edition proves, it was better when it was basic.

## 'Dirty Women'

The lyrical inspiration was close to the studio, as Geezer explained to John Robinson in 2014 (for the *Black Sabbath Ultimate Music Guide*):

The nearest pub was a strip bar. It was walking distance from the studio, so we'd walk down for a beer. There'd be completely nude women dancing in front of you while you were having a beer. It seemed quite weird to us. That's where 'Dirty Women' came from.

It's the track that most closely reflects their past glories, but not without one fault – it's too long and could do with being a minute shorter. The intro is terrific, with Ozzy setting the scene and the band playing a unison riff – the keyboards blending in well here. Ozzy is clearly enjoying himself, giving the words real resonance, such as when he sings 'Out on the streets I watch tomorrow becoming today.'

A repetitive, slightly dull refrain comes in at 1:24. It lasts for nearly 30 seconds the first time, before Tony changes things around and steps up with his first solo at 1:53. Underneath it the band lock into a wicked groove, sounding like the Black Sabbath of old. Then at 2:25, it's back to that dull refrain again for nearly another 30 seconds before the band gear-shift into a fast groove that acts as the middle eight change of dynamics. That is broken at 3:08 by the best bit of the song and the album. Ozzy barks out the words while the band hit that groove again they played earlier, only this time with way more aggression and bite. Tony's fingers squeak on the strings, and it's spine-tingling to hear the band on this form, however briefly.

'Let's go', sings Ozzy at 3:54, and from here on to the outro the track is stunning. Tony overdubs at least two solo parts weaving in and out of the mix. Behind him, there's a rock-solid backing track that features great propulsive drumming and perpetual backing vocals from Ozzy intoning the song title.

For a lot of fans, this is the best song on the album, the Sabbath style with a makeover, but the dark and dirty roots showing through.

## Technical Ecstasy – super-deluxe edition

This was released as two box sets in October 2021 – A four-CD edition and a matching five LP edition. The original album was newly remastered by Andy Pearce and Matt Wortham. Andy Pearce is no stranger to the 'Ozzy years':

We've done them a few times now for Castle, Sanctuary, Universal and BMG. The main reason for the remasters continuing are the advances in analogue to digital conversion. The tapes all sound amazing but going back to the early '80s, the analogue to digital conversion rates were just atrocious. So now we're sampling at 24, 96 and even 192 khz now, which we've just got into in the last couple of years. Of course, the catalogue has transferred to BMG, who thought, 'we own the rights, so we need to put out a new master.' They don't want to rehash old work.

I find the 2021 remaster underwhelming with little discernible improvement, while the remix by Steven Wilson has slightly more of note. 'Back Street Kids' has the drum slur on the end of the riff noticeably higher in the mix and Wilson adds an acapella coda to the end of 'Dirty Women'.

Where things get really interesting are Wilson's mixes of the outtakes and alternative mixes, which are revelatory and establish that one of the key issues with *Technical Ecstasy* is the cluttered final mix. Most of the songs sound better on these outtakes.

The final CD/pair of albums in the set is a live set from the tour, snappily entitled *Live World Tour 1976 – 77* aka Pittsburgh 1976 (reviewed in the chapter *Killing Yourself To Live*).

The packaging is sumptuous, but proper credit to Jez Woodroffe is lacking. He is not listed on the book's front page as a musician on the album, only credited in small print at the back and his name is spelt wrong, as it was on the original album.

## Outtakes and alternative mixes

'Back Street Kids' (alternative mix)
This is a more direct and less busy version of the track. Tony's lead harmony part on the intro is missing so all you get is the basic rhythm track. There are three other main differences: The cymbal slurs at the end of each riff are more pronounced, Ozzy's voice has no reverb on it and he doesn't deliver the song with quite the same attack (but it's an early take) and Woodroffe's keyboards get more focus when they come in. The energy and simplicity here is refreshing.

### 'You Won't Change Me' (alternative mix)
The intro sound effects are louder and more dynamic, making for a more impressive opening. Ozzy's voice isn't double-tracked and he has less presence than on the album version. The denseness of the final mix is missing though, and the song is better for it with more room to breathe.

### 'Gypsy' (alternative mix)
The intro drums sound flatter with no echo. There is no use of reverb on Ozzy's voice and in general, this is a basic but clearer mix lacking the big sound of the album version. Woodroffe's keyboard pattern leading into the gypsy encounter and during it is missing completely. The absent keyboards cause a deadness in the sound at times, and it was a good decision to add them in for the album version in lieu of anything better they might have come up with. There are no backing vocals either, but that's not as great a loss. Tony has worked out the solos, which are pretty much the same.

### 'All Moving Parts (Stand Still)' (alternative mix)
An essential find. Ozzy gets to play the harmonica on this cracking take. The details in the instrumentation have more clarity and the lack of reverb

or double-tracking on Ozzy's voice makes him clearer in the mix too. The other main beneficiary of this mix is Jez Woodroffe, whose clavinet is a surprising essential part of the groove. It's there on the album mix, too but buried deep. Over the outro, Ozzy riffs on some other moving parts which are not standing still while the band are just cooking in a way the album version doesn't get close to. Great stuff!

### 'Rock 'N' Roll Doctor' (alternative mix)

Ozzy sings a guide vocal but gives a storming performance. So do Tony, Geezer and Bill, who are on fire. This is way better than the antiseptic album version. It crunches and grinds with real purpose and is largely stripped of the horrible honky-tonk piano, which is fortunately mixed low. This is still not a great track, but this is the best it has ever been.

### 'She's Gone' (outtake)

Another great discovery. This full band performance has a touching delicacy and texture that is lacking on the album version. Ozzy's vocal is clearer and more personal, and the backing track is beautifully played by all. Woodroffe adds a mellotron choir, giving the song extra sadness. It was a big mistake to leave this version off the album; this is how it should have been.

### 'Dirty Women' (alternative mix)

Ozzy is single-tracked, but this works well; he sounds superb, having already got his vocal pattern worked out. In fact, there is a clarity and directness about this take that appeals strongly. It is punchier and rocks harder than the album version. Witness the final solo which has more bite and none of the dreary backing vocals over it! This mix is vastly better than the album version.

### 'She's Gone' (instrumental)

This has significant differences to the orchestral backing track on the album version. A lead harpsichord picks out the melancholy melody line while the cellos and violins weave around it. The effect is beguiling and the sheer invention of the arrangement shines through. In this form, it makes sense and sounds stunning, but still not a good fit for the album.

# 1977: Sadness kills the superman

Following the Christmas break, Sabbath returned to America in January for rehearsals for the next leg of the American *Technical Ecstasy* tour. They had decided to change their stage production and had signed up with the Showco company. Showco offered a complete touring package of sound, lighting and technicians along with the trucks to transport it all in. So Sabbath flew to Showco's home city of Dallas for rehearsals with the new rig.

The tour began in Miami on 20 January, finally finishing at The L.A. Forum in Inglewood on 23 February. Ted Nugent returned as support on some dates, with Journey playing on some of the others.

The European tour began in Glasgow on 2 March, running through until Gothenburg on 22 April. It was the first tour in the band's history that they did not play a hometown show in Birmingham. The date at Stafford Bingley Hall on 6 March served for that purpose instead. It was also their shortest UK tour to date, comprising of only ten dates, four being at Hammersmith Odeon. Support on the UK leg was by Nutz, while the European dates featured AC/DC (with The Ian Gillan Band also supporting for four nights in West Germany). The tour wasn't supposed to end in Gothenburg but an incident after the show there saw the remaining four gigs cancelled. Details are fuzzy, but it's alleged that Geezer pulled a toy flick-knife out at Malcolm Young as a joke. The combative Young responded by punching Geezer in the face. So that was that, end of the tour for AC/DC and the dates were cancelled.

Back in the studio, but this time not with Sabbath, Tony produced the self-titled debut album by fellow Brummies Quartz. They had wisely changed their name from Bandy Legs and had received a good audience response to their support slot on the UK leg of the *Sabotage* tour. As well as producing it, Tony also contributed guitar solos to two tracks (which sounds to me like 'Street Fighting Lady' and 'Pleasure Seekers') and played flute on 'Sugar Rain'. The latter also featured Ozzy on backing vocals, as did the B-side track 'Circles'. Neither Tony nor Ozzy are officially credited for their musical contributions.

Quartz featured Geoff Nicholls on guitar and keyboards. The link-up with Tony saw the start of a long-running professional relationship between the pair of them in particular. Nicholls eventually left Quartz to join Tony in his endeavours with the Sabbath name for many years.

Time to gather material for a new album and Monrow Valley Studios (which at that time was still a part of the Rockfield Studios site) seemed the best place to get their mojo back. Instead, all it did was focus on their problems. Surprisingly it wasn't Ozzy or Bill who got singled out, but Geezer. He wasn't coming up with anything and it was Bill who was sent to tell Geezer he was fired. It lasted a month before Geezer got the call, from Bill again, asking if he wanted to meet them at the Holiday Inn in Birmingham to discuss coming back. Geezer duly returned, but things remained difficult.

Ozzy went next, worn down by issues with drugs and alcohol, and dissatisfaction with the way Sabbath were going. An additional factor for him was his father Jack's cancer, which had been recently diagnosed. He quit the band on 5 November at Rockfield while they were back together trying to work up songs.

Faced with breaking up without their talismanic singer or finding a new vocalist, Sabbath looked for a replacement. Backs to the wall, they looked among their friends and contacts, coming up with Walsall-born, former Savoy Brown singer Dave Walker. Walker had been known to the band since the late '60s when he was playing on the same circuits as Earth in a band called The Red Caps. Tony made the call to Walker, who accepted the job. Nobody else was apparently auditioned or even considered.

On 26 November, Sabbath announced Walker as Ozzy's replacement. An enthused Walker started writing lyrics on the plane over from San Francisco, and rehearsals commenced with him right away at Bill's home at Fields Farm, Bishampton, near Worcester. Several songs were tried out there with Walker, but there were early warning signs that things might not work out. Walker recalled that a tearful Ozzy joined them at the pub on one occasion and clearly seemed to feel he had made a mistake in leaving. Rather than taking the opportunity to sort out their differences with Ozzy, Sabbath stumbled on with Walker.

# 1978: Don't you ever, don't ever say die

The only thing to come out of the short-lived line-up with Dave Walker was an appearance on the BBC show *Look! Hear!* It was recorded at Pebble Mill Studios in Birmingham on 6 January, but there was no real advance warning of the appearance, other than a mention in the TV schedules in the *Birmingham Evening Mail*. After the briefest of introductions, they were straight on at the top of the show, launching into 'War Pigs'. It was loud, you could tell that, and the band looked introverted, deep in the music they knew well, but no real camera contact. Walker looked uncomfortable, the song cutting short before his vocals would be due to come in. In effect, the band had played an intro overture to the programme. Later in the show, they reappeared for a full new song. No title was announced and it was hard to discern what the title might be. What it musically became later was 'Junior's Eyes'. Walker delivered a throaty bluesy performance. Had they stuck with him, it would have made for the most different-sounding Black Sabbath ever.

Don Arden had been aghast at them replacing Ozzy, making it clear that they needed to get him back or face the consequences of diminishing audiences and record sales. The band, too, were having second thoughts about Walker's suitability. 'It didn't feel right', recalled Tony, and also having second thoughts (as Arden knew) was Ozzy. The death of his father on 20 January had left him inconsolable. He craved the friendship and security of his old friends and wanted to come back.

It was Bill who approached Ozzy on the phone with the offer to come back, and it was also Bill who delivered the news to Dave Walker that he would be leaving. By 28 January, it was done; the UK music press announced Walker had gone and back in was Ozzy. Recording sessions for *Never Say Die* commenced in January and went on until May. The length of the recording made for a stuttering start to what was being billed as the band's tenth anniversary year.

The first six dates of the European tour were cancelled because of the delays in finishing the album. It finally kicked off in the UK, at Sheffield City Hall, on 16 May, with Van Halen supporting, as they did on most of the tour dates. The young and hungry Van Halen were out to dazzle, with Dave Lee Roth and Eddie Van Halen grabbing the headlines. Tony was appreciative of them but noted in his book that, 'They made us look a bit drab really'. Van Halen were a hard act to follow for Sabbath, who were coming off the back of their worst album and the niggling ongoing issues that were bringing them down. The strength of the quality old material in their set and the partisan audiences got them through.

The album was now not due out till September and the setlist initially only contained one new song, the title track, which was released as a taster for the album in May. It saw the band return to *Top Of The Pops* (transmitted on 25 May) for the first time since 1970. They looked and sounded bright on the show with a song and performance that worked well for them but gave a false impression of the state of the band.

Opinions vary on their performances on the UK leg of the tour. There are stories of them being blown off stage by Van Halen and Sabbath looking bloated and tired, but fans who were there seem to have enjoyed the gigs. Sabbath treated them to one of the most career encompassing setlists of their career. They finished off with a filmed show at Hammersmith Odeon on 19 May. A second appearance on *Top Of The Pops* on 22 June concluded part one of the anniversary.

With the album still waiting to be released, they opened the first leg of a North American tour in August, the first confirmed date being at Milwaukee on 22 August. The setlist remained largely unchanged for the duration of the tour, which lasted until Seattle on 30 September. Sylvie Simmons (for a *Sounds* October cover article) caught up with Sabbath at Fresno on 22 September and asked Ozzy why there were so few new songs in the set, and wasn't he tired of playing the old stuff? Ozzy dodged the question about the lack of new material, and of the old material said, 'I love them; it's only now that I realise what an influence we were at the time'.

The album was finally released on 28 September in America, with the UK getting it on 1 October. With just over a week's gap, the band then commenced a short European tour, starting in Hamburg on 9 October. To tie in with these dates, 'Hard Road' was released as a single on 14 October. This European leg finished off in London at the Rainbow Theatre on 22 October, which was the last gig the band played together in Britain for 21 years.

Another short break and then it was back to America for the second leg of touring there. They opened on 3 November in St. Petersburg, Florida, with the tour finally winding down in Albuquerque, New Mexico, on 11 December. The next time the band would play together would be for charity, when they appeared in Philadelphia for the American Live Aid concert in 1985.

## *Never Say Die* *(Vertigo/Warners)*

Personnel:
Ozzy Osbourne: vocals
Tony Iommi: guitars, backing vocals on 'Hard Road'
Geezer Butler: bass, backing vocals on 'Hard Road'
Bill Ward: drums, lead vocals on 'Swinging The Chain', backing vocals on 'Hard Road'
and:
Don Airey: keyboards on 'Johnny Blade', 'Junior's Eyes', 'Air Dance' and 'Over To You'
Jon Elstar: harmonica on 'Swinging The Chain'
Wil Malone: brass arrangements on 'Breakout'
Produced at Sound Interchange, Toronto, January to May 1978, and Rockfield Studios, May 1978 by Tony Iommi
UK release date: 1 October 1978, USA release date: 28 September 1978
Highest chart places: UK: 12, USA: 69
Running time: 45:41
All songs by Black Sabbath

The valedictory title came from Bill. The shock of Ozzy's departure and the relief at his return had created high expectations for *Never Say Die,* but the defiance and fire of the title didn't last. The band chose to record abroad again for a respite from paying taxes in Britain. Sunny Miami had been a good choice for *Technical Ecstasy*, but this time around, there were issues from the moment they arrived in a freezing Toronto to record the songs. The first issue was that Ozzy flatly refused to sing any lyrics written by Dave Walker. Geezer, now back as the main lyricist again, must also have had some misgivings about Walker's less thought-provoking lyrical style. The additional issue for Ozzy was that despite the general enthusiasm for his return, he felt that his relationship with Tony had taken a terminal blow. Additionally, due to the hurried circumstances, Ozzy brought no material along as he hadn't on *Technical Ecstasy.*

Adding to the difficulties, the converted cinema that the band used in the daytime to write and rehearse was extremely cold. Following a day spent there, they would spend the evening recording in Sound Interchange. This became the miserable pattern for the duration of the Toronto sessions.

Don Airey came in to add keyboards and recorded his parts in two days, but it isn't clear if he did that in Toronto or at the hastily added on sessions back in Rockfield. Equally, Jon Elstar added his harmonica late in the sessions.

Having gone to the trouble of recording abroad, it was yet another failing that the production did the now luckless band no favours. The bottom end sounds distant and murky, while the top end sounds thin. Playing again in standard E tuning also contributed to the sound being less Sabbath-like (save perhaps the title track) at a time when they needed it more than ever.

In his autobiography, Ozzy says that while recording the album, he got news that his wife Thelma had miscarried. The band immediately returned home and picked up the sessions at Rockfield Studios. The band are pictured there (in *How Black Was Our Sabbath*) in May 1978, celebrating Bill's birthday. Ozzy says the two songs they finished at Rockfield were 'Breakout' and 'Swinging The Chain'. 'Breakout' does sound better recorded than much of the album, but 'Swinging The Chain' suffers from the same poor sound afflicting the other tracks. That suggests little was done on the latter at Rockfield.

Looking at the quality of the material, there are some good songs, but equally, there are tracks that are plain sub-standard. Tony says in *Iron Man*, 'There are some tracks I liked on it, but it's hard to relate to that album because of the way it was done'. The best tracks are 'Never Say Die', 'Junior's Eyes', 'Johnny Blade' and 'Swinging The Chain'.

There is a stark contrast between side one and side two (or the first and second half in the CD/streaming age). The best songs are mostly loaded onto side one, with side two additionally suffering because Ozzy isn't on two tracks. This contributes to the feeling that they were running out of steam. Side two would have been pepped up by sequencing 'Hard Road' as the album closer. At least then the album would have gone out on a triumphant feel-good vibe. But however you look at it, it's apparent that what made you fall in love with Black Sabbath in the first place is glaringly missing from *Never Say Die*.

There are fans who love the album, and it's certainly an album to discover, explore and find something, because it's nothing if not eclectic. That's great if you can manage it. For me, although it has its moments and it's mostly at least good, nothing here holds up against their earlier work or even much of *Technical Ecstasy*. The band knew it too. Geezer has openly said how much he dislikes it, and they hardly gave it an airing live.

Ozzy expressed his frustrations to Sylvie Simmons (*Sounds*, 21 October 1978), saying: 'On the next album, I really would like to get right back to the roots in respect of writing as a four-piece band. Going into the studio as a four-piece band, that we could totally 100 per cent reproduce on stage.'

The cover art by Hipgnosis wasn't the first concept offered to the band. Sabbath rejected what was then later offered to Rainbow and accepted as the cover for their *Difficult To Cure* album. Instead, we have jet pilots caught next to a plane between missions, their faces sinisterly obscured by masks. In the sky above them the ghosts of former pilots look down from the heavens. It's a striking image but could have done with more drama to it, less colourful tones and a stormy back-drop. There needed to be a more battle-weary quality to the image to reflect the title. The inside record sleeve had blueprint images in the same manner as *Technical Ecstasy.*

## 'Never Say Die'

Tony told Sylvie Simmons (*Sounds*, October 1978) that, 'We just had a rehearsal and it was the first thing we played. We were just playing about, jamming, and just kept it as it was – off the cuff'.

This energetic taster for the album boded well when it was released in advance as a single. It held its own against any punk singles of the time, showing Sabbath nodding to current trends but still sounding like Sabbath. It opens with Tony's barnstorming riff. If it sounds familiar, it's because it's the same riff that Thin Lizzy used on 'The Boys Are Back In Town'. Still, it's more effective here without the Lizzy guitar fills between the chords. With Geezer and Bill also on top form, this is easily the highlight of the whole album. There is a joyous feeling that comes over in the music that is absent on most of the album.

Ozzy puts across the vocal perfectly, with that wonderful melodic instinct he has on the chorus. The middle eight at 2:20 with the change of tempo is delightful, with Tony's sparkling guitar fills perfectly complementing Ozzy. It's one of the most simply effective sections on the album. It also features Tony's best solo, a coruscating affair that takes us all the way to the outro.

The song said Black Sabbath were back, simple as that, but it was short-lived. How they went from the optimism and attack on this to what we get on the bulk of the album is a mystery. It was released as a single backed with 'She's Gone', and reached number 21 on the UK singles chart.

## 'Johnny Blade'

This was developed wholly in Toronto, the title and initial lyrics coming from Ozzy and Bill. Consequently, it's one of the songs that Ozzy had a lot of time for, and he puts in one of his best performances. The lyrical subject matter clearly resonated with him.

It opens with grandiose but uninspiring synth work from Airey, which is broken by a much better synth run from him with real menace. Bill adds busy percussion work to underpin the synth, and it's all set up for the big guitar riff, which is rather underwhelming. Tony adds some jabs of guitar at the 40-second mark, but they fail to cut through the limp tinny production with any bite. Even with Geezer doubling his riff, it's still ineffective. With more dynamics, and better production, this could have been a lot better.

There are flashes of what might have been. Bill is on top of his game, even if he is not best served by the production. At 2:27, there is the best bit of the whole song where it starts to sound like Black Sabbath approaching their best. Cascading riffs from Tony lead into a dirty riff-heavy section that screams out for old school Sabbath dropped tuning. This is as good as it gets anywhere on the album, with Ozzy audibly enjoying wrapping himself around the line, 'Well, you know that Johnny's a spider, and his web is the city at night'. It's one of those moments when the album gets a pulse.

Following a sequence where Airey punctuates Ozzy's vocals with some synth fills, we get Tony's solo. He comes in at 4:58 and solos to the end of the song, but it's lacklustre and distantly recorded to the point you wonder why on earth he didn't try it again. It sounds exactly like a bootleg rehearsal tape.

It's still one of the album's best songs but deserved a better treatment.

## 'Junior's Eyes'

Geezer rewrote the lyrics of this Dave Walker era song, and Ozzy sang what was a tribute to his late father. His extra investment in the song goes some way to making this one of the best on the album, although it could have done with more work on it, as it lacks a little in dynamics.

It opens with a funky bass riff and percussion, a real groove from Geezer and Bill. Tony adds some tasty guitar, but it's noticeable here that it's his guitar that seems to suffer most in the production. Ozzy's vocal is as impassioned as you would expect. Although there are only two short verses and two choruses, there is a lot of emotion here – 'Junior's eyes, they couldn't disguise the pain, His father was leaving and Junior's grieving again'.

The instrumental section from 3:07 onwards cooks nicely, but the guitar solo is sadly the main let-down of the track. It's adequate, but lacks the inspiration and creativity to take things up several notches. Tony tries something again on the outro with two guitar parts weaving around each other and this is quite effective. A great touch at 6:14 is the percussion fills from Bill that escort the song out.

## 'Hard Road'

In America, the track was listed as 'A Hard Road'. Despite the lyrical tone, this is a positive bouncy tune that doesn't sound much like Sabbath at all. It's a good track, but it's fairly samey throughout, with Tony sticking like glue to the riff. There is no way this should be over six minutes long. It's also one of the worst affected tracks in terms of the production – thin, reedy and lacking any bottom end.

Tony gets it going with a reasonable riff and there's terrific swing and snap in Bill's drums and cymbals behind him while Geezer keeps the bass bubbling along. Ozzy, for his part, sings this really well, carrying the melody perfectly.

At 2:45, Tony takes the solo, which is one of the reasons for the track lasting over six minutes. It's one of his best on the album, although it battles to rise above the backing track in the mix. After he's done, we are back into a reprise of the first half of the song again. The extended outro comes in at 4:42 with Ozzy joined on backing vocals by Bill, Geezer and Tony, whose football terrace style contributions work really well. Ozzy scats out an improvised ending while the others sing the main chorus hook repeatedly. Somebody (maybe Bill) adds some woo hoo ad-libbed vocals to the mix too.

This feel-good song could have been even better. It was released as a single, backed with 'Symptom Of The Universe', and reached number 33 on the UK singles chart. The video, recorded at Hammersmith Odeon during a soundcheck, features a different guitar solo.

## 'Shock Wave'

When it came to the live set, this was the only other song from the album to make it. You can see why from the moment Tony's stinging riff comes in. It's his best on the album and gets things off to a good start. It's soon replaced by a second (doubled) riff that is equally as good. Ozzy enters for the first verse and, despite his efforts, it all now seems rather muted as the band battle with the poor recording and soupy mix. Tony's solo at 2:41 is also one of his best on the album, although he could have done with being higher in the mix. There's a nice change of pace after it and Tony continues to shine, adding more lead guitar before we head back into the verses again. The outro is underwhelming, sounding like they had no idea of how to finish the song, it just fizzles out.

There are elements here that work well and it's clear that this is a song that could have been much improved with inclination and a decent sound. It nearly makes my best tracks list and would have done so with more work.

## 'Air Dance'

Some of the band's jazz influences come through, especially in the rhythm section. A nice layered guitars intro from Tony gets it off to a promising start before the switch to a more thoughtful section at 0:34 with creative piano playing from Airey. Ozzy comes in a few seconds later and the melody is carried by his vocal and Airey's piano almost dancing around him.

The middle eight at 2:25 is interesting. We get some introspective lead guitar with Airey complementing it perfectly. Tony changes it around with a heavy riff at 3:31, which sounds promising and suggests we are heading into something even more forceful. Instead, it switches into a full-on jazz workout at 3:54, which comes as a complete surprise. Tony solos away over it sounding for all the world like Duane Allman or Carlos Santana, punctuated by synth and keyboards from Airey. In the background, Bill and Geezer lay down some busy jazz patterns. And so it goes on until the fade, with no real ending.

There are one or two good ideas here. The intro and the moody verses stand out, but there is a sense of sections bolted together that don't actually fit that well. They pulled the totally contrasting sections off really well on 'Symptom', for example, but it just doesn't work here.

## 'Over To You'

Another of the Walker era tracks. Tony's slow grinding riff opens it, but there's little else to get excited about. It's all rather poppy and plodding, livened only by some sparkling piano fills from Airey. In the engine room, there's a throbbing pulse from Geezer, and some bright cymbal heavy percussion from Bill. The brightness of the music hides the bitterness in the lyrics, which refer to a life dominated by those in control - 'I handed my future over to you'. With no middle eight contrasting section to keep things interesting, the song swiftly outstays its welcome. It's little more than an idea that never got properly developed.

## 'Breakout'

It started life during the Dave Walker rehearsals. The most off-the-wall track yet in their catalogue received conflicting views in the autobiographies of Tony and Ozzy. The way it turned out was partly prompted by Ozzy not coming up with any lyrics, says Tony. It's for that reason that the brass section with lead saxes were brought in, he adds. Ozzy has a different take on it. He says it was this track that prompted him to leave the sessions for good because he was disgusted at the brass arrangements taking place. 'F*ck this, I'm off', he said.

Whatever the truth of it, this is a track that adds nothing of consequence to the album. On the plus side, Bill's drums and cymbals have a lovely slow swing feel, and you cannot argue that Wil Malone did his best with the brass arrangement. That being said, the repeating brass melody – da da da dahhh – becomes quickly tiresome, so we are left with the counterpoint brass melodies (which are superb) and a terrific lead saxophone. Listen carefully and you can hear Tony and Geezer low down in the mix, although they add little to the final effect.

It feels like 'Breakout' would never have been considered if they weren't rushing to finish the project and put it to bed. Even If Ozzy had sung on it I doubt it would have been much better.

## 'Swinging The Chain'

One of the tracks that Walker originally wrote the lyrics for, so Ozzy refused to have anything to do with it, says Tony. Stuck for material to finish the album, the others decided to carry on with the track, giving Bill his second lead vocal for the band. Ironically, Bill then re-wrote the lyrics anyway! Ozzy recalled in his autobiography that he had already left the sessions before the track was even started.

In spite of the lo-fi demo sound, the band are audibly on better form and you can't help wondering if Ozzy's absence helped them find their mojo. Bill handles the vocals well, and, had the band carried on with Ozzy, they would have been justified in letting Bill carry on singing one on each album. Tony gets off some tasty solo fills and Jon Elstar adds effective bluesy harmonica, which would have been Ozzy had he stayed around. There is one of those great Sabbath switches at 2:49, the band gear changing pace and riff in a second.

The last part of the track features Bill doing his own backing vocals; he really does put in a great shift on vocals on this track. The attitude and energy of all three make this one of the best tracks. It is the final song on the final Sabbath studio album by (nearly all) the original line-up.

## Related Recording
## 'Junior's Eyes'

It probably would have been credited as written by all of the Dave Walker lineup. The only record of this track comes from the appearance with Walker on the *Look Hear* show at Birmingham's Pebble Mill Studios. Walker gives it a grittier R 'N' B vibe, but musically it's substantially similar to the Ozzy version. Hear it on Youtube.

# 1979 onwards: When it is time to say goodbye

In January, the band regrouped in Bel Air, Los Angeles, for an intended eleven months. Primarily this was for tax reasons, with the 'break' being used to write and record a new album. Don Arden got them an advance from Warners, which should have invigorated them, but the band were floundering.

The main stumbling block was Ozzy, who 'wasn't into it', according to Tony. With their singer demotivated and uninterested, it was also proving hard to keep Warners off their backs. Warners were keen to hear how the band were progressing, and it got increasingly difficult to maintain the illusion that things were going well.

After a few months of lethargy, the band managed to get three ideas for songs together. These went on to become 'Heaven And Hell', 'Children Of The Sea' and 'Lady Evil' on the *Heaven And Hell* album. None of those songs were anywhere near the final finished songs, but this is when they were started. Graham Wright partly corroborates this in the book *How Black Was Our Sabbath:*

> I remember Ozzy asking me to write some lyrics down for him. He wasn't embarrassed about it, it was widely known that he was dyslexic. He was working on the album's title track, 'Heaven And Hell'. It was good to see Oz getting involved in the writing rather than sitting back and leaving it all to Geezer.

That creative period seems to have died after a few weeks, with the band eventually taking the difficult decision to sack Ozzy and save their own careers. Ozzy was sacked on 27 April, and predictably it was Bill who gave him the news. Bill was himself about to go through a difficult patch. Less than a month after Ozzy was sacked, Bill's father, William Frederick Ward, passed away. Then Bill's mother, Beatrice Lilian Ward, also passed away in early 1980.

Ozzy attempted to put a band together with Gary Moore, but that came to nothing. It was Sharon Arden's belief in him and micro-management which saw him commence a solo career. Bob Daisley (ex-Rainbow) was on bass, along with Lee Kerslake (ex-Uriah Heep) on drums. They were the perfect backbone, UK players of his own age and from a similar background. The X-factor was the new, to most people, hot guitarist Randy Rhoads (ex-Quiet Riot). There was a passing thought to call the band Son Of Sabbath, but in the end, it was back to Blizzard Of Ozz, which itself barely lasted past his first solo album and tour. However, the washed-up and rejected Ozzy Osbourne was on his way back to stratospheric success. He earned every plaudit he got.

For Black Sabbath, there would initially be a hugely successful period with former Rainbow singer Ronnie James Dio. But as the '80s progressed, the wheels slowly came off until eventually, only Tony Iommi, of the founding four, was left in the band.

It seemed inevitable that one day they would get back together. Live Aid in 1985 provided the first opportunity, but Ozzy's star was in the ascendant and he had no need for anything more than a one-off reunion.

The bond that held them together since the days of Polka Tulk had been severely tested on many occasions and for many years. But it was that bond which brought them back together eventually. The first reunion was for two encore sets with Ozzy in 1992 at Costa Mesa, California. The second was for two fabulous nights in 1997 at Birmingham's National Exhibition Centre, which were recorded for the *Reunion* album. The band kept going with more gigs, but there were still echoes of past difficulties, most notably with the eventual withdrawal of Bill Ward. But any of those reunion shows with all four present were a glorious reminder of the power and joy of the original, and still the best, Black Sabbath.

**Left:** The site of the former Ladbrooke Sound Studios is still there on Bristol Street in Birmingham. Sabbath recorded there in October 1969. (*Author collection*)

**Right:** Rodger Bain, the producer of the iconic first three Sabbath albums. (*Author collection*)

**Left:** Mike Butcher was at the desk for *Sabbath Bloody Sabbath* and *Sabotage*. (*Mike Butcher*)

**Right:** Thelma and Ozzy on their wedding day in Birmingham, June 1971. (*Birmingham Mail*)

**Right:** This 1969 poster for the first 'official' gig as Black Sabbath still has the band named as Earth. (*Author collection*)

**Left:** Sabbath were back in Malvern in 1970 for this gig 'supported' by the Sidewinder Disco. The image is startlingly prophetic of the *Sabbath Bloody Sabbath* cover. (*Author collection*)

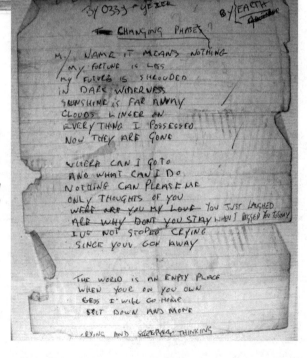

**Left:** Lyrics for 'The Wizard' handwritten by Ozzy, with an extra verse and intriguing running order at the top. (*Sheffield Auction Gallery*)

**Right:** 'Changing Phases'. The original lyrics for 'Solitude' written down by Ozzy some years earlier. (*Sheffield Auction Gallery*)

**Right:** Japanese 'Iron Man' picture sleeve single (*Author collection*)

**Left:** Tomorrow's Dream' European picture sleeve single. (*Author collection*)

**Right:** *Past Lives (2002).* Until the box-set reissue programme, this was the best official live album from the 70s era. (*Sanctuary*)

# Collected works

### Black Sabbath Story Volume One (DVD)

This features all four of the band, plus Jim Simpson, talking about the '70s era. There are copious videos used, all now available elsewhere. Live footage features 'N.I.B' and 'War Pigs' from Brussels 1970 (credited as Paris), 'Paranoid' from Belgian TV 1970, 'Children Of The Grave' from California Jam 1974, 'Never Say Die' from *Top Of The Pops* 1978, 'Snowblind' and 'Symptom Of The Universe' from the Hammersmith 1978 (*Never Say Die*) film.

Four promo films are featured: 'Sabbath Bloody Sabbath', plus 'Rock 'N' Roll Doctor' and 'It's Alright' recorded at a 1976 soundcheck and 'Hard Road' from the Hammersmith Odeon soundcheck in 1978.

It remains a worthwhile package because it was recorded back in 1990/91 and the band's perspectives are different to how they are in recent years.

# Killing Yourself To Live: Black Sabbath live

This section focuses on officially released recordings, key soundboard recordings and some essential audience tapes. Official releases are marked with the releasing company credits. Unofficial releases can be found online via YouTube and rock music blogs and, in many cases, are even sold by the likes of Amazon or HMV.

For Sabbath, the challenge, once they got past *Paranoid,* was what new material to play live, and that was decided by what was possible and its suitability. From *Master Of Reality* onwards, there are songs you would have thought were automatic live choices, such as 'Into The Void' or 'Sabbath Bloody Sabbath', but they never got the traction. By the time they reach *Never Say Die* their confidence in the new material has pretty much evaporated.

Live versions can be notably different to the studio counterparts. Once Sabbath reach the *Volume Four* tour, this is especially noticeable. The number of overdubs and additional fripperies used on record had grown by *Volume Four* onwards, but live, they have to fall back on guitar, drums, bass and vocals. Gerald Woodroffe's arrival in the touring band makes some difference, but not greatly so.

## *Black Sabbath Tour*: 26 August 1969 (Workington, UK) – 20 August 1970 (Stockholm, Sweden)

The arbitrary first date was at Banklands Youth Club when Ozzy announced the change of name to Black Sabbath. Prior to this, the band were still known as Earth. Although this touring period was ostensibly to promote their début album, they quickly introduced songs from *Paranoid,* to the extent that by the time *Paranoid* was recorded (in June) the setlist looks more like it is promoting that album! Setlists are noted under each entry because they evolved and changed so much during the tour.

### Rugman's Youth Club, Dumfries, 16 November 1969
(audience recording)

Setlist: 'Black Sabbath' (cuts in), 'Let Me Love You Baby', 'Song For Jim', 'Warning', 'Wicked World', 'Behind The Wall Of Sleep', 'Early One Morning', 'N.I.B.', 'Blue Coat Man'

The earliest recording of Sabbath live caused great excitement when it emerged in 2005. It wasn't even known to exist until Alex Wilson, who recorded it, made it available. Sabbath played two sets that night and the recording seems to be a composite from both sets. The Osbournes bought the original copies of the tapes, but this compilation is still easy to find online. It's a vitally important historic recording as it straddles the period when Sabbath were changing their sound. The quality is surprisingly good, a comfortable listen, and there is much to enjoy.

There were three new songs to Sabbath fans when this emerged, all of them covers. The first one, 'Let Me Love You Baby', was written by Willie Dixon. It's likely that the band heard it by Buddy Guy, who recorded it as a single in 1961. Sabbath turn in a powerful rendition that reminds me of Led Zeppelin circa 1968.

'Early One Morning' was written by Pete Johnson and Big Joe Turner. The most well-known version is by Little Richard, who recorded it in 1958. It's a blues by numbers track, and again suggestive of Zeppelin playing this kind of material.

'Blue Coat Man' is a cover of an Eddie Boyd song. The version undoubtedly heard by Sabbath would be the 1967 re-recording by Eddie, which featured Peter Green on lead guitar. It's a good workout number and survived in their setlists at least until April 1970, when it appears on the Lausanne recording. This full-tilt number allowed plenty of room for jamming.

The more familiar Sabbath material is broadly similar to the versions on the first album. 'Behind The Wall of Sleep' is an exception with an extended work-out instead of that smooth segue into 'Warning'. 'N.I.B.' comes straight in on the riff, which is fine. It still sounds great, but the addition of the bass intro for the album would prove to be a masterstroke. Ozzy has some trouble with the high vocals on this one.

## John Peel Show, 26 April 1970 (Epic)

'Fairies Wear Boots', 'Behind The Wall Of Sleep', 'Walpurgis', 'Black Sabbath' This first emerged in collectors' circles when Ozzy's *Ozzman Cometh* compilation was issued in 1997. The source was stated as being from his 'basement tapes', and they certainly sounded like they could be early working versions. From comparisons with other sources, it became clear that this was the Peel show with the audience removed. That, and the basement tapes credit, made it look a lot like avoiding paying a licensing fee to the BBC! So this is a somewhat questionable official release.

With *Paranoid* as yet unrecorded, the two from that album would have been new to anyone who had not seen the band in concert. The sound is excellent and it's a notable release because of the quality of the performance and the variations to the album versions. 'Fairies Wear Boots' is close to the album, while 'Behind The Wall Of Sleep' features a 1:30 instrumental coda at the end of the song. 'Walpurgis' is the best-recorded version of the song in its original format, complete with all the original grotesque lyrics. The set concludes with 'Black Sabbath', which features the extra verse. The insertion of a brief version of the galloping outro riff before this verse doesn't work at all. By the time we get to the outro proper, the effect is diminished because we have already heard it. They were wise to keep to the edited arrangement for the album.

### Lausanne Electric Circus, Switzerland, 29 April 1970 (soundboard recording)

Setlist: 'Behind The Wall Of Sleep', 'Walpurgis', 'Fairies Wear Boots', 'Blue Coat Man', 'N.I.B.', 'Black Sabbath', 'Sleeping Village', 'Warning'

A great quality recording and an interesting setlist. 'Behind The Wall Of Sleep' has the jammed ending they were using live at the time. Ozzy introduces 'Fairies Wear Boots' as the opening number, so the running order above (as per download copies) is clearly wrong. 'Blue Coat Man' sounds out of keeping with the rest of the set with its rock 'n' roll stylings but gives some high energy levity in the middle of the set. After the long version of 'Black Sabbath', we get the surprise inclusion of 'Sleeping Village'. Fascinating to hear this one, the quiet opening section, in particular, adds so much to the set. They add a second verse, too, which is, 'Child's crying in its bed, for it's needed to be fed. No-one comes to this child, so it lies there till it sleeps.' As per the album, it segues into 'Warning', the first part of which is listed as still being 'Sleeping Village' on tracklists. There's a cut, which is probably where the tape was turned over, and the track credits now say 'Warning'. Even this 'second half' is a long 27 minutes and includes a bass solo and drum solo as well as an extended guitar solo. Just after the 8-minute mark, they break into a Dave Brubeck 'Take Five' influenced jazz section. Otherwise, much of the rest follows the format of the album version, albeit stretched out! This is an essential recording for your collection.

### Audimax der Freien Universität, West Berlin, Germany, 26 June 1970 (soundboard recording)

Setlist: 'Paranoid', 'Iron Man', 'Black Sabbath', 'Walpurgis', 'Hand Of Doom', 'Rat Salad', 'N.I.B.'

This show was primarily intended for American servicemen in West Berlin, and promoted by U.S. Forces Radio. The even mix and quality suggest that this is a soundboard recording. It's a fabulous performance too. The band kick off with their soon-to-be 'hit' which has a real bite to it, Ozzy changing the words around as he does on a few of the tracks. 'Iron Man' is stunning with an echo effect on Bill's intro drum 'footsteps' that gives it more weight. Ozzy again alters the lyrics to this one. The echo effect is retained for 'Black Sabbath', which also gets the guitar intro piece and the extra verse. 'Walpurgis' is huge, and it's interesting that Ozzy doesn't sing the 'War Pigs' lyrics considering he had only recorded them a few days earlier. 'Hand Of Doom' sees the echo effect back, and Ozzy changing most of the lyrics. Again this is odd; perhaps he couldn't remember them. An abbreviated 'Rat Salad' concludes the set before an encore of 'N.I.B', which is counted straight into the guitar riff.

## *Paranoid Tour*: 11 September 1970 (Swansea, UK) – 26 April 1971 (London, UK)

1970 setlist: 'Paranoid', 'Hand Of Doom', 'Rat Salad', 'Iron Man', 'Black Sabbath', 'N.I.B.', 'Behind The Wall Of Sleep', 'War Pigs', 'Fairies Wear Boots'. 1971 setlist: 'War Pigs', 'Into The Void', 'Iron Man', 'Black Sabbath', 'After Forever', 'Wicked World', 'Fairies Wear Boots', 'Paranoid'

The band start to drop their tuning on this tour, going down from standard E to Eb. This has the effect of making the songs sound even heavier than they were on record. Any significant change of pace and mood rested entirely with the verses of 'Hand Of Doom' and the intro and verses of 'Black Sabbath' itself, otherwise the set was a full-on assault.

Sabbath changed the setlist when they re-commenced touring in January 1971. As they were also working on *Master Of Reality*, the band drop in work-in-progress versions of 'After Forever' and 'Into The Void'. They extended the duration of the set too in 1971, bringing back 'Wicked World' as the basis for their old mid-show jam session.

'War Pigs' took its rightful place at the start of the set for the 1971 dates. It always works at its best opening the show.

### Black Mass, Beat Club 1970 (New Millennium Communications)

The four tracks Sabbath recorded for the *The Beat Club* in 1970 were released in 1999 as a DVD/CD package called *Black Mass*. It was a dubious semi-official release by a company that had picked up the copyright of the old *Beat Club* recordings. This includes the earliest surviving footage of the band performing live.

Interestingly 'Black Sabbath' features the storm and church bells intro from the album. It's taken at a slower pace, enhancing the brooding menace. In complete contrast, 'Blue Suede Shoes' is attacked with joyous intensity. Sabbath played it as part of their soundcheck before recording 'Black Sabbath', but it went so well that the programme producers decided to feature it.

'Paranoid' sounds tinny, reducing the power of the track. 'Iron Man' is also a little thin, but it does have more effective footsteps drumming. Ozzy doesn't perform the intro voice, something he only revisits a few years later in the live domain.

## Montreux Casino, 31 August 1970 (BMG/Rhino)

This soundboard recording was released as part of the *Paranoid Super Deluxe Edition*. The intro features hammering sounds, real heavy metal! Ozzy is high in the mix, but once your ears attune, this is an excellent listen. 'Iron Man' is exceptional, one of the best early versions. 'War Pigs' sees Ozzy wandering off into 'Walpurgis' territory and he also ad-libs on parts of 'Hand Of Doom'.

## RTBF, Brussels, 3 October 1970 (BMG/Rhino)

The video has been often released unofficially, usually credited as being from Paris on 19 December 1970. It was actually a recording made for the Belgian TV show *Pop Shop* and, according to BMG/Rhino, who released the audio as part of the *Paranoid Super Deluxe Edition,* was recorded in Brussels.

Footage has cropped up all over the place in varying quality; it's prominently seen in the *Black Sabbath Story Volume One* DVD. The audio, meanwhile, has done the rounds in its Paris guise for some time, and there are still releases coming out that claim it to be so.

It's excellent quality, with a great sound balance. Ozzy again wanders off on his own version of the lyrics at times on 'Hand Of Doom', which makes for a different listen. Someone in the audience was clearly annoying Ozzy, who invites, 'That bloke to shut his trap' just before 'Black Sabbath'. That song ends with an interlude of more mysterious hammering before they launch into 'N.I.B.'! It's interesting that 'Behind The Wall Of Sleep' is still in the set with the jazz rave-up ending.

## City Hall, Sheffield, 14 January 1971 (audience recording)

An important recording that sees Sabbath trying out material they were working on for *Master Of Reality*. So we get 'Into The Void' (still in its 'Spanish Sid' incarnation) and 'After Forever' – both songs with different lyrics to the later released versions.

It was recorded right up close to the stage and is extremely good quality. It puts you there in front of Sabbath with Tony, in particular, on great form.

## *Master Of Reality Tour*: 2 July 1971 (Cleveland, Ohio) – 2 April 1972 (Passaic, New Jersey)

Typical setlist: 'N.I.B.', 'War Pigs', 'Sweet Leaf', 'Black Sabbath', 'Iron Man', 'Embryo'/ 'Children Of The Grave', 'Wicked World' (including 'Orchid'), 'Guitar Solo', 'Drum Solo', 'Paranoid', 'Fairies Wear Boots'
Occasionally played: 'After Forever', 'Tomorrow's Dream' (different lyrics), 'Snowblind' (different lyrics), 'Cornucopia' (partial)

Following the successful down-tuning for *Master Of Reality*, Tony and Geezer carried it forward into the live shows, tuning down to C#. This worked well for those tracks already in that tuning but makes for a noticeable difference to the tracks from *Black Sabbath* and *Paranoid*. Set opener 'N.I.B.' is a case in point. It sounds slightly odd at a lower tuning, and the difference also included Tony bolting on a guitar intro to it. Deciding what to drop to make way for the *Master Of Reality* songs was always going to be difficult, but it's incredible that only two (not counting 'Orchid' and 'Embryo') made it into the setlist. 'Into The Void' and 'After Forever' had been tried out on the *Paranoid* tour but had not been retained. Given the strength of the new material, it seems like a chance missed, a mistake they didn't repeat for the 1997 reunion dates when the big four tracks all got an airing.

There is no softer material in the set. Bill told *Drum!* In 2012, 'With all the headbangers and everything, it's just like we have to pour it out, and so something with such solitude didn't have much of a chance at being a live song'. So no room for 'Solitude' or others of that ilk, save a burst of 'Orchid'.

Guitar and drum solos were de rigeur for rock bands in the era, so to some extent, they had to stay in the set. 'Wicked World''s time should have passed. This over-extended version could have been dropped for 'Lord Of This World' and 'Into The Void'.

The American dates from 1 March 1972 to the end of the tour were dubbed the 'Iron Man Tour'.

## Borough Of York Stadium, Toronto, 18 July 1971 (audience recording)

This audience recording is generally of a good standard and features a brilliant performance by the band, especially Ozzy, who is on fire. At the 12:46 mark during 'Wicked World' Tony experiments with what will be the riff to 'Cornucopia'. Being from the beginning of the tour, this set showcases early performances of 'Sweet Leaf', 'Embryo' and 'Children Of The Grave'.

## Swing Auditorium, San Bernadino, California, 17 March 1972 (audience recording)

A good quality, fairly clear recording, worth having because of early versions of 'Tomorrow's Dream' and Snowblind' with different lyrics. The only minus point is that Geezer has sound problems and his tuning is a little off for a large part of the set. Despite this, Sabbath are at their best in front of what is a rapturous audience; just listen to 'Iron Man' for evidence. The 'Cornucopia' riff reappears in 'Wicked World'.

## *Volume Four Tour*: 7 July 1972 (Wildwood, New Jersey) – 18 March 1973 (Newcastle, UK)

Typical setlist: 'Tomorrow's Dream', 'Sweet Leaf', 'Snowblind', 'War Pigs', 'Iron Man', 'Cornucopia', 'Killing Yourself To Live', 'Wicked World' (including 'Orchid', 'Into The Void (excerpt)' and 'Sometimes I'm Happy'), 'Guitar Solo', 'Supernaut', 'Drum Solo', 'Wicked World (Reprise)', 'Embryo'/ 'Children Of The Grave', 'Paranoid'
Occasionally played: 'Wheels Of Confusion', 'Changes', 'Under The Sun'

The band kept the C# tuning for this tour. As usual, there are some missed chances in the setlist. Dropping 'Black Sabbath' is brave but odd, and, as always, there is the mid-set dip for the 'Wicked World'/solo section. You hear the intro to 'Into The Void' and wish they would play the whole song. 'Sometimes I'm Happy' first appears on this tour and it's a grooving happy vibe that somewhat surprisingly was never reworked for an album.

It's good to see that *Volume Four* is well-represented in the set. Those wanting more from the tour are best directed to Ngaruawahia Music

Festival, New Zealand, on 7 January 1973, which is reasonable quality and features 'Changes'.

## Live At Last, 1973 (NEMS)

With no studio album due for 1973, Sabbath looked at marking time with that '70s rock staple, a live album. To this end, two concerts were recorded, at Manchester Free Trade Hall (11 March) and The Rainbow, London (16 March), during the UK tour to promote *Volume Four*. However, Tony, at least, wasn't happy with the results and the project was abandoned. With no other recent concerts recorded, and an archive live release (from say 1970), thought to be equally unsatisfactory, there was nothing further heard from the band till the release of *Sabbath Bloody Sabbath*.

The tapes resurfaced in 1980 when Patrick Meehan put them out on NEMS without Sabbath's permission, although legally, he didn't need it. The cheap cash-grab nature of the release is evident in the lacklustre cover of a satellite passing over the lunar surface. Side one was all from Manchester, except 'Embryo'/ 'Children Of The Grave' which was from The Rainbow, along with all of side two.

In spite of the issues, the performances and music have considerable merit and the album got to number 5 in the UK. The band never forgot about the album and it formed part of the later officially sanctioned *Past Lives* release, which was then expanded on for the *Live In The UK 1973* set.

## Live In The UK 1973 (BMG/Rhino)

It features most of the tracks from *Live At Last* and the *Past Lives* update of the same but is sequenced as the setlist they played on the two dates (Manchester, London) in the correct order. However, three tracks are 'alternative' versions; 'Tomorrow's Dream', 'Sweet Leaf' and 'Snowblind' are now the versions from The Rainbow show and thus previously unreleased.

It was released as part of the *Volume Four* deluxe edition in 2021 and benefited from the original multi-track recordings being remixed by Richard Digby Smith, who worked miracles with the tapes:

The main problem was that everything was just so loud on stage. The multi-tracks were transferred over to digital. When I first listened to the vocal line you almost got the whole mix on the vocal mic. I wondered how I was going to get any separation? So I trialled using what's called phase relationship and checked the settings for each mic, vocals, drums, tom-toms. With the toms, for example, I cut them in when they were required, so the leakage was kept down to a minimum.

Then I had to even out the levels and try things with EQ and compression. It was all a bit of a challenge. I separated out the guitar making it slightly more mono but putting the guitar to the left and bass to the right. There's only bass, drums and guitar, so it worked better to give them their own space. I recreated the live set-up so you hear Geezer on his side and Tony on his. Tony had three mics on his cabinet, a cleanish one, a really bright one, and another that was really distorted.

Smith got a friend of his, James Griffiths, to work out where to put the ident points for 'Wicked World', which he guessed incorporated other tunes. Finally, unlike the subsequent live material on deluxe editions issued for *Sabotage* and *Technical Ecstasy*, he got quality tapes to work with. Smith's ideal requirements never waver: 'I always say to them send me them in FLAC, in other words no compression. No reverb, no EQ, just send them to me completely dry.'

What we have here, live at last, is an essential recording that has never sounded better. Sabbath are on blistering form giving the songs extra energy over the studio counterparts, and it sounds like there are no studio overdubs either. Right from the off, they attack 'Tomorrow's Dream' with a more ferocious energy than the studio version. A sniff and 'one up the nose' from Ozzy introduces a piledriving 'Snowblind'. The 'no overdubs' is evident here as Ozzy goes off-key on the end of 'I feel the snowflakes freezing me'. It's live, warts and all, and this is a smoking version.

One of the main attractions here is the prototype 'Killing Yourself To Live' with the original lyrics. They don't sound right, but that may be due to over-familiarity with the album version. Apart from that, the performance has a raw intensity that would have left audiences of the time eagerly anticipating *Sabbath Bloody Sabbath*.

'Wicked World' includes the snippets as noted in the tour overview. There's also a nice light-hearted section where the band get to play the blues together, a little bit of Earth coming back.

While the track selection largely works, you miss 'Black Sabbath' (not played) and 'Iron Man'. It doesn't feel right for a Sabbath live album to miss these two out.

## *Sabbath Bloody Sabbath Tour*: 9 December 1973 (Newcastle, UK) – 16 November 1974 (Sydney, Australia)

Typical setlist: 'Tomorrow's Dream', 'Sweet Leaf', 'Killing Yourself To Live', 'Snowblind', 'War Pigs', 'Sabbra Cadabra', 'Guitar Solo', 'Sometimes I'm Happy', 'Drum Solo', 'Supernaut', 'Iron Man', 'Orchid'/ 'Guitar Solo', 'Sabbra Cadabra (reprise)', 'Black Sabbath', 'Embryo'/ 'Children Of The Grave', 'Paranoid'

Occasionally played: 'Cornucopia', 'Sabbath Bloody Sabbath', 'A National Acrobat', 'Megalomania' (fast section)

The band kept the C# tuning for this tour. A tour preview came when they played at Alexandra Palace in London on 2 August 1973 as part of the London Music Festival. Fans at the show not only got to hear the already previewed 'Killing Yourself To Live', but also 'Cornucopia', 'A National Acrobat' (with different lyrics) and 'Sabbath Bloody Sabbath' in the encore. The latter may have been the intro riffs alone, as the band rarely played it in dates up till 1978. This show was played during their sojourn at Clearwell Castle, a chance to try songs out before the album and ensuing tour.

Considering *Sabbath Bloody Sabbath* is such a strong album, it's a surprise that only two tracks regularly made the live set. Part of the problem was the high register Ozzy used on much of the album. There was no way he could push himself night after night without wrecking his voice, so that ruled out 'Sabbath Bloody Sabbath', arguably the biggest missing track ever live. 'Spiral Architect' made it into the next tour, where Woodroffe covered the string parts, and was a highlight of the reunion tours. That leaves 'A National Acrobat' as the only other viable setlist contender from the album, but it was only played on a few occasions.

'Sometimes I'm Happy' returned to the set, still a grooving jam with simple lyrics from Ozzy. The rest of the set is strong and picks itself for the most part. If they had dropped some of the jam sections, then the likes of 'N.I.B.' could have been retained. 'Black Sabbath' was left out on many dates of the tour too but appears in enough dates to be considered an integral part of the set.

The fast heavy riff section of what would become 'Megalomania' starts to appear in the later setlists for the tour, a good example being a fair recording from Brisbane in July.

The tour also marks the sporadic use of the sirens at the beginning of 'War Pigs' and on the subsequent tours.

## Pittsburgh Civic Arena, 1 February 1974 (audience recording)

There's a shortage of quality releases from this tour, but Pittsburgh makes the cut because the sound is steady, albeit rather flat and at times fuzzy, and Sabbath are on form. We get the best live recording of 'A National Acrobat' as part of this incomplete set, as well as 'Cornucopia'.

## California Jam, Ontario Speedway, 6 April 1974 (soundboard/TV recording)

Sabbath's abbreviated set was recorded by ABC TV, who broadcast five songs. Interview footage with Ozzy, before and after the show, also survives. Audio recordings of Sabbath's set exist in several versions, cuts being variously made to Ozzy's between-song banter.

Sabbath had not played for a while and at times, it gets a little wayward, but their performance is scintillating. Highlights include the bulldozer assault of 'Children Of The Grave' and a spectacular long version of 'Sabbra Cadabra'. The latter has a solid band jam section with Tony playing a devastating lead break over Geezer's wah-wah bass and Bill's drums.

Apart from the wah-wah section on 'Sabbra Cadabra', Geezer's bass is generally too low in the mix, and Ozzy a little too high. In spite of these issues, California Jam remains an essential listen. This is also the first time in the gigs featured here that Ozzy uses the 'I am iron man' introduction, as per the studio version, which he then keeps for every subsequent gig.

## *Sabotage Tour*: 14 July 1975 (Toledo, Ohio) – 13 January 1976 (London, UK)

Typical setlist: '(Intro tape – Supertzar)', 'Killing Yourself To Live', 'Hole In The Sky', 'Snowblind', 'Symptom Of The Universe', 'War Pigs', 'Megalomania', 'Sabbra Cadabra',' Jam/Guitar Solo',' Sometimes I'm Happy', 'Drum Solo', 'Supernaut', 'Iron Man', 'Orchid/ Guitar Solo', 'Rock 'N' Roll Doctor (jam version)', 'Guitar Solo'/'Don't Start Too Late', 'Black Sabbath', 'Spiral Architect', 'Embryo'/ 'Children of the Grave', 'Paranoid'

Jez Woodroffe became the first additional musician to tour with Sabbath. Because his keyboard parts are there mostly for effect, they get away with staying in the lower C# tuning. Woodroffe was positioned to the side of the stage, where, depending on the venue, he was more often than not out of view to the audience. His presence meant they could play 'Megalomania' and the welcome addition of 'Spiral Architect'.

Based on existing recordings, this was the last consistently great tour the band played, with three excellent quality surviving recordings listed here as key evidence. The set choices are generally superb, other than the curious return yet again of 'Sometimes I'm Happy', albeit tweaked since the *Sabbath Bloody Sabbath* tour. Added into the jam section of the set was an early outing for the work-in-progress 'Rock 'N' Roll Doctor'.

The *Sabotage* album was given a prominent airing in the set with all of side one appearing. Intriguingly, nothing from side two was played except for 'Supertzar' as the intro tape. 'The Writ' is the one that got away here as a track that would have suited their live set, but the second half would have been tricky. 'Symptom' is in the wrong place, needing to be somewhere more effective with that destructive riff. It also loses something without the jammed second half.

There would have been room for more oldies if they had cut the mid-set jams and there are several numbers that come to mind as enhancements – 'N.I.B', 'Sweet Leaf' and 'Into The Void' would have been terrific. They would never hit the high standards of this tour with the same consistency again. This was Black Sabbath at their best live.

## Convention Center, Asbury Park, New Jersey, 5 August 1975 (BMG/ Rhino)

Hands down, this is the finest live Black Sabbath album, with so many highlights to pick from! It was at last given a full official release as *North American Tour: Live '75* in June 2021 as part of the *Sabotage* super deluxe edition. Tony stated to *News In 24*, that the songs are 'from different American concerts'. Clearly, nobody wanted to admit that the Asbury Park tapes were used for all of the tracks, possibly due to ownership wrangles. Fans on the Black Sabbath online forum quickly spotted it was all from Asbury Park and that there was no appreciable increase in sound quality, meaning the tracks are taken from the same lossy sources as bootleg copies.

Those sources come from the archives of the King Biscuit Flower Hour radio show, which broadcast five songs from the set but recorded the whole performance. Sabbath used three of those tracks for the *Past Lives* live album – 'Hole In The Sky', 'Symptom Of The Universe' and 'Megalomania'.

The super deluxe version features edits, but the entire set is still out there in the bootleg world. There are many sources for the recording, but the complete show is easy to find online and is a monster.

'Killing Yourself to Live' is awesome. Ozzy rasps on this but gets away with the delivery by sheer willpower. He doesn't have the lyrics quite right yet for the *Sabotage* songs, repeating the first verse in 'Hole In The Sky' for example, but he delivers it with such passion and ferocity it hardly matters. The song has a more open feel too, than its studio counterpart, without losing that overwhelming rhythmic power.

By 'Snowblind', Ozzy has found a comfortable level and this is a colossal version - it really is. Stripped of some of the subtleties, this hits home like a sledgehammer. 'Megalomania' is one of the absolute joys. It sounds even more menacing on the intro because of the more spartan arrangement. This more direct version works well, though Woodroffe is there to pick up the mellotron parts. 'Sabbra Cadabra' is another that benefits from the stripped-back approach, sounding more Sabbath-like than it did on *Sabbath Bloody Sabbath*. Woodroffe gets to approximate Wakeman's work on this one but is fairly low in the mix.

Tony opens the jam/guitar solo with a great chugging riff that could have been the basis for a song. The jam also includes 'Sometimes I'm Happy', which adds welcome variation. The segue from the abbreviated 'Supernaut' into 'Iron Man' is a wonderful set-up for the crowd-pleaser.

The electric solo finale of 'Don't Start, Too Late' acts as the intro to 'Black Sabbath', but would have been more effective in its acoustic incarnation. 'Spiral Architect' is another where the reduced instrumentation makes for a more direct take on the song. The final rush through 'Embryo'/ 'Children Of The Grave'/ 'Paranoid' is a terrific end to this essential recording.

## Civic Center, Santa Monica, 4 September 1975 (TV video and audio)

Twenty-five minutes of their set was filmed for Don Kirshner's Rock Concert TV show, consisting of 'Killing Yourself To Live', 'Hole In The Sky', 'Snowblind', 'War Pigs' and 'Paranoid' The video is easy to find and the audio has started to appear on CD too. The video quality is very good and the audio is excellent. You can hear how Ozzy is pushing himself on the vocals, rasping slightly on the top notes. The audience are artificially too loud on the intro to each song, and close listening suggests it's a loop. But you can't fault the intensity of Sabbath's performances, they are on fire.

## Long Beach Arena, Long Beach, California, 7 September 1975 (audience recording)

Mike Millard is a legend in the concert taping world. He recorded many of the great bands, and by 1975 he was using a stereo recorder. Millard smuggled it into the venues in a wheelchair, which he pretended he needed. He got terrific quality recordings that have the right amount of audience in the levels. How he got that sweet spot is a marvel but any band Millard recorded is worth seeking out. He recorded Sabbath once, and what he got is a rival to the Asbury Park set because of the audience energy. The effect is of being right there at the front of the audience with stunning clarity. Sabbath were at a peak too, so this is a must-have gig. The setlist is the typical one as noted.

### *Technical Ecstasy Tour*: 22 October 1976 (Tulsa, Oklahoma) – 22 April 1977 (Gothenburg, Sweden)

Typical setlist: (Intro tape -'Supertzar'), 'Symptom Of The Universe', 'Snowblind', ' All Moving Parts (Stand Still)', 'War Pigs', 'Gypsy', 'Black Sabbath', 'Dirty Women', 'Drum Solo', 'Guitar Solo/Jam', 'Rock 'N' Roll Doctor', 'Guitar Solo/Jam' , 'Electric Funeral', 'Iron Man', 'Children Of The Grave', 'Paranoid' (Outro tape – 'She's Gone')
Occasionally played: 'Supernaut' (intro only), 'Megalomania', 'N.I.B.' (on some 1976 dates and then all of the 1977 dates).

Sabbath used standard E tuning for this tour. With Woodroffe more prominent now on keyboards (if no more visible) and with the *Technical Ecstasy* tracks being recorded in standard E, it made perfect sense.

'All Moving Parts' was dropped by the 1977 leg, which left three tracks from the new album played on every date. 'Gypsy' is better live than on record but still gets lost in the 'gypsy visit' section, and 'Rock 'N' Roll Doctor' still sounds poor. 'Dirty Women' holds its own and is the one they returned to for the reunion tours.

'Back Street Kids' would have been an excellent track live that could have worked as the opening track, but Sabbath's usual M.O. was to open with a well-known track. 'Symptom' works extremely well as an opener! The only other track they should have considered is 'You Won't Change Me', which would have made for a change of pace and given Tony a chance to shine, hopefully at the expense of a solo spot.

Those solo spots occupy the middle of the set. The first jam is great, with Geezer using his wah-wah, but if they had cut the drum solo out and chopped the second jazzy guitar solo/jam it would have tightened the set considerably or allowed more songs to be featured. *Sabotage*'s representation, apart from a few outings for 'Megalomania', was reduced to 'Symptom', which is a shame, and the likes of 'Sweet Leaf' would have been great inclusions.

Of the old classics that were selected for an airing, the surprise choice was 'Electric Funeral', which, as far as can be ascertained, made its live debut on the tour.

## Civic Arena, Pittsburgh, 8 December 1976 (soundboard recording/BMG & Rhino)

The best unofficial recording (sound quality wise) from the tour, with only 'N.I.B.' and 'Paranoid' missing. Sabbath always seem to get it together in Pittsburgh, witness an exultant 'Gypsy' or 'Snowblind', for example. It's evident that Ozzy is pushing his voice too hard on the opening numbers, he sounds in pain on 'Symptom'. The King Biscuit Flower Hour broadcast four from the set ('Symptom Of The Universe', 'War Pigs', 'Gypsy' and 'Children of The Grave') on their show called The British Biscuit.

The super deluxe edition of *Technical Ecstasy* features most of the tracks from the complete King Biscuit source on disc four called *Live World Tour 1976/77*. Some equaliser work has been done on the selections, and the enhancements make a difference. The running order of the deluxe version is wrong, 'Snowblind' should be track two and 'All Moving Parts' track three. The drum solo has been edited and segued onto the (edited) guitar solo/jazzy jam session following 'Rock 'N; Roll Doctor'. The latter, plus 'Iron Man' and more of the guitar solo/jam sections are missing entirely.

'All Moving Parts' works well and should have been kept in the set throughout on this evidence. Tony gets off a great solo on this version that gives the track a harder edge.

All in all, this is an excellent 'newly official' recording of Sabbath on the tour.

## Olympen, Lund, Sweden, 21 April 1977 (audience recording)

The quality is very good, with Ozzy upfront and clear. It's incomplete, with 'Iron Man' missing though it would have been played, and 'Gypsy' is, for some reason, sequenced out of order. Geezer plays only the last few solo bass bars before the guitar riff comes in on 'N.I.B.' It would have made a great opener! Sabbath are tight, as the set is well drilled, but the declining faith in the new material is evident in the setlist.

## *Never Say Die Tour:* 16 May 1978 (Sheffield, UK) – 11 December 1978 (Albuquerque, New Mexico)

Typical setlist: (Intro tape – 'Supertzar'), 'Symptom Of The Universe', 'War Pigs', 'Snowblind', 'Never Say Die', 'Black Sabbath', 'Dirty Women', 'Drum Solo', 'Rock 'N' Roll Doctor', 'Guitar Solo', 'Jam', 'Electric Funeral', 'Iron Man', 'Fairies Wear Boots', 'Children Of The Grave', 'Paranoid', (Outro tape – 'She's Gone')

Occasionally played: 'N.I.B.', 'Hand Of Doom', 'Orchid', 'Sabbath Bloody Sabbath' (riff only), 'Shock Wave'

Standard E tuning again, but the impact of not down tuning is less noticeable. Only three set regulars were originally down-tuned to C# ('Symptom Of The Universe', 'Children Of The Grave' and 'Snowblind'), so it was obviously thought not worth bothering with a guitar swap for three songs. 'Snowblind' sounds plain wrong played in E, losing a huge amount of its power. Nobody was brought in to play keyboards, but that has a minimal effect.

A tenth anniversary (of the four getting together) tour suggested cherry-picking classics from the back catalogue and throwing in one or two from their new album. In other words, business as usual, but perhaps with more curatorial care?

With the band having mixed feelings about *Never Say Die*, that left the title track as the only strong contender for the set, and it would have been a splendid opening song. You could make a case for the inclusion of 'Johnny Blade' or 'Junior's Eyes' – both would have worked better in a live setting and could have held their own. In the end, the only further addition was 'Shock Wave', which was played late on in the tour on the American dates. There are stories that they also played 'Swinging The Chain' at least once on the tour, but there is no audio or setlist evidence.

The return of 'Rock 'N' Roll Doctor' wasn't a surprise, but it just isn't worthy of making the set. 'Dirty Women' still went down well. The solos and jams were still present and they added to the sense of a flabby and weary band just about hanging on to their mojo. A punchier set would have been a big help.

The first few UK dates saw the main differences to the setlist above. Audiences at those shows got the best (and longest) setlists of the tour because 'N.I.B.' and 'Hand Of Doom' were added in to that typical setlist, coming after 'Electric Funeral'.

## Hammersmith Odeon, 19 June 1978 (Sanctuary DVD)

The second night at Hammersmith Odeon was filmed for official release on VHS and then DVD under the title *Never Say Die*. This was supposed to be on 11 June 1978, but there were problems on the night as photographer Alan Perry recalls:

> When I arrived, there were fire engines with flashing blue lights outside the Odeon. There was an earth problem with the power supply, and it was thought that there was a danger of a serious fire, so the fire brigade ordered that the concert should be postponed.

Perry was there for the rescheduled date on 19 June and photographed the band. Geezer used a Rickenbacker for this show, and not just any old one. He recalled to *Bassplayer* (2013) what happened:

> I used the Rickenbacker on one show, and it was the one that was videotaped. It was the bass Glenn Hughes used in Deep Purple. I bought it just as a collector's piece. We got to that Hammersmith gig, and I had completely forgotten to bring my basses with me. The only one I had with me was the Rickenbacker. I'm not sure why I even had that with me.

The film features ten tracks from the concert lasting an hour, so around half an hour of the set is missing. What we get is excellent quality video and very good sound, albeit a little fuzzy and compressed. It's a good but not great performance, with Sabbath looking and sounding like their killer live edge has gone missing.

## Pittsburgh Civic Arena, 2 September 1978 (soundboard recording)

The King Biscuit Flower Hour broadcast four songs ('Snowblind', 'Black Sabbath', 'Iron Man' and 'Paranoid') on their show called The British Biscuit. However, 64 minutes of the show has made it out onto the internet, including the irregularly played 'Sabbath Bloody Sabbath' intro riff and 'Orchid'. The sound is excellent, and this is a great performance too, much better than Hammersmith.

## Selland Arena, Fresno, California, 22 September 1978 (audience recording)

This has a good sound balance, with Ozzy's vocals in particular coming over well. Because it's from later in the tour, it features 'Shockwaves', as Ozzy calls it. The live ambience gives the song a power it never had on the studio version. This is the best quality complete gig recording from the tour and another great performance. Another gig worth hearing is Abilene, Texas, which is a high hiss level soundboard, only part of the set available but including 'Shock Wave'.

## Miscellaneous
### Past Lives (Sanctuary)

This live compendium was released in 2002 and represented the first official release of *Live At Last*. Disc one was the remastered *Live At Last*, while disc two featured tracks from two TV and radio broadcasts – six from Paris in 1970 (since established to be the Brussels show) and three from Asbury Park in 1975.

So it was disc two that got the attention at the time as it featured new product. The running order is botched with 'Hand Of Doom' opening, followed by the Asbury Park trio, and then back to the 1970 tracks! The album got to number 114 in the American charts.

# On Track series

Alan Parsons Project – Steve Swift 978-1-78952-154-2

Tori Amos – Lisa Torem 978-1-78952-142-9

Asia – Peter Braidis 978-1-78952-099-6

Badfinger – Robert Day-Webb 978-1-878952-176-4

Barclay James Harvest – Keith and Monica Domone  978-1-78952-067-5

The Beatles – Andrew Wild 978-1-78952-009-5

The Beatles Solo 1969-1980 – Andrew Wild 978-1-78952-030-9

Blue Oyster Cult – Jacob Holm-Lupo 978-1-78952-007-1

Blur – Matt Bishop 978-178952-164-1

Marc Bolan and T.Rex – Peter Gallagher 978-1-78952-124-5

Kate Bush – Bill Thomas 978-1-78952-097-2

Camel – Hamish Kuzminski 978-1-78952-040-8

Caravan – Andy Boot  978-1-78952-127-6

Cardiacs – Eric Benac 978-1-78952-131-3

Eric Clapton Solo – Andrew Wild 978-1-78952-141-2

The Clash – Nick Assirati 978-1-78952-077-4

Crosby, Stills and Nash – Andrew Wild 978-1-78952-039-2

The Damned – Morgan Brown 978-1-78952-136-8

Deep Purple and Rainbow 1968-79 – Steve Pilkington 978-1-78952-002-6

Dire Straits – Andrew Wild 978-1-78952-044-6

The Doors – Tony Thompson 978-1-78952-137-5

Dream Theater – Jordan Blum 978-1-78952-050-7

Electric Light Orchestra – Barry Delve 978-1-78952-152-8

Elvis Costello and The Attractions – Georg Purvis 978-1-78952-129-0

Emerson Lake and Palmer – Mike Goode 978-1-78952-000-2

Fairport Convention – Kevan Furbank 978-1-78952-051-4

Peter Gabriel – Graeme Scarfe 978-1-78952-138-2

Genesis – Stuart MacFarlane 978-1-78952-005-7

Gentle Giant – Gary Steel 978-1-78952-058-3

Gong – Kevan Furbank 978-1-78952-082-8

Hall and Oates – Ian Abrahams 978-1-78952-167-2

Hawkwind – Duncan Harris 978-1-78952-052-1

Peter Hammill – Richard Rees Jones 978-1-78952-163-4

Roy Harper – Opher Goodwin 978-1-78952-130-6

Jimi Hendrix – Emma Stott 978-1-78952-175-7

The Hollies – Andrew Darlington 978-1-78952-159-7

Iron Maiden – Steve Pilkington 978-1-78952-061-3

Jefferson Airplane – Richard Butterworth 978-1-78952-143-6

Jethro Tull – Jordan Blum 978-1-78952-016-3

Elton John in the 1970s – Peter Kearns 978-1-78952-034-7

The Incredible String Band – Tim Moon 978-1-78952-107-8

Iron Maiden – Steve Pilkington 978-1-78952-061-3

Judas Priest – John Tucker 978-1-78952-018-7

Kansas – Kevin Cummings 978-1-78952-057-6

The Kinks – Martin Hutchinson 978-1-78952-172-6

Korn – Matt Karpe 978-1-78952-153-5

Led Zeppelin – Steve Pilkington 978-1-78952-151-1

Level 42 – Matt Philips 978-1-78952-102-3

Little Feat – 978-1-78952-168-9

Aimee Mann – Jez Rowden 978-1-78952-036-1

Joni Mitchell – Peter Kearns  978-1-78952-081-1

The Moody Blues – Geoffrey Feakes 978-1-78952-042-2

Motorhead – Duncan Harris 978-1-78952-173-3

Mike Oldfield – Ryan Yard 978-1-78952-060-6

Opeth – Jordan Blum 978-1-78-952-166-5

Tom Petty – Richard James 978-1-78952-128-3

Porcupine Tree – Nick Holmes 978-1-78952-144-3

Queen – Andrew Wild 978-1-78952-003-3

Radiohead – William Allen 978-1-78952-149-8

Renaissance – David Detmer 978-1-78952-062-0

The Rolling Stones 1963-80 – Steve Pilkington 978-1-78952-017-0

The Smiths and Morrissey – Tommy Gunnarsson 978-1-78952-140-5

Status Quo the Frantic Four Years – Richard James 978-1-78952-160-3

Steely Dan – Jez Rowden 978-1-78952-043-9

Steve Hackett – Geoffrey Feakes  978-1-78952-098-9

Thin Lizzy – Graeme Stroud 978-1-78952-064-4

Toto – Jacob Holm-Lupo 978-1-78952-019-4

U2 – Eoghan Lyng 978-1-78952-078-1

UFO – Richard James 978-1-78952-073-6

The Who – Geoffrey Feakes 978-1-78952-076-7

Roy Wood and the Move – James R Turner 978-1-78952-008-8

Van Der Graaf Generator – Dan Coffey 978-1-78952-031-6

Yes – Stephen Lambe 978-1-78952-001-9

Frank Zappa 1966 to 1979 – Eric Benac 978-1-78952-033-0

Warren Zevon – Peter Gallagher 978-1-78952-170-2

10CC – Peter Kearns 978-1-78952-054-5

## Decades Series

The Bee Gees in the 1960s – Andrew Mon Hughes et al 978-1-78952-148-1

The Bee Gees in the 1970s – Andrew Mon Hughes et al 978-1-78952-179-5

Black Sabbath in the 1970s – Chris Sutton 978-1-78952-171-9

Britpop – Peter Richard Adams and Matt Pooler 978-1-78952-169-6

Alice Cooper in the 1970s – Chris Sutton 978-1-78952-104-7

Curved Air in the 1970s – Laura Shenton 978-1-78952-069-9

Bob Dylan in the 1980s – Don Klees 978-1-78952-157-3

Fleetwood Mac in the 1970s – Andrew Wild 978-1-78952-105-4

Focus in the 1970s – Stephen Lambe 978-1-78952-079-8

Free and Bad Company in the 1970s – John Van der Kiste 978-1-78952-178-8

Genesis in the 1970s – Bill Thomas 978178952-146-7

George Harrison in the 1970s – Eoghan Lyng 978-1-78952-174-0

Marillion in the 1980s – Nathaniel Webb 978-1-78952-065-1

Mott the Hoople and Ian Hunter in the 1970s –
John Van der Kiste 978-1-78-952-162-7

Pink Floyd In The 1970s – Georg Purvis 978-1-78952-072-9

Tangerine Dream in the 1970s – Stephen Palmer 978-1-78952-161-0

The Sweet in the 1970s – Darren Johnson 978-1-78952-139-9

Uriah Heep in the 1970s – Steve Pilkington 978-1-78952-103-0

Yes in the 1980s – Stephen Lambe with David Watkinson 978-1-78952-125-2

# On Screen series

Carry On... – Stephen Lambe 978-1-78952-004-0

David Cronenberg – Patrick Chapman 978-1-78952-071-2

Doctor Who: The David Tennant Years – Jamie Hailstone 978-1-78952-066-8

James Bond – Andrew Wild – 978-1-78952-010-1

Monty Python – Steve Pilkington 978-1-78952-047-7

Seinfeld Seasons 1 to 5 – Stephen Lambe 978-1-78952-012-5

# Other Books

1967: A Year In Psychedelic Rock 978-1-78952-155-9

1970: A Year In Rock – John Van der Kiste 978-1-78952-147-4

1973: The Golden Year of Progressive Rock 978-1-78952-165-8

Babysitting A Band On The Rocks – G.D. Praetorius 978-1-78952-106-1

Eric Clapton Sessions – Andrew Wild 978-1-78952-177-1

Derek Taylor: For Your Radioactive Children –
Andrew Darlington 978-1-78952-038-5

The Golden Road: The Recording History of The Grateful Dead –
John Kilbride 978-1-78952-156-6

Iggy and The Stooges On Stage 1967-1974 – Per Nilsen 978-1-78952-101-6

Jon Anderson and the Warriors – the road to Yes –
David Watkinson 978-1-78952-059-0

Nu Metal: A Definitive Guide – Matt Karpe 978-1-78952-063-7

Tommy Bolin: In and Out of Deep Purple – Laura Shenton 978-1-78952-070-5

Maximum Darkness – Deke Leonard 978-1-78952-048-4

Maybe I Should've Stayed In Bed – Deke Leonard 978-1-78952-053-8

Psychedelic Rock in 1967 – Kevan Furbank 978-1-78952-155-9

The Twang Dynasty – Deke Leonard 978-1-78952-049-1

# and many more to come!

# Would you like to write for Sonicbond Publishing?

At Sonicbond Publishing we are always on the look-out for authors, particularly for our two main series:

On Track. Mixing fact with in depth analysis, the On Track series examines the work of a particular musical artist or group. All genres are considered from easy listening and jazz to 60s soul to 90s pop, via rock and metal.

On Screen. This series looks at the world of film and television. Subjects considered include directors, actors and writers, as well as entire television and film series. As with the On Track series, we balance fact with analysis.

While professional writing experience would, of course, be an advantage the most important qualification is to have real enthusiasm and knowledge of your subject. First-time authors are welcomed, but the ability to write well in English is essential.

Sonicbond Publishing has distribution throughout Europe and North America, and all books are also published in E-book form. Authors will be paid a royalty based on sales of their book.

Further details are available from www.sonicbondpublishing.co.uk. To contact us, complete the contact form there or email info@sonicbondpublishing.co.uk